BOUND
IN FLESH

Books by David Thomas Lord

BOUND IN BLOOD

BOUND IN FLESH

Published by Kensington Publishing Corporation

BOUND IN FLESH

DAVID THOMAS LORD

KENSINGTON BOOKS
http://www.kensingtonbooks.com

KENSINGTON BOOKS are published by

Kensington Publishing Corp.
850 Third Avenue
New York, NY 10022

All Kensington titles, imprints, and distributed lines are available at special quantity discounts for bulk purchases for sales promotion, premiums, fund raising, educational, or institutional use.

Special book excerpts or customized printings can also be created to fit specific needs. For details, write or phone the office of the Kensington Special Sales Manager: Kensington Publishing Corp., 850 Third Avenue, New York, NY 10022. Attn: Special Sales Department. Phone: 1-800-221-2647.

Kensington and the K logo Reg. U.S. Pat. & TM Off.

ISBN 1-57566-765-7

First Kensington Trade Paperback Printing: August 2006
10 9 8 7 6 5 4 3 2 1

Printed in the United States of America

ACKNOWLEDGMENTS

Because of physical limitations stemming from a severe accident, I was unable to write for quite some time and that inability led to the delay of BOUND IN FLESH. I want to thank my family, friends, and colleagues for their support through that difficult time, and I also want to thank my readers for their support, understanding, and patience.

I especially wish to thank my editor, John Scognamiglio, and my agent, Lori Perkins, neither of whom lost faith even when I did.

I also wish to thank Mary Madewell and C. J. Hurtt for taking the time to assist me in my research of Las Vegas and its environs.

prologue

I'd taken to drink.

In my disconsolate loneliness, in my unhealable soullessness, in my intolerable soloness, I'd taken to drink.

I'd taken to drink for its restorative powers. That's what I'd told myself, and anyway, I'd taken to drink. And another day began for me, Mike O'Donald. Ex-cop, ex-lover, ex-man.

He's dead and I'm out. Why'd I bother?

Why not?

I woke annoyed. It was impossible for me not to feel the strength of my muscles as I lifted my head from the pillow, my torso from the sheet.

Six foot. One eighty-five. Perfect.

He's dead.

Perfect.

And I'm out.

Perfect.

I'm perfect. Except the week I'd just spent from Christmas to New Year's in bed. Recovering.

Old news. Not even the reporters, bloodsuckers to a man, cared about this story anymore. What story? I told them nothing. Not even in my departmental debriefing did I really tell the complete truth. How could I? Who wouldn't want to put me away permanently for a story like that?

I was chilled to the bone. Again.

Just like every morning for the past twenty-nine, I raced from under my electric blanket and comforters and dashed through my apartment with the radiators steaming full tilt to my hot, tiled bathroom. I turned the faucet full left, pulled the shower curtain closed and in the welcoming fog, I ducked under the blistering spray.

I didn't lower the temperature until my skin had turned bright pink. I promised myself daily that I'd stop doing it as soon as the chill went away. The chill I knew would never go away. Because I'm going to turn into him one day. Jack. The Horror of West Street. One day I'll be just like him. Dead, and still alive. Stealing the lives of young innocents like my Teddy, just to survive for another day. How could I explain *that* to anyone? How could anyone understand? Could anyone believe what I believe? What I know to be true?

I trained the spray on my cold chest and cold belly, my cold thighs and shins. Across cold shoulders, cold back, and cold butt. I never thought of myself as handsome anymore, just cold. Nor well-built. Just cold. I didn't think of myself anymore as one who had been a lover, one who had once been a cop. Not as a son or friend.

Just cold.

I stepped out of the shower and onto the bath mat. I grabbed my towel and turned toward the mirror, its steam-smudged face ignorant of my workout-honed physique. Absently, I wiped the glass surface with one edge of the towel as I rubbed my hair with the other. Slowly, the wet hairs dried lighter to their own shades of ash blond. Hair that had hardly grown a fraction in over a month. Pale blond hair, pale blond brows, pale blond stubble slowly appeared to the mirror. And to my eyes.

My newly sad eyes, their blue now bordering on slate gray. And every day rimmed with red. And each day drawn in despair.

His eyes. Damn it, they're his eyes. I'm turning into him already.

I reached back and caught the neck of my bathrobe, thinking only of my service revolver. Wondering how I'd look when the end finally did happen. How old? How broken? Then I pushed the thought away. I slid the sleeves over my arms and shoulders and cinched it tight in front to obliterate all the muscles I had perfected. *But I haven't had a workout for almost a month. How come I haven't lost definition?* I was growing to love this robe. Because it was long. Long enough to cover all of me. I only brooked the briefest glance anymore. At a body that never seemed to change. At a body that looked exactly like my enemy's. My demonic twin.

I couldn't forget what all the others already had. Hell, it had only been a month since I'd been held captive by the notorious serial killer, "The Horror of West Street," Jean-Luc Courbet.

Old news, Tina'd say.

"Not even a month," I told the cool bathroom tiles, as I rocked my warmed forehead against them. The day after tomorrow, my first month anniversary. I silently cursed all thirty-one day months and sulked from bathroom to kitchen in search of today's first beer.

Wouldn't Teddy laugh at his lover now?

"Here he is, ladies and gentlemen," I announced to amuse the ghost of him in my best W. C. Fields/carney-barker voice, "Mike O'Donald, the teetotaler, snapping open the day's inaugural can of beer. How many, you wonder, would be left before the daily call out for more?"

But Teddy didn't laugh anymore. Or cry, or console. Teddy was dead, a victim of the same brutal, heartless fiend who had victimized me. The creature, I was convinced, who bestowed upon me his same need for bloody sacrifice. The . . .

"Vampire."

I finally said it out loud. The building didn't burst. The sky didn't fall. Nothing changed. Nothing but the assurance that I would become the thing I most feared, the thing I most hated.

I pitched myself toward the bedroom, barely keeping from falling. I flipped on the overhead light and shucked the robe. For the first time in a month, I really looked at myself, long and hard.

"I'm not dead. I am not dead. I. Am. Not. Dead."

I kept repeating it to that tall, muscular blond reflected in the oak framed mirror, as I leaned on the matching bureau. A bachelor chest, I think they call it. The irony found in me.

I stared, for the first time in a long time, at the admirable way that my neck tapered up into my jawline and yet swelled down into my shoulders. How the strong delineation of my deltoids cut into the groove between triceps and biceps. How my radials and extensors had grown to resemble a comic book hero's.

"I'm not dead!"

Just saying it seemed to console me. Seemed.

"I'm not dead," I repeated, this time with less conviction and a noticeable crack in my voice. I said it again and watched the mirrored, single tear hit my right pectoral and slowly slide down toward my abdomen. As it rode over the hills and valleys of my muscles, other salty sledders joined it.

Perversely, I leaned back to watch the pathetic race of my tears to my pubic hairs. Which pitiable drop would go for the gold, which would suffer the agony of defeat in my navel?

Perverse, pathetic, pitiable agony. The mute and hollow walls were the only witness to my groans. My welling, spilling tears.

I whispered to a framed photo as I caressed it lightly with my fingertips, "Teddy, I'm so sorry. I'm sorry I wasn't there to protect you from him. I'm sorry I can't follow you. Be with you. I'm never going to see you again. Not now, not ever. We're never going to meet again. Not in heaven. Nowhere. I'm cursed, Teddy! Cursed."

And I wept.

Hours later, I roused myself from a puddle of my own sweat and tears and nine ounces of undrunk beer. I stumbled out of the bedroom and showered again. As I dried myself, I made my way through to the living room, remotely turning on the television, and back into the kitchen.

I popped open another beer and was caught by the sound of the broadcast, already set for Channel Three's Observation News. I was surprised to find the close-up shot of Hyland Brooke, a sub, at the anchor's desk. I fumbled with the remote to increase the volume.

"...land Brooke, filling in for vacationing Tina Washington. Today's top story is ..."

Vacationing? I spoke to Tina yesterday morning. She's not on vacation. Wait a minute. Where did she say she was going yesterday? Some sort of lesbian fundraiser? Where was it?

"The news, man. Get on with the news," I shouted at the set. "Where the fuck is Tina?" I found myself asking into the handset to my phone, unconsciously speed-dialing.

I waited ring after ring. There was no answer at Tina's. No machine pick-up.

Bzzzzat! I flinched and dropped the phone.

"It's just the doorbell, man, the fucking doorbell. Relax, would ya?" Steadying myself with my words, I went to the intercom.

"Hello?" I heard hesitancy in what I wanted to sound assertive.

"Mike?" I knew the speaker by that one syllable. "It's me. Can I see you?"

"Tina! Where the fuck have you been?" *Where's your key?* I unlocked the apartment door and pulled it open while I buzzed the release of the building's front door. "I mean, yeah, come in."

Why am I sweating? I'm freezing.

"Honey, I'm not alone." Her very recognizable voice refused to be turned into a squawk by the intercom. A hesitation. "Is that okay?"

I looked down at my naked body. *Shit. Two dykes; one naked ex-cop.* "Sure. Come up. I'll leave the door open."

I ran back into the bedroom and grabbed a pair of gray sweatpants. Not that Tina or whichever girlfriend this was would care. But it might seem deliberate. And she might feel uncomfortable around a naked guy.

Shit, I feel uncomfortable around myself naked.

I damned near tripped hurrying to pull the sweatpants on. I was tying the front when I heard them at the apartment door.

"Hello?" she nearly sang it. "Are you there?"

She sounded . . . what? Drunk? High?

Whatthefuck's going on now?

"Tina? Come on in," I managed to call out as I sprinted barefoot from the bedroom.

"I'm with someone."

"Both of you come in, then," I said, pulling the door wide open.

And then I stopped.

My lifelong friend, Tina Washington, from Hell's Kitchen, now Chelsea-Clinton, glowed. And so did her friend.

God help me, I couldn't stop looking at her friend. And forgive me for being surprised that the world's newest most famous lesbian was accompanied by what might be the world's most beautiful man.

"Come in. Please, come in."

Don't act like a jerk, Mike. Take this easy.

"I'm Mi—"

"This is my best friend, Mike O'Donald. He's white Irish; I'm black Irish!"

Tina was radiant. I'd never seen her quite like this. She was beautiful, yes. Always had been to me. But, I'd seen her through chicken pox and braces and pimples. Through her teenage hetero stage. I'd seen her go through everything but this—*what?*—transcendence.

"You look great!"

That's all I could manage to say. But what I was thinking was: this guy's dangerously gorgeous. What's he doing with Tina? And then I felt guilty and tried to suppress the impulse: *he should be with me!*

"Thank you, darling."

Tina never called me darling.

"She's been calling everyone 'darling' since yesterday," the beautiful stranger explained. Like he read my mind. My comfort level was definitely changing for the worse.

"Tina, where were you last night?"

"Clubbing, darling. That's where I met this one. What do you think of him?"

I made the mistake of turning from Tina's eyes—always captivating, ask anyone—to her friend's. Fuck, caught!

Emerald Green. But, emerald green as if it wasn't just a color, but a belief. A social structure. The fucking lottery! I didn't care about his covered shoulders, his concealed biceps and triceps, his camouflaged chest. Not about his hidden thighs or calves. His unseen abs or butt or cock.

Because of his eyes.

Emerald green. It tore at my heart, me, a fine Celtic boy. I heard bagpipes, damn it! I felt the fife and the drum in my temples and in my gut. It was St. Patrick's Day. I was going to pass out.

Then I realized that I was naked with only some flimsy cotton to generate decency. And that it wasn't just goose bumps, everything was hardening.

"I'll be right back," I said as I headed for the bedroom.

"Mikey."

That was all he said, and I froze. "Turn around."

Simple enough, and I did.

Gorgeous. He was simply gorgeous. His halo of blue-black hair radiated in soft curls from his scalp. Too long for my taste, I would have said. But the very look of them excited me.

He smiled. I was too dazzled by the impeccable whiteness to be frightened. I was, I admit, drawn in by the sweet curve of his full lips, a color just short of scarlet. Damned red, yet decidedly manly. My downfall, I admit.

And while I was caught in the visual embrace, he reached for the zipper on his hooded sweatshirt. Tooth-by-tooth, he unzipped. So slowly, it hurt. So seductively, it mesmerized. So surely, I was ashamed.

He loosened the sweatshirt from his frame. He caught it in the crease of his elbows as he exposed his entire torso to me.

Peach. And olive. I could see them. I could smell them. Peaches and olives. Two flavors I never cared for seemed to become the center of my existence. Two essences, so opposed, creating the treat before me.

His skin, which at first glance seemed pale and fragile, glowed with a vibrant flush. His muscles were like peaches, round and fuzzy and full. His eyes, nipples and navel, all ripening olives—

green and beige, bronze and black—breathed a fragrance I had never known. I? Who was I? I of the boiled meats and boiled potatoes and boiled vegetables.

And so, what was this?

The room was rank, redolent of stepped gardens and suppurating black composted soil. An exotic, alien-scented atmosphere, like the landscapes of my dreams. All that I secretly desired. And here.

His sweatshirt shucked, he stood in the middle of my living room, nearly naked. His pants, if I could call them that, were that parachute material, olive drab, and low-slung. Showing him off better than a pair of Speedos would. Not that I then complained.

I have a good body. Damn good! Pale blond hair, not much of it on my frame. Strong muscles, more full than wiry. A sprinkling of freckles, quite pale, across my shoulders and nowhere else. And I stood an inch and a half over this guy easily.

But, goddamn! Look at him!

My guest's arms and shoulders were perfect. His chest and belly flawless. His navel, neither innie nor outie, was as fascinatingly necessary as a pimento in a martini's olive. And in the words of that British agent, I was shaken. I stirred.

"I was just about to change," I heard myself say. I really didn't know why.

"Don't!" It struck me to the marrow. Thrilled me. Stunned me. Scared me.

Please. Don't. I think he said that.

This man was more naked with most of his clothes on, than I have ever been with most of mine off. I knew I was handsome, goddamn it. But, if I was handsome, then what the hell was he? This guy looked like mortal sin.

"Mike, don't get all Irish on us."

The sound of her voice hit me like a shot. Wounded me like a dart. Tina! How could I ever have gotten so caught up in this man that I forgot about Tina? Damn it! I damn near got into it with him right in front of her. What'd gotten into me?

". . . Theater director Patrick Xenpoulos is dead." The television voice-over broke the dense and distracted mood. We each appeared to recognize the name, but it seemed, for different reasons.

"That's Hyland!" Tina exclaimed with honest surprise. "Why'd they give the spot to him?" she added with uncommon contempt.

A black-and-white photograph came on the screen. The man in the standard actor's "head shot" looked to be in his mid-to-late twenties. A very handsome man with thick, dark hair. Pale eyes and a wide forehead dominated his intelligent face. And his sleek, straight nose and full sensuous mouth couldn't be overshadowed by his thick black beard.

He was classically beautiful.

"I know this man, don't I?" I wondered aloud.

"You go to the theater much, Mikey?" my handsome guest asked. Everyone's eyes were glued to the screen.

"Er, no." My answer wasn't hesitant; I just wanted to hear more about the death of this extraordinary-looking man.

As we watched and Hyland spoke, they showed some footage of this Patrick Xenopoulos directing a play with men and women in togas, another scene of him surrounded by actors in the costume of some old-fashioned court. Then, shirtless, demonstrating an action to a group of performers in various stages of undress.

"He's something," I said.

"Was," Tina's friend replied.

"Oh, yeah, right." I was crushed.

"I think I did a story on that guy once," Tina added, making it, uncharacteristically, about her.

"Tragic, how he died," my other guest concluded.

I turned from the mesmerizing figure on the screen to the astonishing one in my living room. *Did he just get taller?*

"I didn't hear them mention how he died." And I knew, at that moment, it was the wrong thing to say.

"They didn't. I'd been listening for it, too. But you know, Mikey, they don't always say when it's homicide."

His air was flippant, his attitude smug. All of a sudden, I didn't like this guy. He excited me still, but I stopped thinking I'd do him. He moved towards me. Not exactly *to* me. I was near the television, Tina at the bar separating the kitchen from the living room, and this guy moved to the center of the floor.

This guy? It was only then that I realized I didn't even know his name.

"Excuse me? What do you know about how they handle murder cases?" I demanded of him. "Are you on the job?"

"You know very well that I'm not a cop, Mikey," he said as he moved closer.

His movements and words were slow. His eyes languid. Hypnotizing as a snake's. I just didn't see them then for what they were.

Mikey? No one calls me Mikey.

Then he touched me.

I hadn't realized that he'd gotten so close. Hadn't seen his hand move. Hadn't time to react before he'd had me in his arms.

The difference between what I'd wanted and what I'd gotten was worlds. Our flesh pressing, chest-to-chest. His grasp was terrible, his touch horrible. Dry and cold. Not only did it have no warmth, it seemed to siphon it. I'd felt this before. This cruel imposition. Once before. And again, I was going to lose control.

"Who are you?" was all I could manage.

"You know who I am."

"I don't! Tell me!" I thought I was screaming, but I heard barely a whisper. I was scared.

He let me go. He released me and I fell to my knees. I had no strength in my legs and couldn't get back up. My vision, insecure. My voice, thwarted. Nothing could I taste, touch, smell or hear, but fear.

"Oh, Mikey," he said in that voice you use when coaxing a child. "Surely, you realize that I killed Patrick Xenopoulos?"

And I knew in my mind that he had.

"Also, and I hate to brag, but you should finally know that I killed Laura Wilcox, too."

And I knew in my heart that he had.

"NO!"

We both turned at once to the woman at the bar. Horrific understanding was pulling her face into a death mask. Tina. We'd both forgotten this time, but he was faster to strike than I was to save.

"Get back, bitch!" he swore as he swung. And he knocked my oldest friend down to the floor beside me.

"Pick her up and tie her to that chair," he instructed in a voice that would broach no contest. For Tina's sake, I went along.

There was a roll of three-eights-inch wide jute cord on the bar. It was not in a viewable position, but somehow he knew it was there. He threw it to me, this killer without a name. This nightmare revisited. I didn't need to know who he was to realize what he was. And I had to do everything I could to save Tina. I was already dead.

I tied her securely. I didn't want her to get all brave on me. Then he threw me the duct tape.

"Gag her," he said, and I did.

"Blindfold."

I did.

"Sit down in the other chair," he demanded.

"Is that really . . ."

"Sit or she'll die right now."

I sat and he tied my wrists to the armrests and my ankles to the front legs. He made a noose, put it around my neck and fastened it to the spindles of the high back of the chair. I loved these chairs. A present from Teddy.

"Who am I?" this demon asked.

"I don't know who you are or what you want. Why don't you tell me?" I was being very brave for a near-naked man tied to a chair.

"My name is Claude Halloran."

But I had already known that.

"Oh, I can see it in your eyes. Jack told you. All about me. And about Noel, too, I guess."

He came to me as he spoke, closer and closer again. I could feel his strong legs and rump as he deliberately settled into my lap. His muscular arms as he laid them over mine. His chest hairs as he teased them over my nipples. He was seducing me! And, I'm ashamed to admit, effectively.

He rocked his crotch closer to mine. He brought me his face. Even at this unbearable nearness, his complexion was like a new-born's. Pure porcelain. Not a wrinkle, not a scar.

His eyes held mine. The whites of them were as pure and cold as new-fallen snow. Not a marring blood vessel anywhere. His lashes, so thick and black. They curled away from their source in perfect arcs. His irises were so green. In them, I saw elegant wine bottles, empty from sharing; pine boughs on a crisp slope. I saw full, ripe zucchini, bursting with life. Deep seas, unfathomable, yet intimate. He was so close.

Then he opened his mouth. To kiss or kill, I didn't know. And there I smelled it again. The olives, the peaches. Rich and lusty and prime. And something else.

I smelled copper. And sulfur. It was blood I smelled. And death and decay.

I jerked away.

"What did he do to you, that I cannot take you?" he screamed at me. Even Tina, blindfolded, bound and gagged, recoiled. "Tell me!"

"I won't."

"Then I will rip it from you brain without your help, the way my secrets were torn from mine."

Anger. And rejection. Good! Underneath it all, I was still a cop and I recognized the betrayal in these emotions.

"You can't, Claude," I told him simply. "If you could've taken them, you'd have my memories already."

"Then I will kill you, Mikey."

"If you wanted to kill me," I reasoned, "you'd have done it by now. What do you really want, Claude?"

"You survived an attack from the strongest vampire in the world. And after Jack, you've kept me from taking you twice."

Twice?

"Oh, yes, Mikey. I was with you in your hospital room on Christmas Day. Don't tell me you've forgotten."

I thought it had to have been a dream. Some subconscious continuation of my earlier torments. I'd first suffered through a devastating abduction by "The Horror of West Street" only to be subjected to a degrading interrogation by my peers.

They knew that Jack had, at least partially, stripped me. And they found a complete set of his clothes, surmising his own nakedness. They assumed that we had sex and hinted at rape, as if Jack needed another crime added to his litany of offenses. They wanted me probed to verify, but I refused.

Then they implied consensual relations. I refused to share more than the barest details with the department representatives, refused any treatment or examination from the hospital staff. I wanted nothing more than to be left alone. It was going to cost me my badge, but they were never going to know completely what had happened on the pier. I never even told Tina. I would take it to my grave. How I had been forced to drink the black blood of the vampire through a slit in his erect penis. How I saved myself by biting it off and swallowing it whole.

Their bullets didn't destroy Jean-Luc Courbet. It was me. Me, and the silver in my fillings. And I'd get this one, too.

"You seem to be remembering, Mikey."

"I remember. I remember someone in my room. In the dark, by my bed."

"What else do you remember about it?" This vampire was eager for acknowledgment.

"The smell. Olives and peaches. It was you."

The room had been darkened when everyone left and the curtains had been drawn around the hospital bed. I remember there had been a moon. I think it was full. Its blue-white light had cast the objects in the room into stark shadow.

Since I had refused all treatment, they left me untranquillized in order to release me later. It was Christmas Day. And I had no one and nothing.

Teddy was dead. Tina was barred from visiting. I hadn't heard from any part of my family since I'd been outed on national television. My days on the force were over. I was completely alone.

It was then, I recalled, that I first noticed the scent.

At first, it seemed unnaturally sweet for a hospital. Fruity, and not antiseptic. Then, when the fragrance started to become cloying, another invaded. This one I didn't like at all.

Overripe and tart and earthy, all at once. The sweet smell was filling my sinuses and lungs like ether, while the dank odor had a different effect. It seemed, like musk, to whisper of sex. And while the first effect was taking me from my conscious self, the second was emphasizing my physical nature.

I thought that I had pushed the covers away, that I had lifted the hospital gown myself. Whether silent phantom or spellbinding enigma, something dreamlike began to overcome me. I felt lusty, in that altered state, in a way I never have conscious. I allowed and experimented in directions I never would have. Never could have. I don't remember if my eyes were open or shut, but my partner, my seducer, my rapist, was faceless. Still, his body I recalled. And here it was before me again.

"So, was it good for you?"

That damnable smirk. If only I was free.

"I will untie you soon enough, Mikey. But first, do you know why I marked you in the way I did and instead of just killing you?"

"You couldn't kill me. You can't now."

"Oh. No. Not in the way I prefer. It is true; my fangs would not grow in your presence. Still won't. I do not know why. But, that is not why you are still alive. There are many, many ways to kill one of you. Watch!"

Before I could blink, Claude was off my lap and at Tina. Before I could open my mouth to shout, I heard the scream escape from hers. Claude stood there showing me his trophies. The duct tape blindfold and gag torn from her eyes and mouth.

"You bastard!" we echoed. But to my relief, Tina seemed unhurt. Just angry and afraid.

"Why are you doing this to us?" Tina asked in unusual supplication.

"Shut up and live."

"What do you want from me, Claude? I'll give you whatever you want, if you let her go."

"As I knew you would. She is just a calling card, Mikey. I really do not need her. And if you cooperate fully, she will be free to go."

"Name it."

"Mike, no!" She was trying to regain her composure through the feisty girl reporter role. But I knew that the only way to save her was to agree.

"You, for my better and your worse, are the exact double of Noel's son, Jean-Luc Courbet."

"I know. We've met."

Claude was growing talkative, knowing that I'd have to submit to his plans.

"His mother keeps me her captive slave . . ."

I interrupted, "But you're here. How can you be captive and free?"

"You were in love and you ask that? Surely you realize that freedom is just an extension of captivity. An illusionary state between commands and demands. I am her prisoner as surely as you are mine."

"You don't control me, Claude."

"No, Mikey, maybe not. But she does control me. And her son's evil ways were nothing compared to hers." And he began to detail Noel's depravity, her iniquity.

Fear was creeping back. And not on tiny cat paws. It was crawling like a leviathan. It slithered. It stomped. It was back. Just at his mention, his invocation, of his mistress.

He started to pace the carpet and the carpet smoldered apace. The air crackled. All the oxygen seemed to be drawn to him and away from us. He continued.

"You have no idea how she caught me up in this. Her cruelty. My misery. I was sent here to destroy her son. That was my pact with her. Kill Jack and I would be released from her service."

"Stop pacing. You'll kill us both."

Claude paused to view the effect of his ramblings on the room and his prisoners.

"Sorry. Unintentional." He stood over Tina. "Sorry, again, but I have to do this."

He muffled her hearing, taping her ears with the blindfold and gag. We could not protest.

"Mikey, if I am to let her live, she cannot know more of the project I have for you. Agreed?"

I nodded. I knew I couldn't trust him, but until I'd served my purpose, Tina would live.

"I'm going to tell you how I met Noel Courbet, how she killed me and then brought me back to life as her undead slave. I will tell you things you could never guess about her son, Jack. And about the amazing things they could do . . ."

He began to chronicle his death, only about seven months ago. *Could you grow so evil in such a short time?* He told me of his kidnapping and torture. Of the continual raping and constant chattering. Of other slaves from other dimensions. Of magic and mayhem. Of desire and death.

He told me of Noel's plan for revenge. How her vampire lord's affection had been stolen away and how her hatred fueled her rage. He told me of how she murdered her husband, Phillipe, and hunted the world for her son. How Jack's death was Noel's primary objective. He told me about the books. The grimoires, he called them.

He told me of their arrival in New York, explained the seduction and destruction of Jack. Described their return to Phillipe's chateau, burned to the ground and then rebuilt by her son over a century ago. A place of magic and mystery and unimaginable wealth.

And through it all, he kept his back to Tina, so that she could not see his lips. So that she could not understand his plan. And through it all, I kept my eyes locked on hers, wordlessly assuring her that I would not let her die. That she would live, even if I did not.

I turned my head away from Claude. Not in revulsion, as he imagined, but to catch the last of a repeated broadcast of the day's top news stories.

"Yes, Mikey," he said when he saw my intent. "I killed him. He was very good-looking. Smart, too. But, he would not give me what I wanted. The role that would have made my trap so much easier to spring. My bait was Laura Wilcox. And this really is strange.

Who'd imagine that two vampires, mother and son, could have virtual doubles in the same city, at the same time? Mind-boggling!

"Patrick Xenopoulos offered me an insignificant role. Theramenes. Then he flirted with Jack in front of me. With his wife in the same theater! Look, Mikey! There she is now."

They had returned to the opening story and the new voice-over described the career of Purity St. Martin, considered to be the most famous witch in America. The Red Witch.

I studied her face. I wanted to remember it.

Finally, he got around to his wretched plan for me. Me, the reflection of the now dead Marquis de Charnac, Jean-Luc Courbet. The doppelganger, he called me.

I agreed to his terms. I'd go with him to France and play the part of Jack's ghost in a conspiracy to torment Noel. Because she was undead, she wouldn't be able to assault a mortal during the day, and Claude pledged his protection at night. It was, after all, to his benefit that I not be caught. He'd rid her of Jack a second time and thereby insure his release from her slavery. In return, Tina'd be left as she was.

He untied me. I got up from the chair and, without looking back, went to the bedroom to dress and pack a bag.

When I came back into the living room, the tape'd been removed from Tina's ears, but she was still bound and newly gagged. I knelt by her chair to whisper to her.

"Don't play the hero, Tina. This guy can hurt us. I'll go with him, then everything'll be okay."

"We have to go, Mikey. It *is* getting early." Claude's humor.

I thought I heard her crying when we left. Still, I pulled the heavy metal door shut and sealed her, helpless, inside. We hurried down the hallway and down the stairs. To the entryway and out the door. Down the brownstone steps.

"What's going to happen to her, Claude?"

"It has all been arranged, Mikey. Once we are away, she will be freed."

"How do you know she won't stir up trouble?"

"Believe me, Miss Washington will not say a word about tonight to anyone. After all, I have you now."

Outside on the street, we both shot a last look up to my second floor window. I didn't know what he knew. Couldn't hear what Claude could. The bitter gnawing at fabric and adhesive. The loud and vulgar expectoration of the gag. The cruel crease of her na-solabial folds as the callous smile began. The simple command, "Burn!"

I could not smell, as he could, the disintegration of those tight jute confines as they obeyed and ignited, flamed and fell away.

I could not imagine, as he could, from his own history, the proud resurrection and the smug self-confidence of my former friend, the newly formed vampiress, Tina Washington.

I could not see, as he could, in his mind's eye, the grin that released her emergent fangs, nor the trouble I was in.

PART ONE

THE DOPPELGANGER

chapter

1

He rose from behind the trash cans, a colorless specter. From beneath the brownstone staircase, like the avenging angel of death. Crisp, calm, cruel. He watched the two figures hurry down the dreary predawn street and away into the cold Manhattan night. Watched as the shorter, dark-haired one clutched, as guardian and guard, the taller blond. The blond, he saw, wore jeans, turtleneck sweater and leather jacket. All black.

New York chic, or is he already beginning to dress as the night?

He noted that the obvious beauty accompanying him wore flimsy parachute pants and an unzipped, hooded sweatshirt. Obvious. That would undo him yet, the watcher thought.

He looked up to the second-story bay window. Smelled the burning jute rope, and knew that she who entered with the dark-haired one, but remained behind, was woman no longer. He could not sense her mortality. There was no taste of her mensed blood in the air, no feel of mortal, anxious salinity. She emitted no human aura whatsoever, and the absence of it assured him that she was indeed undead.

What to do? The former lady or le tigre du papier?

In his usual perversity of nature, Jean-Luc Courbet, The Horror of West Street, decided to allow the fledgling her freedom and bounded down West 46th Street to Ninth Avenue. He picked up the scent of the blond—his twin and his creation—and followed. He listened to the conversation between the two. Listened to the vampire-slave Claude Halloran's plan to ruin Noel Courbet, the former and new Marquise de Charnac, his mother. He listened and approved.

But he would follow, just to be sure. Just to insure.

Jack knew that Claude had not achieved enough supernatural

ability yet to transport this seemingly mortal captive. Following them would be slow and dreary. He wished that he could command the fog, as his mother did, to lend cloak to his pursuit. And yet, commensurate with his fortune, and correspondent to his desire, the first flurries of the Celtic month of Rowan did begin.

"Taxi!"

Claude used his human and vampiric voice to capture the attention of the last unoccupied cab of a snowy night. Just as the Russian driver saw the first flake and consequently reached for the "Off-Duty" switch, Claude lured him.

Married, with three young children, Yuri Lavrovsky had never been attracted to a man in his life. Yet, this blatant young god, a Dionysus half-dressed in the frigid, new snowfall, blinded him. Yuri never even noticed the handsome blond demigod at his side. He screeched to a halt just inches from them.

"LaGuardia!"

Jack heard the instruction and followed through the frosty night, only rarely placing foot to ground. The flurries and light snow at this predawn hour served as a cloak to conceal his advance. He leapt in silence from scant tree to ubiquitous fire escape. From one uniformly spaced airshaft to another random chimney. And all the while, never allowing his eyes to drift from his objective. And as he vaulted above the city, he was reminded of his first such excursion—as a captive himself, stolen away by his first lover, his mother's husband.

The very act of flying made Jack remember Phillipe. It was the floating maneuver—the long and low technique of bounding weightlessly through the eternal night—that contained his dead master's embrace. The very sensation of gliding through the nocturnal environment brought an evocative feeling with it. And that was the remembered touch of Phillipe de Charnac. The maker of vampires.

The moon was full and the evening warm. Phillipe's chin grizzled against Jean-Luc's forehead and cheek. The rasping would have been annoying, the scratching offensive to a conscious Jean-Luc. But in his stupor, the harsh abrading of his stepfather's constant stubble mated with the rib-crushing grasp that held him, soothed him. And drew him closer.

Jack was certain that this hallucination was part of the vampiric disease, the sickness that would destroy him if he didn't fully recreate soon. Noel, his mother, had already spawned Claude. And who knew if she had made others? Even Claude had apparently reproduced in the form of the anchorwoman, Tina Washington, Jack's former darling.

They've taken everything from me. Phillipe and Laura. My chateau and now, Tina. This must end.

"Hope that our paths do not cross, Miss Washington," Jack murmured aloud. "For I will be obliged to destroy you if they should!"

Jack followed Claude and Mike to LaGuardia Airport. Fast and efficient in the early, predawn hours, they traveled across lower Manhattan to Delancey Street and over the Williamsburg Bridge. Up the Brooklyn-Queens Expressway to the Grand Central. And just before the airport, Claude made the driver cut onto and off of Ditmars Boulevard. Just off of Hazen Street, he commanded the driver to stop. Claude abandoned the back seat and got in front with the driver. Jack paused, just meters away, halfway between Astoria Boulevard and Rikers Island, just between the dark and the dawn. One foot on each, both earth and sea.

Jack watched from his secret vantage point as Mike witnessed the horror from up close.

"Take off your clothes," Claude instructed the mesmerized Russian.

Yuri tried to fight, though could not but comply. He slipped out of his coat and tugged the heavy wool sweater over his head. He heard the sorrowful strains of the second act opening of "Swan Lake." The Tchaikovsky plugged his ears, filled his head. Obstructed his eyes. The mournful oboe clouded his defenses; the imagined spotlights blinded him to any audience but his savior, the half-naked Prince Siegfried before him. He knew, in a Russian instant, that he was a captive slave bewitched by an evil spell. His only hope was to shuck these feathers and become human again.

He pulled at the cruel shoes that entrapped him. He undid belt and zipper. No longer leather and denim, but silk and feather and tulle. He was rapturous; he was free. Odette without Odile. He could not feel the cold blast on his bare flesh, so lost was he in the verdant forest of his assailant's eyes.

"Not bad at all."

The audience applauded Claude's admission. They had to agree. This man was still in his prime. None of the copious amounts of Russian vodka and American beer had impacted that frame. The blinis, the borscht, the White Castle's, the Nathan's, all had succumbed to Yuri Lavrovsky's aggressive metabolism. Just as he, now, was succumbing to the incubus, Claude Halloran.

"Stop doing this!" Mike demanded in an attempt at saving the innocent cabbie.

Claude barely looked up from his indulgent driver. "Tell my friend that you are all right."

The Russian complied through his tears, "I am fine."

"He's not all right, Claude," Mike insisted through the plastic barrier. "You're making him say that!"

"Tell him that you are enjoying this."

"It is art, I'm afraid," came the sluggish and sorrowful, suggested reply. Yuri's pleading sobs joined with his demure glow, all from the mixed instructions of overlapping experiences. "One must suffer for art."

"Stop it, Claude, please! He's a married man. Look at the pictures on the dashboard. He has children and a wife. Don't you have any compassion?"

Mike was surprised to find himself hammering on the Plexiglas shield. *That'll bruise; that's gonna hurt.* He rubbed his hand, bit his lip and continued watching as if witnessing a train wreck. He couldn't turn away.

"Kneel on the seat; put your forearms against your side window."

The naked man turned to do as he was told. The delicate ballerina pirouetted. Claude removed his sweatshirt and lowered his pants, pushing the naked driver down to a squat. He enveloped, pushing the man's victimized cheek to the glass pane. Pressing the warm, human flesh with his cold, dead, perfect form. He threw open his jaws, revealing the growing incisors.

"Oh, God, no! Oh, Mary, Mother of Jesus, save him! Oh, you saints . . ."

"Shutthefuckup!" The words were garbled, but only slightly. An apprentice vampire still searching for control.

His curse was a warm wave over the captives. One a lamb brought to slaughter, the other a knight to be exchanged for a queen. But the warmth was incendiary, the wave tidal. And both mortal men succumbed.

Claude inserted his fangs into the Russian without finesse, Jack noted.

What a ghoul! No class at all. Noel has taught him nothing.

The émigré flinched, not understanding that the rape had only just begun. And as Claude drained him, his priapism returned and for its pulsating demand, Claude found an outlet.

Saint-Saens. The Dying Swan.

None turned away.

Mike could not control his reaction to the live sex show before him. One, he knew, that was fast becoming a snuff show. Every engorgeable part of him filled, every ethical part of him failed. This was a scene, an action, he would never forgive himself, never forget. But participate he did, with the hatred of each of his inferior, pre-vampiric thoughts delivered from the beast hidden inside.

Jack's experience was no better and much worse. As difficult as it would be for a sexual man to encounter sexuality in one of its aspects and not react, so much the worse for the blood-dependent vampire, who cannot witness carnage and not engage. He found his incisors throbbing to a time signature of percussive pianissimo, the pulse of fresh human blood. Jack flew off into the pewter twilight, searching for relief.

In a secluded part of the airport, Jack found his Dassault Falcon 900C. The flawless jet was still inscribed with the coat of Charnac. A diplomat's plane with diplomatic privilege. *They've even taken that!*

Jack sought and found a young baggage handler, just out of junior college. A former linebacker for its football team, his dreams for the future had been crushed like his patella. Blown knee, blown hopes. Then Jack.

Refreshed, the vampire Jean-Luc Courbet approached his jet. There were, he knew, secrets to the Chateau Charnac and its ancillary holdings that the new occupants still could not know. Secrets that his mother and her vampire slave could never extract from the wizards who ran his castle, his empire.

Messrs. Baum and White were the perfect fit for their jobs. They were Charnac. Charnac was them. They served their master, Jean-Luc Courbet, after their own fashion. According to their own laws. They had been instructed to allow entrance to the woman who resembled the portrait and any who accompanied her. To serve them well. To allow them full access to the chateau and its holdings. But for the secrets that they held close to their hearts!

Odd creatures, Baum and White. Yet, the perfect foil to a nasty, undying witch who is both mother and huntress. She will not kill them; they were far too clever for that.

Dawn approached and with it, Claude and Mike. Jack secreted himself by the plane.

Noel had already discovered the hidden compartments in the

aft cabin of the jet, Jack realized. He knew that Claude would occupy them for his trip home. One for him and one for his captive.
He knew that they would have dropped fuel to achieve the weight
balance for the return flight.

He also knew that undead, he weighed nothing. And that the
third and most secret compartment was entirely undetectable.
Flying home, he was returning to his native soil. He needed no
more than the earth in his pockets to insure a safe journey.

"Get in!" Claude's voice.

"You can't kidnap an American citizen this way. They won't let
you leave."

Mike.

Jack listened to their ensuing argument.

"No one will know you are gone. This is a diplomatic jet. They
will not search it. And no one is looking for you."

"The pilots. I'll talk to the pilots!"

"The pilots, dear Mikey, are more fucked up than you are. Not
even I can talk to the pilots. Your pal, Jack, could. His mother can.
Us? Knock yourself out!"

The pilot released the security alarm and popped the lock on the
cabin door, allowing entrance to the flushed demon with whom
they'd traveled here and the startling blond American who could
easily have passed for their deceased employer, Jean-Luc, the
Marquis de Charnac.

"*Bon matin, Monsieur 'Allorrahn. Commencer dehors tôt? Permettez-
moi, monsieurs?*" The co-pilot, M. Goriot, greeted both the marquise's intime and his companion and helped them into the jet.

"This is the pilot, Grandet," Claude said to Mike.

"No, *monsieur,*" came his patient reply. And, once again, he explained, "I am not M. Grandet. I am his co-pilot, Goriot."

"Yeah, whatever. Get back in the cockpit and take me back to the
chateau."

"*Oui, monsieur.*" Goriot didn't like turning his back on this one.
The marquis had been strange, but kind. The marquise, his mother,
exuded danger, but was controlled. A lady. This one was trouble.
Still, the marquise must trust him. After all, he knew how to find
the secret compartment that neither he nor Grandet could. Try as
they might. But not too often, and not too strenuously. There were
always Baum and White to consider even when no marquis or marquise was in residence.

Goriot returned to the cockpit and closed the door. He knew that if he turned around and immediately returned to the cabin, he'd find no one there. "Request permission for take-off. We're going back to the chateau," he told Grandet. He didn't mention *le jumeau*, the American who was a twin of the marquis. What did the Americans say: dead ringer? He tried not to think about it; buried himself in his take-off checklist.

Jack lay perfectly still in the secret chamber inside the baggage compartment. Hidden from both the living and the undead, he listened as his pilots prepared for take-off, as his mother's slave drugged his captive twin and sealed him inside a concealed compartment in one of the leather couches in the aft cabin.

"Take this," Claude instructed as he held out the small pills to Mike.

"What is it?" he asked, not taking them.

"Barbiturates. I want you asleep for the flight," Claude answered.

Mike took the two pills, swallowing them dry.

What would be the use of his fighting? Mike would want to see Mother destroyed as much as he wanted me dead. After that, he'll turn on Claude.

Jack settled back and released his mortal coil.

So, to finally go home again. Home to Charnac. Back to Mother. How fitting it seems to see her again at the chateau, in the recreation of the building where she murdered Phillipe. Where Claude thinks he can destroy her. With a human American ghost of me!

He closed his eyes and chuckled silently about best-laid plans. He slowly abandoned Jack and embraced Jean-Luc, the once and future Marquis de Charnac. Never living, never dead.

He drifted into memory as mortals are caught up in dreams. The memory of the last night he saw Claude Halloran, his former lover and his mother's vampire slave. The memory of his last few hours with Michael O'Donald, former policeman and unique entity. Neither fully human nor absolutely inhuman, a being caught between morality and corruption, hunter and victim at once. And in this dream that is not a dream, he heard himself, saw himself, with his human twin.

"I give you something I was never offered, Mike." In his cruelty, Jack unbuckled his belt and unbuttoned the top button of his black jeans. He told the kneeling doppelganger, "Phillipe stripped me of my will and then drained the blood from me." He slowly unzipped and lowered his pants. A punishment? A turn-on? He pulled aside his jock strap, draped his manhood on Mike's mouth and chin, and delivered the smug look resident only

in beings like him. Jack opened a small, razor-sharp, stainless steel knife and, holding the head of his penis just an inch from Mike's face, he inserted the blade a quarter-inch into its tip. He could smell the trepidation, the fear, the horror. Spicy and coppery, acidic and unclean, it smelled of urine and sweat. It smelled of conquest.

The blood, thick and syrupy, gushed from the split organ and drenched the small penknife. The gluey fluid spurted into Mike's face. Unclenching his jaws, he tried to scream, but instead his mouth filled with the vampire's gift. And once receiving, inadvertently demanded more.

"And just like you, I took it."

Jack thrust himself farther into Mike's unconscious mouth and fed him until he could no more. "You see now?" he whispered. "There is no other choice!"

That was when Mike remembered himself and bit down on his oppressor. His jaws and teeth freed him from his captor, as he separated Jack from his penis.

"NO!"

Jean-Luc shifted in his dream state, recalling scream and pain both. He reached down to his unhealing stump and watched Mike inch backwards across the splintery boards of the dilapidated pier. Remembered how he resolutely swallowed Jack's pride.

In his mind's eye, he saw himself adamantly rezip his pants and aggressively taunt his captive. *"Whether you die tonight or tomorrow or seventy-five years from now, my blood cells have already laid claim to yours, and you will become nosferatu at that time. After your death, your teeth will grow long nightly and will demand that you fulfill them with human blood. That is my curse upon you!"*

Jean-Luc remembered the cold night, the flurrying snow and the captive wind. The dark abandoned building that was lit by his will alone. He remembered too, his final cruelty.

"You must make the choice, Michael. Do you spend eternity as you are now, handsome and virile? Or as an old man, crippled and bent? How do you view your immortality, Michael? You can take your own life and be a beautiful suicide forever, or you can be a noble Christian and await your eventual human death. And resurrect as a wizened living corpse! But have a care, Michael! And follow your mortal mother's advice as well as your preternatural father's. Take care of your teeth! If you have none when you die, how will you take your inevitable victims?"

Jack watched Mike's heart harden as well as his will. "No, Jack, you are the one who doesn't understand. My teeth have seen the dentist's drill many times and have many times been refilled with a compound made with silver!"

That was when Jack realized that he had been given the argent sickness! Now, he'd never regrow. Not without extraordinary assistance. And Jack responded in his usual way.

"Burn!" he commanded. And the outer edges of the pier began to burn. The ancient, rotten timbers ignited immediately, their dampness producing overwhelming smoke.

Michael reached for his pistol and fired through the cloud.

"GO!" Jean-Luc remembered shouting. The force knocked Mike to the pier's entrance and he stumbled out of the doorway and onto the wharf.

He heard Tina Washington's shout, "Jesus! Oh my God! Mike!" And Mike's answer, "I shot him. I think I shot him."

Jack remembered how he marshaled his strength and bounded to the rafters and, pale and haggard, appeared in the hayloft window of the deserted pier. He pointed down to his escaping twin and called out in his distinct, yet oddly universal voice.

"Behold, the new Orion. The one among you, who is of you, yet not one of you."

And Mike froze in place and looked up. Voices from above and across the wicked metropolis seemed to echo this chant.

"The new Orion, self-contained and self-contaminated." This hit Mike in the gut.

"The new Orion, who must destroy himself to live off others.

"The new Orion, the self-hunting hunter, the reflection of myself.

"The new Orion, born and yet unborn, living and still undead. The new Orion."

And then the shot rang out. And that shot was shadowed by many. And the lone figure, torn by bullets, fell back from the opening and into the dark, smoking and burning pier.

Jack recalled the next few minutes as if they were eternity. He drove himself away from the hail of bullets and through the open space of the pier. He braced himself and plunged, feet first, through the rotting planks and down into the dark and salty Hudson River. At the base of the farthest piling, Jack shucked his boots and socks, his jacket and jeans and jockstrap. Fully naked, he kept only his key ring and trudged along the riverbed.

It is not true that a vampire cannot travel across running water. Their private legend has it that they can even rest for prolonged periods in it. Wrecked ships and underwater caverns would provide sanctuary from the hateful sun and vengeful masses. There, too, was the speculation that all vampiric things originally came, paradoxically, from the sea, the purported life-giver.

This was the time when Jack justified the conjecture. The Hudson River was bitterly cold, its current swift and treacherous. He knew it would be wrong to ride that current. It led past Manhattan and to the open sea. Jack had to travel north against the flux. He had to remain out of sight and presumably dead.

He made his way upriver at an alarming speed from Pier 45, feeling for and counting each pier along the way. In his mind, Jack ticked off the locations. Pier 46, Perry and Charles Streets. Pier 48, West 11th Street. On and on, through the moving morass, the universal solvent. Forty-nine, fifty, fifty-one. Finally, at Pier 57, he lifted himself out of the river.

Jack rose directly from the riverbed. Fifteenth Street. As all eyes were occupied at another pier, the naked and emasculated Jack bounded, deftly and deliberately, to the warehouse that stored his treasures.

The Sampson Brothers Storage Facility.

Jack eased the key into the Yale lock. The cinderblock hallways were tremendously cold and the corrugated tin of the roll-top door screeched at the indignity of its enforced opening. The infrared cameras never noticed.

Jack slipped inside and lowered the gate back into place. He made his way through the jumbled darkness. His sensitive eyes led his sensitive fingers to a switch. And silently, the cold locker breathed into life.

The storage room, twenty feet by fifteen feet and twelve feet tall, started to cast off its frigid coldness with the effort of the half-dozen space heaters jerry-rigged to a small and almost silent generator.

Sampson Brothers, between Tenth and Eleventh Avenues above Fifteenth Street, was one of his secret hiding places in Manhattan. But of them all, it was the most elaborately equipped, if not the most secure against a being like Jack. The Sampson Brothers catered to the gallery trade and many of the finest artworks in Manhattan were stored here. Stored by some of the most eccentric of patrons, who came and went at the oddest hours. The exorbitant rates reflected the sensitive nature of the warehouse. Many of the priceless works were officially considered missing and lost. Some considered myth and never to have existed. And some, like Jack, both.

Jack surveyed his sanctum. Twin cedar wardrobes held four seasons of clothing. Overcoats and suits, jackets and slacks, sweaters and dress shirts. Tuxedos and leathers and, for every place but the United States, furs. He had three cedar chests. The first contained sport shirts and T-shirts, sweats and jocks, underwear and socks. The second, jeans. Indigo and stonewashed, saltwashed and faded. Blue and black and white. Denim pants and shirts and vests and jackets. And under the jeans, cash.

From England and France. From Russia and China. Japanese, Indian, Brazilian and Greek. Money from Norway, from Canada, from Mexico and Israel. Australian, African, European, Asian, every American. Clean bills, not too crisp, not too new. All negotiable.

Like the bearer bonds and the artwork and the jewels. The third chest.

Jack dressed quickly. He needed to repair himself in, at least, a minimal way. The only way he knew how. He stepped into silver gray silk boxers and charcoal gray wool socks. Gray flannel slacks and a pewter turtleneck sweater. He pulled on a gray cashmere duster and blew out of the storage building like a gathering storm. The night security guard was still asleep, as commanded, and would remain so until Jack gave him permission to awaken.

Jack looked south on Tenth Avenue and decided against a return trip to the Village. The East Side was too far. The hour, too late. Chelsea it was; Chelsea it had to be. The sun would rise soon enough; he had little time. And, on Christmas morning, he would find his lamb, but undoubtedly no shepherds. And, he hoped, no wise men.

West 17th Street between Ninth and Tenth Avenues. The heart of Chelsea. Jack hesitated in front of an old brownstone when he heard the click of the lock.

George Kalamatos opened the front door of the shoddy, sad building. Not quite thirty, George had left Astoria and his parents' house to make it on his own in Manhattan. Except, he had not yet made it, except on his own.

At five feet, eight inches and one hundred fifty-five pounds, George was average. He had medium brown hair, medium brown eyes, average intelligence.

His skin was pale for a Greek, a dusty white with pale rose blush marks at his full cheeks and just a gleam of pink on his nostrils. His eyebrows and moustache were thick, dark and shiny, and even his close shave revealed a blue-black cast above his defined jawline.

His gait was unsteady, sluggish. Not from drink, nor drug, nor exhaustion, nor any external. George was not comfortable in his own body. Jack desired him for the very cleanness of his blood.

"I'm very sorry to bother you," Jack started. "But, are you on your way to Christmas Mass?"

Every nerve ending of George Kalamatos's being sung out, closing his glottis completely.

"I'm sorry," Jack continued, expanding his accent and softening his voice, "I am bothering you."

"No. No, you're not! I just didn't expect anyone else to be around this early." George silently cursed himself for his gracelessness.

"A Catholic Church?" Jack asked, trying to seem nonchalant in face of the nearing morning.

"Greek Orthodox, I'm sorry," George replied.

"Thanks anyway. Merry Christmas."

"Wait!"

George Kalamatos was about to do something he'd never done in twenty-nine years. He was going to pick up a sex partner. He was going to pick up a man. He was finally going to accept he was gay.

"I have a phone book upstairs. I could find the nearest church for you."

Somehow he knew that neither he nor the beautiful blond before him was going anywhere near church today. He doubted that he'd make it to his parents' house later. He would be right.

George's apartment was a small studio with a tiny bedroom alcove. The enclosed alcove, the closet and the bathroom had the only doors. Doors he had apparently installed himself. There were three double-hung windows, all beginning to allow some early prelight. Jack had to work the virgin fast.

"The phone directory?"

George's hopes sunk. "It's in the bedroom. I'll get it."

Jack followed George into the bedroom and sat down on the bed. Between George and the bookcase. George had to reach over him to grab the phone book.

Game.

Jack nuzzled George from clavicle to navel at that reach. The groan indicated enough approval for Jack to ask, "May I close this door?" Jack already knew he'd be trapped in this apartment until the dusk.

"I'm sorry," his host asked, "are you cold?"

"Very."

Soap, over ninety-nine percent pure, scented George's hair and moustache. His armpits and chest and groin. Jack knew which one it was. He inspected it well.

It took little of Jack's time or talent to conquer George. You can't rape the willing. And willing and able he was. Jack sensed much of Phillipe in this other Greek's body and nothing of him in the psyche. Fine!

Jack led the way. Inserting his tongue in George's mouth, he hinted at further insertions. Jack removed George's tie. Unbuttoned his shirt. Opened his belt. He left George with his T-shirt and briefs. New for Christmas. Standing on the bed, he stripped to the waist for George. And witnessing this, George said, "I'm not sure what to do."

"Turn around."

George did.

"Kneel."

He did.

Jack stripped George of the remains of his clothing, ripping them free of his body. Tearing away the remains of his avoidance. And with it, all of his shyness, all of his will to oppose. Jack surprised his host with an inventiveness beyond his mortal imagination, and filled him with all of his knowledge. As gracious receiver, George learned all he ever would, experienced all he ever could, on that day, sealed in his lightfast bedroom with the master of his world, the lord of the undead. He abandoned his body and his fear. Then, he reached around, finally braving the confirmation of his phallus worship.

And the emperor had none.

"What? Oh, my God!"

He sacrificed his life and suffered the loss of it for Jack. The Horror of West Street.

Jack wrapped the desanguinated body in the top sheet and dropped it over the far side of the bed. He covered himself in the king-size comforter and dropped, in the darkness, with a few ounces of French soil from his pocket, into a moribund sleep.

He arose past sunset to the persistent ring of the telephone. He recalled the clean, fresh young man, now enshrouded on the floor at the side of the bed. He rose from the bed and went to the bathroom, never pausing as he listened to the incoming message.

"Georgie? Are you there yet? It's Momma."

Jack took a wash cloth from the sink and wet it under the scalding water.

"How could you do this to us?" another message from George's mother continued in an angry whisper. "Your aunts and uncles, your cousins, they're all talking. 'Where is Georgie? How come Georgie isn't here?' "

Jack wiped the French soil from his besmeared body. His anger grew at the sight of his now genderless form. *I blame you for this, Mother. And you will pay dearly.*

A later message insisted, "I'm sending your brothers right over for you now. They'll talk some sense into you. They'll bring you back," Mrs. Kalamatos continued. "And, believe me, Georgie, you're not going to spend one more day in that apartment. In that city."

Jack redressed quickly. The intercom was active and there were steps on the stairs. Although he'd very much like to entertain George's Greek brothers, perhaps this wasn't the best time. And he had a little matter of his own mother and her vampire slave to deal with. Jack went out the window and into the night.

By the time he'd located where his mother had been staying, under the identity of the Princess Montrovia, she had checked out of the Sherry-Netherland and had disappeared. His only hope was to use the cop, Michael O'Donald, as bait. Surely, she wouldn't ignore him. Certainly, Claude wouldn't.

It took a full month of waiting and watching before Claude finally showed himself. And in the company of Tina Washington, anchorwoman, lesbian, and now formerly of the human race.

The sensation of the jet's descent broke Jack's reverie. It was well past sunset and in order for this hoax to succeed, Noel could not know of the airplane's return.

The almost imperceptible bounce and skidding as the brakes were applied signaled Jack's first return to his homeland in a dozen decades. He would wait, cocooned in the dark, until silence was all that surrounded him. And would reemerge—Jean-Luc, the Marquis de Charnac.

"Charnac welcomes you."

Jean-Luc Courbet de Charnac heard the prescribed greeting at the stroke of midnight. These were the very words he had heard said to Phillipe on the night of his first arrival. The exact and only phrase used by the administrators of Chateau Charnac, the officers of Charnac International, to welcome home their Marquis. The CEO.

Just those words, intoned in the perfect blend of two baritones, introduced Messrs. Baum and White for the first time to Jean-Luc as their new master.

Jean-Luc had been the Marquis de Charnac since the night of Phillipe's death, but had not seen Baum and White since even before that. Jean-Luc had given them the control of Charnac's vast holdings and with that, they rebuilt the chateau.

"I am Charnac!" Jean-Luc responded in the traditional manner as he emerged from the hidden depths of the jet.

"I am yours to command," they answered as one. That was their way. There was no Baum without White. No White without Baum. Phillipe had shared their secret with Jean-Luc after his first meeting with them.

Phillipe had encountered them in Rome on that July night when Nero sang as Rome burned, more than nineteen centuries ago. They were born Greek, like Phillipe, but were slaves in a senator's villa. With chaos ruling the streets of Rome, and the flames that enveloped the capital making the night as bright as day, the lovers were running from their bondage and their torture.

Dentro and Aspros would have been hard to miss in any place at any time. They were each just shy of seven feet tall. Albinos, their coloration was almost the same as Phillipe's. But they also suffered from congenital hypotrichosis, and that condition made them completely and utterly hairless. Totally bald, they had no facial hair, no eyebrows, no lashes. No body hair, not on their chests or legs, in their armpits, nor at their pubis.

The debauched senator kept the teenagers as pets. He wanted them as sex toys to revitalize his flagging abilities, but the two young men had promised themselves to one another only and suffered much physical abuse for their monogamy. Then, on that fateful day when Nero destroyed Rome, they found freedom in the guise of Phillipe.

"What is the problem?" he asked them in Greek.

"Our master has flogged my Aspros," Dentro answered, "for refusing his advances."

Phillipe wondered, "I did not think a slave could shun his master." He pointed to their badges of slavery as proof of their position.

"We have killed him," they said in unison. Strange creatures, fortunate to have found one another.

"They will put you to death for that," Phillipe replied.

The streets were muddy from the attempt to quell the flames. Phillipe, Dentro, and Aspros had attained a normal human look from the flying cinder and ash.

"You are a countryman," Dentro insisted.

"Help us!" Aspros pleaded.

Phillipe looked at the abnormal youths seriously. Abnormally tall and abnormally strong. Perfectly hairless and colorless. "I can give you something in appreciation for your singular devotion to one another. Will you remain as one for eternity?"

"It is what we desire, master," Dentro and Aspros answered in one voice.

"Save for your singular devotion to one another, do you give all else to me?"

"You will be master to us."

"Follow me."

Phillipe took them to his rented villa in a section of Rome unblemished by Nero's fire. He took them into his bedchamber and removed his toga.

They were shocked by his hairiness and his overture. As pale and thin as his skin was, that was how dark and abundant his fur. He was horrific and stunning to the eye. A perfect man, solitary in his beauty and terrifying in his beastliness.

"Undress."

"We . . ." one started to say.

". . . cannot," the other finished

"You will. Dentro undress Aspros. Aspros, remove Dentro's tunic."

The tunics were made from a coarse dark material of three feet and a half. The color, a ruddy, muddy brown, was the symbol of a slave. It was further insulting on the two of them, because it made their pale, hairless condition more obvious still.

"Go to each other. Be with each other, under my watchful eye," Phillipe instructed.

"Master, we cannot do this for you," they replied.

"I do not intend to join you in your lovemaking. I am freeing you because I respect your dedication to one another. Realize that I am not as other men. However, you must follow my instructions to the letter in order to be emancipated for life."

Dentro and Aspros stripped each other without a further word. In silence, lost in one another's eyes, they revealed themselves. The gods had deprived the lovers of much, but had handsomely repaid them in a very private way.

They went to the dais and stretched out on the feather-stuffed mattress covered in Egyptian linen. Glabrous as babes, they intertwined their overlong arms, overlong legs, overlong torsos and penises.

The dark and hirsute stranger watched in rapt stillness. It was like watching marble statues enliven and adore one another. It gave Phillipe the germ of an idea that he would not bring into fruition until they traveled to France and he was awarded the estate at Charnac.

Their lovemaking was like an undulating dance. Like the wind's caress on a field of grain. Like a school of exotic fish swimming in silent accord. Like the conjugation of clouds. It was not sex; it was art.

Quietly, Phillipe advised them.

"I will join you on the pallet now. Fear not. I admire you and will not take any advantage. But, to save your love for eternity, I must take your blood from you and return mine to you both."

Brykolakas.

Both men thought it at once. *A blood monster.*

Phillipe sidled onto the bed. His hairy chest, belly and legs tormenting, disgusting the young lovers. He took the symbols of their manhood, the very things they had killed to preserve for one another alone, and swallowed them simultaneously.

Their eyes flashed widely. This was the assault they had fought to avoid. They struggled, unsuccessfully, against the inhumanly strong creature.

Phillipe pinned them both to their backs by asserting small pressure from the heels of his hands to their sternums. He broke the skin below the swollen heads of their penises with his enlarged incisors. Fluid, their blood, flowed hot and thick from vein and artery. He drank.

Dentro looked longingly into the eyes of Aspros. Aspros returned the look and kissed him deeply and solemnly as they both slowly died.

At that very last moment, Phillipe relinquished their prized possessions and bit into the radial arteries of his wrists. He shoved the left one into Dentro's open mouth and gave the right one to Aspros. And, as all had before, they suckled.

When they regained themselves, Dentro and Aspros knew that they were undead. They bowed to their master and spoke in a new, slightly metallic baritone, "I am yours to command."

Never again did the lovers refer to themselves as other than one entity. Never did they need to hunt as Phillipe did. They shocked Phillipe by feeding on one another.

Simultaneously.

"Remember this always," Phillipe demanded of them. "Never two by one. No others will ever be recreated as you have been. It is my law!"

"I am yours to command," they repeated.

"Hide me from my mother and tell me of her doings," Jean-Luc answered. They nodded. Baum, which means tree in German, as does *"dentro"* in Greek, took his left arm. White—'*aspros*' in Greek— took his right. They led him to the dark and ancient underground chamber where Phillipe, creator of them all, had hidden his books.

"Where is my mother?" Jean-Luc asked with no display of emotion.

"She has taken over part of the old Roman baths. It is there that she plies her magic," their zygotic reply produced of gametic tones.

"Tell me of her. Does she succeed in her learning?"

Baum and White answered, "She learns what I allow and no more. For as long as you walk the earth, you are Charnac."

"*Bon.* Is that all?"

"M. Halloran, her slave, and the strange one, your twin, M. O'Donald, are in residence as well."

"Why do you call him strange?" Jean-Luc understood that they knew much, but what could they know of Michael O'Donald?

"Your doppelganger is not as the other living. And when he passes on, he will not be like you of the undead," they explained.

This was the terrifying truth, the evil and the effect to be played out here at Charnac. All the players and all together. Jean-Luc, the most perfect of vampires, the direct descendant of Phillipe. Noel, his mother. A strong vampiress and a powerful witch who daily grew more puissant. Beautiful and duplicitous Claude. An undead never to be fully trusted, nor ever ignored. Vanity, jealousy and ignorance ruled this revenant.

And Michael O'Donald. The only still-living creature in the vast chateau. Unique though Baum and White were, they were suggesting a new and different creature in him.

What have I done? If Phillipe could convert both of these men simultaneously and create a new species of vampire, what have I made of Michael? He does grow older; I can see it, smell it in him, but at an inhuman slowness. The sun's rays have begun to annoy him. What else?

"What will happen when he dies, *monsieur le Marquis*?" they wanted to know.

"I am not certain," Jean-Luc admitted.

Baum and White looked at each other. "This is not good."

"What do you know, gentlemen?" For, indeed, they were. "What will happen?"

"There is no way to be certain, master. It would have been for the best if your interaction on the pier in New York had never happened. But, there are other things to consider right now."

"Mother?"

"You!"

With that, the hidden underground of the ancient corps-de-logis, the original castle keep, sprang into life. This was no imitation, no replication of the original chateau.

Jean-Luc knew that Baum and White, as caretakers and protectors of Charnac, had rebuilt the castle in exact detail. There had been some changes, naturally, over the years. Modernized electrical system and sprinklers, both inside and out. A state-of-the-art kitchen, though it was rarely used, needed only as exhibit. Of the Roman baths that Phillipe had used for his sculpting hobby, the hot pool had been reverted to its former use, but with modern temperature controls and filters. The warm and cold pool areas they had refurbished with new appeal.

But none of the recreation of Chateau Charnac was like this. Here, in the hidden vault where Phillipe had discovered the secret knowledge of the known world, Baum and White had preserved the spirit, if not the letter.

The floors were of polished black marble. The original granite walls were also polished to a gleaming sheen. Row upon row of crisp halogen lighting subdued the glinting little ambers and rubies and emeralds. This was still the heart and head of Charnac, yet now completely automated.

Massive computer mainframes lined the walls. Expansive workstations occupied the center of the cavern. Everything glistened, so sleek, so cool, so clean. Charnac was as aloof and inhuman as it had ever been. But the ancient seat of iniquity had entered yet a new millennium.

"*Excellent! Magnifique!* Bold and beautiful at once! Phillipe should have seen this!"

All three creatures were overtaken by the mild stirring of their former human responses to the master of vampires. A personal sadness caught at each of them. And any vampire overcome by emotion is a lost thing. Jean-Luc first broke free.

"*Allons-y!*"

"Yes," they agreed, his tone reclaiming them, "let us get on with it. Remove your clothing. Let me see the damage."

Jack stripped completely. His color was rapidly approaching theirs.

They inspected the remaining stump of his penis, barely a flaccid inch. The cut end was concave and elliptical, echoing the shape of Mike's bite mark. Not bleeding, it was not healing. The rough, raw edges were not damp, but crystallized.

"The argent sickness," Baum and White pronounced. "Have you fed regularly since this happened?"

"Daily."

"Drained each one?"

"I always do."

The lovers were still sickened by this remark. Although they knew, in theory, how their masters had continued to live, they had never been directly confronted with the reality since the night they were changed.

"That's good," they finally managed to say. "I will keep you in good supply until I can achieve a reversal."

"I have always hunted for myself," Jean-Luc insisted. Then they reminded him of his first victim, in this very chateau. He conceded and went on to ask, "Is it possible then? To regrow?"

"I have no reason to doubt it. You have taken good care and I have already done the research."

"That is good news. Now, what do we do about the others?"

"Master, I have a plan . . ."

Baum and White outlined their plan to stop Noel from her final and greatest occult commitment. She must be stopped, they insisted, before her power was ultimate.

They explained how Jean-Luc's role would fit into Claude's plan to "gaslight" Noel. Jack should replace his own imposter. By using his supernatural abilities, he should torment Noel and deceive Claude until the full moon, the night of the greatest gambit.

"Your mother must be destroyed. This you must already know. She is much too strong and selfish to remain a private immortal. She wishes to be worshiped as a goddess and if she succeeds in her Black Mass, she will achieve her goal."

Reluctantly, Jean-Luc agreed. What else could be done? She could be kept trapped in a silver cage, her victims brought to her for eternity. But that would give her more time to grow and more reason for revenge. No, Jean-Luc admitted, there can be no more of Noel. *Maman est finis. Elle est morte.*

"Agreed, then. I will take care of Noel and Claude," said the resigned master of Charnac.

"You may wish to spare M. Halloran a while longer," they suggested.

"Why?"

"*Monsieur le Marquis,* I will attempt to cause your regrowth with what I have learned over the centuries. If, however, I fail, you will still need some lure for your victims. Claude, as you well know, is a splendid snare. And, once he has witnessed the destruction of your mother by your own hand, I am certain that M. Halloran will become . . . docile. And, possibly more."

"He tried to kill me."

"Only as a means of preserving himself. To protect himself from your mother. That is all."

Jean-Luc had to recognize the logic behind this. Claude could certainly attract victims. And things would have worked out nicely with him had it not been for Mother.

"And what do we do with M. O'Donald?" Jean-Luc asked, tying up loose ends.

"He will be left here with me. He will not bother you, nor any other. He will grow old as a mortal and when he is no more, then I shall see what becomes of him. He will be safe and protected from harm and will live to grow ancient. I believe that he is better off here."

Jean-Luc almost agreed, and then realized, "How can I keep him here with me at the chateau? He would be a daily reminder of what I had done."

Baum and White looked at each other. It seemed an eternity that they met, held and explored each other's gaze. When they at last spoke, naturally, they spoke as one.

"You are not to remain, *Monsieur le Marquis*. Charnac is no place for you. Even if you did not keep M. Halloran, you alone would require more than a hundred victims yearly. Possibly double or triple that. How could all those disappearances be hidden in a place so small?

"And with the additional needs of M. Halloran? The countryside would be decimated in half the time. No, you must go on as you have before, to large, anonymous communities where you are not so well noticed. And neither are your activities. Meanwhile . . ."

They turned as one. Two extremely tall, two extremely strong, two extremely pale men. Their all-black suits—identical—were expensive and immaculate. Their matching silk shirts as crisp as their demeanor and as starkly white as their flesh. The unblemished Bruno Magli oxfords on their feet made little noise as they walked solemnly to a secreted door.

They returned in a moment with a youth of about nineteen. He walked between them, aware and erect and totally undressed. A farm worker, no doubt, for the size of his muscles. An angel, undoubtedly, for the naive beauty of him.

He was Jean-Luc's height, but much broader. His chest and shoulders, arms and lats, back and abdomen and legs attesting to the congregation of hard work and heavy loads.

His hair was brown, the color of a new fawn. And the ridge of his nose was mottled with a spray of coppery freckles. His eyes were the color of a deepening summer sky and his lips and his nipples were very full and very pink.

"Is he drugged?" Jean-Luc asked in suspicion as he felt his incisors growing.

"Not narcotized, hypnotized!" they answered in a single voice. A single mind. A single intent.

"Quesque vous-appelez vous?" Jean-Luc asked.

"Mathieu."

"And do you know who I am, Mathieu?"

"You are the master of Charnac," Mathieu replied evenly, too evenly, "the marquis."

This is a good state for the victims. This one does not even note my loss. Was he instructed not to notice? Or, maybe he doesn't look at men down there. Nevertheless . . .

"What do you want from me, Mathieu?"

"To serve you, lord."

Jean-Luc stepped in closer. They nearly touched.

"You are beautiful, Mathieu."

"No, *seigneur*. I am a common man."

"Embrace me, Mathieu."

Jean-Luc watched the closed cells of the young man's pupils crack into an awakening. The innocent schoolboy's smile drooped, ever so slightly, as compliance questioned.

Good.

"I should not embrace you, sir."

"Why is that, Mathieu?" Jean-Luc asked in mock concern. In total alert.

"You are naked."

"You are naked as well. Have you never embraced a friend after bathing in the river?"

Jean-Luc was playing with his food again. A nasty habit from a spoiled childhood. Or was he merely showing off for the audience?

"If I promise not to touch you below the waist, will you not give me a hug? Come, Mathieu, we're all men here! Do not be such a child!"

And Mathieu Rorchet gave himself up like a man. The room where he'd been kept was cold. This computer room was cold. The blond man holding him didn't seem much colder than he already felt. The man put his lips to Mathieu's neck. Unconsciously, Mathieu put his head on the marquis's shoulder. His neck suddenly began to warm where the marquis kissed it. Maybe he would warm all of me, Mathieu wondered absently. He had grown so very cold. So very cold. So . . .

"I will become the doppelganger now! Where is he kept?" Jean-Luc barely needed to swipe a backhand at his lips. He drained so well.

"The chapel, lord," the indivisible reply. "He is sequestered there until he is needed."

"Hide me!"

Baum and White took Jean-Luc to the chamber where the victim, Mathieu, had been secluded earlier. A huge box, four feet wide, seven feet long and three feet deep, was salted with the soil of Charnac. Made from the cedars of Lebanon for a Crusading knight, it was also strewn with lavender and cinnamon, lemon peel and myrrh. A welcome home gift from his devoted servants.

Jean-Luc Courbet, Marquis de Charnac, settled himself naked into his perfumed nest. The heavy lid closed and he released himself into the night. Disembodied, he drifted back into the recreated chateau. He passed through the public rooms on the main floor and, invisible, entered into the chapel.

Rough-hewn granite and solid mahogany beams. Brass flambeaus and incensors. Stained glass of deepest amethyst and brightest topaz. The colors of Charnac. The grape and the grain. The body and the blood.

And cowering in the midst of it, the doppelganger.

He was awake.

chapter

I wasn't alone in this darkness.

I knew that the single entrance to the chapel hadn't opened, but there was someone, no, some*thing*, else with me. This was the Chateau Charnac after all. Not the creature who brought me, or the creatures who greeted me, or the one I was here to destroy could I ever consider people.

Could I be? Would other men consider me, Michael Flannery O'Donald, human?

All I've learned, from Jack before his death on the pier and from Claude on the way to the plane, assured me that my intended victim, Noel Courbet, was dangerous. Deadly. She was the worst thing here and so had to be dealt with first. Claude'd be next. For the way he treated Tina. For what he did to Laura. He deserved it. The two tall, strange men, Baum and White? Well, there's got to be something wrong with them to work here. They'll have to go, too.

But who, or what, was in the room with me? How did it get here? And what does it want?

Soon it would be daylight. I could see the stained glass begin its illumination from outside. No undead thing would travel outside this close to dawn. Could this be Claude performing one last check? No, he'd be too busy placating Noel. It had to be Baum or White.

I disobeyed my instructions and lit one of the beeswax tapers. The chapel was a revelation. And I was alone in it.

It was a place too beautiful for these godless monsters. And way too good for me. Built of gray granite blocks, it wasn't exactly circular, but constructed of twelve flat-sided walls. One, I noticed, for each month of the year, each one representing an apostle or an angel, one for each sign of the zodiac. Each, I didn't know then, a decade of youth and vitality for the vampire.

I judged each wall to be about six and a half feet wide and roughly fifteen feet high. Each had a thick brass disk of its zodiacal symbol, three feet in diameter, embedded in the wall and centered exactly five feet from the floor. These shields looked to be very old. It made me sorry that I never learned about art and architecture and their history. The heavy brazen saucers were very ornate and vulgar, bordering on pornography. The ones that had only human figures were explicit enough, but the ones involving animals were disgusting. A few feet above each shield was a pointed stained glass window. I remembered the shape from my altar boy days. A lancet arch. Thank you, Father Connelly, for being such a stickler for details. It was the most common style window for a chapel. Maybe that's why I remembered it.

These windows were mostly purple and yellow glass, and each represented a month of the year. I don't remember much of my high school French, but as I looked around, I noticed that they were inscribed with *septembre, octobre, novembre* and *decembre.* Anyone could have figured that out, and I could also count backwards.

Each of them had a different flower in the center. Some I could identify. A rose, a bunch of violets, a daisy. Most I couldn't. Something else I realized I had never learned. I remembered my mother saying something about each month having its own flower. I guessed then that she'd been right.

Each window also held its own birthstone. And every one of those stones was leaded in as just another piece of glass. But I knew just by looking at them that those fist-sized additions weren't glass. They were real. A huge diamond at April, a sapphire at September, emerald in May's window. I can't remember the names for them all. Yet another sin of omission on my part.

From the altar at the center of the room, the disks and the windows looked pretty much the same. Except for the wall with the thick and heavy wooden door. July.

It was Leo. And Leo I had reason to remember.

In the tall arched window above the door, again mostly purple and yellow glass, a sunflower was portrayed in the middle. And just below the flower, there was a ruby about the size of a navel orange. Larger than a baseball, it was the most beautiful object I'd ever seen.

I remembered too little of Laura Wilcox, but I clearly remembered her ruby pendant. And as magnificent as that was, and as much as I coveted it, this stone here was a monster. I couldn't even have desired it. It belonged in the forehead of some pagan idol in some remote and exotic place. I was certain that it had been stolen from a place just like that.

The astrological plate embedded in the door was the same size and shape as the others. It gleamed, however, in a way that the others didn't. It was clear to me that the big, heavy shield was made of solid gold. Gold and gruesome.

The dozen shields around the chapel all depicted sexual activities. Soloed and partnered and grouped. Every aspect of carnal peccadillo from the imperfectly human to the bestially cruel, from lovingly self-agonistic to perversely polymorphic existed in exhibition on these works of overwrought art. There in *septembre*, a round and luscious virgin was caught in the arms of a hairy Satyr. She screamed at the knowing that she would be one no longer. The Gemini twins of *juin* did all that two men could to each other in one frozen moment.

As I inspected further, I realized why Pisces meant fish. And why *avril* was the cruelest month. But I had to turn back to the segment that held the door. The month and sign that represented me. The odd man out.

The huge medallion consisted of two handsomely well-built and well-endowed naked men. They stretched between them a male lion on a bed of flames. Its heart was pierced by something sharp. And smoke from its dying carcass rose into a starry and fully moonlit night. Except for the men's erections, there didn't seem to be anything expressly sexual about the image on the shield. But it remained the most disturbing.

Michael O'Donald, I must speak with you.

I heard the voice inside my head. And I knew that voice. I'd never forget it.

Yes, Mike, it's me. Jack.

I shook with the fear that this was imagined. I sobbed with the realization that this was indeed real.

"Where are you, you bastard? Come out where I can see you, you fucking bastard!"

I cannot show myself to you at present. I am not yet arisen.

I barely recognized the quote—the mockery of it—for the terror and rage I felt. But he was here, this I knew for certain. He was here and, I had begun to suspect, inside of my head.

Very good, Mike! I see that my blood has already begun to give you some gifts of observation.

"Gift? You call this a gift, you monster? I've lost everything because of you. My lover, my job, my life, maybe even my best friend!"

I started easing around the chapel, perversely hoping that Jean-Luc Courbet, the owner of the chateau, was truly, physically, here. In this odd chapel, one with a dozen edging pews. This strange chapel with its polished granite slab of an altar set directly in the center. One way in and one way out.

"I'll tell them that you're here, that you're alive."

Why would you want to do that, Michael? Claude could do nothing about it. Baum and White already know. And my mother? Are you ready to face the creature that I have hidden from for twelve decades?

The laughter in my head was cruel and terrifying. I knew then what madness was. Or thought that I did. And in my madness, I threatened.

"I can go out in the daytime, when you can't. I'll take care of all of you then," I promised.

And how do you expect to get out of a locked room?

"Then, at night. Your mother is awake then. She'll hear my screams. She'll come."

I didn't know how it happened exactly, but in the next moment I flew upon the altar stone. My hands were held down to the corners near my head and my ankles held to the opposing corners. I couldn't turn my head left or right. Try as I might, I couldn't pull away. And yet I knew, there was no one else in this room.

When I surrendered the fight to the force that held me, the terrible thing happened. My right hand lifted from the granite and moved, by itself, towards my head. I was not in control. It came at me, an alien thing.

I began to sweat and the hand that used to belong to me wiped it from my forehead. Then it began to caress my face. It slipped lower down my chin onto my neck. I watched as it slid under the neck of my black sweater and over the skin of my chest. My own right forefinger rasped and prodded at my nipple. And when I began to respond, I also began to cry.

My estranged hand reacted to my sobs and withdrew. He does have a conscience, I thought. My hand drifted slowly from my body and rose until it was fully outstretched above me. I assumed that it would go back to its pinned, captive position. But how wrong I was.

It sank slowly forward, torturously slow. In my imagining, there were many things he could have done with my traitor hand, and none of them I wanted to see. I shut my eyes.

He opened them.

He controlled my body, every part of it. This I realized. He grabbed the fabric of my sweater between my fingers and my thumb and pulled it free of my black jeans. He played with my belly, rubbing it, slapping it. Hard. He lifted the end tab of my belt and pulled it free of its buckle.

I began to shout, "no," but he clenched my jaws. It was only my tear ducts he couldn't control. Or didn't care to.

I watched him open the waist button with my own hand and unzip me. He used my own hand to cup me. He plied me until I was erect and achy, but he wasn't finished. He wasn't interested in my pleasure, in the one I'd deprived him of ever having again. It was my humiliation he wanted and total dominance. And I do not care to reveal how he achieved it.

Evening came.

I must have slept, but I don't remember. All I recall is the sudden knowledge that I was free of his controlling mind. Slowly, cautiously, I sat up on the altar. On the twelfth wall, the door was ajar.

I jumped down from the stone slab and the soft sound of my feet hitting the floor alerted my captor, my jailer.

"You sleep like the dead!" Claude's idea of a joke.

"This isn't going to work, Claude."

"So, you do remember, Mikey! Good! Put these on!" Claude ordered.

It was a single-piece outfit like a speed skater would wear. Black silk. The bottom was like panty hose; it continued up as a body suit with long sleeves, a turtleneck with masklike hood.

"No."

"It's cold outside, Mikey! If you're going to pull this off, you'll have to save your energy."

Of course, Claude was right. It annoyed me to no end that he was. He watched me strip off my black sweater, my boots and socks and jeans. I reached for the elastic band of my shorts, but . . .

"Relax, Romeo. You're only here to do a job," he told me.

I sat on the floor to put on the leggings of the garment that looked like Peter Pan's shadow. I stood and pulled the crotch up to mine and put my arms into the sleeves. I pulled the nearly invisible zipper up from the navel to the neck. I was warm. Really warm.

"Put your clothes back on over it," Claude instructed. I honestly didn't know where this was going. I redressed.

"Here, use these, not your boots." Claude handed me a pair of very soft leather shoes. Suede, maybe, with soft felt soles. Black.

"We do not make sound when we walk. Neither should you. Remember: you will only live as long as your impersonation is believable." Claude smiled with his eyes only. A look that was an invitation as well as a dare. Cat's eyes and cruel. "Come!"

And the game, I thought, was afoot.

Claude led me down a corridor made of the same gray granite blocks. The walls were punctuated with gilt-edged mirrors and sconces. The high ceilings interrupted every eight feet or so by large stained glass lamps—purple and gold—hung from massive chains. The floors were covered in a thick patterned runner about six feet wide and continuing the entire length of the hallway. Purple and gold in color. Wheat and grape in design.

The hall ended at what seemed to be the main foyer of the chateau.

"This is the main floor and these are the public rooms," Claude whispered. "The game room, the library, the armory and the formal dining room are on this floor. Down that way"—he pointed to a massive stone staircase leading down to a wooden double door—"is the entrance floor. The formal courtyard and the bridge that separates the chateau from the rest of the estate are there. Do not cross the bridge!"

"Why?" I wanted to know.

"Because I will kill you if you do, Mikey."

I shook. I was certain that Claude could smell the fear on me. I certainly could. Then, his smirk confirmed it.

"It is good to be afraid of death, Mikey. That will keep you alive!"

The idiot! It isn't dying I'm afraid of, it's not dying! It's never being able to die!

"The other way," Claude disrupted my thoughts to finish his tour, "leads to the garden. You will do most of your work there. Come."

"I'm hungry."

"Shit!"

Claude had forgotten mortal needs in a very short time. "Shit," he said again. His deliberate attempt to speak in the same faultless fashion as the others didn't extend to curse words apparently.

"Mister Halloran?"

Out of the shadows, Baum and White appeared. Dressed, as always, in their black suits, they looked like funeral directors from the surreal. They frightened Claude—I could tell by the way he reacted to the sound of his name—these strange men who spoke as one.

"What do you want?" Claude barked, recovering.

"I have prepared dinner for your companion. Is he ready to dine?"

I knew then that Claude suspected something of the supernatural in their catering. But I knew, just by looking at them, that they were accustomed to a servile life and that providing for guests of the chateau was second nature to them.

Claude left me to the strange pair's ministrations. I followed Baum and White past the armory hall and on to the kitchen and dining hall. I noted, in passing, the solid antique furnishings, the tapestries and rugs. Porcelain vases and gold plates, paintings and sculptures that looked as if they belonged in a museum. I also made note of the arsenal of weapons stored here.

"All these things are very expensive, aren't they?" I asked my guards.

"Priceless," they said.

"How much is Jean-Luc worth, then?"

"If he had lived, *Monsieur le marquis* would be worth a great many million. Some billions U.S. perhaps," they answered.

"You know, don't you?" I said it quietly, although I wanted to shout. "You know that he's alive, that he's here." I might not have a supernatural ability to read their minds, but I was still a damn good cop. These guys knew.

"Have a care. *Madame la marquise* may be distracted with her project right now, Mister O'Donald, but still, it is best not to tempt fate and draw attention to yourself. After all, you have not yet accomplished what you set out to do, have you?"

I stared up at their bald heads, their colorless faces, their pink and naked eyes. These men were more human than any other being in this house. More human, I thought, than I was anymore. And they knew that Claude's plan wasn't my plan. And there was more than that.

"You're lovers, aren't you?"

And they answered in that disconcerting way of theirs, in one voice and referring to themselves as one person. "I, Michael, am more than you can possibly grasp right now. I am more Charnac than I am *of* Charnac. A subtle distinction, to be sure, but one you will one day appreciate. Eat now."

I hadn't realized that we'd continued walking. I didn't know exactly where in the house we were. The dining hall, like all of the public rooms, was massive. And all of the furniture and effects were in proportion to the room.

The head of the dining table was set with more food than I could ever imagine eating. A full roast turkey, a whole smoked ham, a standing rib roast. Cold shrimp, salmon and caviar. Halved avocados holding quartered lemons. Potatoes roasted with beets, carrots and leeks. Asparagus and broccoli in creamy sauces. Green beans and peas floating in butter and smelling of mint. Freshly baked bread and chilled water. And wine—at the correct temperature, I was certain.

"You don't expect me to eat all of this, do you?"

They spoke and each time they did, I got chills. They never seemed to have to consult nor take clues from each other to speak in a perfect blend of their two voices.

"Need I remind you that Noel Courbet is busy now? Too busy to take note of you. But understand, she will notice a banquet prepared in a house where nothing living dwells. I prepared everything at once, for it must last some time. Or I will be hard pressed to explain a second time why I cooked."

"You're both like them, then?"

"No, I am not as they are. Nor, I believe, will you be when your time comes."

"Jack told you?"

"I knew before the master said a word. He does not know what he created in you."

"But you guys do? You know what will happen to me?"

They smiled at me and suddenly I didn't find them grotesque anymore. Their hairless heads and faces took on a quality like classical sculpture, a sense of masculine beauty I'd never seen before. No longer seeming thin, they looked to possess the perfect balance of wiry muscle for their long frames. And immediately, they didn't seem to be unnaturally tall either. No more so than a professional basketball player. These guys were actually riveting.

"Thank you, Michael. This must be the first time in my long history that I was not thought repulsive and, in fact, handsome."

As I ate, Baum and White told me their story. An extraordinary, yet fully believable tale of ancient times and modern wonders. Of the sad childhoods of Aspros and Dentro and their cruel slavery and the means by which they escaped it. Of their servitude over the ages to the Greek, Phillipe, the maker of vampires. From the fall of Rome through the Dark Ages to the Renaissance. Of Marco Polo and Christopher Columbus. Old worlds and new. Of wars and peace. Wealth and poverty. Life and death. And how that vampire evolved to become the first Marquis de Charnac.

They told me how Noel had murdered Phillipe and how Jack had destroyed the chateau in an attempt to kill his mother. Of his flight, her pursuit and of their own reconstruction of Charnac. Of how they remained as stewards to a new wealth and of how they repulsed the Nazis and embraced the Silicon Valley. They explained how they, albino spiders, used the Worldwide Web to lure their victims.

"You *are* killers then!"

They smirked like schoolboys. "Raider, not killer. *Corporate* raider, Michael. I have no need of another man's blood. I am self-sustaining."

I studied them while I ate. What was it that they wanted? Why allow this plan to go through and even aid it?

"I want to know . . ."

"Why I am assisting you."

Interesting, they can read my mind and Claude can't.

"Claude Halloran is a relatively new undead. He has not developed much of his abilities. He can read simple things, surface things. But, he is too impatient to learn much and is content to live as a pretty boy eternally. He is no threat."

"Maybe not to you. But that still doesn't answer my question."

"I do have abilities beyond Claude's. Beyond Jean-Luc's or his mother's. Although she has attained other powers and continues to grow stronger nightly. She desires what none of her kind, not even Phillipe, dared. For that, she must be stopped."

"Why didn't you destroy her when she first got here?"

Baum and White rose from their chairs. I hadn't realized until then that they'd sat to make me comfortable, so I wouldn't have to look up at them. Now, I did. And I was, for the first time, aware of the strange beast that hid behind their strange beauty.

"I cannot destroy one of the master's blood," they said. "It is my undying oath. When Aspros and Dentro were saved from certain death, Phillipe made a promise, as did I. He would never again recreate as he did that night. It is written in his book. Never two by one. It is anathema. As forbidden as what the present marquis did to you."

I took this in, piecing together the parts of their story, their pledge.

"You can't destroy Noel."

"That is correct."

"You can't destroy Jack or Claude."

"They are all descended of the same blood."

"You can't destroy me."

"I am here to preserve you. You are foretold."

"Does it have to be me? Am I supposed to destroy them all?"

They looked at each other. I'd never seen two people look at each other like that. They truly were one person. They didn't, I saw then, resemble each other as much as I first thought. Not nearly like my vampire twin and me. But there was a sense of harmony—of oneness—that I'd never witnessed before. Not mine with Teddy, not my grandparents. Never.

"You will do what you will do, Michael O'Donald. You are controlled by no destiny, no fate but of your own making. I will assist you when I can. When you request. What you do about the other creatures abiding here is your decision."

And they were gone.

I felt as if the room had grown larger, the candlelight dimmer. The house haunted and full of hate. Terrors crept from every corner. Every shadow held a vile promise, a veritable protest. The fireplace still roared with the immolation of thick timbers, perfectly weathered. But for all the flames, there was no warmth. I shuddered.

"Break's over, Mikey!"

I shook again at the announcement of Claude's return. I knew that he thought it was from fear of him. Good. Let him. He makes it easy.

"Let's go," I told him. "I have your dirty work to do."

Claude led me on a winding tour around the house, leading out the rear doors and onto the patio that overlooked the formal gardens. Although the moon was no longer totally full, there was more than enough of it to fully light the area. I'd seen places like this before—in movies and on television. But I'd never been allowed to freely wander around anything like this.

It was like being in your own private park. The terrace and its railings and stairs looked like they were made of white marble, not granite like the main building. It glowed in the moonlight. So did the many full-size statues that peopled the gardens.

Claude leapt from the deck to the walkway, without touching the broad, wide steps. I knew he did it to impress me with his powers, and I admit I was. Not that I'd ever let him know. I walked down to him as slowly as I could.

"You will have to learn to keep up!"

"And if you want my help, you're going to have to stop showing off!" *Going to, not gonna.* It was then that I first noticed a subtle change in my speech pattern, the enhancement of my vocabulary. The poetic leaning released. When had that started? I was changing.

"This way!" he said. He grabbed my hand and fled, pulling me into the darkest part of the garden.

Behind a grove of thick-branched evergreens, hidden from any casual glance, was the entrance to a cave. Barely ten feet tall and roughly eight feet at its widest, it tapered like a feather, a gaping wound. A slit in the face of the earth. And though it was naturally accessible, there was something repellent about this entry. Claude passed through as if it didn't exist. It was then that I understood its nature. It was evil. The evil of Noel Courbet.

A palpable force, as real and tangible as the dirt and stones at my feet. As cold as the January air, as unswerving as addiction. There was dragon here, but I was no St. George. Yet, whether savior or sacrifice, agent or agnus, I was the only thing stationed to impede this unseen and immortal monster. I had defeated her son, and now I was to confront her.

I followed Claude. Matched his silence. His mute footsteps mated to my muffled own. I heard my heart and wondered if they would as well, for I knew that she was near.

The suffocating blackness of the cavern dissipated. And my anxiety grew. Claude's cockiness crumbled, leaving the humanistic residue of one accustomed to subservience. Actor. Model. Tool.

The passageway grew larger. It was swelling into a monstrous space. Something hidden, something hollow, something hateful. And as its size increased, so did the languorous golden light.

I could smell the burning, greasy torches before I saw them. Smell the chemicals and botanicals, their essences commingling, filling the cavern. Still, there was something else in here. Beyond the beeswax and basil, the sage and the smudge. There was the feeling—no, the knowledge—that I was encountering something as ancient as life. As merciless as death. As unequivocal as passion.

I peered around the corner and witnessed the glorious face of Noel Courbet.

Her eyebrows were as faint and innocent as a schoolgirl's. Only if and when they lifted would trouble signal. The bony arch above her eyelid remained centered and dogmatic, while her upper lids feigned and flagged. She had not scented me yet. Still an actress at heart, Noel dusted, rather than penciled, her brows and then powdered pink and peppered copper her lids, before smudging her mascara with a smoky signet that lined her eyes. Her eyes.

Each salty or neophyte sailor scavenging the Caribbean was aware of and afraid of that color. Seafoam. Neither gray nor green, less a color than an oblique memory. Less a memory than a warning. Less a warning than a trap. Seafoam. From whence Venus was born and seamen sacrificed.

She stood naked in the center of a horseshoe of oaken tables, tables laden with common and curious things. The books and beakers and bowls, I recognized. The crystals and candles and cloths. I identified pieces of fur and feather and fin.

Somehow, I understood the symbolism. She was depicting the elements: earth, water, fire, and air. And in her soft, solemn chanting, she bent them to her will.

She stood naked in the center of the cavern. I had not seen many adult women fully undressed before this. Not by accident, not by design. Certainly never one like this. She was, simply put, gorgeous. Naturally, she had to be a generation older than her son. He was almost a hundred and sixty years old. She? Could she be nearing two hundred?

She must have been something special in her time, her beautiful body out of fashion. At about five foot-six, she had retained a slim frame. Her luxuriant, pale copper hair did not so much fall as cascade in insouciant tendrils down past her shoulders. Her breasts were a Park Avenue plastic surgeon's dream; her hips, a West Village drag queen's frustration. Her legs were soft, yet stubborn as a panther's. Each muscle in her body acknowledged, yet undeclarative. And she moved this formidable frame with the cunning grace of a prima ballerina or a coke whore.

Her skin did not have that cold, milky whiteness of the vampire, but was a warm, soft and human pink. She must have recently fed. Her lips and nipples were a fuller, deeper color. Not that pastel, poached salmon of her skin, they stood out against it, engorged. They matched, in shade and swelling, the ridges of her labia, dark pink and unfolding deeper. Her copper pubic hairs—scant as her brows—framed her sex like a metallic lace. An engraved invitation. But, for all its invitation, still a trap.

Here was a creature built for pleasure. I easily understood how men would be attracted to her. Even die for her. She combined all aspects of womanhood at each moment, in every part. A man could get lost in there, even one like me.

She spoke.

"Entrez-vous, s'il vous plaît!"

Shit! I had been found out! Mere moments into our seemingly well-conceived plan, I had been caught. I knew at that moment what an actor meant by "flop sweat." I had failed, big time, and every pore on my body told me so. I wanted to scream out loud one last time before my destruction.

And she beckoned. Not so much with her voice, nor with her eyes, nor even her attitude, yet nonetheless she beckoned.

And they obeyed.

"Besom and Clovis, Chaner and Letti. Hopsimom and Trylee and Shpy. Come. Come nearer, dears, and give witness."

And they came. Whatever they were, they came. Globes or globules, maybe. They were gassy or waxen. They manifested warmth, yet the space grew colder. They seemed to arise from the corners of the cave or from the air itself. Each a blue-green, yet sickly white light. All the size of a softball or grapefruit. Every one bobbing and drifting towards their daemon queen.

They shifted and cruised around like a hellish solar system, and she their epicenter. They appeared to be, all at once, evil and real, yet vague and absent of vice or virtue.

And as I watched in relief, knowing that she sought them and not me, they surrounded Noel and headed intently for her.

"Besom, you, and Clovis attend." And automatically, the slave spirits of light caressed her breasts. They flattened and elongated and moved apart and then together, covered by these aquamarine non-beings. "Chaner and Letti attend." And instantly, these bits of St. Elmo's fire entwined themselves into her hair, creating a classical upsweep of her loose and neglected locks. They swept down her back, leaving faint tendrils of themselves and rested happily upon her buttocks. They gripped the cheeks in a lover's grasp, and as they pushed and pulled and pummeled, they did so in rhythm with the sprites at her breasts. And before me, I witnessed the non-corporal phantoms physically debauching this vampire witch.

"Trylee and Shpy, attend." And they did so, each bizarre squirming light recognizing its own name and function. They descended to the floor and wove between her toes. They circled her ankles and licked up her calves. They tickled behind her knees and lapped their way up her thighs. I was growing nauseous.

Noel rose, yet she did not stand. Her faint familiars carried her inches above the floor. Prodding and poking. Sucking and succoring.

Attending.

"Hopsimom," she finally called to the spirit reminiscent of a view caught by the Hubble telescope. "Attend," came the throaty voice that no longer seemed to belong to her.

Hopsimom, the final personality, elongated to do his lady's bidding.

From its grapefruit shape, it stretched to the size of an over-ripened zucchini. It floated to and nuzzled her neck. It dropped down and teased both Besom and Clovis as well as their charges. As it further lowered, Hopsimom delivered feelers from its base end. Like a green gaseous bat, it spread these wings and fingers to his mistress's wrists and elbows and shoulders. It went first to her armpits and then, pushing aside Chaner and Letti, went to her waist and hips. It insinuated itself around her ankles, unsettling Trylee and Shpy.

Hopsimom, from his vantage point, nuzzled his queen's navel and belly, her inner thighs and groin. And ever-nosing himself, entered her.

She rocked as she chanted, chanted as she rocked. Louder and faster. Moans and screeches. In her rapturous rhapsody, she lolled her head to the side and saw. Me.

"Stop!"

I knew she was commanding the creatures, but I could have been caught up in the command had I not turned and run. That was another thing about the invading vampiric cells; I was faster and stronger and less easily manipulated now.

I ran out of the cave and into the garden. The moonlight coated Claude. Intensified his ivory, ironic smirk.

"Go!"

That's all he said and we were off and through the garden. Up the marble stairs and through the chateau. Back to the chapel.

The leonine door was shut and bolted before I could catch my breath. I was alone in the darkness again. My first mission as the ghost of Jean-Luc Courbet was complete.

I shucked my shoes and clothing. I stripped off the one-piece silk undergarment that had kept me warm outside. And while I was in my shorts alone, the candles ignited, as if by their own accord.

"You did well."

And there I was, face-to-face once again with my destroyer, my twin.

"You're no ghost! You're really here." Not my best speech, but exactly what I meant. I hadn't wanted to believe it. Couldn't, until I saw for myself.

 He stepped fully out of the shadow, not Jack, but Jean-Luc Courbet, Marquis de Charnac. I had not seen many important people in my life, but I did recognize when someone knew he was important. And this one knew.

How could I have ever even thought of him as my twin? We had the same height and build, but not the same imposition. We had the same hair and eyes and features, but not the same effect. Even now, with me almost naked and him entirely, we look like an original and a reproduction. It might take a trained eye to tell us apart, but not too trained, not for very long. This scheme would not work.

"What do you want, Jack?"

"I want," he said as he hung his left leg over an oaken pew, "what you want."

He had situated himself in the most flaunting way. His taut, cockless balls were positioned freely away from his body and his muscles tightened into their most appreciable display. Except for what I'd stolen from him, he looked exactly the same. But, seduction be damned, I knew something he didn't. I was not turned on by my own type.

"I am not trying to seduce you."

The mind reading again. *What do you want, then?*

"I want to make you a deal. But understand, Mike, I cannot help but read your mind."

Will you always be able to read it?

"Yes, I will. Until . . ."

Until after I'm dead.

He stood and came to me in an instant. Barely an inch away, he paused. We were eye-to-eye, nose-to-nose, chin-to-chin. Our shoulders spread to the same width. Our nipples reached for each other's exactly. Navel-to-navel. Knee-to-knee. His hands grasped mine at our sides.

"No," he said so softly I wasn't certain he spoke. "It will not be until after you are *un*dead."

My knees buckled, but he held me as if nothing had happened. He was not just strong, I realized, he was immutable. He would never, ever, change. And one day, he had assured me, I would be exactly the same.

Still, there was a frightening splendor to being held by him, a staggering seduction, an overwhelming comfort and excitement. I could have, would have, died for him then and there with no remorse, but for the one thing.

"You are already dead, Mike."

And all illusion evaporated. Our imbroglio no longer embrace.

I understood Jack finally. I did not like him, did not accept him. But I did finally understand.

And then I even surprised myself. I kissed him. Deeply and softly. Firmly and simply. With reticence and resignation. I kissed him.

And he kissed me back.

"I cannot do this," I whispered into his ear. I was not at all certain which of my situations I meant.

He understood and answered, "I will do it for you, if you will assist me." He meant the impersonation.

"How can you?"

We did stand as lovers, I am ashamed to say. I did not wish, could not conceive of separating from him. We slowly rubbed our chests against each other's. Our bellies, our thighs. We held each other's hands in a death grip.

"I will enter you," he whispered.

He answered my reaction before I had the chance to voice it. "The way I did earlier."

I understood.

"I will take over the control of your body each night when Claude leaves you. I will use your body to become my own ghost. I can protect your physical being better than Claude could and better than you could by yourself. I know the chateau and my mother best."

I protested. "Where do I go when you take me over?"

"There are three avenues. I can keep you inside with me . . ."

"That is what I prefer."

"Sans doubt! But it is the most difficult to control should you decide to fight me on a decision."

I realized how precarious that could be. "What else?"

"I could place you inside of my inert body while I was in yours."

"Trap me in a prison of dead flesh?"

"That is not how I would have put it. But I can appreciate your reticence."

"The third way, Jack?"

"You can remain free as an astral being, on a separate plane, separate dimension."

No more conversation.

"Then that's what I'll do. That's my decision."

Jack explained the problems of the astral plane to me. How I would be prone to attack from psychic forces and how my senses would tend to jumble making sounds visible and sights tactile, a paler version of the vampiric existence. And how only the slimmest of threads would hold me to myself. If the thread broke, I would perish.

Wordlessly, he led me to the altar stone and made me lie down. He reclined in the other direction, his feet near my head, mine near his. I felt the fevered burning of my left side to his cool left. The subtle slumping of his muscles when his spirit ascended. I felt the tug, not physically, as he drew me up from myself. I saw the stars.

Jack glowed in front of me, solidly transparent. From his navel, an ethereal umbilical attached him still to his corporal self. It seemed metallic, but at the same time, made of pure light. Just like him.

I looked down at the reclining figures. Geminic in their beauty. Jack spoke.

Not with words or even gestures, but I knew what he was communicating. He looked up. I looked up. We ascended.

Through the ceiling and the roof, we were free of the chapel and flying in the midnight sky. The stars.

My God, the stars sang. And I understood their song! Pine trees shuddered in the wind, and I saw the sound as rustling colors. Much like the dance of oil on water. The River Charnac murmured against the shore below and I saw every lap as a hue of angelic intensity. This is heaven!

This is just a taste of what your nights will be forever once you have finally turned. Jack's thoughts spoke to me.

Your seductions are cruel, Jack.

It is to be your reality, too, Mike. You will have to get used to it to survive.

I will not be like you and Claude, Jack. Forever destroying others to contribute to my own vanity. I will end it all before I let that happen.

The next moment we were back in our bodies and Jack was getting up from the altar. He strode down the only aisle toward the lion's door. He turned sharply away from it and disappeared behind the single pew that marked the Cancer segment. I ran to it, but he was gone. He hadn't made a sound, but somehow he'd escaped this locked chapel without using the door. But, before I could locate a secret panel or hidden door, the candles extinguished and I was left alone again in the dark.

It continued like this for four or five days. First came Claude's cruel abductions followed by Jack's canny invasions to create small torments of Noel. And finally, the late visits in the chapel from her inhuman son. The same pattern for days. I was torturer and tortured at once. I wasn't sure any longer whom I hated most. Maybe it was me.

Just before the next sunset, Baum and White brought me my daily meal. I ate as much as I could, since I only eat once a day.

"Do you know what's going on here?" I asked them.

"It is my conception, my plan."

"And what if it goes wrong?"

"This scheme of mine is going to work out best for all involved," they answered.

I wanted to probe further, but Claude pulled open the chapel door and we were again underway. The moon was past its quarter; I'd been here over a week.

He instructed me, again, about Noel's peculiarities. The best way to approach and avoid her. He led me to the cave's entrance and abandoned me. I felt cheated. Then I felt spectacularly free.

Jack spoke in his voice, but out of my mouth, "Don't go far! This shouldn't take long." And he vanished into the mouth of the cave and to the belly of the beast.

I should not have followed, but my training was to do just that. I had been patient long enough. I knew I could not be seen, and so, I admit, it was not very brave.

I watched Jack walk my body towards the light. Noel was involved with her chants and her charms. Her green floating attendants were assisting with her labor. Jack waited until she was caught up in the throes of her work and whispered, *"Bon soir, maman. Me manquez-vous?"*

"Evidemment! Mais non deux fois," she spat back.

I wasn't certain of the words, but I damn well knew what they were saying. Jack was tormenting his mother and she wasn't having it. Not on the surface. But a trained eye could see her fright. The all-powerful Noel Courbet couldn't rid herself of her hated son.

"Aidez-moi!" was all she said to those translucent green bubbles and they floated slowly towards where Jack stood—*I* stood.

Jack flew past my astral self and out of the cave. My body had never moved that fast; I was amazed. Just outside the cave's entrance, he paused, looked up and winked. In that split second, I wondered how he knew where I was. And a split second later, I was back in my own body, looking up at the cold French sky.

Jack grabbed me from behind and said, "Let's go!"

He grabbed me by my collar and belt and must have carried me. I swear I never touched the ground. Jack bounded fifty yards, then eighty yards, and thirty yards more. Zigzagging this way and that all through the grounds of the chateau. Here, we were in the statuary garden; here, the vineyards. Back to the chateau.

I was beginning to realize the immensity of the property, the vastness of the building itself. But, Jack knew every inch. We clambered over the rooftops and scampered under the trees. And at every moment, at each setting, they followed

Besom and Clovis. Chaner and Letti. Hopsimom and Trylee and Shpy. Her seven demons.

They had no faces or distinguishing marks. They ranged in size from a large grapefruit to a regulation soccer ball. They glowed with a muted internal light, like electrified lime gelatinous minds. They displayed personality, but only the witch who summoned could distinguish them.

We ceased our escape in a small clearing amid tall evergreens.

We stood still and I knew we were waiting for them. And I hoped one of us had a plan.

The underside of the pine branches lit up with a sickly glow. Faint at first, it grew brighter until I could see the things bobbing through the trees. They approached us on more than three-quarters of the clearing. Their bodies began to stretch and grow. Their glow intensified.

"They want to surround us. They're trying to capture us," I told Jack as calmly as I could.

"A moment more," is all he answered.

At ten or twelve feet away, Jack commanded the creatures.

"Burn!"

And they did.

But they did not burn as other things burn. These weren't the simple St. Elmo's fires that Jack had called into the pier in New York. They were living things of some sort. Hellish, without a doubt, but alive. And he killed them, as he had killed many times before, without remorse.

When it was over, I asked him what he had said to his mother in the cave.

"I asked her if she missed me. She said, 'Evidently! But not twice!' "

I was not relieved.

And so it went on, almost daily, for the next weeks. Full moon to fourth quarter. From fourth to new moon. New moon to second. I was marking time the way they did.

Baum and White would feed me and tell me of the things I should not know. Claude would come for me and tell me what he wanted me to know. And lead me to one place or another where I might torment Noel without getting caught. Jack would enter me there and play at being his own tortured, vengeful spirit. Four men, all long dead, using the one living being who could not refuse them to rid themselves of a woman eternally undead.

It was just past dusk. The gibbous moon had begun to rise into the magenta-to-indigo sky. The brightest of the stars began to show against the velvety backdrop.

How could I know this from inside my darkened cell?

Baum and White were later than usual, but I was already accustomed to eating just once a day. I was never really hungry or thirsty anymore. I no longer sweated, rarely used the toilet, did not cry.

My hair seemed to have stopped growing and I had only needed to shave once since my arrival.

The lock clicked and the door swung open throwing a swath of light into the chapel.

"Burn!"

God help me, I recognized the voice and it wasn't Jack's.

All the candles and torches simultaneously burst into flame and illuminated the chapel and its new occupant. Noel Courbet, Marquise de Charnac. And I discovered that I could still sweat and piss.

chapter

3

She brushed back the hood of the black velvet robe and revealed her pale radiance to me. Perfect complexion just flushed from alabaster. Like a newborn's. Not a pore, not a wrinkle. Flawless. She wasn't wearing makeup and her bare, expressionless face was more beautiful and more terrifying because of it. Mostly terrifying for its singular resemblance to Laura Wilcox.

"Michael O'Donald."

That was all she said. Not a question, nor a statement. Neither invitation nor dismissal. I had been reduced to five syllables and those of little-to-no meaning for her. She moved closer as she studied me. Studied me closer the nearer she came.

I had never felt so exposed.

I had been sleeping in just my undershorts for the last week or so, not dressing until Baum and White arrived. I was often undressed when Claude showed. My small way of controlling my situation. And I had been growing less self-conscious about my body. But this woman looked at me, through me, the way only one other person had before. Like mother, like son.

"Your eyes have far too much blue, not fully gray. Your hair, almost a shade too dark. Your coloring, too human to be my son's. You did well to keep your distance. Only not distant enough."

"When did you guess?" I dared.

"Do not speak!" she commanded. And the flames trembled on their beeswax tapers. And all of my hairs stood at attention. And the smell of fear hung on me like the clothing of a hapless drunk.

"That wretched American accent! How did you perfect the French phrases and my son's voice?"

"Il vraiment n'importante pas, n'est pas?" I replied in the language I hadn't spoken once since my junior year of high school. I thought

that I noticed her reaction to the palpable change in me. But no, I was the only one who knew that Jack resided in me.

She laughed. On the surface, it was like the tinkling of little bells. But down deeper there was a hollow echo, an unintentional essence she could not disguise. Like her beauty, her grace and charm, like her wit and her talent, Noel's laughter was a mask, a tool she used toward her own dark ends.

"No," she answered in English, "it no longer matters at all.

"When I find Messrs. Baum and White, they will be dealt with for their role in this hoax. As for your other accomplice . . . Claude?"

She called and he entered the chapel. This was not the sinfully handsome man who had entered my apartment in New York and taken me hostage. This was the cowering slave he had risked everything to avoid becoming. His beauty had not been damaged, but his psyche had. This was a mere shell of Claude Halloran.

"Now, there is the question of you, Mister O'Donald. What to do with you?" she purred with the self-content of pure malice.

She continued, as much for her own enjoyment as my persecution, "My attendants have all been destroyed. You could not have done that. Claude would have confessed if he had. That leaves only the vampire freaks; cowards that they are. That is why they abandoned you to your fate."

"Which is?" I dared to ask.

"Show him, Claude."

Claude pulled four matching weights into the chapel. Iron or steel and quite heavy-looking. Attached to each was a stout and hefty chain. To each chain, a manacle.

He clamped one to each of my wrists, the other two to my ankles. There was no wisdom in resisting.

He lifted me, weights, chains and all, over to the altar. He laid me on my back and pulled my arms over my head, so that my wrists and ankles just barely hung over the opposite ends of the stone slab. The weights apparently touched the ground with only a link or two to spare. I couldn't move my hands or feet over to the corners. I was not quite spread-eagled, but close enough for discomfort.

"Claude, you are forgetting." Her dictate was terse and unimpeachable. Claude looked at me with distant, sad eyes. Yet I knew the sorrow caught there was not wasted on me. He tore at my waistband and rent my shorts. He pulled my last semblance of protection away.

I looked at her with what I attempted as a dare. I knew she did not credit it as such. She curled her lips and blinked her eyes in a strangely feline fashion.

"Lovely. My last need."

I wasn't sure what she meant, but I didn't like it, any way I considered it. She drifted to the altar. She stretched out her small hands. Small, but her fingers were very long. She reached over my body, hovering barely an inch away from my flesh. I craned my neck and saw each of the hairs beneath her palms standing upright. Reaching for her! Not that it was the worst of what I saw.

The glow!

Between the palms of her hands and the surface of my skin, a light existed. It was like the aura surrounding a candle, a halo effect. No particular color, but a brightness nonetheless.

Noel went down to my feet. I could feel them rise off the altar stone, restrained by the chains alone. She moved up my shins to my knees, my thighs. I was rising.

She moved along the altar's edge, silently as a shadow. She separated her hands to go to my hips and they rose from the table. No hair below my waist was lying flat. All drew for the ceiling. My genitals followed suit.

My abdomen lifted. My chest rose and nipples distended. The hairs of my armpits stood straight up. My arms tugged at their restraints. I was no longer on the altar, but arched in the air above it. She came around the corner and stood over my head.

Noel undid the jeweled clasp at her neck and the belt at her waist. Her robe draped open. I could see the smirk in her eyes, unaccompanied by her lips. This was getting worse. She leaned over me, rubbed her cold breasts on my face, and then looked me in the eyes.

"Asroath, come!" And from her opened mouth a sort of cloud emerged.

Slowly, at first, like the first gum bubble of a tentative child. It was the same pale pink as her forehead. As it exited, it grew in shape and shade. A brighter color now, like pink champagne. And effervescent as well. Larger, too, it took on a mutable jewellike tone. And I did not doubt that this thing lived as her now-dead demons had. And lived solely to do her bidding.

"Xltita! Now you." And another emerged in the exact same way. Growing in form and in facet, displaying its evil, it floated down my body to join its sister wraith.

"Mazul," she called. Then, "Cymdular." And when all four were fully emerged and fully formed, she dropped her robe and rose up to greet them. Directly over my midsection, they joined their mistress, aped her and adapted her form. Asroath. Xltita. Mazul. Cymdular.

Four pale pink plasmic replicas of the witch danced with their paler queen. Holding each other's newly formed hands, they wove in and out of each other's embrace as if in gruesome mockery of a medieval or ancient pavane. And, as I was to discover, an element of the sexual took precedence in all of Noel's rites.

With Xltita and Mazul at her hands, Cymdular and Asroath went to Noel's feet. Delicate tendrils extended from their female forms, their fingers waxing ever longer. They grew like vines. Xltita and Mazul entwined their way to Noel's breasts. Cymdular and Asroath climbed up her calves and thighs and squirmed into her delta. And slowly they brought her sex to my face.

I turned my head to the side as far as I could. The last time I'd been in a position this heinous was with her son and I was still imbued with that particular gift. Noel's contribution to my fate was bound to be even worse. Still, from the corner of my eye, I could not help but watch.

Each rosy, glowing, fatal femme throbbed. And in pulsating, pinched and pulled at her labia, her nipples. And their rhythms repercussed on their mistress. And so she moaned. She contracted. She gloried.

They drifted her in a semi-circle over me. We were face to crotch. If my electrostatic manliness intrigued her, it was of no use. It was not standing of its own accord. I laughed.

Xltita and Mazul jerked her torso up, while Cymdular and Asroath held her legs in place. She was kneeling in midair, spread-eagle, above my head. Her moans had become screams; her contractions, spasms. Wider and wilder, they drew her thighs apart. Her mound of Venus flexed and convulsed. Faster and faster. Her screams became a single shrill shriek.

"Oh, my God," was all I could whisper. I was too afraid to say more, think more. And still, the attendant sprites pulled her further apart.

"No, no, no," was all I remember screaming, when her shriek became a siren and the convulsions erupted.

Blood.

That terrible black blood of the undead spewed from inside of her. Dousing me. She lurched with them, spattering me the way Pollock splattered his canvas: hauntedly, madly, gleefully. Baptizing me from head to foot.

Her blood wasn't liquid, more like a paste. So thick, so gruesome. And everywhere it touched, it burnt. An acidic onyx gel.

Never one by two! Jack shouted above the chaos inside my head.

And it was over.

Her personal demons wrapped themselves about her, creating a pink, transparent cocoon. Together they drifted—four feet above the floor—out the single door. A single tendril, callous vine, floated back into the chapel and roped itself around Claude's neck. And led him, tethered, out the door.

It slammed shut. Locked. The flames extinguished. I was alone.

"Stay still. Do not speak. Do not move. Do not even breathe!" I heard his hushed, physical voice. He was in the chapel. "Above all, do not swallow!"

One by one the candles relit and the torches flared. Jack hurried from the Cancer segment and up the single aisle. Baum and White were at his heels.

Baum was carrying two large buckets overbrimming with water. White, armfuls of white towels. Jack, ever the marquis, carried nothing.

He was instructing me, but I heard nothing. I was caught again by the look of him. The beauty that I resisted and overlooked on the pier two months ago—was it only two months?—caught at me like an embracing mirror. This is what I will become.

He pushed the hood of his tunic from his face. The coarse material was a strange, dark brown, like an aged penny. But its plainness just emphasized his beauty. His pale hair, pale skin, pale eyes. Its shapelessness accentuated his delineation, the fine lines of his cheeks and jaw and nose and neck.

"I am going to wash away her blood, Mike. Do not move until I have finished. I do not want you to swallow any of her blood."

Why? I thought rather than spoke.

"Never one by two," Baum and White recited. "Phillipe's instructions in his death throes."

What does it mean? Despite my anger and disgust, I had to know what they knew. It would be my only protection, my only defense. And possibly my best weapon.

"*Intermenstruus, intermundia, interior latibulum,*" they recited.

"English, please?" Jack requested for my sake, no doubt.

Baum and White began the strange recitation that I came to know as Phillipe's swan song. His final instructions before he was no more. "Between the moons, between the worlds, my innermost sanctuary. Vellum enclosed in leather inside of a skin. Flesh in a layer of flesh in a layer of flesh. Surmounted by a rib cage of bone. Bone painted with hooves. Hooves covered by bone. Enclosed in earth. Moon covered by moon counseled by moon. Each into its fullness. In its fullness is each made full. Never two by one. Never one by two. Never one by the master. But at times by the master none. No moon fatal but full. Ten dozen in reproduction. Earth's bones by the dozen."

There was silence then. Almost reverential. Until I said, "That is the stupidest poem I ever heard!"

Jack's eyes flared and shock stung all of their faces.

"Do not swallow!" Jack commanded as he poured water into my open mouth. "Rinse and spit! Do not swallow any of it!"

I did as I was told.

"Did any of it go down?"

"I'm not sure," I answered. My mouth and throat burned like my flesh. But was it starting to burn going down? Burn the way Jack's blood burned? I was certain then that it did, but I wasn't ready to give up that information. Not before I knew what it meant.

"I hope not," Baum and White said together.

"What will happen if some did?" I asked them.

The three looked at each other. They could have been silently agreeing not to tell me, or they could have been searching for an answer in each other's eyes. I didn't know.

"Probably nothing more than what has already been done," Jack decided.

"Well then, nothing more to worry about. Why don't you tell me about the poem? You've all been running around for a hundred years trying to figure out what it means."

"First, M. O'Donald, it is not truly a poem. It is more like a coded message. And what it means is that we vampires exist from one full moon to the next, between the living and the dead. Phillipe said that his grimoires were hidden under the earth's bones. Rocks. That these stones were glued together, mortared. One course upon another. Under which his secret was buried.

"As for the monthly phases: only at the full moon can a vampire be created. And only one creation per phase. Two vampires cannot feed from the same victim. A vampire cannot kill its master, its creator. In every one-hundred-and-twenty-year cycle, a vampire must create anew."

"They mean one hundred and twenty vampire years. We do not count time as mortals," Jack added.

Baum and White continued. "Twelve layers, or courses, of stonework hide the books. It was Phillipe's way of pointing to his secret library without the marquise discovering them.

"Secondly, I have not been trying to find or decipher the books for the last century, I have always had control of all but the last book. Much of my power has come from the practice of those spells for hundreds of years. Noel Courbet de Charnac is now in possession of them."

"So, she figured out the code?" I asked them.

"No. She may not even remember the whole of Phillipe's song. I gave them to her."

"You *gave* them to her?" I couldn't believe that they would deliberately empower her.

"It was her son's instruction. I simply obey."

I turned my head to look at Jack. I never thought it odd that he hadn't released me from my chains. Or that he had turned up his sleeves and was still washing me free of Noel's blood throughout the explanation.

"You just let her have them?"

"What did I care if Noel had more of her little magick tricks?"

"Little magick tricks? She summons beings from other dimensions!"

"She will be able to do more than that after the Black Mass!"

My Irish Catholic upbringing had more than prepared me for a concept like a black mass. For every silver lining that they held onto, Catholics believed in, feared, and were controlled by the massive black clouds. Even the lapsed ones and the ones who claimed new or no religions. Even the fallen faithful who denied God. Satan, Hell, and evil stayed with us long past the release of God, His angels, and Heaven.

I knew now that Noel Courbet represented everything that was vile in this world. And that this Black Mass of hers was the final step in ensuring the totality of her evil reign.

"Tell me what I have to do."

"Nothing."

Jack replied to me as if I was an afterthought. A commodity. A tool to be used in his never-ending combat with his mother. How easily they seduce and gain trust! How easily we are deceived! I hated him with the same intensity I did when I saw Teddy's lifeless body. The same as I did that night on the pier when he cursed me.

More.

He turned abruptly to look at me. His face was a blank paper, a darkened screen, a void. He showed no anxiety, no remorse. No interest. Whether he killed Noel or Noel sacrificed me, whether Claude or the lovers lived or died, none of it mattered. Nothing but the continuation of his own infernal existence. Nothing ever mattered to Jack but Jack.

"Noel," he began, "will wait until the time of the full moon for her ceremony." I did not know if he was talking to me, Baum and White, or himself.

"Her sacrifice must remain on the altar until she returns. She will immediately notice that the blood has been cleansed and will suspect the two of you. Mother will want her vengeance. Seal yourselves in the hidden place with the true grimoire until I come for you. If I am not there before dawn, you will know that I have failed and that only she survived. You know what you must do then."

He went on with further instructions to them, but I heard nothing but my pulse pounding in my temples. Felt nothing but the burning on my skin while it waned to a tingling. And the burning in my throat as it waxed slowly to my stomach. And from there began its spread.

I looked up and saw stars. Again. But I knew that I wasn't leaving my body. I was not traveling outside. Still, I saw stars. And recognized them for what they were.

The ceiling of the chapel was covered in deep blue tiles. Some precious mineral, no doubt, judging from the rest of the place. And the tiles were inset with diamonds. I knew in my heart that they were genuine.

Diamonds! Singularly set and in clusters. Solo stars and constellations. Some as large as eggs, some so small they could barely be seen. It was the entire night sky set in the most expensive way possible. And then as I watched, they dimmed.

At first, I thought it was my eyes. I turned to look back at Jack and his servants. They were gone. And each of the torches and all of the candles were gutting, shrinking, snuffing.

I was in darkness, again alone. And again I suffered the torture that I alone of all men had to suffer twice. The complete transmutation of my blood cells. The cruel overcoming of my blood by the

Santa Clara County Library

Milpitas Library

Patron: 23305013031782

		Due Date
1	Bound in flesh / 33305212849842	09/29/10
2	One night stand / 33305208090542	09/29/10
3	Same cell organism (yaoi) / 33305211391226	09/29/10

09.08.2010 14:28:52

Thank you for visiting the Milpitas Library

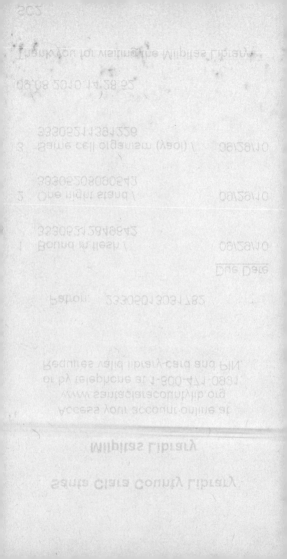

blood of yet another vampire. The only living man with the blood of the undead coursing through my veins.

At just past dusk, the Quickening Moon rose fully into the cold, February night sky. Claude entered the chapel. Two torches flamed into life. He wore a long, hooded, black velvet robe and carried a large sack and more of the same black material. A robe for me?

No. It was a black velvet altar cloth. He separated my feet and placed the cloth on the granite slab between them. He began to unfold it, revealing the gold, embroidered, arcane designs. He lifted me, weights, chains and all, and spread the cloth over the altar. He placed two candlestick holders on either side of my head. They were about eighteen inches tall. Solid gold, to be sure. And ornate in that Gothic way. Then, two on either side of my chest, two on either side of my hips and two more at my feet. Each of the eight held a thick, black candle. He lit them and the torches guttered and died.

From his sack, Claude pulled a six-sided quartz crystal, as thick as my wrist, and placed it on my forehead. He took another stone, smoky brown and shot through with golden threads, and placed it on my solar plexus. A jet-black one he placed upon my pubic hairs and the last one, milky white, across my ankles.

He lifted my balls and insinuated a golden chalice between my thighs. Lifted my dick and placed a wooden stick under it. It was about twenty inches long and only about a quarter-inch thick. It tapered naturally to a point and still had its bark. It looked like the kind of switch they thrashed schoolchildren with many years ago. He draped my penis over my scrotum to hold it in place.

He took a small copper pot, and balanced it over my navel. It was almost perfectly round, about six inches in diameter and had three little legs like an old cauldron. It felt heavy for its size.

Finally, he took out a knife. It must have been steel and the double-edged blade was about nine inches long and honed to a perfect sharpness. The hilt was made of some sort of black stone. Onyx, maybe. Claude placed it—the tip towards my neck—directly over my heart. I got the point.

I was the altar and I was the sacrifice. I was the representation of all mankind and of her only begotten. She would take control over all existence, living and undead. But if she killed me, what then? What would I become? I was certain that she didn't know all about me.

Throughout his duties, Claude refused to answer my questions. He remained perfectly mute. He never looked me in the eyes, nor acknowledged that I was anything more than the apparent altar for his mistress. But every few minutes, he would take out a leather wineskin and cram it into my mouth. Between each of his various tasks, he would force-feed me at least half a pint of this astringent liquid.

It must have contained wine or liquor, because I began to feel lightheaded. But even as I grew more woozy, I still wanted more. With each completed task, Claude offered the skin. And with each offering, I drank. More and more. Over and over again. I remembered that old adage about the man taking the drink and then the drink taking the man. But I did not care.

I awakened, hours later, to Noel's rant.

"Who cleansed him?" Her words crackled through the already charged atmosphere. They slithered, snakelike. They clouded and they stung.

"It wasn't me, Noel," Claude cringed. "It must have been Baum and White."

"I will deal with them in due time. It's almost eleven o'clock. We must begin."

It was then that she pushed back her heavy hood, then that I saw her. Then that my eyes focused. And then that I could earnestly say that I'd stared into the face of hell.

She was beautiful. Radiant. I knew she was naked under that thick, rich robe of black velvet. It made her pale skin and coppery hair glow even richer. Her glimmering green eyes and deep pink lips more entrapping. This creature was seduction in its most primal form. So what if she was taking over the earth, she damned well deserved it.

"End it, Claude. Say it."

"*Gratias Deo*," he intoned in his new, peculiar monotone.

"*Est Missa Ite*," she responded. And each time she did, her volume grew.

Him: "*Tuo Spiritu cum et.*"

And her, louder still: "*Vobiscum Dominus.*"

Amen, I thought and they chanted together. Thanks be to God. Go, the Mass is ended. And with thy spirit. The Lord be with you. Amen.

It was the mass. In Latin. And backwards. The Black Mass.

Whether it was my upbringing or my fear, my desire or my determination, I heard the Latin, but understood the English. Heard it backwards and reversed the words.

"Saeculorum saecula in regnas et vivis qui." Who livest and reignest forever and ever. *"Sacramenta refecerunt sancta et pura quem."* Who have been fed with this pure and holy sacrament. *". . . macula scelerum remaneat non me in ut et praesta . . ."* And grant that no stain of sin remain in me. *"Meis visceribus adhaereat povati quem. Sanguis et sumpsi quod Domine tuum Corpus."* Cleave to my innermost heart . . . and Thy Blood which I have drunk . . . which I have received . . . May Thy Body O Lord.

Amen!

It wasn't so much said as understood. Her creatures unimaginable, her creations invisible, envoiced the last "so be it!"

Her look, too resplendent to be smug, too regal to be contemptuous, justified all. She was not the Marquise de Charnac; she *was* the Queen of the Night.

"In your name, O Lord God Adonay, who reigns over the earth, who lords over the world, I implore you to grant your ominous power to me! So mote it be! O Satan, O Lucifer, O you Prince of Darkness, throw open the gates of Hell and arise from the abyss to greet me as your sister and friend! Grant me the gifts of which I speak! I take you unto myself! Take me as your bride! So mote it be! I am the lowest of creatures; I glory in all things of the flesh! By Hel, God of the Pit, the Eternal Baal, I beg that these things I desire shall come to pass! And in exchange, I give to you all of my being eternally! Consent and be favorable unto me. So mote it be! O Grand and Powerful Adonay, make yourself present and give form on these spirits whereby our work shall be accomplished! Come forth, O Beelzebub, Mephistopheles, you Archfiend and Lord of the Flies, and answer to your names and by so doing, manifest my wishes. Asroath, I call you forth! Xltita, approach. You, Mazul, come hither. Cymdular, I beckon you. By favor of these names, I adorn myself. So mote it be!"

The air thickened. In four separate patches, it seemed to shimmer into mass. No longer just air, it condensed from transparent to translucent. From barely there to quite unclear. The spirits appeared in the chapel. Asroath. Xltita. Mazul. Cymdular. No longer confined to their soft pink shapes, they had crystallized into a hard rubelline crust. Gemlike, they floated, no longer like things born of air, but like things borne on air. They had mass now. My troubles never end.

Her voice reverberated throughout the chapel. "I accord this victim to thee, O Grand and Powerful Adonay, the Lord God, Lord of all Spirits, Lord of the Flies! To thee, all-powerful Eloi, Lord of all flesh, to, Laziel, the Almighty, and Jehopetam Transcendent, to the honor, glory and power of thy name, which is superior to all other Spirits. O Grand Adonay! Suffer to receive it as a worthy tribute. So mote it be!"

Here, she removed the chalice from between my upper thighs, took my penis in her hands and milked the urine from my distended bladder. I could not hold back.

She took the brimming cup, at the same time repeating the words, "It is to the honor, glory and dominion of thy name, O Grand and Powerful Adonay, the Lord God, Lord of all Spirits, Lord of the Flies, Eloi, Laziel, Jehopetam, that I drink the water of this offering! Grant, O Grand and Powerful Adonay, the Lord God, Lord of all Spirits, Lord of the Flies, to receive it as a suitable gift. So mote it be!"

She drank from the chalice, draining it. I admit I hadn't finished wetting myself. I was ill.

She took the athame, her sacred knife, from my sternum. She lifted it to the ceiling. The air crackled. All of her creatures, all undead, cackled with the crackling air. All were electrified and emancipated. Parasites waiting upon their hostess.

Noel shouted, upstretched, to the unseen above her, dagger pointed to the heavens. "It is to the honor, glory and dominion of Thy Name, O Grand and Powerful Adonay, Eloi, Laziel, Jehopetam, that I spill the blood of this sacrifice! Vouchsafe, O Thou Grand Adonay, to receive its ashes as an acceptable tribute. So mote it be!"

A flutter. Like pigeons' wings.

"C'est fini, Maman!"

Those words cut through the charged atmosphere. They carved and cleaved, pierced and penetrated. "It is ended," said the son of Noel Courbet. And with those words, and during those words, he had moved. And she had moved toward him.

A simple shift, a cutting curl. A toss, a thrust, a touch.

And from his fist, all thickly clad in thickest leather, he had released a solid silver paten. The fluttering wings of pigeons.

That dish, eight inches in diameter only, was beveled precisely at its edge. It was honed to razor sharpness. And I watched as it sliced through incense and air, through devotion and deception, and finally through flesh and cartilage and bone. The bone, cartilage and flesh of the strongest vampiress in the world.

It severed head from body, existence from oblivion. Dominatrix from domain.

The silver paten, eight inches wide, dug into the chapel wall. Just far enough to create of itself a ledge. A shelf to support what it had carried, auspiciously, along with it. The witch's head, the head of Noel Courbet.

It jutted from the twelfth wall of the chapel. The Capricorn wall. Her wall. It lodged just beneath the brass medallion of the antlered goat. For a moment only, Noel's head was haloed by its brazen aura.

And those horns seemed to grow from her own head.

And, at that moment, she reminded no one in the chapel of anyone more than Laura Wilcox at her death. Not Claude, who certainly engineered it. Not Jack, who apparently regretted it. Nor I, who truly lament it still.

"It is ended," he seemed to say for no one's benefit but his own.

Her inhuman slaves blew throughout the chapel, flaming filaments, like a child's holiday sparkler. Then they simply winked out of existence. Her undead slave slumped to the floor.

Jean-Luc, Marquis de Charnac, strode from behind the Cancerian pew, down the center aisle, to the altar. He looked down at me. Not to see if I was all right, oh no, not him. To see if I was alive!

We stared eye to eye.

"Where is she?"

His mouth never moved, it was Claude's voice I heard.

"Shit! Jack! It's really you! You're alive!"

Claude had just come to realize that the standing, clothed blond was not me. The death of his mistress disoriented him for a moment only.

"Do nothing stupid, Claude! Noel is no more. You are free of her."

And then he added, "Burn!"

The chapel burst into light. Every one of the torches flamed. Each of the hundreds of votives ignited.

Jack pulled off the leather gloves and inspected them. They were severely burned and smoldering at the palms and the fingers. He revealed pale white hands free of blister. He had protected himself well.

He went from my side, around my feet, to the other side of the altar, all the while looking at and speaking to Claude.

"You are free to go, Claude. Free to roam the earth as you choose. Free until the end of all days."

The chilling words seemed to have a warming effect on Claude.

He rose up from the floor, no longer a slave. His eyes shone bright again. His lips relinquished their grasp and relaxed into their natural sensuous curl. His shoulders dropped and his chest thrust. Even his robe seemed to tent between his hips. The old Claude was back.

"But before you do, I have a proposition for you."

Jack stopped on the other side of the altar near my waist. Right next to where Noel had stood. He turned his back on the room and looked down. I could see from my vantage point the small, soft mound of dust that had been the single most beautiful embodiment of pure evil. The remains of Noel Courbet.

"*A tout a l'heure, Maman.* It was a frightening world with you in it. But, what will it be now that you are gone? Cold and empty. And pointless, sans doubt! Like yesterday, last month and last year. Just more so."

That was more about Jean-Luc Courbet than I had ever wished to know. I did not want to feel for him. I wanted to destroy him.

"What's your offer?" Claude asked. This guy's timing sucked.

"This one here," Jack said, motioning to me, "managed to hurt me when we were on the pier together. I need your assistance until I can heal."

"Heal? What could he do to you?"

Jack released his belt and zipper and whisked his slacks and underwear down to his knees.

"This!"

Dressed all in black, his deathly whiteness seemed all the more so. And in the same way, the handsomeness and strength of his leg and stomach muscles all pointed to the groaning absence I'd left there. This wasn't just the sanitized sexlessness of a child's doll. It was a crime against manliness, against beauty.

I couldn't look at Jack, so I shifted my head towards Claude.

His pretty emeralds had darkened. Wine bottle. Green still, but dark. The impossible whites of his eyes were clouded, too. Then, from the corners of his eyes, bleak cranberry droplets formed. He was crying. He was crying blood!

"I had no idea, Jack. No idea who she was or who you were. I would never have gone along with her if I had known you first."

Rubies. Sad, sick droplets of deep, dark blood dripped from his tear ducts. Not human, but humanish still.

"I know."

Shit. What was this? A vampire mating dance?

"Claude, I must leave here. I need to regrow what I have lost. And I need your help."

"Anything, Jack."

"Come with me while I use Phillipe's grimoires to become whole again. If, after that, you want to go on your own, I will not stop you."

"Jack, I never wanted to leave you! Your mother . . ."

"Never mind that now, Claude," Jack started as he made his way for the altar. "Finish up here. I must see Baum and White. I will meet you at the jet. We do not have much time."

They kissed.

I'd never seen a kiss like that. I knew I'd never have a kiss like that. They were both beautiful, and complacent in their beauty. Immortal and assured. Two perfect creatures knowing that they would remain perfect. Forever.

Jack went out. Claude turned to me. A smile caught at the edges of his lips and eyes. Caught there and gripped me. It was the fulfillment of fear.

He came to me.

chapter

4

Jack Courbet left the chapel and moved into the hall, once again the master of Charnac. Every few meters, he saw himself reflected in one of the many mirrors. He loved the hall of mirrors. They were like him. Cold and aloof. Unremitting and relentless.

Jack moved slowly through the recreation of the chateau he had destroyed. Slowly, because his mother was dead. Slowly, because his creator was dead. Slowly, because he was for the first time seeing Charnac as his. And his lordship had become sure.

He swept through the hall leading from the chapel. The gold and purple runners needlessly absorbing his cat steps. He charged through the great hall and stopped-still in the game room.

Baum and White had reproduced it to its tiniest detail. Bull elephants and newborn shrews. Hyenas and jackals, foxes and wolves. Lions from Africa and tigers from India. European bears and bucks. All manner of animal, great and small.

Jack saw each of the reestablished taxidermies as a link to the past. But, the vampiric memory was not the best. The present and past smudged. The future collided. He was here with Phillipe, but Phillipe was no more.

Did he run from his mother still?

Yet, the game room was the same, perfect in reproduction. With one exception.

The small alcoves knitted into the beams above his head.

Empty.

The unicorn heads were gone. Destroyed and never replaced.

How could they be? With what? Phillipe acquired the Charnac lands in order to encompass the last herd of them. Hunted and destroyed them all. The rebuilt alcoves stood in mute testament to the erasure of their like. Their kind.

Jack flew from the gallery and back into the great hall.

Much of the original armaments had been exactly replaced. Many pieces added from private collections. Mostly, it had become a greater exhibit.

Jack finally appreciated the models of power and of mastery. Of the hunt and of the kill. He had finally become Charnac. And as such, much more dangerous.

He drifted into the dining room and through the screened passage into the kitchen. On the outside wall of the kitchen, the voussoir arch still stood.

Jack saw the imitation as he approached, but his memory supplied the rest. He passed through and descended the staircase.

It was still—again?—constructed of stout stone. But the torches did not need his command to ignite. Motion-sensitive, they felt his presence and responded. At each of his steps they sparked, grew and dimmed. Down he went, to Phillipe's domain, with the sconces adapting to his every move.

He entered the subterranean grotto and rewitnessed the tiled caldarium. Exact in every way, yet modernized to require no care.

A state-of-the-art heating and filtration system had been added to the pool to keep its waters pristine and blistering. Heat lamps had been installed into the ceiling casting a coppery glow on the ancient tiles.

Jack longed to shuck his clothes and float towards relaxation and away from regret in the scalding waters. But there was much to do. He must get to Baum and White.

He swept past the pool and through the ancient columns on into the vaulted tepidarium. Again, the lights lit as he approached. But this was not a recreation of Phillipe's "art studio." The lights here were now filtered in blue. The gelled spotlights could range in intensity from the palest sky to the darkest indigo. And what they lit amazed Jack.

Phillipe's sizing pool was gone. And mercifully with it, the wretched odor of isinglass. The cavern had been paneled in solid mahogany, the floors redone as a checkerboard of black and white marble, each a meter square. Every three meters there stood a monument to Phillipe, a gift from his eternal servants.

Baum and White had recreated Phillipe's "sculptures" out of solid Carrara marble. Each was, naturally, life-size and amazingly exact. How exacting were the minds and fingers of this immortal

pair of lovers to have recalled every detail of each of Phillipe's preserved victims and to reinvent them in solid stone. How fabulous
their devotion. They had retained every nuance of gesture and expression flawlessly.

Jack remembered each one. Stances innocent and vulgar, personalities heroic and insipid. Nude men and women and children.
Works of art never to be seen by living eyes. He took a moment to
stop by each. He lingered longer at the reproduction of Etienne du
Mont, the chevalier who was his first blood host. Still beautiful in
face and form, his overwhelming masculinity oddly reinforced by
the subtly effeminate way he played with his hair.

He turned to the next sculpture, the centerpiece. Phillipe.

Fittingly, the lovers had sculpted their master at half again life-
size. Although they had surely not seen Phillipe fully naked again
since the night of their turning, Baum and White had captured him
perfectly. Here was, indeed, the original model for Michelangelo's
David. Although the Italian artist had chosen to give a less aggressive nose to his sculpture and to remove almost all of Phillipe's
body hair, there was no doubt that this was him. And the way nature had created him. The long and aquiline nose that was
Phillipe's now matched the sex organ that Michelangelo had also
truncated.

And the hair. Swirls of hair, mats of hair, masses of hair. From
the top of his scalp to the last phalanges, they had restored his magnificent pelt hair by hair. The eroticism of it was unbearable. Jack
turned away.

The final work. At exactly life-size. Jean-Luc Courbet de Charnac.
Stunning.

The cold, hard stone showed him as he truly was. Only marble
could mirror that ineffable beauty, that eternal magnetism. How
and when Baum and White had a chance to study him naked
seemed not the point. That they had captured and preserved the
very essence of Jean-Luc was astounding. Jack was well pleased.

He turned away to the secret passage that would bring him to
the original castle keep, the ancient corp-de-logis.

Twelve courses of stone led from Phillipe's former studio to the
secret heart of the castle. Each course was made of granite blocks
and each block was a cubic meter. There were four steep steps to
each course—one for each season, each direction, each element—
and each rise was twenty-five centimeters. And each step two me-

ters wide and set at twenty-two and a half degrees from the preceding.

Jack descended counterclockwise. By the time he reached the bottom, he'd turned three times around. At each completed full turn, he faced west again. Away from the rising sun.

He entered the domain of Baum and White. The home of Aspros and Dentro. He walked amid the megahertz and gigabytes, the hard drives and compact discs. Communication etheric and plastic. He passed through the ultra-modern sanctuary to the arcane vault.

"I am Charnac."

He said it simply. As he should. With recognition comes power and with power comes quietude. The vault could not open without calm.

"Master! Charnac welcomes you," they said as one.

"She is no more," he simply replied. The orphan magister of Charnac. The king without claim.

"All is arranged. Your new home, new identity, new occupation. All is arranged."

He trusted them as he had never trusted. They had never failed him. As his mother had, as had Phillipe. Laura. And Claude. He trusted only them.

"When?" It was all he asked and all he needed to ask. They were Charnac. They knew what he wanted to know.

"Now, master. Leave now. All is prepared. The jet is waiting. M. Halloran is aboard."

A faint smile softened his lips.

"You work quickly, gentlemen. But have you solved my problem?"

They stood as one.

They dropped the single sheet that clothed them and stood as Aspros and Dentro. Naked, they glowed in the soft light. They had just fed. Their mated sexuality sung out as complete as a farrago of grain, a pod of whales, a murder of crows.

Naked, they stood head and shoulders above their lord. Living Modiglianis, breathing El Grecos, they were two perfect models of manhood stretched and blanched. They held between them the book.

Phillipe's grimoire was an antique work. Just at a glance, Jack knew it was far older than he. But hundreds of years? Dozens of centuries? More?

The leather cover had probably been soft once. Had hardened throughout the ages. The raised dimpling of the rough-hewn skin was darkened. By age and environment, Jack knew. Neither Phillipe, nor the lovers, nor he himself secreted oils that would dampen and darken the surface.

The vellum pages were also old, yet perversely preserved. No cracks, no splits, no yellowing from the original eggshell color. And there were hundreds of them. Each with a special instruction or an invincible spell.

And each writ in the dark blood of a vampire.

This was not a book to lose.

"I have the transformation spell in here. With it, I can regrow what you have lost and provide a new identity for you and M. Halloran."

"But I am content with my own identity. And, I like the look of M. Halloran."

The perfect sculptures replied, "And so will each and every detection agency. Listen to our plan."

And they explained what they had achieved over the Internet as they brought their master to his diplomatic transport. His new house in his new country. His new occupation and that of his companion. Their new names.

"And, when the spell is done, your new bodies."

Jean-Luc Courbet, Marquis de Charnac, listened to the plan and approved. They accompanied him into the jet.

Claude saw the two men for the first time as just that. Two men. Baum and White had not redressed.

At less than six feet, he was already apprehensive of men bordering seven feet tall. As a new undead, he feared their aged knowledge.

"Your berth is salted with American soil, Claude Halloran. Strip and lie down."

Claude did not, could not, broach their authority. He stripped naked and reclined in the hollow leather couch.

"Master, it is now your turn. The soil of Charnac is present. There is more where you will reside. It is time to reform and transform."

Without a word of farewell, the marquis stretched out full into his box. He had no doubt that all was as to his wishes. All would be well. He was, after all, the king of the undead.

Baum and White spoke the ritual of transformation to provoke the regrowth. They exited the jet assured.

Claude, listen to me.

Yes, Jack?

From this moment on you will be known as Loki. You will remain the same, just more so. Just enough to disguise you.

But, I like the way I look.

Good. Then you will love your new look.

What about you?

I am about to change as well. I will be known as Apollo. I, too, will alter, but only significantly enough to ward off unwanted recognition. You will see, and, certainly approve.

Where are we going?

We will hide, as they say, "in plain sight." We are going to the most visual place on earth. The city where it is commonplace to be outrageous. Where the more we stand out, the more we blend in. Where night is day.

Jack? Are we going to Vegas?

Las Vegas it is, Claude.

I always loved Vegas.

You will love it more now. You will be a cult figure, a superstar. You will own Las Vegas from now on. I learned one thing in America. Your celebrities are like our royalty in the way they are regarded by common people. But they do not have the restrictions of having to behave like true royals. They can be as snobbish, petulant and indulgent as they please. And they are thought all the more of for it. We are entering a world of ego and excess, Claude, as the icons of it! As its definition. Are you ready for that, Claude?

I was born for that, Jack.

One last thing, Claude, before we rest to let the transformation take place. How was Michael O'Donald when you left him for Baum and White?

I didn't leave the freaks a headache, if that's what you mean.

What are you saying, Claude?

You asked me to take care of him. I took care of him, Jack.

How? How exactly did you take care of him?

I didn't suck his blood, if that's what's bothering you. I just smothered him. Don't worry about him anymore, Jack. I know I left him dead.

Jean-Luc Courbet, the Horror of West Street, the Marquis of Charnac, and the new Apollo, hid his thoughts from his untrustworthy partner, his false lover. He knew that the thing that Claude had done had not left Michael O'Donald dead. Claude had joined in sharing the responsibility for creating a new undead. A new form of vampire. One of whom he could not guess the extent or properties of his power.

"*Que sera . . .*" And he abandoned his physical shell, knowing it would grow in size and power and beauty as he slept the mock death.

PART TWO

THE DEAD OF LAS VEGAS

chapter
5

It rarely went to freezing in Las Vegas. And as the sun set, it was a comfortable sixty degrees. The vampire awoke from his communal sleep. Unlike the accustomed relation he had with Phillipe, Jack, now Apollo, shared his berth daily with his consort Loki, the late Claude Halloran.

The newly very blond Apollo stretched from his proscribed slumber on the half of their shared bed strewn with French soil. "Light," he whispered in consideration for the muscular beauty who inhabited the American-dusted side. Just enough light to show his reflection on the mirrored walls and ceiling. His newly regained complete reflection.

At an increased height, Apollo had increased in stature as well. And his perfectly muscled body had amplified in size and mass. Each evident muscle more aggressive. Every subtle delineation now dramatically cut. His ash blond hair had transformed into longer and brighter tresses. And his silver gray eyes had become positively platinum. A lily gilded.

Claude had become Loki. And as Loki, had become godly.

His untamed black curls reached toward his shoulders. His formerly full muscles had become archetype, the emphasis, as ever, on the sexual.

His hairs from navel to sternum had dissipated, but those remaining had coarsened and multiplied. His now-larger chest was carpeted with whorls of thick black short hairs leaving only his nipples exposed. They were still a hue between fleshy pink and olive brown, but now as large as silver dollars and as prominent as the eraser on a new number two pencil. Tiny colorless hairs downed his magnificent six-pack of abdominal muscles. Only halfway down his perfectly formed belly did they begin again to grow darker and thicker. The perfect coils enhanced the only original part of Claude that remained. Baum and White could not improve with their magic the most private of Claude's parts. As big as they were, they were still all Claude.

"Rise and shine, Loki."

Claude's hand rose and caught at Jack, clasping his scrotum. He worked his way down the thick long inches of Jack's reformed penis to its large plum head. Claude smiled without opening his eyes. He recalled the immensity of Jack's victim from last night. The young man who had donated the replication of his penis along with his life's blood. It was the only fault in Baum and White's spell. Jack would take on the penile form of his last victim. That shape would last until Jack fed again.

Their images were multiplied on every wall, and each of them reproduced on the ceiling. Every mirror reflected the others consumed in vampiric foreplay, creating a kaleidoscope of impeccably formed men. The light and the dark. Classical statuary as pale and perfect as the finest mined marble. Smoldering coal and glittering gold. Flesh that was flesh no longer. The intimate embrace of the unliving. Of the undead.

Claude's ministration on Jack resounded in color and scent. Jack's reciprocal performance was rendered as visual and aural, visceral and oral. These two flawless examples of neoclassical art danced the waltz of the little death with the conscious gravity of a Rodin and the airy impertinence of a Calder.

"You make me hungry," the dark one snarled through lust-induced incisors.

"Then let us go feed," the blond growled in reply.

They left the concealed basement room and went up the stairs of their very private home bordering the Tropicana Wash about midway between the University campus and the MGM Grand Hotel.

Baum and White had to be congratulated again on their selection. Their charges were firmly ensconced between The Strip on the west with its losers willing to exchange their sexual convictions for a financial recoup and a renowned athletic department to the east. There boasted an impressive array of adolescent and post-adolescent wannabes and hangers-on free of curfew restrictions. North of them was the Sheraton Desert Inn Golf Club and the Las Vegas Country Club. And just to the south, the McCarran International Airport.

So many men, so much time.

Steam clouded their eight foot by eight foot pink marble bath and shower. There were five steps down from the doorway to the base of the pool. Hot water could be jetted and aerated by the two dozen nozzles that lined the bath just below the watermark. And it also could be sprayed from the twelve showerheads, seven feet above the floor. The ceiling, mirrored in fog-resistant glass, held the small pin-spots gelled in a soft pink. They washed away their chill in a heated embrace.

"Why did you take me with you? Why not kill me like your mother?"

"Baum and White said I would need you. However, they did not say in what way or how long. When I was first whole again, I did think to dispose of you. I did not know that I would need to daily regrow what I had lost."

"That's all?"

"You are a little monster, Claude. Granted. But I am a much larger one. The truth is: I have been lonely and you are the perfect mate. Understand?"

"Let's eat, Jack."

"Yes, we must feed. But you must now call me Apollo in private as well as in public. There can be no association between who we are and who we were. You are Loki to me now. I am your Apollo. Agreed?"

"Agreed."

"Let's dress for the hunt then, Loki." Apollo consciously altered his speech pattern.

"Are we going out together?" This was a treat; it was Apollo's way to hunt alone. "What should I wear?" Loki asked.

He'd never had so much as this. A regally unpretentious home in the center of a city sprawling away from its nucleus. The very best of cars, serviced and awaiting. Clothes. From the most assiduously formal to the trashiest of casual. Replenished at whim. More jewelry than he could wear, more money than he could spend, more pleasure than he had ever anticipated. Without end.

"I think we can dress down tonight. Leather? Denim? Chains, if you like."

Loki sparkled. His full lips spread into a tantalizing smile. His grin beckoned, his white teeth dazzled. His full intent.

They entered the master bedroom. The motion-sensitive lights warmed to their approach. Loki threw open his closet, Apollo his.

In the original floor plan there had been three bedrooms in a row. The outer two had been sealed from the hallway, reopened from the central room, and recreated as two huge closets. The clothing had been arranged identically in both, yet with subtle differences reflecting their personalities and corresponding to their preferences.

Beginning with evening wear—the morning coats and cutaways and tuxedos, formal shirts and vests hung above satin ties and cummerbunds, silken underclothes and stockings and patent leather shoes. Suits came next, ranging from black to gray, blue to brown. Darkest to lightest. Isaia. Varvatos. Dolce & Gabbana and Armani. Three-piece, then two-piece, then blazers and slacks. Corneliani, Hermes and Brioni. Cubbied beneath were undershirts and shorts and socks. Bruno Magli shoes. Prada shoes. Ferragamo. Sportswear was next.

Polo shirts of every hue and description. Turtlenecks and crew necks. Sweaters by the dozens. Solids and stripes, argyles and cable-knits. Merino, vicuna, cashmere. One hundred percent cotton socks in every conceivable color and style. Each thing in its own cedar cupboard or drawer. Softer leathers in natural, brushed and suede, laced and slip-on shoes. Deck shoes. Tennis. Loafers.

Gym gear.

Sweatshirts and sweatpants and shorts. Swimsuits. Athletic socks. Jockstraps and sneakers. T-shirts and A-shirts and H-shirts and briefs. Black, white and gray.

The big closet.

Leather.

Both Loki and Apollo owned a full array of black leather. A battery of jackets and pants. Vests and chaps. Shirts pullover and button-down. Jocks and thongs and body harness. Custom designed and handmade.

They had black leather belts and boots. Caps and visors. Cuffs and clamps and masks. Black leather leashes and black leather whips. Earplugs, gags, buttplugs.

Black leather wallets attached to stainless steel chains. Black leather wallets inside of wrist cuffs, ankle cuffs, belts.

And denim. Yards of denim. Shirts and jeans and jackets and vests. Indigo, faded and black.

And boots. Motorman's and workman's and cowboy's.

They dressed apart. As always. They both liked to surprise.

"I'm ready!" Apollo called to his partner.

"Almost!" Loki answered. A script polished from rehearsal.

Apollo strode into the central room. His shiny gold tresses were swept back from his face. He wore a gray T-shirt, too small for his frame. Skin-tight, faded blue jeans and a black leather jacket with the sleeves removed.

He added dark aviator sunglasses and a commissioned solid gold watch. He was ready.

Loki entered from the other room.

He left off the Levi's and went for the leather. Not much of it.

He wore black leather combat boots that laced-up just above his ankles. Black leather chaps, skin-tight, and no jeans. A black leather codpiece. Studded. Black leather vest. A studded, black leather collar. And from clavicle to umbilical, shoulder to finger, hard-etched flesh and soft fur.

He turned and revealed two perfect cheeks. Naked mounds of muscle. Flawless.

"The Jag or the Mercedes, Apollo?"

"Bikes, Loki!"

This was to be down and dirty, then. The twin Harley-Davidson motorcycles. So much muscle. Such an impression. And, they could each carry two. The distinct message sent. Apollo and Loki might travel together, live together, but they didn't always play together. The perfect message for this haunt.

North on Paradise, east on Flamingo, past I-515, it took them almost twenty minutes to get to the notorious Raptor's Nest. If there had once been a beaten track to this place, the track had long grown over. It was as un-Vegas as Las Vegas could get.

A stout, squat stucco, half-timbered building with small mullioned windows, "The Rap" had other sensibilities. No neon signs to advertise liquor or beer; its parking lot was twice the size of the building. And, strange for a degenerate locale, not a sound emitted.

Apollo and Loki parked their bikes away from the other motorcycles. This was not the recognition they wanted. They carried helmets, but never wore them. Apollo stood off his hog.

He combed his fingers through his hair and nodded to his consort.

Loki dismounted and dropped his black leather vest over the seat. He'd enter the club naked to the waist.

Apollo blasted the door open to get the full attention of the doorman. No point in entering if an entrance isn't made.

"Fuck!" The doorman.

His mouth was at Apollo's nipple level. His expression, a declaration. His declaration, a desire. Sitting on a stool, he'd kneel a
slave.

Apollo cruised past, allowing no connection, savoring the full
effect. Loki grabbed the man in a semi-playful headlock, enveloping him in the heady spice that is the scent of the hunting vampire's
blood. A victim marked.

The Raptor had an oval bar, more than fifteen feet wide and almost forty feet long. Two bartenders worked it together on the
weekday nights and four on the weekends. They never stopped
pouring except for a piss, a drug or a blow job. And they didn't
necessarily leave the bar to do any of them.

The lighting tended to be more amber over the bar and indis-
tinctly red in the rest of the room, but for the heavily shaded white
light over the pool table.

The Rap was like its kin all over. Quintessential gay leather bar.
The prefab deejay tapes vacillated between heavy metal and mournful country. Very loud inside a soundproofed building. Invisible
speakers everywhere. A sea of masculinity in half-light.

The men ranged from five and a half feet to well over six feet
tall. One hundred and sixty pounds to more than twice that. The
shaven hirsute to close-cropped and bearded to hairless. The very
fit to the formerly fit. Cubs and papa bears. In denim and leather.
Chests exposed and butts exposed. And sometimes more.

Shaded eyes, hooded eyes, glassed eyes.

Sneers that passed for smiles.

Rampant, desperate loneliness. Pervasive, reckless horniness.

And into this barren twilight, the birth of a brand-new day. Into
this mock boot camp, artificial bunkhouse, counterfeit motorcyclist
den, two gods walked.

They looked like the cover of the romance novels that no one
here would admit to having read or seen. Everything about them
was overstated—the hair, the muscles, the beauty, the manliness.
Yet, they were the most genuine beings in the room. They didn't
belong, but the room belonged to them.

"Two Buds."

The bartenders and the patrons scrambled. Everyone wanted to
be noticed by the two men that everyone noticed.

"Mike, that's on—"

"I want to . . ."

"Those drinks are with . . ."

Mike "Silver" Fox opened two from his reserve of extremely cold bottles. At sixteen, he'd started graying. And in compensation, the high school sophomore started pumping iron. He had grown some from five-six at the sight of his first gray. From the one hundred twenty-four pounds. By his senior year, he was five feet, eleven inches. Salt and pepper. One ninety.

Now, perfectly gray, he hit just over six foot. Just over two-twenty.

"Gentlemen," he said in his commanding baritone, "these are with The Raptor. Welcome."

Apollo could sense Loki's interest without looking. Silently, he sent him away.

Go over past the pool table. See what's going on there.

I like this one, Apollo!

Too obvious! What did I say about that?

I'm gone.

Apollo marked him for his own.

The room pulsed. For Apollo and Loki, the aural intrusion was a flow to be controlled. They had to feed in order to mute the influences of the physical world.

Vampirism was something that each member had to deal with alone. With or without a mentor, the experience was different for all. Jack had no base support. His was a situation that he'd partaken with Phillipe. Comprehended in Claude. Understood in Noel.

But vampirism could not truly be shared.

Each vampire had to feed. More than one in a feeding ground led to increased awareness. So, each of the undead needed to travel alone. Yet, their residual humanity craved a mate.

Apollo stood silently in the shadows as he watched Loki set his net of seduction.

Loki went to the pool table. He placed quarters in line on the table's rim for a chance to play. The light caught his leather and his muscles. As he intended. The heat carried his scent. As he expected. Loki nonchalantly adjusted his hair to expose his underarms. A vampire can call with his armpits when he chooses. Pheremones be damned!

Loki was well on his way.

"You know, you big guys with all your hair and muscles usually bore me."

Apollo looked out of the corner of his eye to see the five-foot seven inch firecracker who'd come up to him. This one was self-satisfied to within an inch of his life.

"Your attention? I'm Cody Daly. You're . . . ?"

If a redheaded, freckled-faced ventriloquist's dummy in cowboy drag had grown up to be Las Vegas's hottest weatherman, he'd surely have been Cody Daly.

There had been hardly a moment since his hiring that the news station or Cody couldn't figure out an episode when Cody could appear shirtless or pantless. In Speedos or gym shorts or tights. And for all the right network reasons.

Cody at ballet class in dance belt and tights. Cody's Mardi Gras installment wearing a toga and beads and not much else. There was that segment on massage therapy when he wore only a towel. The Swedish spa part when he didn't. His ski report in boots, boxer shorts, earmuffs and skis. His UV warning about sunscreen with his smile suggesting that it was all he had on. Cody Daly was a whore to be reckoned with. And he usually got what he wanted.

But Apollo had not responded.

"I could do you right here."

"No, actually, you could not."

"I'm Cody Daly!"

"I'm leaving," was all Apollo replied to the self-satisfied weatherman.

He walked away from Cody and approached Loki. "Take your pick. I'm leaving. The little one is following."

"I want that one."

Loki's intended prey was all that a master could dress to be.

His black leather jackboots pushed him up that extra inch to a height of six foot. The black leather pants hugged his solid calves and bulging thighs. This guy worked hard for the look.

A thick, black Garrison belt encircled his hips two inches below his navel. And studded leather belts held at his sternum by a large stainless steel cockring crossed his torso. Matching leather bands separated his biceps from his deltoids.

He wore a black leather motorcycle cap with a patent leather visor. His heavy beard was trimmed to half an inch, as were the back and sides of his head. Aviator sunglasses hid his eyes. Eyes, Loki knew were watching.

They were more alike than different, this vampire and this victim, and Loki wished to play with that. They seemed to be an equal size and weight. Both muscular and hairy. But, Loki's hair was longer and he was clean-shaven, and that's where their appearances began to diverge.

The man wasn't classically handsome, still he was alluring in a dangerous way. Damned good-looking, and damned just the same.

The close trim of his head and beard revealed a few errant and quite gray hairs among the nut brown. And whereas Loki's muscularity was entrancingly unreal, Steve Leeds had a body built by hard work and perseverance.

His hair was now, at thirty-four, beginning to recede, but not in an unattractive way. But because of the perceptions attached to it, he fought harder to push back the invading calendar and retain his claim.

Steven J. Leeds was, in his workaday life, "Mr. Easter Bunny." He was the springtime chocolatier of choice for the affluent of the Western Hemisphere. His rabbits appeared every year after Mardi Gras, not as the commonplace standing bunny-and-basket, but as fat and robust lapins worthy of the Feast of Resurrection.

If it was a Leeds's chocolate rabbit, it had to be skinned first. Freed from a fine flaky fur of spun sugar or nougat or coconut. Cinnamon sugar or strawberry shreds or licorice curls. The chocolate bodies under sweet frothy pelts were a further surprise. Some were white chocolate based, some milk chocolate, some dark. Yet to these three basic profiles, Leeds worked his particular confectionary magic. With dozens—hundreds—of herbals and botanicals at his disposal, he created for each new rabbit a singular "genetic code." White chocolates took best to the lightest fruits and berries and pretty botanicals like violet and rose. The milk chocolate favored expanded culinary spices and particular homey fruits, like cinnamon and apple, orange and clove, ginger with pear. The deep chocolates braved his strongest inventions. Venturing into heavier botanicals like sun-ripened tomato and pumpkin, he introduced the liquors and liqueurs and the most exotic and demanding of flavors. Each Leeds's rabbit was one of a kind. And perfect. As was Steven James Leeds. Arrogant and sinful and ultimately semisweet.

Loki felt his nearness as he reached across the pool table, bridging his fingers to access the cue ball. A scholarly shot, all geometry, English and composition, Loki turned away from it before the spectators could tell he'd won.

He flourished his stick and with it his scent. He bought it down, over and around Steve Leeds, trapping him within his massive arms.

"It seems I've won twice tonight," Loki told the businessman.

"You've got the wrong guy," Steve answered. "I'm the hunter, not the prey."

Loki released his stick, pivoted and relinquished his naked back and backside to his intended.

"Is that better?" he whispered over his shoulder.

"Much."

"Meet me in the parking lot."

Men are caught in traps of their own making. They are the assistants of their own demise. Ego is self-supplied bait. Steven J. Leeds was going to get his, but not as he had planned.

Once outside, Steve searched the dark corners of the parking lot for Loki. He came up to him, introduced himself and asked, "Didn't you come in with that guy over there? The blond on the bike with the hot redhead?"

"We are together and not together," Loki answered in an imitation of Euro-trash. An answer that is not an answer. A seduction that he'd learned from Noel Courbet.

It was enough for Steve, whose leather-clad crotch was pushing against Loki's bare-flesh buns.

"Should we follow them back to the house, Steve, or travel on by ourselves?"

Leeds recognized the weatherman clutching the big blond. This is the kind of party you dream about, he thought. Not the kind he got invited to.

"Let's join them." Steve jumped on the bike.

Loki blasted out of the parking lot. He surged past Apollo on the road. A signal. Apollo let him go. Loki would have Steve into the hot tub by the time they entered. Cody wouldn't resist the tub if he thought the rest would be private. Cody was mostly a show-off.

They all took Flamingo back to Maryland, Maryland to Tropicana, Tropicana to Paradise. They went off Paradise and back to the Wash. Very private.

Loki and Steve were nowhere to be seen when Apollo entered the house with Cody.

"Wow! This is quite a house. I didn't even know it was here," Cody confided in his host.

"We were fortunate to have found it, Cody."

"We?"

"You must have noticed my partner, Loki, at the pool table. The half-naked slut with the black hair and sinful body?"

"He's your lover?" Cody asked, disbelieving that he could possibly live up to the competition.

"We don't use terms like that. We share our time for the moment," Apollo started to unbutton Cody's checkered shirt, "but we don't always share our interests." Apollo pulled Cody's shirt free of his jeans and dropped it to the floor. He unzipped his own leather jacket and began to reveal himself to Cody. He pulled off his T-shirt. The television weatherman faltered with appreciation.

Cody Daly had gotten away with his "cute" look for most of his life. He was very aggressive both in his business and social life. He was intelligent and witty. His aquamarine eyes glowed with a wattage only overshadowed by his dazzling smile. And he knew it. He kept out of the sun to reduce his freckling and inside the gym to increase his marketability—both professionally and personally. On the short side of average in his height and his length, the freckled redhead compensated by showing off his honed physique.

Cody had a big chest for his frame and finely formed. Lightly peppered with sunny copper hairs and punctuated with assertive bright pink nipples. He knew he had good arms and lats and abs. Good shoulders and back. But how, when he removed his jeans, was he to measure up to dark-haired hunk or to this blond beauty, this god, this—

"Apollo."

"What?" Cody couldn't believe his ears.

"I forgot to tell you my name, Cody. I'm Apollo."

He pulled off his boots and shucked his jeans and stood before Cody in heavy gray socks and black briefs. Nothing on this guy wasn't perfect, Cody thought.

Apollo came over and reached for Cody's belt buckle. The weatherman's hormones kicked in with a "flight-or-delight" response. The big blond knelt before him and started for his zipper. Cody was going nowhere.

Apollo undid Cody's buckle and button and zipper. He tugged at the rear pockets and pushed the jeans down to his guest's knees.

Apollo felt him, front and back, with his left hand and right. He was perfectly muscled and perfectly shaped. And, in keeping with his overall frame, a little small.

Apollo stood up quickly and in doing so, swooped Cody off his feet. Cradling him in his massive arms, Apollo popped off Cody's cowboy boots, peeled off his jeans and pulled off his socks. Cody Daly had not worn underwear his adult life.

"Can we do this in the bedroom?" Cody asked.

"How about a little time in the hot tub first?" Apollo countered.

"Yeah, okay. You do seem a little cold. One thing first . . ."

Cody slid out of the blond's arms and slipped his hands inside the waistband of Apollo's briefs. He pushed them down over the rock-solid buttocks and slim hips, down the impressive thighs, oddly delicate knees and bulging calves. Apollo stepped out of them and stood, naked, before Cody.

"Ohmygod, what does that thing look like hard?" Cody wondered aloud.

"Let's get hot and find out."

Apollo carried Cody to the marble bath. He kicked open the door.

Half a dozen bottles of Cristal champagne littered the ledges of the hot tub and two lusty satyrs loitered in the steaming waters. Their chest hairs were sodden and dripping in the humidity. Their faces flushed with erotic tension. But it was the overwhelming aroma of musk that eroded Cody's apprehension. The heady scent of manliness that was stewing in this enclosure.

He slipped out of Apollo's arms and into hot water.

Steve and Loki turned their mutual attentions to the new addition. They wore large gloves made of natural sea sponge and introduced the weatherman to their touch-sensitive game. Together they lathered and fondled the redhead, soully teased and sweetly tortured him. Adoration makes for swift coercion.

And yet, all eyes were on Apollo, the blond god who descended into the bath at a mesmerizingly slow rate. Even in the soft rosy lighting, he remained starkly pale. A whiteness that commanded attention from a pool of onlookers poached pink.

They went to him, all three.

Soon, warmed by their attentions, Apollo's skin lost some of its coolness and took on some color from the hot waters and blasting jets. When the physical excitement of the guests became apparent, Loki whispered to Steve.

"I have another game for you. A little hotter than this bath. Let's leave them."

"Maybe they'd like to join us?" Steve asked in return.

"Perhaps later," Apollo answered for both himself and Cody. "We'd like to get to know each other first."

Cody demonstrated obvious relief and unmitigated pleasure at this. A rub-a-dub in the tub was one thing, a four-way fuckfest was quite another and definitely too much for him.

"We'll be in the game room, if you want to come by later." And they stepped up and out of the tub together, already hot and wet.

When the dark-haired and muscular naked men shut the door, Cody turned to Apollo and said, "Thank you. I'm glad you weren't into it either."

"Oh, I do play cruel games with Loki now and then. But he knows I don't like to share as he does. And my games tend to be more cerebral than physical."

Cody was starting to get confused. Cautious. He conversed to overcome anxiety.

"Well, for whatever reason, I'm grateful."

"Come show me how grateful."

Cody waded over to the most handsome man he'd ever known. He straddled Apollo's lap and held him close, belly to belly, chest to chest, mouth to mouth.

Apollo slipped his arms under Cody's buoyant thighs and lifted the television personality's crotch to his mouth. Cody draped his legs over Apollo's shoulders and, with the blond's hands and arms providing support, floated on his back in the torrid bath.

"I could do this every day," he whispered to the god he adored.

The rhythmic lapping lulled Cody into an altered state. He was overcome by the headiness of the enclosure. The scents and sensations. He was manipulated, up and down the scale, by a virtuoso. Overture through coda. From pianissimo to allegretto, from presto to crescendo. He was fully orchestrated by a maestro.

"I'm almost there," he murmured to his host. He sung, his strings humming.

And so am I.

Apollo swallowed him whole. And inserting his fangs into the deep dorsal vein of Cody's most private part, he took all the weatherman had to give. In his spasms, Cody did not feel the secondary ache of the puncture. Until he at last called, "Enough! You're killing me." And discovered, at that moment, that indeed, Apollo was.

Cody tried, but weakened by the blood loss, couldn't pull out of his postcoital languor, couldn't pull away from the apparent death grip Apollo had on him. The fight remained in his mind only, his muscles bereft of their abilities.

He sunk into the heated waters resigned, his last anemic thought, his final pallid word, "Why?" And with it, the cruel compliment he carried into his afterlife—*because you're beautiful.*

And at war with his vile intrusion, Apollo decided to give something back to Cody Daly. Love? Certainly not, for what he was about to do was not loving. He punctured the corona of his own penis—now remarkably identical to Cody's own—and fed the adorable redhead, rescued him from death. He pondered amazed all through the process of converting Cody. Apollo did not know why he did it.

He hurried at preternatural speed to secrete the regenerating corpse of Cody Daly, flew to The Raptor's Nest and commandeered Cody's BMW convertible with Steve Leeds's motorcycle loaded into the backseat.

He took a new victim. To replenish the blood he'd given to Cody and to reconstruct a sex organ larger than the one Cody had gifted to him. He drew a big, black bear of a man behind the club, and was rewarded in his kill with a superlative example. The distinctly contrasting flesh tone amused him.

He hurried home to add fuel to Loki's fire.

The game room was well heated for Apollo's return. Only fifteen feet by fifteen feet wide, it had high ceilings and no windows. The walls and floor were foam rubber padded and covered in tanned pigskin. The room smelled like an expensive new car. The ultimate aphrodisiac.

The lighting and sound systems were embedded into the ceiling. Gelled lights ranging from straw and saffron to amber and honey, from palest pink to deepest rose. All for a reason and to a purpose.

In the midst of it stood Steve Leeds. Ironically, like a kid in a candy shop. For there were things in this torture chamber that defied even his knowledge of the art form.

Apollo watched in stealthy observance as Steve experimented with apparatus grand and gratuitous. Torments apparent and appalling, tortures obvious and obdurate.

Loki was enjoying the attention. Shackled naked to a leather-covered incline, he was blindfolded by a black leather hood and tantalized by small devices.

Rubber-clad clips of stalwart tensile strength were fastened to his nipples. His scrotum and penis were caught in a cat's-cradle of wet rawhide that clenched as it dried.

Loki's arms and chest, his belly and thighs, were striated with a crosshatching of raised welts. The signature of a scrupulous whip-master.

Loki sensed his partner's return and spoke.

"The cage."

Steve Leeds had wondered about the centerpiece of the collection since he first entered the room. It was made of solid steel tubing. Seven feet high, wide and deep. An indestructible latticework cube with immeasurable menace. But how to work it?

Both closed sides of the cage were grids of stainless steel. Fine, fingerlike needles of steel could be swung to the center of the cage, singularly or in groups. Electrodes coiled from the grid at the top of the cube, snaking in elasticity toward any prey.

Padded, leather-cuffed and chained manacles intended for wrists and ankles seemed to complete the setup. But still, Steve couldn't unravel the intent of its design.

"The cage," Loki repeated; he knew Apollo looked on.

"This is your playroom," Steve finally conceded, eager to get on with the show. "You'll have to show me how to use it."

Men only enter traps of their own making.

"Free me and let's go to the cage."

Loki stayed perfectly still as Steve Leeds untied, unclasped, unfastened and unfettered him. Loki peeled off his mask and said, "C'mon, I want to show you this."

He took Steve by the hand and demonstrated.

"Pull and release. Like this! It frees the mechanism. Then you can draw the manacle to where you want it."

Misdirection.

The art and the law of Las Vegas.

Steve watched one manacle and was caught up in the other.

"What the ..." And as he swung for Loki, his strong right roundhouse was rendered immobile by the vampire's left hand.

Steve Leeds found himself caught, left and right, in the manacles of the cage. Although insulted by the assault, he brought himself to say, "What's this? Am I *your* slave now? You can't even get that thing hard!"

"No, not me, not yet, Steve," the dark beauty answered. "But he can."

Apollo came out of the shadows.

Everything about him was big. But what Steve Leeds most feared was the very large spongy muscle that reached for the ceiling. The very dark brown organ that stood apart in grave contrast to the fevered blush of Apollo's ordinarily pale white muscles. This was not a perfect situation for rapacious Leeds.

"No. Don't do this to me," he broached. "How about a safe word?" he bargained. "We need to stop!" he begged.

Apollo approached in all his new miscegenated glory. A big blond with big muscles, everything about him was big. Including his hard and aching black dick.

"This isn't right!" Steve was displaying a calm in the face of a huge dilemma. "There's something wrong here. I can't do this. Not like this."

He was starting to jabber and he knew it. Steve Leeds had been in charge his whole life and found himself jockeying for third place in a contest he didn't want. Couldn't win.

Wordlessly, Loki and Apollo approached. They were beautiful-looking men with perfect bodies and massive members. One, the blond, a rock-hard, if mismatched, terror. The dark-haired one was normal, but still flaccid and still the more frightening for it.

Steve did a mental critique of Apollo.

Over six feet tall and probably two-eighty by the size of him, his muscles were like a synthetic shell. He looked like some pumped-up gay action figure in his flawless exaggeration. Apollo's reproductive organ was certainly as long as Steve's forearm and nearly as wide as his wrist. And black! This big, beautiful blond had a big, black dick and that *wasn't* the one he had in the hot tub earlier.

Drugs, he thought. Did they drug me? No, he didn't think so. I *need* drugs. Drugs would help. He did a mental inventory of the contents in his special black leather wallet. But, didn't he leave that wallet hidden in his motorcycle still parked at The Raptor's Nest?

"No, Steve, I went back and got your bike," Apollo settled the unvoiced question. "I could have left it in the lot, but I thought that sooner or later you or Cody would be missed. Someone would eventually start looking for one or both of you. They might even trace you to The Raptor's Nest. Someone there would certainly remember us. And, although we weren't seen leaving together, the authorities would eventually come to question us. We can't have that."

"What kind of game are you guys playing?" Steve barely recognized his voice for the squeaky tremors. "Kidnapping locals and holding them as sex slaves?"

"Oh, nothing as permanent as that," Loki responded. "My partner here has already made fast work of the weatherman. Now he's here with one last thrill while I get one more kill."

Fear. Smells of ammonia, the candyman thought. His vision blurred with welling tears. And his choked-back cries closed his glottis and muffled his hearing. Fear.

Smells of ammonia. And of urine. He realized by the warm back splash that he was emptying his bladder onto the expensive leather floor.

Loki knelt in the puddle between Steve's legs and licked the wetness from Steve's feet and calves and thighs. He encircled the source of the stream with his lips.

Apollo stepped behind Steve and knelt for a reflective service on his captive's posterior. Steve began to respond to their attentions. The wrong head was doing Steve's thinking.

I get it. This is their game. First a mind-fuck and then the real one.

Steve's shoulders slumped in relief. He expelled a relaxed sigh. If this was the way it was going to be, he'd give his gorgeous hosts a hell of a ride. They both certainly knew what they were doing and if you can't beat 'em . . .

They manipulated their guest into a delicious dynamic tension. His muscles and nerves were electrified. He simply couldn't hold out any longer. The spasms rocked him, shaking him violently. An explosive initial quake followed by a series of tingling aftershocks.

Loki slowly rose from his crouch. He dragged his tongue over Steve's belly, his navel, his abs. He teased each nipple and then raised his head to look into Steve's satisfied face.

Loki smiled.

It wasn't a look that Steve ever wanted to see again. The broader Loki smiled, the less he looked like a beautiful man. The grin that grew out of it contained a grimace. The perfectly dazzling white teeth were growing into grotesqueries that belonged to some sort of wild animal.

"Jesus Christ!" was the last thing Steven J. Leeds ever said. He made one last horrible scream as Apollo fulfilled his initial menace and invaded what he had primed. And atrocity followed outrage as Loki tore at Steve's exposed neck with his huge canines.

Steve could feel his blood spurting out of his neck in rhythm matched with Apollo's assault and mated by Loki's theft.

Then he felt no more.

chapter

6

When Jack left the chapel after killing his mother, Claude came to me. He cradled my head in his hands.

I saw, in his face, a kaleidoscope of conflicted emotions. He couldn't drink from me, which I knew was what he wanted. But he obviously didn't need me around anymore. He was free of his enslaver and reunited with his lover.

"Don't kill me. Please, Claude," I said as quietly and rationally as I could.

"Jack said to take care of things in here. And that means you."

"You don't know what you're doing. He doesn't want me dead. Just ask him. Killing me would just . . ."

He covered my mouth with one hand. Just to quiet me, I think. It must have been the very look of it that gave him the idea. And he pinched my nostrils with his other hand.

I fought desperately to get free. Free of his hands, free of my manacled restraints. But even as I struggled, I knew it was no use. Claude was like all vampires, inhumanly strong. And my death was what he wanted.

I knew then what it was to die. To die and survive death. I can put to lie the silliness of the bright white light and of the spiral tunnel leading to it. Of angelic choirs announcing the arrival of a new saint. The feeling of lightness, of floating. The feelings of harmony and of peace. Any sense of completion, all sense of serenity. It is all a lie.

At least for me. And those like me.

When Claude snuffed out my life with his brutal, beastly strength, all I felt was his hatred of me and a compact with the cold. I burst quickly from the realm of the living, never savoring the slow passage I expected. Wanted. I did not go gently, nor did I rage.

My lungs simply burned from the inability to inhale or expel. Then, they just stopped. Like my heart.

There was a brilliant, momentary burst of light behind my eyelids. Just a flash that ended in darkness. Then an oozing warmth throughout me, like fresh blood seeping over my belly or hot urine running down my leg. But, as the warming sensation grew, so did the overlaying chill. I couldn't see, my hearing dimmed. I felt nothing.

I do not know how long I slept there, if indeed sleep it was. I thought that I opened my eyes to the pitch-black chapel. Had I only imagined that Claude murdered me? I wished I could see.

Instantly, flames appeared at each wick. The chapel was brightly lit and Baum and White were sitting together on a pew. Natty as ever. Dressed to kill?

"You did that well, master." Of course, they spoke as one, but this time I could distinguish their individual voices. "Psychokinetic immolation is usually an acquired talent, not a birthright."

"Am I dead? Am I one of you now? One of them?" My voice rose with my anger. I felt angrier than I ever had in life. And my very anger affected the surroundings. I felt it.

The precious stained glass windows shook, the wooden pews trembled.

Yes, I knew it now, I was dead. Well, undead.

"Get me out of these manacles!"

"You can free yourself, master."

And I discovered that I could.

Why are you calling me master?

Neither Baum nor White showed any reaction to my unspoken question.

"You can no longer read my mind, can you?"

"No. Nor will Jean-Luc Courbet nor his lover, Claude Halloran."

"Where are they?"

"It is forbidden to tell you, master, nor may I assist you in finding them."

"Why do you call me master?"

Baum and White rose as one. They seemed to float up the aisle to the altar, but I could finally discern their movements. They held a thick terry cloth bathrobe between them. I put it on gladly. Not that I minded being naked and aroused in front of them—a development that surprised me. But I was cold and it helped.

"Come with me and everything will be explained."

I followed them out of the chapel and down the hall. I knew that I had changed forever. I noticed each of my muscles in a way I never had before. The feeling was as intense as a cramp, but the sensation was sweet. And, too, I perceived things differently than I had as a human. The entire earth and everything on it took on a new beauty. Or possibly revealed a beauty that I could not know without vampiric senses.

"Are you seeing sounds yet, master?"

"Yes, that is it exactly!"

"You will hear and taste colors as well. And the tactile will become aromatic as you begin to experience the fullness of every sensation for each stimulus. The life of the vampire is at its core sensual. And it is greatly heightened from mortal existence. That is why men become monsters. To fuel this divine fire. The existence is all-consuming, and the vampire's blood must consume as well. To preserve, to continue."

We walked from the side hall, down the main hall and back through the dining room to the kitchen. They took me down a secret passageway and ancient stone stairs into a cavernous subfloor with a huge heated pool.

"Go ahead, master, get in. It really does help ease the chill that is now a constant in your existence."

I dropped my robe and waded into the pool. The water was incredibly hot. But it did help, they were right. I no longer felt cold. For the first time in months, I felt good.

I looked back up at the two strange men who stood at the pool's edge.

"Will you come in?"

"I control my chill at first dark," came the haunting singularity of their reply. "As soon as the sun sets."

I continued to tread water, although I could easily have stood. The pool was only about five feet deep. But the small movements of my arms and legs were creating stimulating sensations. Exquisite colors and sounds and scents. I never wanted to leave this water. But there was still much I needed to know.

"When you say you control your chill, you mean you drink blood."

"Yes, master. But not like the one who took your life nor the other who claimed your afterlife."

"Will I be like them?"

"Let us find out."

Baum and White left me luxuriating in the pool and went through another archway out of the cavern. They came back with a beautiful man, Spanish by the look of him, who was about my age.

He wore a robe identical to mine. When Baum and White introduced him, he removed it, shucking it much the way I had. He was naked underneath his, too.

"Master? This is Bernardo Santiago. He is here for you."

Bernardo was shorter than me, about five ten or so. He wore his hair longer than I did, but not much. Its thick blackness was reflected in his moustache and again on his chest. And, judging by the fullness of his muscles, he must have been some kind of weightlifter. He had a bronzy complexion and the biggest, blackest eyes I had ever seen. Baum and White must have read my mind at some point. He stepped into the pool.

"Mi Madre!"

"Yes, it's hot. You'll get used to it though," I said, reverting to my former style of speech.

"You speak English. I didn't think you French ever spoke anything but French."

"I'm not . . ."

"Monsieur le marquis?" Baum and White interrupted with intent. "I will not be far, should you need me."

Bernardo made his way to me at the center of the pool. The only man I had ever been totally naked with was Teddy. The only one I had really made love to. I had not had sex since he died. Not counting Jack or Claude. But I had the feeling I might be able to count this one.

He put his arms around me. His left under my right armpit and his right over my left shoulder. He was strong. He brought his face to mine.

Something unnaturally strong drew me to him. I entered a kind of dream state. Like I had been drugged. When I looked at this beautiful man, I experienced so much more than I ever had looking at one. I gently touched his chest and felt his heart beat through his skin. I ran my tongue over his neck and heard its salinity. I felt his heat. And his heat came from his blood. I had turned.

His blood fascinated me. I could smell the unique perfume of it. Hear the music of its flow. I felt its pulse as a gentle massage and as a roaring stream. I could see his vitality as it rushed into dilating capillaries, showing his excitement.

His excitement was filling him as his blood rushed to his skin layer. It engorged him. The blood and with it his hormones. That was the sweet high note to counterbalance the deep darkness of his blood. His testosterone called to me, a siren's song in baritone. I must possess this manliness. Own him.

He was hot and we were both ready.

It was sex as I had never had it before. Few, I imagine, had. Certainly no one living. As lovely as it may have been before, it was extraordinarily tantalizing as a vampire. Each touch reverberated into my other senses. Each taste, every murmur. The sight of him— not just his butt or his cock, but his wrist, his small toe, his knee— thrilled me as much as an erotic stroke. The very scent of him, especially at his armpit or his crotch, had intensified in my reception to a supernatural degree. It was not merely an orgasm, but ecstasy on a divine level. I exploded and nearly shook us both apart.

When he finally realized that no harm would be done, he looked very pleased with himself. Afterwards, he left for another appointment. This guy, as it turned out, was a pro. Baum and White confided that they hired him to test me. I will always think kindly about them for the gift of the Spaniard in the pool. If I had grown fangs and went for his neck, they would have had their answer.

"You never smelled his blood?" they asked.

"I smelled all of him. But I did *not* want to drink from him. Not his blood anyway."

"Master, have you no hunger?"

"I could eat. But only if you call me Mike."

"Michael it is, then," was all they would relinquish.

I put on the clothes they laid out for me. Perfectly fit, but not clinging. And soft. As only really expensive clothing is. I followed them back upstairs to the dining room.

They made me my favorite meal, a surf and turf comprised of a two-inch-thick filet mignon and a sixteen-ounce lobster tail. Steamed asparagus and a baked potato crowned with bleu cheese.

"How is your meal?" they wondered.

"Perfect."

"Are you enjoying it?"

"You can see that I am."

I drank the best of the estate wine with my meal. Baum and White watched me as if they'd never seen anyone eat before. Each bite, every sip peppered with questions about my enjoyment. Salted with inquiries about my health.

I discovered shortly after finishing why. Why vampires never eat food. Why they rarely drink.

I passed my entire meal in the exact pieces I had consumed. Pissed a deep red and expensive vintage. My body rejected it just like any other vampire would. I could eat and drink, I could even enjoy the process, but I could no longer sustain myself as I had.

I found out, just before sunrise, how it was that I would.

Hidden in one of the exterior walls was a circular stone staircase. They led me up through it to the second story. Directly in the center was a windowless room.

Its walls were stout granite lined with antique tapestries and expensive furniture. Bookshelves filled with rare editions and rarer parchments. Pedestals holding beautiful bronze and marble statues still unseen by the contemporary art world.

Baum and White pushed aside a large, heavy wardrobe to reveal a secondary room.

"This was the berth of the marquis. Phillipe's bedchamber. It is where he died."

But that felt wrong to me.

"I thought Jack destroyed the entire chateau when he left. How could this be the original bedchamber?"

Baum and White looked to each other first. No doubt silently agreeing to tell me what I wanted to know.

"Much of the chateau was totally devastated by Jean-Luc's blaze. The original corps-de-logis was spared, as were certain full and partial rooms. Ours, for instance. Remarkably, Phillipe's chambers had no fire damage, nor were the stones crushed in the collapse. These are the original rooms, albeit reconstructed. Some things cannot die."

"But, this is where Noel killed him," I insisted.

"She did destroy the maker here."

A cop to the core, I struggled to fit the pieces of this puzzle together. But it was still not meshing.

"If Phillipe created Noel," I started, hoping that the right words would come, "then he would be her master, right? And if he was her master, and his poem says you can not kill your master, then how could Noel possibly kill Phillipe?"

I had never seen them smile before, I was sure no one had. I was starting to like these guys.

"You have realized what the rest never questioned, Michael. If Phillipe had been Noel's true creator, she would have been incapable of rising up against him. Phillipe told me that he did not turn Noel directly. According to Phillipe, he first transformed the child, Desiree. This tiny vampiress, Desiree, was used to convert Noel and then, after Noel's rebirth, he destroyed the little girl."

They told me the whole story. They told me that Noel fully knew what Phillipe was and demanded the black blood from him. She craved eternal beauty. Phillipe was so apprehensive of a mortal who would gleefully abandon her humanity to gratify her vanity, that he created a bridge between his superior blood and what would be Noel's, diluted by being filtered through Desiree's.

"Jean-Luc is the only true heir to Phillipe's gift. A sole recipient of the master's pure blood."

"Wait a minute! Phillipe changed you two as well!"

"Yes, but Phillipe changed Aspros and Dentro simultaneously by his single blood. What would amount to a half dosage apiece. Neither simply bound in flesh nor just bound in spirit, I am completely bound in blood."

"And that is why you are unlike the others."

"I am as immortal as the rest, but only half as powerful. And, conversely, without some of their restrictions."

"Restrictions? I think we should talk about . . ."

I suddenly lurched forward with a gut-wrenching spasm. I was burning and torn at the same time. I felt clammy and nauseous. Headachy and blind. There was a terrible buzzing in my ears and a foul smell of rotten eggs everywhere.

"What is happening to me?" I screamed.

"You have not fed, master. You require blood."

Baum tore off his jacket and snapped off the right cuff button of his impeccable and expensive dress shirt. He pushed his wrist to my mouth as White held me near.

I heard the *lub-dub* of his vital fluid coursing through his veins. I heard the sound as if it was the center of my existence. But for all my desire, my fangs would not grow. I could not receive his ultimate gift.

I pulled away from the lovers' grasp and rolled into a fetal ball on the wood floor. I covered my eyes with my fists to weep. And suddenly the frantic howling and the diabolical drumming stopped. I smelled a redemptive scent. The blazing red blindness cooled down to a refreshing blue-green.

I felt the ancient, uncanny force press my jaws open, elongate my canines. Far from painful, it was like an erotic, dental erection. My enamel tumescence sought its own goal and I sank the razor-sharp projections into my own wrist. I sucked at my own lifeblood.

At the end of my rapture, I lifted my head to see the lovers standing hand-in-hand on the other side of the room. "Is it like this for you?"

Again they smiled. And I knew.

Baum pointed to my crotch and said, "The priapism is usually a result of the feeding. As I said, vampirism is a world of the senses."

I realized then that the preternatural orgasm I just had was not on the physical plane. I thought that the Spaniard, Bernardo, was the cause of that riotous sex earlier. Now, I knew for certain. It was a vampiric condition.

"Is it always like this?"

White spoke alone, for a change, "I have always found it to be so. You appear to be different. I cannot speak for the others who are true vampires."

"I am not a true vampire, then?"

"You feed from yourself," they said, once again in harmony. "I feed from my selves. That is how we are different from the hunter vampires. Neither you nor I ever need kill a human to survive. But you are different in other ways."

"How? Tell me so that I know."

Baum and White sat together on the edge of the giant four-poster that dominated the room. I noticed then the eternal horni-ness that existed in them as well.

"You had silver amalgam dental work in your teeth when you changed. You are the first to be so."

"What does that mean?"

"You alone are immune to the argent sickness. When the vam-piric cells invaded and changed you, the silver was incorporated into your bodily structure. Neither Noel nor her son had these fill-ings, certainly not Phillipe nor I. Claude's teeth had been filled with porcelain, an actor's vanity. We are all subject to the argent sickness, even to a deadly level. But not you.

"Then, too, is the sun. I cannot be certain that its rays will harm you. Roses? Wooden stakes of maple, hawthorn or aspen? Garlic? It is possible that none of these will affect you in any way. You, Michael, were a vampire *before* you died. You were not brought back, not saved from death. I do not know if you can ever truly die."

There it was. My final judgment. Jack's ultimate, unwitting curse. I am doomed to forever roam the earth.

"Tell me more, gentlemen," I said in a voice I had to get used to as my own.

Baum and White took a moment to look at each other in silent accord. Then they proceeded.

"At the time of the full moon, we are all at the height of our strength. We are weakest at the new moon. Unlike humans, who mark their calendars in a solar cycle of three hundred and sixty-five and one-quarter days, we are on a lunar cycle of thirteen lunar months. We are never without our powers, but they do wax and wane with those phases."

"I have noticed as much in the others. What else?"

"A vampire can only be killed or created during the full moon. It was true for the creation of Phillipe all the way through to your recent transformation. All of the creatures of the night are subject to the moon."

I turned abruptly to confront their expressionless faces. The faint glimmer of a smile that passed over their faces like a momentary break in the clouds told me that they knew what I wanted to know.

"All of the creatures of the night? Please explain all."

"Michael, a vampire must recreate once every one hundred and thirty human years. I do not yet know why, but that is the span. Perhaps Phillipe did not know either. But at least once every thirteen decades, he made a new vampire. And oftentimes, many, many more. I believe that is why mortals have considered the number thirteen unlucky far into prehistory. Why thirteen at a table is considered so terrible that it was incorporated into the legend of Jesus's last supper. If you know which face to look for, you can see Phillipe in Leonardo's painting, one of the master's many puzzles.

"Phillipe was an amazing individual. Who can be sure how long he had been undead prior to our encounter in Rome almost twenty human centuries ago? How many others might he have engendered before then? Do any of his other offspring survive today? Who can say? The odds are against them certainly. This is not an easy existence to sustain. But if even one lived, could not that vampire have given birth to more? And those to still others?

"Yes, I understand," I said just to stop them. It was like those tests about rabbits or fruit flies. How many generations could be created in a given set of time?

It was likely that Phillipe had created at least twenty descen-
dants. If, that is, he had only made one for each of the centuries we
knew he existed. But, he had made Baum and White at the same
moment, Noel and Jack within months of each other.

"This is mind-boggling!"

"You see my predicament, then. I try to monitor news and
events to see if I can spot an anomaly."

"Anomaly?"

"Death by hemodetriment. If an unusual number of mortals die
in a confined area due to extreme blood loss, I have reason to believe a vampire exists there."

"And what do you do about it?"

"I watch, Michael. It is my role. I intercede when it is the only solution."

"Oh, yes," I said. "I remember. You cannot harm anyone of
Phillipe's bloodline."

"And what makes you think that Phillipe was the only master
vampire to have existed?"

There was no need to read my mind. Surely, the expression on
my face told them that I had not yet considered the possibility. I
had a lot to learn and not a lot of time. I wanted to find Jack and
Claude and rid the world of them. But, I simply did not know how.

"I need your help. I have to find Jack and Claude. To know how
to destroy them. But on the more practical side, I need to survive
long enough to do this. I have no money and very little other re-
sources. Shit, I have to have a passport! How do I get them if they
left the country?"

"It has all been arranged." I had no idea at that moment what
Baum and White were capable of doing. I have never known the
full extent of their extraordinary faculties. I have never been less
than astonished. And I learned, over time, to expect the impossible.

"Rest now, Michael. We'll speak again at sunset."

And they were gone.

When I awoke the following evening, Baum and White, in their
signature black suits, awaited me. We went down to the game
room together and my amazement began in earnest.

"These must be signed first, of course."

They handed me a pen and a stack of what appeared to be legal
documents. They were all in French, but they looked like a lawyer
had prepared them.

"What are they?"

"These are for the legal transfer of the lands, the estate and the title of Charnac to the new heir. This one is the contract for the new CEO of Charnac Internationale. This, for various credit cards, and this, a driver's license, and finally, here a marriage certificate . . ."

"And who would be signing these?"

"This is his birth certificate."

I looked at the filled-in blanks of the paper. "Michel de Charnac. Who is Michel de Charnac?"

Then I noticed his date of birth. We were born on the same day at the same time.

"Am I Michel de Charnac?"

"The deceased marquis's younger brother. After his demise in America, you have come to the estate to succeed him."

"This will never work!"

"Michael, in every generation I prepare new marriage certificates and birth certificates for the marquis. Do you really think that the locals would countenance a landowner who is unchanged for a century and a half?

"And what of Phillipe? He lived here for hundreds of years! How do you imagine we justified that? We have remained very private and sent out periodic announcements of births and marriages and deaths. Just often enough to allay suspicion and not frequently enough to breed an intrusive interest."

Without another word, I affixed my signature to the papers, each and every one. I never asked which was which. But I did ask whom I married.

"I do not know. Yet. You are very young. You have time. And who knows, Michael," they added slyly, "unlike the true vampire, all of your equipment still works humanly. The feeding is not the only cause of your erections. You might want to start a family one day."

"Only if you can find me a man with a uterus!"

We moved on to our other business. I was measured for my wardrobe. I was photographed for the basis of my formal oil portrait. Invested with the signet of Charnac. Amethyst and topaz and diamond, I called it my Super Bowl ring.

I was shown the inner sanctum of the house of Charnac.

The mainframes and computer terminals, the telecommunications and the fax machines. I could determine, in an instant, what the weather was like on Calle Luna in Old San Juan or how heavy the traffic was at Regent and Oxford Streets outside the London

Palladium. I could view all of my new holdings simultaneously. And, I could find out who had died. When and where and how. I was becoming the master of Charnac, even though the former one still existed. And even though I could find all of the Charnac real estate and expenditures, I could not determine which ones he used.

I woke each evening just as the sun set and wiped the French and American dust from my naked flesh. I went down immediately to the caldarium and into the pool, leaving Baum and White alone to their mutual maintenance in their room. I supposed that they wore those regimentally formal black suits to camouflage their massive hard-ons. Erections that remained until near daybreak. I preferred to go the opposite route and slept through the day with my vampiric one.

After my bath, I joined Baum and White. In some sort of psychic accord, we always met up at an unvoiced location. The gardens or the game room, the library or the armory.

Never the chapel, nor ever the cave of the witch.

They taught me how to move so quickly that I neither cast a shadow nor created an afterimage. To speak like a vampire, above mortal discern. I learned how to fly. The floating maneuvers, they called them. And how to transform myself as Jack did. How, like Phillipe, to move objects and manipulate the minds of lesser animals, humans included. I could call the elements as Noel could. I understood the seduction of this kind of power. I even understood what men would do to retain it. And was thankful that I did not have to make that sacrifice.

From the Cold Moon of December, when I was given the black blood of the vampire, to the Wolf Moon of January, when I was abducted from my home. From February's Quickening Moon, the full moon of my rebirth, to the March moon, the Storm Moon, I learned. First, about desperation and despair. Next, about danger and death. And finally, I learned about Charnac, learned about vampires, learned about power and the means for revenge.

"I am ready for them. I will find them now and do what has to be done."

"Yes, Michael, you are ready. And although I cannot hint or help, I will ask you to consider your secular training. Become what they call a profiler. If you were Jean-Luc and you had Claude with you, where would you hide?"

And I thought I knew.

chapter

7

He stood alone, just past dusk, on Sixth Street between Park Paseo and Charleston Boulevard. He stood invisible in his anonymity for the final time. He watched the night crew enter to prepare for the opening night as the last of the day laborers left the completed renovation.

He followed one, a nineteen-year-old with jet-black hair and crystal-blue eyes and the newly emergent muscles of his first full-time job.

Kenny Logan strolled slowly into nearby Dutton Park. Eager to be accepted as a real carpenter by the old hands, Kenny spent too much of his last hour on that job with a beer in his hand instead of a hammer. Whatthehell! The new owner was some rich Euro-trash pervert, they said. Gay, probably. Spent all his time in the gym and the beauty parlor, by the looks of him. They said. Kenny never saw him, try as he might.

Kenny followed Park Paseo to 9th Street and entered the park. He traveled diagonally towards 7th Street looking for a place to take a private piss. He could have waited and gone with the guys to The Beaver Dam, the seediest of the low-end Vegas strip clubs. But even with the $10 admission and the $10 all-you-could-drink, the tips were breaking him. And it wouldn't be much longer before they got tired of his shy act and he'd have to put up or shut up.

It wasn't that he was gay, Apollo sensed that. He knew that Kenny had yet to show any outward signs of sexuality. Not men, not women, not much of himself. He just wasn't physical in an erotic way. And that increased his desirability.

In the darkest and most private area he could find, Kenny stopped and unzipped. He fumbled trying to free himself of his jockey's and finally unbuttoned his top button as well. He tugged at the elastic and pulled his privates over the top. He closed his eyes and after a moment, he let loose.

When the forcefulness of his flow abated, Kenny remembered to be more observant. He'd been caught at this before and didn't relish the idea of another embarrassing encounter with the LVPD. Especially not Officer Freitag.

But what he saw amazed him. Just as Apollo intended.

Seven, maybe eight yards away, a big, muscular blond was doing the same thing. The guy must have drunk a gallon by the extent of the whiz he was taking. Or maybe it just seemed louder coming from a faucet like that.

Apollo positioned himself so that the light would hit all the right spots and throw a shadow of stark contrast. His arms and shoulders, chest and abdomen, thighs and calves glinted in the dappled light.

All he wore were work boots, heavy socks, very short cutoff jeans and an insulated vest. His very blond hair caught the available light, as did the perfect bone structure of his chin and cheeks, his forehead and nose.

Kenny hadn't realized that he'd stopped pissing and that he was just standing, *en flagrante,* in a secluded section of an out-of-the-way park, with his joint in his hand, staring at a stranger.

A handsome stranger who turned and winked. And disappeared.

"You're drunk, Logan!" he told himself.

He cupped his privates to redeposit them and found his hand covered as well.

"Let's see how drunk you are, Kenny."

Fuck, he thought, but "Shit," he said.

"Mister," he said, trying to sound reasonable, "you're gonna have to let go of me or . . ."

Kenny finally turned to look at his captor. The big strong blond had him in the palm of his big hand. Their bodies were barely apart. The big guy's chest was wider than Kenny's shoulders, each of his shoulders as big as Kenny's head, his abs like a six-pack of Kenny's fists.

"Mister, let go please?" was all the still-teenaged Kenny got out before fear finished what he had started with the part of him that the blond held.

"Oh, mister!" Fear shrouded Kenny Logan as he realized what he had done. It was Officer Freitag all over again. "I'm so sorry. I'm really sorry. I didn't mean to . . ."

Apollo never released his prey, but bent down and licked at his wrist and forearm and lapped at the small stream that the man-boy couldn't stop. He rose and pressed his urine-stained lips to Kenny's trembling ones. He pushed his tongue into Kenny's mouth and brought with it the taste of recycled beer. He inserted his mind into Kenny as well. The beginning of all the rapes the teen would ever know. Ever could know.

I'm going to die. And death tastes of piss.

I'm going to die and it feels like a baseball bat shoved up inside of you. I'm going to die and I don't even know why. I'm going to die now and I haven't even begun to live.

I should have done it once with one of the strippers. Just once before I . . .

Apollo returned to the commercially zoned building he'd purchased just a block off the Strip. Neither downtown nor mid-Strip, the old building had been ignored for decades. Apollo had it rebuilt to his own specifications. Designed to his own rules.

No parking was the first one. This business would be carriage trade only.

The motif, coal and ocher, which prefaced on the theater's exterior, blossomed in.

Black and gold. Gothic and glamorous. Rich and deadly.

Alate ebony bars fully enveloped the lobby of Las Vegas's newest theater. Huge double bats seemed to engulf and devour. And the sinister creatures did their job well. They compelled the audience towards the bars where the patron's drinks were always gratis. Any drink. Only top shelf. A Venus's-fly trap.

The lobby walls were covered in black-flocked gold paper. The pattern, a fleur-de-lis. A gilt-edged black lily that again suggested the bat. The windows were cloaked in black velvet curtains, tied back by golden ropes. Art Nouveau met Rococo in the Asiatic swirls and non-Arayan excesses.

The gold-and-black motif was mirrored in the thick black carpeting edged with Escher-like reflections of golden fledermaus and fleur-de-lis. And again in the Art Nouveau period works, notably the Aubrey Beardsleys and Alphonse Muchas. All original. Then, the coup-de-grace.

There were black-and-white photos of famous, infamous, and nefarious horror writers in ornate gilt frames and circumspect placements. One of a brooding Beai. Of Taylor taunting. Ferrenz caught in her furs. The notorious cigar photo of Platt, Santoro, and Nassise. The legendary nude of LeBlanc, Cacek, Rohrig, Addison, and Jens. The scandalous one of Pelan, Alexander, and O'Rourke that destroyed more than a few marriages. Phillips en flagrante. And the picture Castle claimed didn't exist. None identified. Unnecessary.

The good-looking, uniformed attendants were everywhere, and not one bested by the opulent decor. Not a median pigment on any, the men were either very black or very blond. Dressed in black leather trousers that hugged the buttocks and groin and billowed like harem pants to the cinched cuff, the only other thing the barefoot staff wore were gold lame ties. Nothing else.

This formal wear was for the public viewing areas alone. Inside the new *"theatre du magique,"* they were less than shirtless. Trouserless here, a new leather garment—a baroque codpiece, a hybrid of a thong and swim trunks—was universal.

And still, there were neither brunets nor redheads. All members of the Vows and Secrets staff were black or golden. And if they were good-looking in the lobby, they were glorious inside the theater.

Vows and Secrets. Theater of Magic.

Showtime!

The arrogance of the setting, neither downtown nor Las Vegas Strip, the conceit of the ticket price, the audacity of the single show time—midnight, every night—all blended into a Vegas event. A must-see!

Eighty percent of the opening night crowd had been comped for the weekend. Private jets, flawless suites, chauffeured cars, dining intime. Booze and drugs and studs and babes. Old Vegas; new Hollywood; everyday New York

Vows and Secrets.

Where to be seen was to be accepted. Where seen and accepted were considered commandments. Where consideration was king.

Loaded, luded, and lauded, they entered the arena.

If the lobby was stunning, it was still no prelude to the theater itself.

Every seat was double-size. Expensive black leather covered

overstuffed cushions on gilt frames. Each armrest had a drink holder, an ashtray and a call button. And a near-naked attendant answered every signal immediately.

The space was like a Faberge egg. Overwhelming in every intricate detail. Gilt palm tree pillars punctuated the gold and black lozenged walls and lifted their fronds into the dark night of a predominantly black ceiling. Each segment was defined by the pillowed, cushioned effect caused by gilt banding and discreet pinlights. The heavens, indeed. But, mercifully organized.

It was a Russian onion dome of a theater with the stage set in center. A magical theater in the round. This was certainly a first, and the celebrity magicians in the audience were noticeably chagrined. Counter to the perks and the publicity of opening night attendance, one walked out. The others did not, could not dare.

The attention shifted as the house lights relinquished to stage lighting. The show was about to begin.

"Ladies and gentlemen," a disembodied voice intoned. "Prepare to be astonished!"

From mid-space between the stage and the ceiling's apex a shirtless figure in a white cutaway formal appeared. He slowly descended to the stage to the soft, sweet strains of angelic harps. The lighting and the small puffs of smoke were set to prove that there were no wires. The applause was tumultuous for the unknown magician. Maybe it was because of the drink and the drugs. Maybe it was because most of the first night attendees were performers themselves. Maybe it was because he was beautiful.

He touched down upon the center stage. He lifted his arms in a sign of welcome.

"I am Apollo."

That was all he said before the theater was thrown into uproar. The door to the lobby burst open and a figure clad in black leather tore down the center aisle on an impressive classic Indian motorcycle. With an assault of techno-rock music to match.

He hit the ramp to the stage at an impossible speed. The entire circumference exploded into flames. There were screams from the audience as the bike itself took a vertical spin and the rider was tossed into the air.

The big blond in the white formal wear caught the heavy, vaulted motorcycle in midair. He let the driver drop to his side.

Clad in a one-piece and skintight leather jumpsuit, the rider landed on his feet like an accomplished gymnast. To much applause.

"I am Loki!" he said as he removed his helmet, shook out his locks and showed the opening night crowd his startling good looks. He turned and tore the jacket off the blond.

Apollo never stopped balancing the appreciably heavy motorcycle as Loki stripped him down to a gilded leather codpiece. It did not simply suggest, it testified to the encased.

Apollo put the bike down.

He tore at Loki's collar and cuffs. Ripped his leather sleeves from his massive arms. He mauled the leather from Loki's chest and rent his staunch outfit in two. He left his partner nearly naked on the stage.

The show had begun.

"Thank you all for coming to our opening night," Loki said. "We'd like to entertain you with a magic we call 'Birth.' For, as you know, all things originally came from the sea."

He glanced at Apollo and with that, the lighting changed, music altered, and the show began in earnest.

The stage was ringed with blue-white and laser-intense lights that shot up from the edge of the circular floor.

At center stage, a dozen young men appeared from nowhere. Their very brief costumes were skin-colored. Each was alternately night-shaded black or sun-kissed blond. And all were stunning. The largest of them approached the still larger Apollo.

Apollo waved his hands about the muscular black man. He rose off the floor and as he did, he transformed.

The ring of lights became jets of sprayed water. The stage filled like a pool with no apparent walls. As the waters rose within their own membrane, the rest of the men altered as well. Their legs conjoined and grew scaly. They floated up upon the rising waters and frolicked in its depths.

The stage had become an aquarium and the performers, mermen.

Although he was completely submerged inside an invisible film, the audience could still clearly hear Apollo.

"Behold!"

And one of his chorus members transformed into a menacing gray shark. He pushed at the water's edge and threatened the audience.

"Encore!" Apollo shouted. Not one audience member questioned his ability to speak, much less breathe, underwater.

And with Apollo's command, his partner, the darkly beautiful Loki, changed.

His thighs grew together, becoming a single tail. His feet flared into fins. And then he grew.

His chest expanded first. It encompassed Loki's head and neck and arms. His belly and more. His hair smoothed in incorporation and he bloated beyond any sense of human. Loki had become a monstrous beluga whale.

Great white whales were rarely captive; none appeared in magic shows. Certainly none in-the-round. With celebrities in attendance.

The crowd went wild.

Apollo dispersed all of the attendant mermen. The fish and the sharks. He floated alone with the great white. His lover.

Together they performed a pas de deux so erotic the audience could no longer tell the difference between the species. If indeed a difference there was.

Loki, the whale, rasped and nuzzled. Apollo massaged and brushed. They tickled, pampered, and teased each other. Each audience member would later swear that he alone had the perfect view for the sexual interplay.

The gigantic pink tongue prodded the blond magician. Tickling his armpits, taunting his nipples, tormenting his groin. The huge whale made love to the blond in full view of five hundred audience members.

And then, in an instant, it swallowed him whole.

The waters dispersed and the music subsided and the beluga floundered loudly on the hollow stage. Coughed from its considerable depths was the master magician, Apollo. He turned to the whale, stroked it once, and in doing so, returned it to its previous form. The beautiful Loki.

A seemingly innocent and overlooked shell remained on stage as Apollo and Loki took their bows, received their deserved ovation. They were nearly naked in their leather thongs. Gold for Apollo and black on Loki. The more the young gods bowed, the larger the shell grew. As the shell enlarged, the audience applauded the more. When they quieted, the shell subsided. It took them little time to realize that they were controlling the creature. They went wild. And it grew.

The magicians seemed oblivious to the magic the audience was creating behind their backs with their tumultuous applause. And the crowd loved it. They increased their ovation until the thing had become as large as the men it threatened.

A strange amalgam of lobster, crab and scorpion, the mutant creature was certainly menacing. It stood on its hind legs and brandished its claws. One of the performers came on stage to protect his employers with a lance the size of an oar. The monster neatly snapped it in two.

Apollo and Loki turned to the creature.

They separated, attempting to outmaneuver the hungering crustacean. They attacked and retreated. Threatened and backed away.

The entity was beginning to exhibit stunning speed and apparent reasoning. There was no escape for the duo. It hunkered down. It struck.

Its pincers seemed to elongate as they extended. Simultaneously, they sliced the air with audible torque. They clipped within a hair's-breadth of the magicians, grazing their bellies and capturing their codpieces. Rendering them naked.

The theater went black.

Instantly, the glaring house lights popped up; the stage was empty.

The uproar was palpable. Did the stars of this show just do Las Vegas's most elaborate striptease? Were those private things that they revealed for real?

The audience left the theater in fervent chatter. Each one wanted to be the first to describe the show to the unfortunates who couldn't be at opening night. Each one had an amazing story to tell.

The most beautiful theater in Vegas. The most beautiful men in the world appearing nearly naked on stage. Huge, impossible illusions performed with the audience encircling the action. A stage flooded from floor to ceiling with no apparent encasement. Sharks and whales and mermen. Hideous mutant creatures and naked magicians. It sent shockwaves through the entertainment industry. It was the "must-have" ticket.

And no performance was like another.

And no one was absolutely sure of what they'd seen.

It was pure theater. Pure magic.

Young men came from all over to become part of Vows and Secrets. Gymnasts and dancers, bodybuilders and acrobats. Teenage runaways and seasoned pros showed for the constant casting calls. Many were culled, few were chastened.

Loki was having a field day. For the first time in his history, he was in charge. He was the buyer and not the bought. For all the years of being looked over or turned down, he was extracting full reparation.

Whether gay, straight or undecided, Loki looked at them all. All of them. When they entered his casting office—one at a time—Loki gave each man a thong to wear. There was no place to change but in front of him. Points were deducted, he assured them, for procrastination and timidity.

"This is an all-man revue. If you're not all-man, leave now."

If the applicant's naked self did not measure up to Loki's standards, he gave each a moment to "show all he had to give."

Do it or else.

Base pay was two hundred-fifty dollars per shift for waiters and bartenders, who also earned much more in tips. The dozen onstage performers were paid a thousand dollars a performance. The turnover, however, was big.

The rumor amongst the straight men of the crew maintained that guys left either because of the majority of predatory gays or because they wouldn't perform privately for the owners. The gay staff heard that once you did succumb, you couldn't walk properly for a few weeks. Every employee publicly hoped that Apollo or Loki wouldn't call upon him. Many privately wished they would.

In every sector of the entertainment industry—insider or outsider, gay or straight—the Twin Gods were becoming the most talked about act in show business.

And their publicity was a dropped gauntlet about to be retrieved.

chapter

8

I went through two evolutionary processes during my stay at the chateau. One physical, the other intellectual. Neither distinct from the other.

I had become vampyr, yes, with all powers and abilities attendant. My strength? Uncanny. My body and my mind achieved things that no human's ever could.

My skin was difficult to pierce. It took strong jaws and sharp fangs like mine to break the surface. My bones and muscles were equally substantial. And my new recuperative powers were amazing.

And like all of the others before me, the vampiric cells perfected all of my physical faults and flaws. No tiny wrinkles, no enlarged pores. No blackheads, no whiteheads nor broken capillaries. My freckles were gone and so were my scars. I had achieved full perfection of my form. A necessity for those blood-dependant vampires who needed flawless beauty in order to seduce and destroy, but mostly a detriment for one such as I.

Especially since my transformation had separated me from my humanness. The only quality that had kept me from being the exact duplicate of Jean-Luc Courbet.

My eyes retained none of their blue. They had started turning gray from the time that I took Jack into my mouth. Now they were completely changed. They sparkled, at times, like newly polished sterling silver or clouded into a dark metallic like marcasite or pewter.

Even my facial features had subtly changed, losing their singular "Irishness." My slightly pugged nose had almost imperceptibly elongated and thinned. My "smiling" eyes lost the crinkle at the outer edges. The creases of my vague dimples had filled to become a solid plane.

Whereas I had thought of myself as handsome in a normal, casual way, I now saw myself as beautiful in conventional, classical form. The worst of my many new gifts.

And with the gifts, I had inherited some of the vampire's deficiencies.

The sun was one enemy. I tolerated the early and late rays of dawn and dusk, but from midmorning to late afternoon, I received a painful and burning blistering. Not fatal, but fearsome. I avoided completely the strong rays of noon. I was not ready. Not yet. Not until my mission was complete.

I detected a new allergy to roses and garlic. Not nearly as fearful as the true vampire's reaction, but both effected me nonetheless. So, too, were my responses to certain woods—aspen and hawthorn and maple—dreadful in quantity, a little chancy in the slightest exposure. They could break my skin with an ease that steel could not. And my reparation time was greatly slowed.

But my biggest disappointment was my encounter with the mirror.

I did not care to witness my rebirth undead. But vampires do have reflections and shadows as any solid does. The doubt of it was hysterical, religious fantasy, which, accepted as fact, lived on in myth. Sanguinolent exchange cannot so easily overcome the scientific principals of reflection and refraction. Bram Stoker! You have to love the guy!

The undead refer to him as "the Irishman." He was wrong, too, about hosts and holy water, about churches and crucifixes. Wrong might be too strong a word, considering his source. Still, he did no favor by his poetic licensing. Like most people, what I knew of the vampire came more or less directly from him. And Baum and White assured me that the success of his novel *Dracula* was no mistake. They, along with Noel and Jean-Luc, had used him for the purpose of "misinformation." Charnac International continued to invest in the furthering of fabulous vampire legends, in print and on film.

Any one of these four could have been a high-level spook, I told them.

"What makes you think that we have not been?" they asked.

I was no fool. I did not rush.

"Tell me more about *Dracula* and Stoker," I told the lovers. I was becoming more the master of Charnac with each passing hour.

They spoke to me first of Jack the Ripper. London 1888. And of Noel's actions against her son. When Jean-Luc fled, Noel remained. Always the actress.

As the Marquise of Charnac, she was accepted everywhere. Her look reminded people of a young Noel Courbet, the late, celebrated French actress. She had youth and beauty and charm and funds. She was accepted everywhere. Imagined, by some, to be her own daughter.

There had been rumors about her, of course. Mme. de Charnac and this actor or that chanteuse. With a poet, painter or playwright. Some true, mostly not. Ellen Terry fell under her sway. And with Mrs. Kelly came Mr. Irving. And with Henry Irving, the trap was set for the Irishman.

She already had the ear of Oscar Wilde, who had known her son. She inspired Wilde to immortalize Jean-Luc, but he would not concede the ultimate evil upon him. Not nosferatu. Instead he tried to seduce the shadowy gift from her by appealing to her actress's ego and using her as an inspiration for characters, over and again, in "Lady Windermere's Fan," "A Woman of No Importance," "The Ideal Husband" and in "The Importance of Being Earnest." Ultimately, he damned her with his *"Impression du Matin."*

But, as femininely as he might behave, Wilde was a man. An aggressor who would not succumb to Noel. She used women as fodder and men as tender. He used them both as grist.

And so, it came down to Stoker.

But, artiste though she was, Noel never expected literary inventiveness from Stoker. His Count Dracula was not the tall, handsome blond that Noel had described to him, but a more Eastern foreigner. Dark of hair, eye and soul. She offered him a Dorian Gray; he found, instead, a Vlad Tepes.

"Go figure!" I told them.

"Invention and artistry are the magic of mortals," they answered.

The magic of mortals.

It somehow seemed so important.

Magic mortals!

"I have to go!"

I flew by Baum and White and headed upstairs.

"Pack for me and arrange a flight."

"Where are you going, master?"

"You know where. It is time to go home."

Baum and White had already told me that they had kept up my apartment. That everything in New York was all right. But I had to ask.

"Tina?"

It was not as appreciable as a glance, as understandable as a gesture, but still I knew that they were reluctant to confide something.

I thought I knew.

"Is she dead?"

"Miss Washington, Master?"

"You know damn well 'Miss Washington.' "

There is something human in my skin still that does not correlate completely with my vampiric blood. For when I started to cry, the blood-infused tears tore rosily down my cheeks and seared my flesh with sadness.

"I could tell you that she is dead, or that she walks the earth still. Either way, master, she is no longer for you to know.

"You are one who should not be touched, should not be reckoned with. How would you explain yourself to an intelligent, imaginative, investigative reporter?"

The point pierced me. I could not.

"Please tell me that she is unharmed."

"Master, she is unchanged from the last you saw of her. This I swear!"

The Dassault Falcon 900C was primed and ready. My clothes packed and my papers arranged for the banks. I was Michael O'Donald no longer. I would take off before French dusk and arrive just after dusk in New York. As necessary. I would not seek Tina out. I was looking for someone else. Someone I had only ever seen once, briefly, on television.

The flight was uneventful. Each flight bearing the Charnac coat of arms was. Baum and White had salted the hidden sarcophagus with both American and French soil. They still did not know which one might apply to me. They themselves always slept on a mattress stuffed with Greek and Italian soil. One for where they were born, one for where they died.

But I was not even a vampire of their ilk. They passed from life before they received the master's blood. I was infected by Jean-

Luc's serum long before I died. And then again with his mother's blood the day before Claude killed me. I will attempt, one day, to rest with either one soil or the other. Perhaps with neither. Just to see.

Flying against the trade winds, it took longer to return to New York than it did to escape it. Still, even having left Charnac with the setting sun, we simply chased it west and landed slightly behind it in Eastern Standard Time.

For safety's sake, I called the elements as we approached Montauk. By the time the jet was cleared for landing, a thick fog lumbered in from Jamaica Bay.

The Falcon was given every diplomatic privilege despite the very strict security. But neither pilot was leaving the plane, and no one was boarding. Their mission of record was to pick up pre-cleared, crated antiques for their noble collector. So, the jet was never challenged. It was a simple turnaround.

Only one human had seen me since my transformation. And the Spaniard suspected nothing. Still, I was apprehensive about blowing past the airport security.

I emerged from the hidden coffer and secreted myself in the baggage compartment. I heard voices. I knew there were others about. When the outer door opened, I willed the fog to flood in as I passed out.

Simple really. I was getting good at this.

Home.

I could smell New York.

I was never an outer borough boy, so I hurried off the western-most part of Long Island and into downtown Manhattan.

Home.

I had to rein my excitement. Drop back to human appreciation. I did not want to suddenly appear in the midst of a group. Perversely, I refused to slow my vampiric stride until I had reached the West Village. Just north of Christopher Street on the far side of West Street.

I came back to human realization in the exact same spot where I had stopped being one.

The pier.

The notoriety it had received when I was its most famous captive had not dissuaded the hungering eager from its black and rotten depths. I was not alone.

The moans and the grunts, the muffled gags and the slap of one thigh against another commingled into sexual orchestra. Again, the auditory found reflection in the visual and the tactile. I could smell them, taste them. These invisible men.

My jaw began to ache. My fangs hungered to emerge.

This was my reaction to sexuality forevermore.

Lust was bloodlust.

I had to find a safe place to feed. There was much to do. I went. Home.

I let myself in and found my apartment unchanged from the time I left it. I could tell without opening it that the refrigerator had been cleaned and stocked. Certainly, the rooms needed to be more thoroughly vacuumed and dusted and aired. I was not going to accept a crypt quite yet. But I was finally home again.

Out of habit, I turned on the television. It was still set for channel three, but the Observation News broadcast was well over by the time I tuned in. I watched for a while, channel surfing to a cable show about a group of gay friends. It was set in a place that people who are not New Yorkers call a city. Still, it had a city's worth of explicit sex and nudity. Of banality and cruelty. I took off my clothes and stretched out on the couch. It was well past midnight in France and I felt the need to feed.

I bent my left elbow and sunk my fangs into my wrist. I drank.

And as I did, the evidence of my successful feeding grew. The more I fed, the more it filled. I stopped only when the throbbing in my jaw and in my heart was overcome by the throbbing in my groin.

I had released that discomfort alone in the Chateau Charnac. I could not speak the language properly, so picking up Frenchmen on my own proved too difficult. And I had a problem with Baum and White pimping for me.

But I knew New York, and I wanted to go out.

First, I looked for my Manhattan White Pages. I found the "X's" and ran down the list. Was he too much a celebrity to list himself? No. There it was: Patrick Xenopoulos. An upper West Side address near The Dakota, if I judged right. I picked up the phone and dialed.

After a half dozen rings, I heard, "Hello?"

Her voice was not hesitant, was not even bruised, which I would have expected. Not sleepy, nor annoyed. It was as if she expected the call. As if she had been waiting for me.

"I'm sorry to call this late. Are you Purity St. Martin?"

"You know that I am, and yet you dialed my late husband's phone number. Would you care to identify yourself?"

"I'm a retired police officer. My name's Mike O'Donald. I . . ."

"I know who you are."

That's all she said, but I knew there was more coming. She drew me, just as I lured her.

"What is it you want of me, O'Donald? We both know that you truly are no longer he."

"I know who killed your husband."

There was a momentary silence. I tried to picture the woman whose face I saw on television. The Red Witch. What did the rest of her look like? How did she dress? Was her face fraught with mourning, worry venting her tears?

"No, O'Donald, I'm not crying. I'm picturing you as you are attempting to do with me."

That stunned me. She was not an undead, yet she could do that to me. No. Even that is untrue. Not even the undead can read my mind. I am not exactly vampire or human.

"I know . . ."

"Yes, you know that Claude Halloran killed my husband. You know that his partner, Jack Courbet, is not dead, as the world believes, but together with him. You are seeking their destruction and want my assistance."

"Yes!"

"No, O'Donald. Apparently what you do not know is that I cannot harm a living thing. I cannot avenge my husband's death in that way."

"Mrs. Xenopoulos? Miss St. Martin?"

"Call me Purity, O'Donald. Everyone does."

"Purity. Neither Jack nor Claude are living beings. Claude has been dead for nearly a year and Jack for much more than a century. 'Do no harm.' That's it, right? That's why. But you can prevent *them* from doing harm! Wouldn't that fall under your oath too?"

"Come see me, O'Donald, and we'll talk. It's the garden apartment. I'll leave the French doors in the rear unlocked and open. You'll have no trouble."

"I'll be there in about an hour," I said, noticing that there was a physical problem I had to solve first.

"Well, take care of your business. I'll be waiting."

The line went dead. I shuddered with embarrassment knowing that somehow that woman had just seen me completely naked in all my glory.

I dressed quickly and went out into the velvet night.

It was warm for this time of night, for this date in March. I wore construction worker's boots and faded jeans. A gray pullover hooded sweatshirt and a brown leather bomber jacket. And it was a little too much. I left the jacket open and showed off what I barely camouflaged in denim and fleece.

I hurried down Bleecker Street, turned onto Christopher and went down to Hudson. I barely turned the corner when I saw what I wanted.

His hair was dark brown and expensively cut. His eyes, a rich sapphire blue. His lips and cheeks were flushed and full pink.

He had that pretty, snotty, angry look that I normally would have loved to have busted for vagrancy or pot possession. But tonight this cute bad boy looked just like sex to me. I caught him with a look and like a petulant butterfly, he wriggled, but could not free himself of the inhuman specimen pin.

"How ya doin'?" he asked, never taking his half-lidded eyes from mine.

"Good," I said.

"You look like you're lookin' for trouble," he ventured.

"I'm just lookin' for a little fun," I admitted. Switching back and forth between speech patterns had become easy for me. Unconscious.

He gestured over his shoulder to the tavern behind him. It had been a hangout for writers, painters and actors for about a century. I put him squarely into the last category.

"I have some friends inside. I don't want them to see us together. Meet me around the block." He left.

He went clockwise; I went the other way. We met around the block near Bank Street.

"I don't usually do guys," was his greeting.

"Why me?" I asked.

"You look straight. I'll only do it with a straight-looking guy. Just so no one thinks anything, y'know?"

I sized him up at maybe twenty-two. Baby face and lush black lashes framing glittering blue eyes. There was a chemical behind that glitter. You did not have to be a cop to see that. He had a great ass and the rest of him was okay in a way that would mature nicely over the years. A swimmer's body or a runner's. He would fill out. Nicely.

"I live a few blocks from here," I told him.

"I live right upstairs," he said. "But my roommates will be back soon. They'll run out of money for beer in an hour or so. I don't want to have to explain you."

"I won't shower."

"I like it that way."

It was a third floor walk-up with a living room, a kitchen, a bath and two bedrooms. Without offering me a drink, he started undressing on his way to one of the bedrooms. I followed suit.

He turned on a lamp with a red light bulb. Mood lighting, I guess. I was not like this at twenty-two.

He had peeled off his denim shirt and was pulling his black undershirt over his head. His skin was quite pale. The only body hair he showed was a surprisingly full tuft in each armpit, a small snake of dark hairs reaching up from behind his belt buckle and crawling into his navel and a faint ring of hairs surrounding each pretty pink nipple.

He threw himself down on the bed, undid his jeans and wriggled out of them. He was just what I expected. What I wanted. I stripped for him. First, my jacket and sweatshirt.

"Fuck! You must work out a lot!"

"No, not anymore," was all I said.

"Seriously, what can you press?"

He was nervous. Talking around the subject. I popped open the button on my jeans and unzipped. I faced him as I took off my boots and socks. I deliberately turned my back to him to show off my butt, the backs of my thighs and my calves. I removed my jeans and turned around.

"Jesus!"

"You're not so bad yourself."

"Look, I'm gonna have to work up to that slowly."

I knelt on the bed and slowly lowered myself onto him. Kissing, licking and sucking at him the whole way up. I stretched myself full length over him. He squirmed and moaned with delight at my advances. Toe to toe, knee to knee, cock to cock, belly to belly, chest to chest, and face to face.

"Wait. I don't kiss."

Well, *c'est la vie*. But he did manage every other thing.

John Cabot Cox became my most usual outlet from that time on. I was his deep dark secret and he was mine. He had learned a lot in the few years that he had been sexually active. And, boy, could that boy fuck.

I hurried up the West Side Highway to Riverside Park. I crossed the park and exited at Seventy-second Street. I scaled a tall apartment house on Riverside Drive and from its roof began my version of the floating maneuver.

I bounded into an air current and glided towards West End Avenue. Bounded from one building to the next until I came to the rooftop of The Ansonia. From the residential hotel, I soared to the roof of the freestanding bank across the street. From the northern point of "Needle Park," I flew over Amsterdam Avenue. I bounced and floated down Seventy-third Street and drifted high over Columbus Avenue.

From the roof of the apartment building that housed a supermarket on the ground floor, I saw the loveliest little Eden imaginable for the center of Manhattan.

I balanced on the high wall on the north side of the garden. It was dun-colored concrete with a few stress fractures. But someone had recreated, in chalk or pastel, the moment from the Sistine Chapel when God enlivened Adam. I dropped silently into the lightless garden.

She had set the framework in evergreens, dwarf pine, yew and fir, arborvitae, holly and ivy. All embedded in cedar tubs or boxes that had weathered into a glorious gray.

Awaiting in their rest were the fruit trees—apple and peach and fig and pear.

There were a few dozen burlap-covered, oaken half-barrels, each bearing a name etched into a brass plate. I did not need to near them to know that they were roses. The neighboring half-dozen full barrels contained the winter skeletons of grapevine.

The center of the garden held an eight-foot structure made up of four two-feet tall, tiered, circular, terracotta planters. The base planter was eight feet in diameter. The next, six feet. The third, four feet, and the uppermost only two feet wide. Each cardinal point held a series of steps barely a foot wide with a six-inch rise. This was her herb garden. And, as the garden was protected from the elements by high walls, the perennial varieties were very much intact.

Small copper plaques announced the planting space for each of the witch's herbs. The lowest tier had twenty spaces, each about a foot square. These plantings I mostly knew.

Lavender and thyme, carnation and marjoram, basil, violet, peppermint and sage. There was a space for pansy, parsley and onion, for garlic, lemon balm and anise. This is about where my knowledge left me. I saw signs for lovage and borage, lemon verbena and hyssop, rue and vervain. They sounded barely edible to me.

The next tier threw me almost completely. I did recognize clover and chamomile and heather, but the rest had me baffled. Valerian, pennyroyal, cinquefoil, angelica. She had woodruff, cyclamen, comfrey, agrimony, maidenhair, yarrow and nettle.

At the six-foot level, purposely over most people's heads, were the really weird ones. Some of these names I did know. And I didn't like the looks of them. Deadly nightshade, belladonna, and hemlock. These were poisonous, I knew. But what were foxglove and periwinkle doing here? My mother had grown them. But with mandrake, wormwood and mugwort my suspicions were confirmed. I had to see the final level. I rose.

There was only one plant on the highest tier, covered in a glass bubble like a small greenhouse. It stood about two feet tall and the same in diameter. Its trunk and branches were woody, but its leaves were spiky, leathery and small. They looked somehow familiar, but like something I saw in a jar and not growing.

"Where a woman rules, rosemary grows."

I turned toward the sound of her voice. A voice simultaneously throaty and girlish. With a peal of maturity and the tinkle of laughter. A voice like another I had heard. The other witch, Noel Courbet. At once, classic and casual, determined and flighty, commanding and coy.

And like Laura Wilcox.

I saw her and knew her immediately. How right I was to compare her to the only two women I had grown to know in the last six months. How alike they were!

Three voices of regal lassitude, sexual and soft. A genteel growl. Then, too, was the red hair.

Here, Purity St. Martin differed from her sisters. Laura and Noel both had pale copper hair. The reds were distinct and dominant, but the soft blonde undertones deceived the viewer into underjudgment.

Purity St. Martin had a red that demanded attention. Like a copper penny, yes, but one that had been around, one that had been tendered. Hers had an overlay of expensive ruby velvet, of vintage Bordeaux. And the soft waves lacked intention, and so were the more attention-getting still.

"You make quite the entrance," was all she said. But her voice held the convivial amusement of an old shared joy. She turned on the garden light. Stunning woman.

"So do you," I added.

I thought her eyes would be green, but I was wrong and not disappointed. They were like caramel. Not like the candy, mind you, not that soft and sweet. But the way marshmallows get when you roast them to perfection. The way onions get when they reveal their true nature. Brown, certainly. But the brown that a precious metal would be if it only had the chance. Not rusty, either. No ruddiness at all. And they did not glitter as my eyes now did, but shone. There was a light in this woman that I have never before seen.

She was all that she claimed she was.

"It's too chilly out for this outfit. I'm going in. What about you?"

Her outfit.

If you could cross a robe with pajamas, make it out of shiny black satin, have it fall off of both shoulders and show at least fifty percent of your breasts, ninety percent of your legs and still look like you could go anywhere in town in it, then you have it.

It showed her off to her fullest advantage. Swanlike neck, creamy shoulders and the bosom Dolly Parton would have chosen for herself. A cinched waist. Not in a sick, Barbie doll way, but a woman's waist. One that suggests belly and hips and behind.

She turned and went back into the apartment.

I followed.

Almost.

I got right to the lintel and I could move no more. It was if a plasmic, plastic wrap barred my way. I pushed hard and was repelled harder. I tried to break through, squeeze through, force my way through. To no avail.

"Hey!" I shouted. "What gives?"

She turned in the full light of her living room. Her hip length, deep red hair bounced in coils around her. Her black satin dressing gown slipped and for a moment, she was gloriously pale from the nape of her neck to the nape of her back. Her hands gathered the fabric forward towards decency.

"I had to be sure. I still didn't believe it was true."

"I thought you'd help me," I complained, darkening.

She looked at me for a moment and said, "You may enter my dwelling."

The resistance was simply gone. Vanished.

I entered.

"What the hell was that?"

She was trying to place a cigarette between her lips, trying to light it. She knew she was shaking, knew I knew, knew she still had to.

"Light," I said with small resign. And her cigarette lit.

She accepted it gratefully, not at all surprised that it lit on command.

"I wasn't sure until this moment that I hadn't made this all up. I wasn't certain that there actually were vampires, that anyone would believe there were vampires, that anyone would consider me more than the oddity, the joke I've been."

I am not good with women. I do not like to see them cry. I do not like crying. Period. I did not like this.

"The doorway? What was the deal with the doorway?"

Her cheeks puckered, pushed by her smile. She shook her head. In the way that says: no. Yes. But also in the way that says: I have been a fool.

She looked at me.

"You're not like them. I can see that. I'm sorry."

"How did you keep me out?"

She draped herself over the sofa. The coffee table held two bottles of 1989 Chianti Classico, one mostly full and the other quite empty. And two stemmed crystal goblets mirroring the fullness and emptiness of the bottles.

She saw me looking and offered me a glass. "I had taken them both out when you called. I didn't think you'd be this late. I polished off the first one alone."

I poured half a glass to be polite and the smell was delicious.

I put the bottle back down between the overlarge goblet that served as a fish bowl and the book-size sand box with the tiny silver rake that acted as a miniature Zen garden. A large seashell functioned as the incense burner. It was filled with dried herbs. Basil and sage and bay leaf, I recognized. The others I did not.

The table also held a feathered fan and five lit candles—silver, pink, purple, yellow and black. They determined the points of the pentacle as the other objects represented earth, fire, water and air. My time with Baum and White was well spent.

"Do you know why I agreed to see you, O'Donald?"

"Because I told you that Jack and Claude were undead and so you would not be breaking your oath."

"No, not really."

She stood and started to move around the room. She coaxed the logs in the fireplace; she added more herbs to the incense. She filled my glass. Added food to the fish bowl. Drew in the sand.

Simple things, ordinary things. But there was nothing simple or ordinary about this woman.

"I want to see these creatures dead. I want to see it with my own eyes.

"My husband did not deserve this treatment. This cruel libel to his name. The police as much as told me that he must have had a secret gay life in order to fall into the hands of the copycat killer who was reenacting the 'Horror of West Street' crimes."

My dead heart nearly broke at the expression, verbal and physical, of her devotion.

"Patrick loved all people! Every one of them! I don't think he ever knew if someone was gay or straight, trustworthy or criminal, good or evil. He walked blindly around in a world of his own making. He was just a big kid. A storyteller who believed everyone's story."

She turned with a quickness and a flow that belied her drinking and made me wonder if she had ever turned away.

Her bottom lip was quivering and she seemed all the more beautiful for it. Her amber eyes glinted with the tears she did not wish to fall.

"I have to avenge him somehow, O'Donald. I let him down. I didn't protect him. Me, Purity St. Martin. The famous Red Witch. I couldn't even help my own husband! The only man I'd ever loved."

She started to cry and I was at a loss for what to do. Do I hug her? Not one of the things I like; not one of the things I do well. But I really liked her and she was really sad.

I went to her. She put her head on my chest and I held her.

She was naked under this black satin thing. I knew because I couldn't feel anything under it. That feel will get me thrown out of the gay vampire club. Certainly.

"Purity?" I said when a respectful time had passed. "You can't come with me. They're just too dangerous. I have to find them and deal with them on my own."

"You'll never find them alone."

"No, I know that. I need your help for that. You can find them, can't you?"

"Come sit down, O'Donald. I'm okay now."

She sat back on the sofa and I sat with her. She took an atlas out from behind a pillow.

"I've been using this to locate them. Do it again with me."

She shifted her weight and pressed her right knee to the sofa back. I corresponded and put my left knee there. We formed a sort of table where she could balance the maps.

She took a large crystal out of her pocket. It was easily four inches long and certainly over two wide. It was six-sided and almost perfectly clear at the point of one end and cloudy, roughly broken at the other. It was heavier, much heavier, than it looked.

"I'll show you how this works."

She opened to the map of the world and asked aloud, "From where did O'Donald recently come?"

We put our fingers on either side of the crystal and it began to move. Out of the mid-Atlantic and onto the European continent.

"Europe!"

She changed pages and found the map of Europe. We continued. Found France. Changed maps again. Found the Cognac region.

Charnac is too small and intentionally unimportant to find its way onto most maps. But I conceded the point to her.

"Okay, let's find Jack and Claude."

"I'll do it, but you have to take me with you, O'Donald."

"I can't, Purity. It's too dangerous."

"But you can't do this alone! Just a very short time ago, you were Mike O'Donald, cop. You're not prepared for this encounter. I am!"

I rose to show her just how prepared I was.

"Watch this!"

I stripped off my brown leather jacket and my pullover sweatshirt.

"I'm sorry," I apologized for my half-nakedness. "Sometimes my clothing gets imbued with this scent and I can't get it out later."

I looked at her dining room table and called, "Light!" And the candles did.

"*Basta!*" she said, and they extinguished. "O'Donald, that's nothing!"

"How about this?" I asked. I rose from the floor and floated above the room.

She rose off the sofa.

I tried each thing I had learned, and she matched me show for show. There was one last thing to present to this talented witch.

I dropped to the floor, naked to the waist and called.

"Bineal, Padula, Kistengue, Altabour! Arise!"

Her pretty, perfect Eden diminished. A sulphured fog replaced it. And in that yellowed cloud, violent indigo lightning flashed.

Bineal appeared. His enormous, dank blue form branded the oaken floor where he touched it, besmirched the pretty wallpaper where he leaned.

Padula came. Another godlike creation. A huge man, muscular and aggressive like his brother. Yet lacking, too, facial and genital features. Kistengue and Altabour, the twins, filed into the room.

Each was over eight feet tall. More than a yard wide. They had sensuality without sexuality. An objective without the subjective. I had succeeded in creating really big, strong, sexless dolls. No wonder they were angry.

Purity was close to wetting herself.

"What can they do?" she asked, barely aloud.

"Probably just rearrange furniture. I'm not very good at this."

She picked up the pink candle and wrapped it in basil leaves.

"Goodly spirits," she began. "I thank you for your attention and I free you to go." She blew out the candle and my creations extinguished as well.

"Thanks. That was really good!" A small snicker escaped my lips. "I had no idea how to get rid of them."

"I should have kept them around for my yard work," she joked back.

"Well, you wouldn't have caught them dicking around. I forgot to finish them," I laughed.

"They had nice butts though," Purity countered.

We were holding each other to keep from falling. My magic! How funny! I stopped laughing when I saw her staring at the tinged tears that stained my cheeks.

"This is really real. My husband's been murdered by something and you're a . . . what?"

I took her in my arms and she punched me full in the face with fists embellished with silver rings.

"Good instincts. It would have worked on the others, however."

She gave me that smug, injured-yet-enticing look. The girl thing. It must have worked every other time.

"We need each other, Purity. You have to help me find Jack and Claude. Get the map!"

"You don't need the map!"

"I need your help. I can't find them without you."

"Then take me with you!"

"I can't!"

"Then go to hell with yourself!"

She threw a magazine at me. Did she think it would hurt me? I think not. Insult me? She had already done a good job of that. Annoy me? She had done that too.

"What the fuck is this?"

"Pick it up, asshole."

I wanted to burn it where it lay. Sprawled open on the floor. But I did pick it up.

"The cover, O'Donald," she said in a simple, resigned way.

I inverted the magazine and saw what she intended for me to see all along.

I had never seen *U.S. Entertainment Magazine.* I never wanted to again. It was a cheap, celebrity tabloid with only one redeeming article. The cover piece on the magicians Apollo and Loki. A gold colored, satin mask hid the blond Apollo's face. The dark-haired one had on a black leather mask that covered his whole head. The inside story included photographs of their club, Vows and Secrets, but no pictures of them unmasked.

"You think this is them, Purity?"

"Don't you?"

It wasn't as much a question as a demand. She wanted back up, validation for her theory. But I wasn't sure, and I couldn't make a mistake.

"If you think you've already found them, why didn't you go after them?"

"I had to wait for you."

I had been pulling my sweatshirt back on. The question popped out before my head.

"How could you even know I'd come here? How could you possibly know anything about me?"

Purity explained how it was she worked her magic. Since she had met Jack and Claude before, seen them on a few occasions, she suspected that it had been Claude who killed her husband. She sensed that they were "cut of the same cloth" ever since she first met them.

She searched for Patrick's killer and found him in France. She found a great deal of evil in a small area in Cognac. Supernatural forces at loggerheads. An evil witch, to be sure.

I told her about Jack's mother. About Claude's plot to destroy her and obtain his freedom. I related the whole experience at Charnac to her. Much of which she had already accurately sensed. I told her about Jack's reappearance and how he used my body to portray the ghost of himself. About Noel and the black mass. About Baum and White.

"They seem to be more like you than like the others," was all she said in response to my admittedly bizarre story. Purity St. Martin had apparently witnessed some strange things in her own life. I figured that I might as well be perfectly honest with her.

"Phillipe created them differently than any of his other vampires. And I was just a mistake. An undead who isn't truly a vampire."

"Can you die?"

It was a strange and abrupt question, one that I sensed hid the thing she really wanted to ask. But after all this time with creatures that routinely hid their motives and underlying intents, it was refreshing. So I told her the truth.

"I don't know. There are only a few ways to destroy a vampire, Purity. Silver doesn't bother me as it does the others. Neither does weak or filtered sunlight. I can spend much of the day awake, if I'm out of the direct rays. There's a serious lack of unicorn horns nowadays and I'm not certain about roses. I'm not brave enough to cut off my own head or push a wooden stake through my heart, but I'm sure that eventually I'll find some way to do it."

That turn in the conversation proved more awkward than I intended. Here she was a recent widow, and I was ticking off the many and varied ways I had considered suicide.

"Don't look for death, O'Donald. It will find you soon enough. Consider Noel. She wanted to live forever and rule the world. What is left of her now? She is barely even remembered as an actress. Let's worry about Jack and Claude instead. I've scryed and meditated on the photo of Apollo. I'm convinced that it's Jack. He's changed and is changing still. He wants now what his mother wanted. To be worshiped. I think he'll soon go the same route and invite the truly dangerous demons to share the earth with him."

"You think that Jack will perform the black mass, don't you?"

"As soon as he can get the proper sacrifice."

"And that would again be me."

"Or me."

Looking at her, I realized that she was right. And that she had not gone to Vegas by herself for the same reason that she did not want me to go by myself. It was simply too dangerous to go alone. I needed someone to watch my back. And that someone could only be Purity St. Martin.

The doppelganger and the red witch. What a pair.

chapter

9

Paris may call itself the "City of Lights," but Las Vegas's rebuke was to rebuild Paris as a hotel and casino. And Venice and New York. Any place that took itself too seriously, flaunted itself too mightily, was subject to gaudy recreation in this desert place called "The Meadows."

And compared to the glittering Las Vegan night, daylight shone less lustrous. At night, the colors were no longer earthbound. No longer controlled by a pragmatic nature. They glowed with intention. With the arrogance and hubris that belonged to man alone. The headlights and tail lights of the thousands of cars that daily flooded Vegas could not compete with the crystalline grandeur that scintillated above.

The Strip.

Luxor.

What could possibly be more brazen in scope for usurping Las Vegas than all of the Egyptian dynasties? The Luxor's enormous Sphinx and stunning thirty-story jet black pyramid—topped by the light of thirty-nine xenox lamps to create a beam of over three hundred thousand watts—defied classification as a footnote at the foot of the Strip.

The blond vampire noted the sharp and deep shadows thrown by the brilliance of the intense lighting. He filed away those dim recesses for later use. For a time when chiaroscuro might be the only magic he needed. He shifted his glance to appreciate the black-haired charmer who accompanied him and the attention he was attracting. Burgeoning fame and flawless beauty would do that.

Apollo and Loki were both dressed all in black. Apollo in a simple, elegant pullover silk shirt by Corneliani which complemented classic Hermes linen trousers topped by a voluminous, matching duster. His partner's tastes tended towards the hip and cutting edge. Loki's outfit, shirt, jacket and slacks, all by John Varvatos.

They walked Las Vegas Boulevard, "The Strip," northward from the Luxor. Although they were heading for a club nearby their residence, it was too early to make an entrance at Stoker, Las Vegas's notorious Goth club. And an entrance was what they needed to make on their initial excursion into the world of the cosmetic vampire.

"On a later date, Loki, we shall go 'Egyptian' and show them what immortality really looks like!"

Loki laughed. Filled with his vampiric sensory-overstimulation and his lack of comprehension.

The night held the master magicians as if in a lover's embrace. As vampiric lovers, they were bound by the night alone. By the hunt. By the blood. Such is the relationship of the homosexual. The self-sustaining narcissism of the undead precludes all else. A paired mating is one of residual intellectual and emotional need. They served as one another's mirrors. As the journals and recorders of each other's conquests. But ultimately, the vampire needs no one. None but the victim, the blood host.

Still, old habits die hard, and a novice undead has many dormant issues that only many decades of revenance will allay.

"What are your plans for the redhead, Apollo?"

"What redhead would that be, Loki?"

Loki turned full toward Apollo and his gesture and intent forced all nearby to unconsciously turn away.

"Cody Daly!" And the wind changed.

"The weatherman?"

"The vampire," Loki hissed. And air masses clashed.

To know that jealousy is born of fear, one need not look further than the pathos borne on Loki's face. And Apollo knew that fear is the father of retribution as well. He also knew that since another vampire had transformed Loki, he owed no blood-fealty, and therefore was dangerous. Perhaps lethal.

"Try to remember Phillipe's command, Loki. If I did not recreate within thirteen decades, I would die. I only had a matter of months to do so. I saw the opportunity and took it.

"You, on the other hand, have over a quarter millennium to concern yourself with another recreation. You bear no pressing concern."

Loki, ever circumspect, demanded, "What do you mean? I have no concern?" Wariness is the other child of fear.

"You have already engendered a fledgling. Do not pretend that you did not!"

It took Loki a moment to comprehend the inference. Another to recall Tina Washington and apply it to her. Still another to understand that Apollo had known all along.

"I . . ."

"Do not explain. I know why you used her as you did. In your situation, I might have done the same. But, Loki, you have left Miss Washington as an untrained rogue. What has become of her? What will she reveal if she is found out?"

Apollo went on to explain the difficulties of vampire life for an unsupervised fledgling. The uncertainties, the missteps, the dangers. He described many of the attributes and detriments of the vampiric life that Noel had never detailed.

Apollo was certain that she had given to her slave only the basic information that a fledgling vampire would need to know. The harmful attributes of sunlight, the need to sleep on native soil and the horror of silver poisoning. Those things she had been taught by Phillipe or had gleaned over her years. She taught him only the things she had cared to share. But she had never trained her protégé in the floating technique, in mind control, in elemental command. Noel Courbet had been content for Claude Halloran to remain zombie-like in his undeath. A revenant, a walking dead with few abilities and no will of his own.

"Come, Loki, there is much you need to learn. And we still have a performance to give, a party to attend."

Apollo began the instruction with the floating maneuver. He coupled it with vampiric speech. Both ambulation and diction too fast, too specific, for human perception.

He brought Loki atop the head of the sphinx. From there to the turrets of Excalibur. The cityscape of New York, New York and across to the MGM Grand.

They flew off to the tip of the recreated Eiffel Tower at Paris and admired from above the beautiful Bellagio and its pas de deux of fountains and lights. Over to Caesar's, to the Mirage, and on to the Venetian, the pair toured the Strip the way no others could.

After cruising the Venetian's gondoliers, they ogled the pirates battling before Treasure Island. Up the Strip they drifted, two sensors, one sensation. Two demands, one command.

When the stimuli exceeded the impedance, the vampires silently agreed. It was time to make their entrance. Time to appear at the vampire club and see how they were revered.

Stoker was as dreary a location as one could find. Just a few blocks off the Strip, it was a strip mall in its architectural design, fallout shelter in execution and grade "B" horror movie in ambiance. The Stoker had but one saving grace. And that, overlooked, misunderstood and generally ignored by its clientele.

Bob Maverick Taylor was more than a deejay. More than a musician. More than a sound engineer. But, he would have accepted any of those appellations, rather than have to explain what it was that he actually did. What it was that he liked. What it was that he employed to influence his clientele.

But influence he did, now that he had accepted his hippie mother's christening, a reflection of her affection for John Cougar Mellencamp. Bart and Bret, move over! He'd played at being plain Bob Taylor long enough. Now he was the "ear to hear."

At just past his thirtieth birthday, "The Maverick" controlled what was listened to in ultra-hip, neo-underground Vegas. Taylor was a man who couldn't be bought. If he liked it, he played it. If he hated it and there was money behind it, he mocked it unmercifully. If you had a request? You were cordially invited to curl up and die. His new radio show broadcast from this secret location. He played for the Goth set because they allowed for his classical bent without interfering. Feeling that it lent a sense of gravitas to their lack of respectability. Taylor also enjoyed that they never seemed to notice when he mocked their capricious role-playing. And, at five-eleven and one hundred twenty-six of the city's palest pounds, the gaunt, petulant misfit finally seemed to fit in. Or, at least not to stand out too far.

He started his set, each and every night, with the beginning of Bach's *Toccata and Fugue in D Minor*. It was a great intro and he lived in the land of great intros. Just under a minute of Bach. His mystery and his menace. Those who didn't like it, be damned!

Then, he segued into Sea of Souls' "Out of My Wrist," a vamp favorite with a strident guitar collapsing into nascent, nasal angst. Whining and demanding, it was the plaintive anthem of the lost young adult. The young Goths ate it up like stage blood. Maverick was their troubadour. Their Pied Piper. The Goth Gabriel who would trumpet the arrival of their messiah.

Ave.

The entrance doors blew open at the silent announcement. The doorman was blasted from his perch. Hail.

The fog on the dance floor clouded, thickened, condensed and compressed. Doubling upon itself to overshadow the inhabitants. The club lights muted in supplication. All to The Maverick's coincidental choice of Inside Scarlet's "Gently."

The rock dirge was hypnotic in its despair. As spellbinding as the true vampires who appeared on the landing. With preternaturally languorous steps, they descended the entrance stairs. And along with them, desperation and desire also settled upon the room. In this den of pasty-faced post-pubescents, Apollo and Loki shone as certain gods. In the face of the makeup and the make-believe, they were stunningly authentic. They surveyed the room as they negotiated the stairs.

Club Stoker was little more than one large square basement room. The bar was opposite the entrance stairs with the DJ booth on the north wall between them.

Four massive cinder block columns supported the upper floors of the building and outlined a dance floor in the center of the room. They also served to delineate a perimeter consisting of the four important territories of this, the most important Goth hangout in underground Las Vegas.

Stoker's bar served only bottled water and juices, wines, brandies and cordials. To emphasize its management of the symbolic grape, it was lit with deep violet-colored lights. This was the area peopled by the Clan Dracul. These were the older, yet not the oldest, patrons. Bored by the other role-playing games which first drew them out of their uninspired isolation, this jaded family drifted into drink and drugs to shore up their flagging egos. They were the wealthiest, if not the wisest patrons. Some Dracul members had gone through the pain and expense of implanted fangs, but most just slipped-on teeth as false as their golden or red-tinged contact lenses. Multiply pierced and tattooed, they were, for the most part, irresponsible and amoral, preying, sexual aggressors. And none too fussy about gender. And all salivated obviously for the two new arrivals.

Maverick attracted the Clan Tepes to the quarter where both his booth and the sapphire blue lights dominated. Tepes was peopled mostly with poseurs. The club kids. Few had any type of permanent alteration to recreate them as pseudo-nosferatu. Most of their establishing costume was cosmetic or theatrical. The affect effect. Their asocial masquerade was a direct appeal for acceptance, for applause. "Show me you love me, and I won't do this." Clan Tepes was to Goth what Lurex and spandex were to Disco. Pins and razors to Punk. Not necessarily the point, but a pretty eyeful. Even the undead need divas.

And even divas need a supreme deity.

The third group clung to the shadowy green-gelled entrance area at the base of the stairs. Officially called Clan Vladimir, they were known disdainfully to the rest of the patrons as the "Vladmirers." They wore the black leather and French lace of the Goth kith and kin. Many of the women and a few of the men wore the obligatory black nail lacquer and merlot-dark lipstick. But, for all the fripperies, all the trappings, they were only Junior Leaguers hell-bent on proving they weren't. They were the day-trippers, the hemo-curious. The ones who were looking for a place to belong. This place, any place.

"In the Hall of the Mountain King" from Grieg's "Peer Gynt" Suite No.1 teased the Goth crowd, as Maverick knew it would. It ended just as Apollo and Loki finished descending the staircase.

Apollo knew the most influential of the patrons were also the most intelligent and the most knowledgeable. He knew that an opening magick would get their attention and their identities would be known in a rippling effect.

"Let there be light!" he intoned in a voice that seemed to include its own echo.

Dormant candelabras sparked into life. From behind and upon the bar top they ignited. A dozen pieces each holding a dozen tapers. From the four corners of the room the unused candles erupted. Freestanding floor versions held three dozen candles each. From behind the deejay booth they flared. From the sconces on the walls and on the columns they flamed. Dozens upon dozens, gross upon gross of inky black beeswax candles burnt with a single intent. To announce the arrival of the deliverer.

Bob Maverick Taylor threw his "pissed" look out to the dance floor and his watery blues met the electric green eyes of the raven-haired god. The rest of the room disappeared with all active thought. Apollo chose Beethoven's "Moonlight" Sonata, and Loki transmitted his request telepathically to the deejay.

Apollo turned his back on the booth and faced the final sector of the vampire club, those crimson-colored, velvet-covered banquettes and tables of the undisputed leaders, The Brahmins. Lit in deepest ruby. Masked in black lace.

The most unobstructed path led to the center niche, and yet it was the least approachable. Higher backed and more ornate than the booths of the left or right phalanx, it was clearly the dominant site. The throne. And centered in the dark cushions, the undisputed leader—not only of Clan Brahmin, but of all the subservient families as well—was casting his imperious sneer at Apollo.

"I am the High King Kieron, the sovereign Vampyre," the prepotent poseur hissed through his impedent dental additions. "All who enter here pay fealty to me!"

"I am the god Apollo," the lone blond on the dance floor countered. "And as such, I believe I will not. Therefore, kneel before me, Kieron, and live."

Herbert Mietus had been challenged many times in his life, both before and after becoming the Vampire Kieron. And whether to his credit or not, all contenders had eventually wished they hadn't. He rose from his berth, disrupting his lounging, half naked lovers, the Lady Justelle and her brother, the Lord Consort Athanas.

High King Kieron stood to his full height. Six feet, four inches. He knew that he made such an impression in standing that he always initially greeted people from a sitting or reclining position. No gymnasium had refined his genetic structure. He had been blessed with a fine, slim frame, and a lithe, strong body with only moderate hairiness. And although he was secretly over forty, he showed but one sign of advancing age in a chosen culture that revered agelessness. His hairline was receding.

To capitalize on a cruelty of nature he could not captain, he shaved his hairline even farther back to shape a perfectly sculpted widow's peak. He tweezed his eyebrows into the same artificial angle from where they appeared to meet at his long thin nose upwards.

Kieron wore black satin pants that hung from his waist and a black satin robe with velvet collar and cuffs. He moved slowly towards the usurper. He threw his hands to his hips in pure Yul Brenner style, exposing his taut body from clavicle to near-pubis. He shook his head and sent an ornate barrette flying, freeing his two-foot long, sable ponytail into a sheer, silken storm. He arched his lips into that self-same snarl that captivated and controlled each of his underlings, and flourished the long, thin, off-white fangs that he'd had permanently affixed. He set his dead-black eyes on

Apollo's platinum and lost all his audacity in the hellish hall of mirrors that was the core of Charnac.

He melted to his knees right in front of the beautiful blond. He might be the reason for being to a small clubhouse of forgettable wannabes, but he was no more than a snack to this divinity.

"Master, I am yours."

"Receive me," was all that Apollo deigned.

Kieron was accustomed to debasing all comers in this, his small fiefdom. He never even yielded to reciprocal sex play in private. He was the master of his world and everyone in it. Nevertheless, he unzipped his new deity, took him in his mouth, and demonstrated his abject subservience to all present.

But Apollo had not come here for the king alone. If he was to be god in word and deed, all must comply. All must pledge. To him and to Loki both.

High King Kieron was loath to release the divine organ from his mouth, but he did as was required and presented his horrified and repulsed queen.

"My God, The Lady Justelle."

Apollo met her eyes and she could not but follow the pattern set by her Goth king. She arose, approached and serviced the god Apollo. As did her brother, her masculine image, Lord Athanas, and after him the War Lord Cadwellen together with his lover, Lord Emlin. Then, Lord Counsel Osred, the Ladies Letitia and Malvinia, the Lord Treasurer Morvren and his wife, Lady Fenella.

The entire High Council took a turn sucking greedily at the overlarge penis of the beautiful vampire god.

The patrons looked on enrapt as the rest of Clan Brahmin abased itself in a most significantly understood way. There was not a single member of any clan here who had not been forced through an identical covenant to The High King.

During their initial ritual fellates, High King Kieron gave to each his or her vampire name and allegiance to a particular family. The High Priestess Vashti was Kieron's first "star." When she betrayed him with a new lover and brought him into the club, Kieron not only organized the four clans, but also established the "sacrament of fealty," the "Gothic baptism." While he was being satisfied, High King Kieron pronounced the new, vampire name. More often than not, wholly mocking. No one protested with a full mouth.

So, Vashti's new lover became the second of Clan Dracul, The High Priest Jervis. The spear servant. Flavio and Aneurin were so dedicated in their ministrations that all he noticed was their yellow and golden hair. Cordelia was named for her heart. Tadzio was courageous. Sirgo, a servant; Riordan, a poet. Each of the fourteen permanent members of Clan Dracul was so named.

The same held true for Clan Tepes.

Zandra and Julian were helpful and young. They organized the pretty ones. Charmaine was a delight; Auriela and Xanthus were both golden as well. Wolf and Talbot used their teeth. Zared and Scanlon were so good as to be called "trap" and "little trapper." Mina and Lucy were hardheaded and light. Dugald, "the dark stranger," took his medicine and then kept to himself and with his eleven siblings.

Clan Vladimir was shepherded by an Italian woman renamed Sabina. She brought along her friend, Parris. And Parris was no stranger to French. Clarinda was the bright one. Big, brawny Volker was the people's defender. Tristan remained sad from the time of his first and only blow job. Perdita seemed lost. Alethina was very sincere, but lacked technique. Ondine gave a little wave. Zigana dressed as a gypsy, her gold coins tinkling with every bob of her head. Sven was very young. The last, Colborn, was a big black bear not easily understood.

These were the sixty vamp-aspirers who nightly inhabited Club Stoker. There were many others in attendance on the weekends, but they were merely onlookers, not family like these. And after each had paid homage to Apollo, it was Loki's turn.

Loki had stripped naked to display his perfection to the pretenders and drew them all to him at once. Each of them adored him. He blessed each of them in his own way. The doorman, the bartender and the deejay were the only mortals left untouched. Still, one clan member was affected more than any other.

Loki finally nodded to a giant made of ebony. Colborn.

Even in the flickering, indistinct lights of the club, this mighty dark man glistened.

Sure, Stoker was a white club, weren't they all? But here color prejudice was clouded by lighting design and skin tone veiled by vampiric cosmetic. And being a dark man in a predominantly pale club didn't bother Charles Worthington III. He was accustomed to being an outstanding black man in a mundane white world. A big black buck running amid albino fawns. He'd never forgotten what he was taught at home—he was a champion, an Olympian on a field of amateurs.

Tall and talented, his black skin was the only thing that didn't bewilder him at what he privately thought of as the "University of Nevada at Lily Virgins." Many times a week, he snuck out from his enforced curfew and left his dorm at the university to enjoy, in secret, the only liberty he'd ever really known.

The first time he was admitted into The Stoker, he only ventured as far as the landing just inside the main door and watched the players below. The second time, he moved down past the doorman to the base of the stairs. From then on, he went all the way to the bar, got a drink and returned to his dark corner beneath the stairs. Separate even from his own clan. Until he saw Loki.

Here at last, Charles decided, was a man worth enjoining.

He was the only son of a widowed mother, a teacher who thought it best that her fatherless son spend his free time in athletic programs. No pick-up street games for the son of Mrs. Charles Worthington Jr. So, from age five, Charles the Third, as he was now known to the collegiate sports world, spent all of his time in a strictly man's world overseen by his stricter mother. St. Jude's Roman Catholic Church's altar and choir recruited him first on Sundays and special occasions as a server and boy soprano. St. Jude's School for Boys' football, basketball, baseball and track teams all staked their claims throughout the school years. The programs sponsored by the police department taught Charles swimming and diving, archery and bowling, judo and gymnastics. And between the city police and the Pope's police, Charles thrived.

No acting classes for him. No poetry, no painting. Charles was going to be a man's man. His mother was going to see to that.

Charles's religious insulation and social isolation molded a self-involved, self-absorbed clay. As the clay hardened, it was etched with a narcissistic chisel of manly desire and virile resolve. Fired in a kiln of guilt and remorse.

Then, the athletic scholar, the collegiate super-jock, cooled to the adoration of his own image. He looked around at his fellow athletes at the university. Some fine specimens, yes. But with each, a flaw. The interested ones were not manly enough. The manly ones, not interesting enough. One beautiful body had a baby face. Another owned a rugged face without physique. All brawn or all brains, all bereft of the magic.

Then Loki.

He was pulled, along with the others, by a desire inexplicable, a command inescapable, a destiny inevitable. But Charles Worthington, called the Vampire Colborn, was too self-possessed to play "sloppy sixtieth" to the only man he'd ever wanted. The only one who deserved him.

Instead of waiting, Charles Worthington III stripped as naked as Loki. Attention must be paid.

Maverick segued unconsciously into a ritual mating dance fit for nosferatu.

Carl Orff. *Carmina Burana*. Secular songs.

When the gathering got their first look at the naked Colborn, the opening appeal to the goddess of fate registered as a superfluous echo. He stepped from the shadows and neared the nude god, Loki. In his unfed state, Loki was nearly as pale as Carrara marble, and his stunning whiteness exposed his exorbitant muscles in dramatic definition. But it was Colborn's rich blackness that created the drama.

In a room where black was the single most common color for eyes, hair, clothing, lips and nails, black—truly black—skin was not just a novelty, it was a rarity.

All members of all Goth clans avoided the sun and cosmetically whitened their skin. All but Colborn. All favored an anemic, listless demeanor. Movements slow and languid. Sluggish, studied and sibilant speech teamed with sloe-eyed gazes, lazy and lethargic. Every detail that was not Colborn.

And it was Colborn who dominated the moment.

The hundreds of flickering candles that surrounded the room gutted on Loki's unspoken command, leaving just the somber gobos of theatrical light undulating across the dance floor, licking and tickling, tickling and teasing the superior musculature of the undressed men.

The interplay between Loki and Colborn was like the mating of acrobats. Each was capable of lifting, carrying and manipulating the other wholly. And athlete and performer both knew how to partner for effect. Their erotic joust was unabashedly masculine, lacking softness of design or intent. They fit together absolutely. Unashamedly. Entirely.

Colborn balanced the beautiful Loki on his crouched thighs. He inserted himself deeply. Loki did the same.

Although the present company had surely witnessed ritualized blood hosting, none had ever seen the true growth of a true vampire's fangs. None had ever observed the tender, desensitized merging of dento-hemo coitus. Not one had ever given over to another so completely, so egolessly.

Each man's mutual, rhythmic pulsing satisfied, completed the other. Colborn gave himself to Loki as completely as Loki gave of himself.

Loki drained Charles Worthington III completely dry. It was his way. He slowly released the perfect form to the floor.

To a release of repressed applause.

Apollo and Loki caught each other's eye. The son of Charnac was well pleased at his lover's restraint. No longer the ghoul of months ago, Loki was a godling. A new rule had begun.

Apollo spoke.

"As you see, Loki required a willing sacrifice to sustain his godhead. Now I require no less.

"Who will yield to his god?"

From every sector of the room, eyes sidled, eyes darted, eyes froze and closed. The lethal display of a moment ago had charged each of them, yet none wished to relinquish a life. All prized the ability to continue under the rule of the living gods. The undead deities.

Like the others, James Foster was still standing in now silent honor to Loki. As Ludovic, "The Lion," one of the twelve secondary Brahmins, his position was at one of the six pawn tables before the throne of Kieron. His partner at the table was his occasional bedmate, Kostas, the "steadfast" Turk.

Jimmy was a chorus boy at one of the nightclub shows on the Strip, a vaudeville-cum-circus performed semi-nude in grotesque masks. As soon as Apollo and Loki first arrived at Club Stoker, he had recognized them from their descriptions. The "weapons of mass seduction" as they were called by the performers of Vegas. He desperately wanted to audition for their show. Now was his time.

"Me," he said simply. "Take me."

Apollo turned and looked upon him with favor. The Vampire Ludovic was tall for a dancer, over six feet. He was buff and aggressive. Dressed in a flowing, Byronesque satin shirt and tight black leather pants, he looked more like a Gothic hero than a Goth.

"Jimmy!" his on-again-off-again boyfriend whispered. "Don't!"

But he was already pulling the dandified shirt over his head to reveal the body he built up for hours each day. He lifted his feet, one at a time, to pull off his buccaneer boots. He peeled off his leather pants and stood in his bikini briefs and socks in a room of the fully dressed. Nothing new to Jimmy.

"Jimmy, for me?" Dean, the vampire Kostas, pleaded quietly.

"For *me!*" was the last human sound his occasional lover ever shared with him.

James Foster had always been willing to sacrifice a good situation for a better one, a fine lover for a superior. Whether in dwelling, employment or social status, he was always inclined to trade up. He saw an opportunity before Kieron did, and moved on it before he could.

He stood face-to-face with Apollo and said, "Take me and give me your love."

"I have much to give," the vampire responded.

"I can take it all."

And from nowhere but the combined intent of the offering and the celebrant plus the skill of a master musicologist, a Bose turntable and a dozen Daewoo speakers, the zarzuela began.

Jimmy pushed Apollo's long black linen duster from his shoulders and let it drop to the floor. He eased his broad hands inside the vampire's waistband and slid the silk shirt over Apollo's torso and head. He could not help but smell the scent released and found himself aching.

He knelt to remove Apollo's pants, undoing the belt buckle and worrying the zipper. He removed Apollo's shoes and leg after leg took the trousers to himself. Apollo stepped out and raised Ludovic off the floor.

He dropped his black satin shorts and showed again to the assembly what each of them had received. Flaccid, yet fulsome. Sizeable still in its softness.

"Turn around!" the master vampire said in a ringmaster's voice. Venom in the vibrato.

Jimmy turned even as he said, "But I don't . . ."

"You do now."

Apollo rent Jimmy's briefs. Not since his diapering days had he intentionally allowed many to see his penis. And still, it was an adorable little thing, its head like an acorn, the shaft, a fish stick. And hanging from it, two cherries. Eminently edible. A snack.

Apollo massaged him from waist to nape, forcing him to bend over. He dropped his own silk shorts and positioned himself between Jimmy's thighs.

He teased his member between the chorus boy's cheeks. He

rested his abdomen on Jimmy's back. He wrapped his hands around Jimmy's chest and tormented his nipples. He rasped his tongue along Jimmy's spine and up to his neck. He drew aside Jimmy's long blond hair and threw up his own chin to display his dominant fangs to his spectators.

Jimmy clenched at the crowd's reaction and felt the unique pain of a nosferatu's passion.

Apollo commanded the lights to brighten. If he was finally to have an audience, he would not be denied his dramatic moment. Still his mother's son.

He curled his lips to allow for the witnessing of the insertion, the osculation. And he drew back his hips to demonstrate the effect of the blood sacrifice on his manhood. And in another moment, he sunk them both back into Jimmy. Repeatedly and rhythmically.

Until Jimmy was no more.

He pulled his blood-soaked mouth and chin from Jimmy's bloodstained neck. He pulled his engorged member—magically identical to his victim's—from the site of his other assault. His spellbound audience applauded his conquest, but Apollo held up his hand for silence. He alone knew the drama had just begun.

He slit the tip of his penis with his sharp fingernail and shoved the violating member into Jimmy's mouth. And Jimmy Foster responded in the same greedy way that Jean-Luc Courbet did many years ago. The way Phillipe once had. And Aspros and Dentro. As Claude had. As Cody had.

All had taken and drunk.

And the formerly lovely golden brown eyes of the six-foot-something, blond singer/dancer opened to reveal glittering tiger's eyes. Hard and cold and cruel. No longer mirrors to his soul, simply parallel reflections of the horror that surrounded him. The captivated legions of Apollo and Loki were grinning, glorying in the transformation of one of their own. The Vampire Ludovic was reborn.

To melting apprehension and more, mad applause.

chapter

10

Purity St. Martin counted time the way I now did. Perhaps she always had.

We met in March, between the full Storm Moon, which was so important to me in my state, and the Spring Equinox, Ostara, which is a source of strength to those of her kind. If I had met Purity six months earlier, I would have dismissed her. A kook. Delusional. I wonder what she might have thought of me back then.

Me, Michael Flannery O'Donald, still and forevermore awaiting my twenty-ninth birthday. Me, the son of an abandoned mother who drinks a bit too much and an irresponsible father who walked out too many years ago to matter any longer. Me, the only brother of two adult sisters, Mary Pat, whom I call Missy, and Margaret Ann, from whom I withheld both nickname and my complete affection. Three Irish-American women who have again been abandoned by the man of their family, their protector.

Me, the unread teetotaler with no sense of style, no taste to speak of, no philosophy on life or love, politics or religion. Me, the man with no favorite book nor movie, actor nor singer. Me, without a favorite food, a favorite drink or flavor. Never a favorite color, never a favorite television show, flower or article of clothing.

I had a favorite guy once. Possibly my only deliberate preference ever, my only true choice. The only stimulus I truly responded to.

"But he's dead now.

"And I'm dead, too."

"What did you say?" came the sleepy murmur.

Shit! And I am well on my way to screwing this up as well. I had forgotten where I was.

My whole frame, damn near two hundred naked pounds of it, had encircled John Cabot Cox. This stormy evening and almost every evening. I held him again like something to protect. Someone like Teddy.

"I was saying how good this felt."

"Liar," he said in that flat, creaky, lazy voice of the sleeper awake.

"Oh, it's come to name-calling, has it?" I teased, nuzzling my chin at the nape of his neck, chucking my knuckles under his chin, into his armpits, his waist, his groin.

He was terribly sensitive to tickling, this John Cabot Cox. This man of still a boyish twenty-two. My inhuman, feathery touch was anathema to him. But, affliction and affection both. Bane and boon.

A deep, rich manly basso groaned in contradiction from the very depths of his post-adolescent body. An erotic growl from a grown-up Gerber baby. It drove me wild, as he knew it would.

He reached over to the nightstand on his side of the bed.

His side.

I was already in this too deep. We had no future. This was just wrong.

I thought he was reaching for his alarm clock, set an hour before his waiter/actor roommates were due home, or perhaps for the overly thick roach he had left unfinished when our foreplay evolved. But he reached further and pressed the play button of his combination radio/cassette/CD player.

"Before These Crowded Sheets." The Dave Matthews Band. He played it because I loathed it. It was like the tickling.

He played it for hours while we played. As counterpoint to the storm outside. Over and over. It stopped long after we had. After he had fallen asleep.

I turned it off myself, because I loathed it. Hell, Dave Matthews can probably get laid just for being Dave Matthews. But I doubt that even Dave Matthews fucks to Dave Matthews's music. I refuse to see how he could.

Some of it came off like jazz to my ears. And I do not like jazz. "The Last Stop" sounded Middle Eastern. Tents and camels and belly dancers. I hate tents, camels and belly dancers. The track before it, "Rapunzel," sounded like jazz-interpreted Celtic music. And, God-forgive-me, I cannot stomach that New Age-y Celtic crap. Or most any other Celtic crap. I will burn in Hell for that.

I can listen to "Danny Boy"—the world's single most depressing song—on St. Patrick's Day or at a funeral dinner. Ditto "The Wearing O' the Green." Any song with "Irish" in the title—whether it's a great day, a little bit, or eyes smiling. The same goes for songs with Irish towns or counties in them. Unless someone in the room is painted green or dead, I don't want to hear it. I am not a good Mick. Fine! I admit it.

"I'm losing you, Mike."

"I'm sorry, John. I have a lot on my mind."

"About us?" He tried to sound noncommittal, but it came out accusatory anyway.

I had not had this argument before in my decidedly paltry love life. But I knew about it. Everyone does. Whether they admit it or not. And everyone has had it. Now it was my turn.

Why don't you love me like I love you?

Whether reprover or reproved, the argument is the same. Only the perspective changes.

"John . . ."

I started, but it was worse that I had. I should never have opened my mouth. Never have tried. For surely he saw through me. And we both hated me for it.

"I want you to go, Mike. Get out."

He did not even yell it. Did not even wait for recantation. He pulled on sweatpants and left the room. It was clear that I should do the same.

I threw my clothes on and flew out the window. I could not bear a last glance. I landed at the base of his fire escape in a crouch and bounded up again. Strong emotion set off a vampiric response. The floating maneuver carried me automatically into the dark night, careless of John's reaction to my disappearance. I drifted northward unconscious of my destination. I was enjoying the storm; it matched my mood.

I played with the clouds and the lightning and the rain until I tired of it. I dropped down on the steps of a brownstone. I got caught up in the ornate curlicues of the wrought iron ornamentation on the front door. Knowing it without recognizing it.

"You are capable of entering my home by yourself, O'Donald."

I was soaked. April showers and all. I turned to see her standing there on the sidewalk. The people who had given her a ride were spraying their departure over the cold April curb.

"I didn't want to frighten you when you walked in."

Her laugh.

The bright tinkling came not from just her mouth, but from every part of her being. From her torso, womanly and ethereal both. From her eyes and the way she squinted them. Her nose and its wrinkle. From her outstretched fingertips and her arched neck.

From the way she swayed and the way she stepped. From her assurance.

And from her concern.

"C'mon, O'Donald. Let's get you dry." Purity unlocked the building's door and walked to the end of the hall to her front door.

"Don't you want to know why I'm here?"

"To apologize for missing Patrick's memorial service?" she called back as a taunt as she entered her apartment.

I had forgotten. Her husband died three months ago. Most memorials are after forty days, but Purity insisted on ninety. Some private belief of hers, I imagined. I was at her side in an instant.

"I'm really sorry."

"No matter. I wasn't really for Patrick anyway. And it wasn't for me. Theater people love a great show of emotion. Especially if they can completely divorce it from affection."

"Purity, I hope this doesn't sound insensitive, but I had the impression that your husband was very well liked."

"Oh. Of course he was, O'Donald. But Patrick is gone now. He can't help anyone's career anymore, but neither can he deny anyone's claims. So, all the performers and designers who were there tonight will feel entitled to allege that they worked with Patrick. And the directors and producers can all maintain that they taught him everything he knew. There's not a single one who would exchange a perfect photo-op or a beneficial sound bite for a moment of telltale concern.

"It's the theater, O' Donald. Comedy and tragedy *are* just masks. And something else you should know? The quarry you're after? They live by the same commandments. Remember that."

She went to the linen closet near the entrance of her co-op. She handed me an oversize, white towel.

"I'm going to change. I'm coming back with a sherry or port. Which do you prefer?"

I said port because it took less time to say than sherry. I think she knew.

This upstairs bathroom was fairly small. Maybe eight feet by eight. Sink, toilet and tub. Neat and trim. And disappointingly sterile. Very much the guest bathroom for people who did not often have guests.

The porcelain fixtures were all white, as were the tiled walls and floor. The guest towels, soap, toothpaste and toothbrushes were white as well. The exposed pipe, faucets, curtain rod, towel bars and bath accessories were stainless steel or chrome. The light bulbs were decorator, but bare; the shower curtain, clear.

I turned the hot water tap fully counterclockwise, stripped and got in.

The thick, foggy mist that escaped from the overhead nozzle was a graying white. It enveloped me. Then captured the room. When its warmth finally caught up with me, I turned off the tap.

"O'Donald?"

All of the water evaporated at my reaction to the sound of her voice. Nothing dripped from the faucet, nothing clung to the curtain. Nothing pooled in the tub, hung from the mirror, embraced the towels.

The room was dry.

"Your sherry?"

She displayed neither surprise nor embarrassment as she placed it on the ledge of the sink. None as she pivoted back towards the hall. Her rain-darkened hair was drying into brighter, unyielding curls that bounced in counterpoint to the terry cloth that swung from her hips.

"Uh-huh. Just as I remembered!" she smirked under her breath.

In her absence, I caught sight of myself in the bathroom mirror. I was smiling much too broadly at the thought of this highly professional and celebrated—not to mention recently widowed—woman sneaking a peek at a well-built, very homosexual—not to mention recently undead—former cop.

Naturally, my clothes had completely dried when my hair and body did, but it seemed adolescent to redress when she was just in a robe. Childish and mistrusting. I wrapped the generous terry cloth towel around my waist, neatly folded my clothes and picked up my drink to join her.

"Didn't I ask for port?"

"You wanted sherry."

"I did," I admitted.

"Wow!" was all she said.

Although the towel covered me from just under my navel to just under my knees and its thickness obscured all that it covered, all the rest of me was still showing. Workout or no, my body had retained its development and seemed to have improved upon it by itself.

"Does Mr. Courbet look *exactly* like this?" she asked.

"As far as I remember."

"Well, talk about a body to die for!"

"Just keep reminding yourself that a lot of people did die for it. And he has the capability of changing it, magically, if he desires."

"Like this?" she asked. Then, amazingly, she transformed herself into a fine replica of Julianne Moore, morphed into Nicole Kidman, into Gillian Anderson, then Rita Hayworth. She drew her fingers through her hair and went from red to blonde. Marilyn, Madonna, Mae West. A sweep of her hand and she went brunette from Ava Gardner to Liv Tyler.

She brushed her hands over her face, down her neck and over her cleavage. And as she touched, her peaches and cream skin deepened, darkened. She was Lena Horne. Halle Berry. Iman. Grace Jones.

"Stop!" I said and Purity reappeared. "It's a glamour! You're not really changing. You're just *apparently* changing!"

"Of course, O'Donald," she tried to explain. "You can't reinvent bone and muscle. You can't alter melanin levels. All you can do, all *Jack* can do, is change perception!"

"Do you really think so? Do you think that's all he can do?"

"Naturally! What you're suggesting of him is impossible!"

"Then this will surprise you."

I went and sat down beside her. I took her hands and placed them on my cold, hard face. I did the facial alterations described in the vampire maker's books. I first drew my eyes in deeper, furrowed my brow, let my facial muscles go slack at the edges of my eyes and my nasolabial folds. My nose became more classically shaped, my cheekbones higher and broader. I drew in my ears closer to my head and pushed out my lips to a more sensual fullness. I let my hair darken and curl. My newly darkened beard grow. My eyes shifted from a clear, sky blue to a pale honey-amber. I could not pull the sound of Patrick from Purity's mind, but unspeaking, I was her husband.

She never took a breath.

I finally altered the tautness of my vocal chords to my best approximation and spoke, "Are you surprised?"

"Shit!" She started to cry.

I released the change and she withdrew her fingers from my facial rippling.

"That was so cruel."

I knew it was. Maybe that was my intent. I just cannot imagine why.

"I'm sorry, Purity. You had to see what they're capable of doing. They can look into anyone's mind and be whomever they think will prove most attractive."

"I would never have known it was you, O'Donald. Can they both do this?"

"I learned it from Baum and White. Jack's had access to the same books as well as to their writer, so I'm sure that he's as good or better. And sure, he may have taught Claude."

"How will we ever find them?"

"Well, and I hate to acknowledge this, there is one attribute common to all vampires that will be a help to us."

I stopped. This was killing me to admit.

"Are you going to continue, O'Donald?"

"Self-satisfaction."

"What?"

"All vampires seem to have loved their human looks. It's the sin of Pride. They are all ultimately undone by their egos."

Purity St. Martin burst out in peals of laughter. She sloshed her sherry over us both. She was choking on her own private amusement. And each time she was about to speak, she flew again into a fit of hysterics. She pushed me from the couch, from her sight.

I went into the kitchen, just as pleased to rid myself of her.

This was no ordinary kitchen. There was more brewing here than Mom's chicken soup. I looked at the breakfront that served as her spice rack.

The hutch was four feet wide and six tall. It carried dozens of small bottles on its three tiers of shelves. I knew many of the herbal names, the simple ones like mint and basil and rosemary. Some I could read well enough, but still did not understand. Like ylang-ylang, trefoil and fumitory. Then there were the others I could not read at all. Little labels covered with undecipherable signs.

"They're sigils," she said simply in her usual calm voice.

"I can't read them."

"You're not supposed to understand them, O'Donald. They were only put there so that Patrick wouldn't confuse one thing with another when he cooked.

"He once was making a barbecue sauce on the Fourth of July, and created a downpour instead. When he realized how many people all over the tri-state area were indirectly furious at him, he asked me to clearly mark the things he shouldn't touch."

I went to brush back her hair with my hand. To ask her why she'd started laughing earlier.

She pulled away.

"Don't, O'Donald. You shouldn't touch me. I shouldn't be so near to you."

"What's wrong?"

She took a step back before she answered.

"I'm not sure. It could be that you unconsciously will seduction. As you would need to do, if you were a hunter vampire. Or, you could be producing an inhuman amount of pheremones. Or, I could just be a horny widow and you could be just too damned good-looking."

I wanted to explain to her that what she was hinting at would be unthinkable for me. With the exception of a small teenage exploration with Tina, a brief mistake with a distant cousin who looked alarmingly like her brother, and an idiotic need to "prove" myself at the Academy, I had singularly no interest in the other sex.

But, before I could say a word, Purity said, "This will never happen again. Put your clothes on, O'Donald."

"Fine with me. So, tell me what were you laughing at before."

"Before?"

"Why did you burst out laughing before I ran into the kitchen?"

"Oh, that. It was what you said."

I tried to search my memory, but I could not recall a funny comment.

"O'Donald! You said that all vampires are undone by their own egos!"

"Yeah?"

"All *men* are undone by their egos! Caesar ignored the warning to beware the Ides. Kennedy ignored the pleas not to go to Dallas. All through history, men are undone by their egos."

"Women, too, Purity! Joan of Arc trusted that her inner voice would protect her. Marilyn Monroe, her fame . . ."

"Yes, of course, I meant women, too."

"But, what I meant earlier was that Jack and Claude are too narcissistic to adopt false fronts for long. They both assume that their own faces, their own bodies, will be the best way to attract the victim they want most. They could assume the likeness of a Brad Pitt or a Tom Cruise if they chose, but they feel as if they are already more attractive. That's how we'll find them!"

"And then that's how we'll destroy them. I'm going to throw on some sweats, then I want you to look at something."

We both came back into the living room dressed appropriately. I sat down on one side of the couch, she on the other, with the *U.S. Entertainment Magazine* and a collection of newspapers between us.

"Okay, what've you got?"

"This is that story on the new master magicians, Apollo and Loki . . ."

"Whom you believe are Jack and Claude," I interrupted. "You showed me that."

"The inside story," she continued, flipping pages to the corresponding article, "was a short, fluff piece about the two of them.

"It's deliberately inaccurate, O'Donald. Those magicians played this reporter. They overdid this 'aura of mystery' that magicians use as a way of keeping the techniques of their illusions secret. She writes that they insisted that the interviews be conducted in the dead of night, after the shows. The reporter was never allowed backstage, in the basement or dressing rooms of the theater.

"And, she was not allowed to photograph or see their house. She never even learned its location!"

"All of which makes perfect sense for a magician," I added. "They all jealously guard the construction of their tricks. Every magician in the world insists that really good engineering and theatrics is actually magic."

"That's just it!" Purity yelled. "The others claim to be doing *magick*! Apollo and Loki maintain that they are just illusionists!"

I filled in the end of her thought. "And all the while, they really are creating true magick."

"Magi pretending to be magicians! It's about the best disguise you can get, O'Donald. No one would ever believe the truth."

"It makes perfect sense. And their secrecy and stringent privacy would serve their vampires' need while it was being interpreted as a theatrical ploy to heighten their persona and a magicians' requisite to guard his repertoire."

"Clever vampires we have here," Purity said as she gave me the collection of newspaper clippings. Each contained an article about a strange death or disappearance in Las Vegas. In silence, I read them all.

All men. All between seventeen and fifty. All healthy, most robust or athletic. A great many of the men were single. Some were local, either businessmen or performers; the rest tourists. Some had already turned up dead. And when LVPD chose to report it—desanguinated.

If you were looking, you could see the pattern emerge. But, we were the only ones looking. LVPD was not going to be any better than NYPD in determining the correct profile. No better at narrowing down the possibilities. Because this was not a possibility. And Jack and Claude knew it.

"Yes, Purity. Clever and lethal. But not indestructible. If Phillipe could die, then so can they."

I told her everything I had learned from Baum and White about Phillipe, the vampire maker. Phillipe had been an undead for a period of time unknown to them before he encountered and changed them. He may have been nosferatu for centuries prior. And that he may have been thousands of years old before turning Noel and Jean-Luc, before Noel killed him.

But destroy him she did. And I explained how.

"You don't happen to have any unicorn horn on you, do you?" she asked.

"No"—I smiled grimly—"there are none left. But there are other ways to kill one of us, and here I can teach you."

I explained the lethal effect wooden stakes—aspen, hawthorn, and maple. The deadliness of garlic and rose. The toxic effect of silver. We had been over much of this before. No doubt, we would go over it again.

I revealed to her the vampiric reactions to the sun, how much could be tolerated, how it was avoided. The moon, and its quarterly effect upon our strength and abilities, our bodies and our minds. And of all the ways these parts of the solar system controlled our lives.

I told her of the nosferatu's loathing of food and drink. I confided his dependence upon his native soil. I betrayed our very existence to her.

"What about cooked garlic?" she asked.

"We'd all certainly avoid it. It's one way of telling the players, but it's just as easy to confuse one of us with an innocent that way. Not everyone likes garlic."

"Yes. Of course. I see."

"They sell a garlic concentrate in liquid form at the grocery store, Purity. I suggest you stock up on it. Maybe fill a water pistol with it."

"What about rose essence, O'Donald? Attar of roses?"

"Sure, that too."

"Can I combine them?"

"I don't see why not. It might make it easier for you to stand the garlic odor. And you'd have double the protection."

"Could I kill with it?"

"I don't think so, Purity. But you would hurt one of us with it. Think of it as a vampiric stun gun."

Then I described for her a new kind of weapon I had designed. It would be strapped to her forearm and hidden beneath long sleeves. A combination miniature crossbow and dart gun. Only these darts would be about seven and a half inches long and about three-eighths of an inch wide. And they would be made of solid maple, or aspen, or hawthorn. And tipped in silver.

"These would be lethal."

"Isn't it kind of overkill, O'Donald? Silver and wood?"

"The silver tip wouldn't necessarily kill a vampire, Purity. And the wooden dart without the metal tip might not penetrate his flesh deeply enough. It's the combination that's deadly. And it's also a precaution against the possibility that your aim won't be true."

Purity looked at me for the first time with deadly serious eyes. Eyes that recognized the consequence of failure.

"What if I do miss?"

"That's another reason for the silver. All you have to do is wound the vampire, break his skin. He won't die, but he will develop the argent sickness, which is almost as effective."

Without her asking, I began explaining what it is that the element *argyros* does to an afflicted undead. And by explaining the argent sickness, I revealed mysteries inherent in the existence of the nosferatu. And in explaining, seduced her with the concepts as I was enchanted by the blood.

I told her how a vampire lives eternally in a state between the conscious and the unconscious, the imagined and the concrete. Even as he deceives others, he walks his own path between duplicity and deceit. Nothing in the vampiric order is as it was in the mortal realm. It is eternal synesthesia.

The vampire smells colors, tastes images, feels sounds. Every sensation is interchanged, enhanced by the others. Each vampire is caught in a vast web of sensuality where a single stimulus suggests several perceptions. The undead cannot see a mere photograph of an apple without tasting its juices, smelling its flesh, hearing it ripen, and feeling its decay.

And so it is with every living thing. Each human is of necessity victim to the vampire. On first sight, the subject reveals all of his nature—yes, even unto his own demise—to the creature who is at once both dead and not.

This is all part of the grand hallucination of the vampire. Even what is real is unreal. Surreal. Paradigm *and* paradox. Concept and contradiction, all at the same time. Death is life and blood is the spice that makes it palatable.

Consciousness and accountability are vital facilities for those who need to transverse the mortal world. Survival demands it. But unfortunately for the undead, dream is interchangeable with sentience. He must cling, tenaciously, to mortal landmarks each waking moment. If not, he would fall prey to the everlasting torment that is confirmed and ensured by the argent sickness. That hell of never knowing wake from sleep. True from imagined. Certainty from artifice.

A vampire's night is for eternity. And that in itself becomes horror enough. But, to float adrift, guyless, never to supercede the complexity of conjecture, always hampered, hamstrung by perception. That is what the nosferatu fears more than death. To be lost forever wandering the inescapable halls of mythos and memory.

"Jesus! That's what you want me to do to them?"

"Yes, Purity. If you can't kill them outright, trap them within their own minds and senses with silver. Silver intensifies the normal state of the vampiric disease into the argent sickness. They will eventually seek their own deaths just to escape it."

"It's cruel. I can't do it."

"Purity!"

She turned to face me and I knew that she was listening hard.

"Each moment I'm with you and every instant I'm not, I spend evading the vampiric tendency to overwhelm myself with my past or my perceptions. I can never be sure that when I pass a stranger, she won't be wearing my mother's perfume and thereby send me into a tizzy of recollection. A newspaper reminds me it's my birthday, and I disappear into my history. A song, a flavor, a texture. Any of these will trap me, possibly into a fatal error. Only human blood will counteract the vampiric disease. Sometimes, I think, the vampire kills just not to be reminded."

I heard the tear in her voice before she actually spoke.

"I'm sorry, O'Donald. I truly am sorry for you."

"It's too late for that, Purity. Perhaps it was fate. I tried to avenge Teddy's death on my own and it ended up turning me into this. But, if it hadn't happened, I wouldn't have the strength, the means or the wherewithal to destroy these creatures.

"I can't get the argent sickness, because the silver in my fillings incorporated into my dead self. I'm immune. And because I was already infected with vampiric blood before I died, many—if not most—of the cautions for the undead do not apply to me.

"Unlike the others, sunlight does not bother me in small or muted exposures. Only the sustained maximum strength of the sun's rays—from just before to just after noon—will seriously harm, perhaps kill me.

"Roses and other herbals normally dangerous to the vampire merely annoy me. Like a slight allergy. But, I'm pretty sure that if you cut off my head, shove a stake through my heart, or trap me out in the sun, I'm a goner."

"But it's all theoretical, isn't it, O'Donald?"

"What is?"

"Your ability to die. We know how ordinary vampires, created in the usual way, can be killed. That's not theory, it's been practiced. But there's always the possibility that you are a true immortal."

She found the secret as surely as any archer finds his mark. She might seem otherworldly, even flighty, but Purity St. Martin always managed to find what she set out for. And her prize for the bull's-eye was my complete unraveling.

I did not wish to live forever! I did not want what the others desired. I wanted to be normal. Human. I wanted to flee.

"O'Donald. Let me tell you something," she began in a tone that assured me that she knew exactly what I was going through.

"I never asked to be 'Purity St. Martin, The Famous Red Witch.' I just sort of ended up as her.

"I knew, even as a small child, that I could do things. Heal a fallen baby bird and float her back into her nest. Stop the rain on my seventh birthday. Get a date for the prom . . ."

I couldn't help the knee-jerk reaction to her girly insecurities. My head did not just politely swivel towards her, it snapped in disbelief.

"Oh, don't be such a man! There isn't a woman alive who thinks she's beautiful. Women aren't like men, O'Donald."

"I have noticed that."

"Stop it, O'Donald! What I mean is women are different from men in ways men can't know. Can't comprehend."

She did not so much sit on the overstuffed velvet sofa as become part of it. An earth mother linking her flesh to the furniture to the floor to the building to the planet itself. In her simple act of sitting, she described the nature of womanhood. The ability of a woman to become so much more than herself. To become more than simply human, to realize the infinite. The eternal. Like the Earth, women were nurturing, sustaining.

"I'm going to tell you something about women, O'Donald. There's barely a woman alive who doesn't want to kick gay men right in the ass!"

"What?" This was a comment beyond belief!

"Except for lesbians, of course. Although I'm sure that the one and only thing that lesbians like about gay men is that they don't hit on them!"

I was certain that the look on my face was more than just simple astonishment. But I also knew that if I interrupted her right now, I was in big trouble. I was not at all sure where this was going, but I knew better than not to follow along.

"Gay men, O'Donald, are the personification of what women hate about the unfairness of life! Every insecurity a woman has about herself stares back at her in the beautiful face of a man who prefers men. Every instance when she's settled for less is mocked by gay men's obsession with grooming and fitness. With *male*ness.

"Gay men are ideal men because they're *idealized* men. They attend to the details that women find desirable in a man. A fit body, well groomed and well dressed. Interests in theater, art, music and literature. In fine wines and in good food. In fashionable clothing and in quality furniture . . ."

"Purity!"

I had to stop her. I did not like the way this conversation was heading. The way it would mar our relationship.

"What is it, O'Donald?" she yelled at me. "What could you possibly have to say?"

"I have absolutely no interest in any of those things."

It stopped her. Cold. I could see that this irritated her, that she was preparing an argument for her stance. I had to continue before she regained steam.

"Teddy used to get annoyed at me because I didn't know about plays and movies or actors and actresses. I didn't know any of the gossip about celebrities, or who was singing what song on the radio . . . much less who wrote it!

"I have no taste in clothes. Other than my uniform, I wore jeans and sweats. I owned one suit—navy blue—for occasions when I had to dress, but shouldn't wear my uniform.

"I don't really read books. I don't know a single poem. I've never seen any Shakespeare or opera or ballet. I don't like classical music. I don't think I particularly like any particular type of music. I can't recall the words or tune to a single song."

Her argument was bursting from her. "But, O'Donald . . ."

I would not be deterred.

"But nothing, Purity! As sophisticated as you are, you make the same mistakes, cater to the same stereotypes as everyone else. 'Gay men are cultured.' It's just not true.

"There's not a single solitary difference between a gay man and a straight man, except in individual behavior. My personal enter- tainment preferences run towards baseball, basketball, football and boxing. Hiking, biking and, yes, working out. But I worked out to be better at my job, Purity, not to parade up and down Chelsea."

"I'm sorry, O'Donald. I only meant . . ."

I knew she was ashamed and was trying to apologize, but I was not finished. I had only just realized that I wanted to say this to someone for a very long time. Someone who mattered.

"I always feared that I'd lose Teddy because I wasn't 'gay' enough. Teddy was smart and I wasn't. He knew about all the arts and entertainment, and I didn't. He was fun and funny, and I. Just. Wasn't."

Purity came to me and put her arms around me. How do I tell her I am just not a hugger? Not me, but I suspected she was. Like Teddy. She started to comfort me with her words, too. Not whis- pered, but soft, just the same.

"It's all right, O'Donald. I'm certain that it was your very 'un- commonness' that Teddy loved." Maybe she sensed my discom- fort, because she broke away with businesslike, "Let's get to work!"

"Good! Pack whatever you'll need, Purity. Leave anything that we can get there," I said as I started moving towards the door.

"Pack? What, now? We're leaving now?"

* * *

I could hear the anxiety in her voice. Her obvious attempt to suppress it pained me. But I couldn't relent. Not now.

"There's no reason not to leave now. We know where they are. We think we know *who* they are. We can't stop them from here. Any more preparation can be made there."

"It's so soon."

The sound barely passed her lips, caught as it was by her clenched throat. I could smell the fear, taste the insecurity. This was the first time she ever had to deal with creatures not of her own creation, with powers mightier than her own. Other than an improbably benign one like myself.

"Fear is good, Purity. It will keep you sharp. You don't want to let your guard down or underestimate them."

Her eyes grew huge, magnified by the tears welling in them. They were no longer the mirrors of her soul, they were microscopes peering inside. The weight of her commitment had finally landed upon her. She was faltering.

"I talk a great game, O'Donald . . ."

"You can do this."

She inched backwards.

"I'm always so sure of myself . . ."

"You can do this, Purity," I said as I moved towards her.

"Always so sure," she murmured either to me or to herself. "Always the one who prodded and poked and spurred others on."

She stopped when she got to the shallow corner of the living room between the entrance to her bedroom and the glass doors to the garden. She stopped because there was no other place to go. No place further to retreat.

"I cannot go, O'Donald. I'm a coward."

I grabbed her upper arms and drew her towards me.

"Purity, I don't blame you. These opponents of ours aren't human. It's too much to ask of anyone. I didn't want to die, so I can't ask you to face the possibility."

"Then you'll stay?"

"No, Purity, I'll leave tonight if I can arrange it."

The cracks in her ego cobwebbed, grew and shattered. All emotion and excuse flowed from her. She needed to convince herself that it was all right to abandon me to this quest alone.

"O'Donald, I'm so sorry. I just can't do it. The thought of killing someone, of being killed . . ."

"It's okay. Don't worry. Hey, I didn't want you to come in the first place." It was a poor attempt at a joke, but I said it with a smile.

She smiled back. Not a cheery one, but wistful and a little distracted. She did not want to excuse herself, but was glad that I did.

"Is there anything I can do for you?"

"Yeah. Teach me all the magic you know!" I caught the look in her eye. The one that says: I-deceived-you, I-lied-to-you, I'm-a-phony-and-you-caught-me. Addressing that was not going to make it better; I had to try to make her useful.

"I'd like to use your phone, if that's okay?"

"Of course. Don't be silly. Here."

As she handed the handset to me, I said, "It's long distance," teasing that her freedom would be expensive. She was in no mood to joke. I dialed the number that few did. The voice that answered said what it always did.

As per the ritual, I said, *"Je suis Charnac!"* The rare vampire on the other end responded in the approved rejoinder. I continued in French, a habit and ability I picked up from Baum and White.

"Allo? Baum? C'est moi."

I proceeded to instruct the large albino undead genius of my needs. The jet for a trip from New York to Las Vegas. A furnished place once I got there. Neither too big nor small. Centrally located. Secure sleeping arrangements—he knew what that meant. Clothing, accessories, cash and a line of credit. A new identity—I didn't want Jack to note a recent arrival of an O'Donald or a de Charnac. I needed, above all, privacy and security. Baum assured me that he had anticipated as much. Everything I would need was already in waiting.

I thought I could no longer be astonished by their perceptions. Since there was nothing more to arrange, I hung up the phone. And when I turned to say good-bye to Purity, there she stood with her bag packed.

"What's this?"

"I changed my mind."

"It's not that simple, Purity."

"Don't make this harder, O'Donald. Let's just say I've come to my senses. Or chalk it up to a woman's prerogative. You need me there and I need to be there. C'mon. Let's go."

We shut down her apartment without a further word. I knew Purity was mentally ticking off the arrangements she would need to make to run her affairs while she was gone. We left the building to find a limousine waiting to take us to the airport, courtesy of Baum and White. The first of Purity's surprises. When we arrived at the airport, the driver went directly to the small jet terminal. The Dassault Falcon 900C bearing the Charnac coat-of-arms was waiting for take-off. We got on the plane—my plane—with a brief hello to the pilots.

There was no time to lose. If we left as soon as we had clearance, we could be in downtown Vegas before sunrise. And I could rest before the work at hand.

M. Grandet, the pilot, announced our take-off. The expression that shadowed Purity's face was that of the commercial traveler. The prompt broadcast confirmed for her that this was no pleasure trip, no matter how impressive the trappings. We were in a hurry and we meant business.

Purity was content to stay in the brass and cherry wood entry-way/galley. I had to point out what a finely furnished diplomatic transport looked like. The interior layout of the Falcon 900C was most impressive. This one, designed by Jack, Baum and White was stunning. The severity of Jack's Virgoan tastes for dark wood and neutral colors was lifted by the lush and stunning deep-pile carpet in the Charnac colors—purple background and a gold wheat border. I gave Purity the grand tour as we taxied.

Because of its large cabin, at six feet, two inches of headroom and a thirty-three foot length, the two of us could easily get away from each other. And the amenities were as impressive as the size. The telephones, fax, data link, copier, computers, video screens, television, custom executive desk and conference tables made it a flying research center. Purity looked once at her outmoded laptop and tossed it into the nearest overstuffed, gray leather chair of the forward cabin.

The molded cherry wood cabin was divided into three separate seating areas. The forward cabin, the mid-cabin and the aft cabin. Purity immediately laid claim to the forward as her territory and we agreed that the mid-cabin would be communal. This left the aft, and its well-concealed coffins, for me.

I believe that it was the full-service galley, fully equipped and fully stocked, that made the difference. Baum and White had known Purity's mind better than she did, anticipated her change of mind and paid much attention to her needs and tastes in filling the pantry, the refrigerator and the liquor cabinets. She needed for nothing.

The twenty-four panoramic windows stretching the length of the cabin—a dozen to each side—revealed the airport environs as we sped from them. But the screens that could be brought down to block the light were of a very special design for a very special purpose. No natural daylight ever need enter the cabin.

Now Purity had almost five and a half hours to show me her bag of tricks. She had packed no clothing except for ceremonial robes. She did, however, bring her crystals, runes and tarot cards, wands and botanicals. And her laptop. The grimoire of the new millennium.

She laid them out quickly and even more quickly explained their usage. Undead, I am the student I never was in life. I absorb information readily and completely. But, not a natural witch, I had to relearn the core lesson taught to me by Baum and White.

Relax and let it come. Nothing flows with tension, with greedy demand.

Before we got down to serious study, I interrupted to bring her a snack.

Although not strictly vegetarian—Purity did eat certain seafood and some fowl—the jet's refrigerator had been stocked for her with a great assortment of fruits and vegetables. Bowls of hummus, vegetable pate and guacamole sat side-by-side with a mound of cooked, chilled jumbo shrimp. A duck comfit in aspic. Two giant turkey legs roasted to perfection. Cheese upon imported cheese.

There were chilled bottles of sparkling and spring waters. Fruit and vegetable juices. The chilled wines, beers and spirits were in a special compartment below. Here, too, the lovers thought of everything.

The pantry doors hid breads and rolls and crackers. Condiments, spices and dressings. Tins of various epicurean delights as well as box upon box of cookies and candies and bag after bag of snacks. Vampires adore the decorative value of junk food.

I made it simple.

I grabbed a tray and dropped on two types of grapes, a Red Delicious and a Granny Smith apple. To this I added Gouda and Roquefort cheeses. A box of crackers. I grabbed a bottle of Perrier, a St. Emilion and a Pouilly-Fume. I grabbed a beer for myself. St. Pauli Girl. I knew I would just piss it out, but whatthehell, I did the same alive.

I carried the bounty mid-cabin where Purity lounged on one of the divans.

"Here. Eat."

She looked, pointedly, at the open beer.

"I never said I *couldn't* eat and drink. It's just wasted on me."

"And what about the possibility that it could induce a memory?" she asked.

"Nah. Not with Pauli Girl. Bud, maybe."

We both laughed. She was starting to know my tastes, my sense of humor. She was getting like Tina.

Tina.

I thought it without realizing. I had never thought about Tina. Sure, I had promised Baum and White that I would avoid contact with her, but I never meant to keep that promise. Tina was my best friend. Still, I had not thought of her once while I was in the city. Not until I was in the air and away. Did Baum and White put some kind of spell on me to keep me from Tina?

And what about Tina? Did they keep her from contacting me? There were no notes, no letters, not a single message on my answering machine.

Where was she? Could she contact me? Why . . . ?

"O'Donald?"

I slid back into reality. Purity.

"I'm here."

"Are you sure? It's like you froze or something."

"I was thinking about Tina." I did not want to get into this conversation. We were on a mission and that was all that mattered.

"Yeah, it is strange that she didn't get in touch with you."

I stared at Purity. Into Purity. How would she know whether Tina spoke to me? What did I really know about Purity St. Martin?

"Did you try to reach her?"

No, I had not.

"Did you watch her TV program, O'Donald? Just to check on her?"

No, not that either. And now the things I neglected to do were beginning to pile upon me like bricks.

"O'Donald, are you just worrying over nothing?" And bang! The bricks were gone.

"Yeah, Purity. I think I am. Eat up."

The vampiric nature was essentially self-involved. My own doubts devastated me, my convictions buoyed me. I was getting sick of the roller coaster. Eternity sucked.

"This is really excellent," she said as she simultaneously stuffed cheese in her mouth and unwrapped her deck of cards from some velvety fabric.

Purity explained the history of the tarot while she ate. She described for me the interpretation of each card.

"But, O'Donald, there are *two* uses for the cards."

I knew by her inflection that there was something more for me to understand, something I was missing. I could then see in her expression that she knew I missed it.

"Tarot cards are active as well as passive."

"I honestly have no idea what that means, Purity."

"In their passive, most common mode, the cards are used for interpretation. That's reading the tarot cards, the thing most of us are aware of. Anybody can do that; everyone has that level of psychic ability. But a trained witch can use the cards to *do* magick, not just to interpret their fall."

I shifted in my chair. I was uncomfortable and wondered why. There was something very wrong here.

"Okay, O'Donald, I'll show you." She splayed her deck on the table before me.

"Pick a card." I did. Two X's. Number twenty. The Judgment card.

"This card usually represents transformation. Something that is very much on your mind. Not just your own transformation, but also that of Jack and Claude. If, indeed, they have changed their identities, we'll have some difficulty finding them. You say you'll be able to tell whether the magicians are human or not by scenting their blood. But that will only work if we are alone with them. Correct?"

"Yes."

"Then, O'Donald, let me show you what proactive tarot is all about."

Purity took the card and held it to her closed eyes.

"Envision both Jack and Claude, O'Donald." I did. And she began to chant while she stared at the tarot card.

"This I pray: so mote it be:

"Release the shade like night to day.

"Fade all masks that hide true face,

"And in my scope, façade replace,

"Reveal the hunter to the prey.

"Grant my prayer: so mote it be!"

I felt the pulse as if a ripple proceeded from Purity and spread around and past her. A concentric wave that continued on and on.

"What did you just do?"

Purity shook her head in the way that you dispel a bad thought or a dog dries itself.

"I used the transformation card to cast a spell. Now, whenever I am near either of them, they will look like their original selves. No matter what form they've taken!"

Okay. Now this was good. This would help.

"I'll be able to see it too, right?"

Purity looked as if I had just caught her deer form in my headlights. That look that says the keys *and* the baby are locked in the car.

"Oh my God, O'Donald! What did I do?"

"I think you just locked me out of your spell. And I think you have to fix it before we get off this plane."

There is nothing so unnervingly charming as a confident woman reduced to her girlish self by an accidental blunder. All the more so when her fair skin deepens with her discomfort.

"You should see yourself."

"Why?" was her dulled response.

"You really are 'The Red Witch' now. You're blushing like crazy."

But that caught deer quickly evolved from clumsy girl to terrified woman.

"I can't fix the spell, O'Donald."

"Of course you can."

Her eyes searched mine for a loophole, an escape. A place where she could find protection from her error. A safe harbor. But, hers was a living art form and no commiseration was to be found in dead eyes. We sat in silence across the still table in the soundless jet. Chastened, she shared her misery and opened her mind to me. And I saw.

A spell, well performed, is a living thing. It had life; it had legs. It would do as bid and only that. It was like bearing a child. You could not just append more desirable attributes, if it was not exactly what you wanted. It was that child and none other.

Purity's most potent spells were set for her alone. She did not give away keys to perception. She never had. And so, it never occurred to her to include another, not even her new partner, in this undertaking.

Yet, in opening her mind to me, we both saw an unintended avenue. Just as she would be able to recognize Jack and Claude and know them for who they were, so too would they know her.

Although we each looked into the other's eyes, we both were lost in our own thoughts. What's to be done about this? How do we fix this?

"I suppose there's only one thing to be done now."

"I agree, O'Donald."

"I'm sorry to have to ask you to make this sacrifice."

"There's no other option."

"I'll have them turn the plane around, Purity."

The look on her face could scarcely be called disbelief. It was as if shock and anger could be mated into another strong emotion.

"Turn the plane around?" she yelled at me.

"Purity, what are you yelling about? You just agreed to go home!"

"O'Donald, I agreed to be the sacrifice! I thought that you were going to use me as bait."

If I had ever thought that we understood each other, knew each other, I was proved wrong. She had no intention of giving up and going home, she was going forward with her plan.

"Purity, I can't let you do this. This is not the plan."

"It is now, O'Donald. I'm sorry, it wasn't deliberate, but here it is. As soon as I'm near enough to Jack and Claude to recognize them, they'll also recognize me. Not just as Patrick's wife whom they met briefly at the theater in New York, and not only as 'The Red Witch.' They will know for a fact that I'm there to destroy them."

I hated this idea as much as I marveled at her resolution. Even if I sent her home, she would come back and try alone. We had to work together. And within the spell.

"Okay, then. Where do we start?"

"Well, either I first begin to teach you magick or we decide on a plan of action. And second, we do the other one."

"Okay, Purity, the magick can wait a minute. Let's talk about what we should do in Vegas."

"Fine. Do we know where we're going when we get off the plane?"

I told her what Baum explained to me.

We would go to a residence that they picked out. Like the jet, our new quarters would have everything, mortal and vampiric, that we needed while we were here. Food, money, and clothing enough for whatever the length of our stay. A car and maps. New identities in the form of credit cards and drivers' licenses.

"I'll need to know where to get certain supplies, O'Donald."

"I'm sure Baum and White have thought of that, Purity. Once we've settled in, we'll need tickets to Apollo and Loki's magic show. We need to know if they are really Jack and Claude."

"I think we should sit separately. If they are able to recognize the fact that I'm there to kill them, you shouldn't be near.

I agreed. We should not be seen together. But the first trip should just be for reconnaissance. We should only identify them.

Purity reluctantly agreed. She wanted to prevent any further victims as soon as she could, but getting herself killed was not the way.

We touched down at the Executive Airport in Henderson less than twenty miles from McCarren International. Baum and White would never chance Jack noticing the arrival of the Charnac diplomatic jet or a new vampire named O'Donald. They had a helicopter waiting for us. I could just about see Purity acknowledge the onset of our "adventure" with a determined set of her eyes and jaw as we boarded the bird and strapped ourselves in.

"I'm going to miss that jet," she said.

"Not if I know Baum and White."

It was just a short trip over the Las Vegas Strip. It would be day soon enough, but the city still glittered like a Christmas tree from above. We landed on top of a very modern office building in the older part of Vegas near the North Strip. We could see no other lights in the vast glass and steel building, but I could smell people working below.

"Where are we?" Purity shouted over the deafening whirr of the helicopter.

"Top of the world, Ma."

No response.

"Either you didn't hear the joke, didn't get the joke or didn't think it was one. Which?"

But still she was responseless. I motioned her away from the helipad and to the door of the building. I opened the door with the keys that M. Grandet had given me. We stood inside the tinted glass ceiling-to-floor windows and watched the helicopter fly off. Then we turned to look at the darkened residence.

"Money may not be able to buy everything, O'Donald, but it does pretty well for itself."

"Hold on, Purity. Watch this!"

I pressed the touch pad just inside the door and the penthouse lit up. It was an outlandish display of wealth, especially for the House of Charnac, even for Las Vegas.

The exterior walls were all tinted glass, mirrored and with the highest UV protection. People who live in glass houses should throw parties; this three-hundred-and-sixty-degree view was unbelievable. I pushed another button and the same type of shields that the jet employed descended from the ceiling, completely blocking natural sunlight. And, perhaps, to keep out even more.

The "house on the hill," as Baum and White referred to it, was an interesting design. The public rooms—kitchen, dining room and living room—ran the outer circle of the penthouse. The bedrooms, bathrooms and closets formed the inner circle, along with the very private elevator and staircase. We were the only beings to ever visit the penthouse; Purity was the only human to enter since the last workman left.

It was situated on top of the Whitetree Genetics Laboratory and Research Center. Privately owned by Charnac International, all of the lab's work was secret. Whitetree never applied for grants or patents and published few papers. Neither Jack nor Claude was informed of its purpose or existence. A few members of the lab's senior management knew about the top floor, but the penthouse and heliport could only be reached by the private elevator or stairs. It was inaccessible and off-limits to all but Purity and I.

Unless, of course, one could fly.

PART THREE

THE HUNTER AND THE RED WITCH

chapter

11

He was not the natural performer that his mother was. Never even as desirous of the profession as his lover had been. Yet, as he stood backstage, Apollo felt what they had felt.

He could sense the arrival of the audience, feel their apprehension. The quick pat to a stray hair. The pull at errant thread before exiting the car. The stroll into the theater. Deliberate, concise, grand. The cranings and flexings to see and be seen, note and be noticed. Tucked and taut and botoxed, they entered Vows and Secrets in silks and satins, velvets and lames. They came to him. Came as supplicants all.

They merged their anticipation with the escalated business of his staff and crew. Each ticket-taker, bartender and attendant was flawlessly turned out in uniform. Gold lame bow ties and black leather harem pants only. And broad, bare chests and bulging biceps. All at a minimum of six feet tall. And every one a beauty. For the scene-makers, the show had already begun. And for the watcher as well.

Apollo turned his attention to the last minute changes and adjustments of the cast. To their warm-up and their makeup. Their primping and obsessing. Backstage at Vows and Secrets was no different from backstage anywhere else in the world. But for the abilities of its stars. And perhaps in the nonexistent rehearsals and sets.

The master magician, Apollo, who had been Jean-Luc Courbet de Charnac until scant months ago, stood alone backstage and watched the pre-spectacle as it unfolded all about him. Gaffers and tailors orbited around his celestial center as a busy asteroid belt—a show biz solar system. The chorus boys—dancers and gymnasts and acrobats all—warmed their muscles, stretched their ligaments

and tendons, and checked their own hair and makeup in reciprocal, unconscious response to the arriving audience.

Jack saw here, saw now, as he had never before. He had at-
tended the theater nightly when his mother, the famed Noel Courbet,
had enlivened Parisian culture with her performance. It had always
seemed so hopeless, helpless, hapless, to him. Always one disaster
or another. One hold-up, one delay, one unwinding. Misfortune in
the making.

Here a pulled muscle or, there, a misplaced wig. A missing cast
member, or a worrisome review. Or a temper tantrum. Always a
temper tantrum.

Jack recalled how his mother had always seemed so aloof from
it all. Above it, even when she had been the cause of the conflict.
She reminded him of the moon. Serene Celene. She of many phases
showing but one face. Cool and imperious goddess, consistent and
inconstant both. And of all the celestial bodies, the only one likely
to drive men mad.

Was she, too, distracted endlessly? Was that the essence of her
inscrutability? Performance fueled by anxiety? He stood as she
had, the center of a self-created universe, and experienced as she
did.

He smelled what she had once. The sweet greasepaint and the
talced powders of her makeup. The pungent horsehair, glue and
lacquer of her wigs. Acrid bleach and gummy starch and lavender
soap crept into the fabric of her costume, while floury sizing and
blunt lead and eggy tempera paint covered the canvas of the sets.
He could scent the heat-softened gelatin that colored the stage
lights. The stage manager's gamy tobacco and sour gamay tossed
carelessly over his carawayed sausage dinner. And, oh! What's this?
Delightful distaste and a pretty poignant fear, as an ammonia, wafting across the nose of the new ingenue! Jack saw what Noel saw.

In her dressing mirror. Abundant, auburn hair piled high upon
her head and glimmering in the gaslight. A forty-year-old face
camouflaged with a portraitist's exacting brushstroke. Her sallows
and grays colored pink and peach. Her cooling eyes painted to a
twinkle. Slender bosoms and boyish hips teased into archetype
through the art of primping and prodding and padding. Stunning
jewels—gifts from admirers—glinting from neckline and earlobe,
bodice and finger and wrist. Clear and cool diamond, burning
bright ruby, sage sapphire, and verdant emerald. All framed and
glorified in gilt setting. And moreover, an exquisite costume—royal

amethyst velvet, gleaming platinum satin and rich ivory lace—more befitting her station than her role. He heard what his mother heard.

A single line repeated again and again, its inflection varying from one word to another upon each repetition. And each time in search of the perfect intent. Musical scales sung for fluidity, tongue twisters for flexibility, tea mixed with brandy and honey for courage as much as any other thing. Whispered gossip. Spoken gossip. Cackled gossip. Barked orders to a stagehand. Strangled imprecations to a fickle lover. Murmured prayers to a remembered patron saint.

And Apollo heard one thing more.

"Places!"

Apollo looked down upon himself automatically. With no need. Everything about him was perfect. His hair fell in a thick soft wave from his center part to his massive naked shoulders. His body was big and beautiful; his costume, what there was of it, was beautiful as well. A loincloth of perfectly matched silver fox tails, it covered very little. Loki, he knew, was at the opposite side of the stage in an almost identical costume, a bit briefer, tails of black sable.

They and their cast moved out upon the circular stage in complete silence, total blackness. The opening strains of Igor Stravinsky's "The Firebird" called to them. Over the mournful woodwinds, puzzled strings and frightened percussion, they could hear the nervous rattling of their audience. A shift in a seat here, a throat-clearing there. Everyone anticipated a performance by Apollo and Loki. To date, no two had been the same. Two things could be certain at a Vows and Secrets performance. One was that the beautiful and near-naked men of the cast would display—sometimes subtly, sometimes not—homoerotic behavior. The other was that the magic was unbelievable and original.

The lights slowly brightened. A soft blue and pale yellow tone that mimicked daybreak revealed a community of primitive men, impeccably muscled, in loincloths of fur and hide. They slept, singularly, in couples and in groups. A dark clan on one side of the stage and the fairer on the other. The day had not yet called to them.

The lights intensified and they stirred. They awakened as lovers do, rising to themselves, each other, and the day. And as they grew out of their sleep, the set grew out of the stage.

Small stones developed into large boulders, mounds into mountains, ferns into forests. A palmful of water swelled into a small pond in the center of the stage. Cast members netted fish and crustaceans from the water and released them. Some fell to the stage and became various mammals, some rose into the air as birds.

Small tensions began to develop over the possession of this food or that trinket. Disagreement became dispute, conflict arose into combat. Amity devolved into violent animosity. As the orchestra thundered and clashed, so did the cast. Their discord escalated into armed contest with stones and clubs. The din provoked their totems, their djinn.

Apollo appeared from the cave of the light warriors, Loki from the cave of the dark. They performed a pas de deux, a duet comprised of individual dances. Achingly slow, artfully deliberate. Each solo performance suggested autoeroticism, divine self-involvement. The lead performers mirrored one another in their steps, in their magic. As members of each tribe awarded individual offerings to their gods, Apollo and Loki took the objects and changed them. Shells and stones became rare and precious jewelry. Leaves and fronds were turned into rich pelts. The simple offerings transformed into precious sacrifices in the hands of the twin gods. All to Stravinsky's slow, swirling, sensuous strains. A delicious, decadent diorama of prehistory.

But even as man invented his gods, these divinities were subject to the desires of their creators. The conflict must be resolved, the bloodlust satisfied. The gods must satisfy their objectives as archetype. The savior must be sacrificed.

Apollo and Loki began their transformations into the totems of their respective clans. As they circled the stage and each other, Loki's broad, hairy chest grew more expansive and hirsute. His hands and feet broadened and splayed into huge paws. His hair and the pelt he wore converged into a dark, rich fur. Loki had become a huge brown bear, more than twice the size of a man. Apollo, at the same time, expanded as well. His long, blond hair grew into a veritable mane. His body, sleek and muscular, enlarged with a feline grace. As Loki turned himself into a giant bear, Apollo became an immense golden lion. And as bear and lion, natural enemies. They enacted, in single combat, the war between the tribes. The sheer energy of their conflict scattering the tribesmen, forcing them into the caves.

Loki's ursine power dominated the vertical aspect of the stage, while Apollo's catlike crawl ruled the horizontal. They measured each other in a primitive dance of death. Now snarling, now clawing. From opposing sides they drew nearer and nearer, two awesome planets pulling into each other's orbit. Closer and closer they came. The audience could feel the heat of their anger, the chill of their swipes, the pulse of their growls.

But neither the customers nor the cast and crew could hear the conversation between the undead magicians. Michael O'Donald alone was privy to their secret.

"What's wrong?" Loki asked Apollo. He could sense distraction in his partner on stage in a way he never could off of it.

"We have company," Apollo replied in that same vampiric tone that eluded human hearing. They continued their theatrical battle, snarls and stomps covering conversation.

"I don't understand. Who's here?" the giant bear, Loki, asked.

"Your friend, the Red Witch, for one," Apollo, the great golden lion answered, swiping his gigantic paw at Loki's massive chest.

"Purity St. Martin is here?" Loki craned his thick, muscular neck over the apron of the stage, terrifying the first few rows.

Apollo pounced upon him. "And if I'm not mistaken, Michael O'Donald is here with her!"

Loki batted the huge lion off his chest. This was not just play-acting. Apollo had accused him of not doing his duty at Charnac. O'Donald was dead, he was certain of it.

"O'Donald is dead, Apollo! I know I killed him!"

The big brown bear and the giant golden lion had outgrown their intentions. They were bigger than they needed to be for the magic, growing larger than the stage would allow.

"He is vampyr! I never intended for you to kill him at the chateau. You were supposed to see that he remained shackled. Now he has escaped the chateau and found us."

The argument was witnessed as a monumental clash between two unnatural beasts. A terrified fascination kept the audience taut in their seats. None dared move. There was no way of telling if this fight had already gotten out of hand and might overrun the stage.

"Why would Baum and White have transformed him?"

"It was not Baum and White, Loki. We did it! You and I! I forced him to drink my blood on the pier last Christmas morning. It was my punishment to him. He was a living human with vampiric blood. It was not until you killed him at the chateau, months later, that he became vampyr."

"Then who is his master? Who controls him, Apollo?"

"No one, I believe. I did not kill him before I gave him the black gift. You had not fed him your blood after he died."

"He has no master?"

"I am not sure if anything that rules us applies to him, Loki."

"What are you saying? He can't be hurt by the sun or garlic or anything?"

"I am saying that I do not know. If I had to guess, I would say that he is vulnerable to nothing."

"What do we do now?"

"We have a show to finish. I have an idea. I will take your role in the second half. You go and make sure they have not found our lair."

"But . . ."

"No, Loki, it must be this way. Let us finish this."

Each hunkered back to an opposite side of the stage. And to flash and fanfare they charged one another. And disappeared.

Slow mournful horns emerged from the darkness, from the silence. Strings joined adding an atmosphere of mystery, ominous and hopeful. The near-naked tribesmen emerged from their caves and moved through the fog-shrouded stage to its edges. The cloud rose from the floor. And as it rose, it swirled. The lights and the music became brighter, quicker. And as the shadow reached the ceiling, the tone had become joyous.

From the cloud, the firebird burst forth. It unfurled its massive wings and revealed its glorious plumage. Brightly feathered as a parrot, the firebird shone like a perfect flame. Simultaneously pale and intense, its feathers flashed yellow and orange, red and magenta. And all overlaid with an iridescent quality that vacillated in the theatrical lights. It dripped rainbow colored crystals upon the stage and the theater. Rained its essence upon the cast, converting each primitive tribesman into a more perfected human, each glowing with inherited divinity.

It gave until it could give no more. It gave until it was gone.

The theater went black.

In the uproar of the applause, the audience could not hear the cast readying themselves for the next bit of magic.

The lights grew back in less than a moment. Dim and soft they barely revealed the primitive landscape of the stage. Prehistoric, but unlike the previous. This was the prehistory of legend. Not totems and icons of a lost civilization, but the race memory of mythos. A memory tapped into by visionaries like Maxfield Parrish.

Down from the dim recess of the uppermost part of the theater, deep indigo blues faded to clear, clean cobalts and then to pale and vague aquamarines. This skyscape set the background for the deep siennas and vibrant ochers of the dusty and claylike earth that emerged from the stage floor. The growing mammoth rocks and boulders were picked out in dark brown sepias and various deep purples of eggplant and plum. Deciduous and conifer trees extended their beryl-green branches past their gnarled and wrinkled umber barks towards the center stage. Asiatic wisteria lolled its soft pastel clusters of pink and rose and white, while tropical flamboyan wept its bouquets of flame-colored flowers over the setting.

And amid this set design that was apparently there and yet evidently not, an image emerged.

According to the program, this was the role that Loki was to have taken. Yet, this fully naked performer was Apollo, and Apollo was different somehow. The gleaming, shoulder-length blond hair was unmistakable. His large, muscular shoulders and broad, perfect back testified to his identity. But as the lights brightened, the discrepancies grew into focus.

Apollo's smooth, hairless form was sprouting hair in full view of the audience. Not Loki's dark sable wires, but a burnished gold. It began below his waist as a lone, low velvety flute awakened as well. He shuddered, a somnambulist. And with a harp's glissando, all of his naked, supine body became apparent. As did the musical composition. The harp repeated and he shuddered.

His perfectly muscled rear grew hairy as the melody passed from one languorous air to another. Dark golden hairs erupted on his gluteus maximus. The hairs grew longer and coarser until they curled like wool. Muted strings. Harp and horns. Odd and interesting percussion. The growth continued down his thighs to his knees, his knees to his claves. To his ankles.

When the harmonies grew rich and hypnotic, Apollo's feet turned into hooves.

He stood from the languor of his sleep. A dream awakened. The "Afternoon of the Faun." He was the perfect realization of a myth. No longer the sun god, Apollo, but the father of dreams, Faunus roused.

He reached for his pipes, a collection of phallic reeds strung together, as if in an attempt to recall his lustful dreams.

He put them to his lips and summoned.

And from the trees, and from the stones, and from the air itself, his fantasies came into being.

Called as woodwinds, called as strings, these creatures could not but come as called. Babies appeared at every part of the stage. They rose from leaves and petals. Broke free from clay and rock. Emerged from cloud and puddle. Like little cherubs from some forgotten fantasia, they crawled and stood from their birthplaces.

And as he called, they grew.

Babies to toddlers to boys. To tall and muscled, lithe and proud, naked men.

Big black men. Big blond men. And the men themselves began to change. Every one transforming into either satyr or a centaur. All moving as slowly as a dream to the pipes of their Pan. An extraordinary, hallucinogenic magic.

Each centaur and satyr displayed an obvious and outstanding physical interest in the divine man-beast; their nakedness displayed to all. Each cast member touched every other one on his way towards the central attraction. And all the strokes were joyous, sensual, erotic. Giving and demanding. All roles played on each one. Every kiss, touch, and embrace experienced. Innocent as the play of kittens, carnal as an ancient bacchanalia. Each one experienced the others as he drew closer to the desired one, the eternal one. The deity who is half-man. And half-beast.

Apollo knew that this new magic—not as it was originally planned—would have a more desirable effect on the intended audience member. And just like Faunus, he spoke to the somnolent inner spirit of his doppelganger.

You are a god now, Michael. No longer a mortal. Dead and not dead. Human and not. Watch what happens to the objects of your affection. See eternity from a god's point of view.

As each excited cast member approached the godhead, he began to dissipate. With each step, each one aged. His muscles grew slack, his hair thinned and grayed. And when he touched his god, he shattered, blown asunder like the umbels of a dandelion.

The faun beckoned to each and each in turn responded, approached and disintegrated until Apollo, the faun, was left alone.

You love a dream, Michael! And this is how you will end!

And Apollo did what Nijinsky had done in May of 1912. Left alone onstage with no one to partner his advanced state of erotic tension, he acted alone. As the lights and music faded, the magician massaged himself, his still-hairless chest, his fresh furry belly, his animal genitals.

And when the house lights came back up, an entire dazed audience sat stock-still in dazzled disbelief. All but two.

chapter

12

I heard him clearly inside my head. There was no mistake. He knew we were there, Purity and me. This rude little display was his way of showing off his knowledge and his power. I had to get her away from the theater. Off his radar.

Before the lights had completely dimmed on Apollo, I was at Purity's side. Afraid to communicate telepathically, I touched her arm. She trembled, but to her credit, she did not scream.

"O'Donald!" she whispered. "Are you trying to give me a heart attack?"

"We have to go. Right now," I answered in the same hushed tone.

I hustled her out of the theater and around the corner onto Park Paseo. Some of the employees caught a glimpse of me and thought I resembled Apollo too closely. But I knew that they had seen stranger things. After I hid Purity safely behind a parked car on the south side of the street, I stopped. Maybe it was the look in her eyes.

"You heard him?"

"Every word."

She was suppressing the shudder, but the fear was clear. She understood magick and just saw a whole theater full.

"Well?"

"Well, my magick worked, O'Donald. He saw me as his hunter. And I saw him as he really is."

She did not continue. Could not. She could not even look at me.

"You saw me."

"I'm so sorry, O'Donald. The magick worked too well. You and he look exactly the same to me."

"At least we know we have the right targets."

Her eyes flashed in a singular aspect. I'd never seen her look this way before. Ordinarily so kind, so compassionate, so understanding, Purity looked like a felon. I had seen that look often enough before. And my cop's instinct was to find out why.

"Target, O'Donald. One vampire."

Okay, now this baffled me.

"Are you saying that you only saw one vampire on that stage?"

"No," she said too calmly for my taste. "I saw three. Apollo . . ."

"Jack."

"Exactly. And another big blond guy in the chorus. I could sense evil in him and couldn't see a human aura."

Shit! He is repopulating with more vampires. Jack has recreated. He will be immortal for another hundred and thirty years.

"And the last one. The one who calls himself Loki. He's the one I want. The one who killed my husband."

"We have to kill them all, Purity, not just Claude. This is not just about revenge."

"I know, O'Donald. But I want him first. Before I do anything else."

Before I could explain to her that we would take them as we could get them, the stage door opened.

We had managed two purposes in hiding here. Avoiding the audience as it left the theater and lying in wait for our enemies to emerge. The cast came out in groups, singly and in pairs. I could scent their blood and they were all human. Jack and Claude still chose well. These were beautiful men. They eventually trickled down to just a few and then no one else exited.

"Do you think they have another way out, O'Donald?"

Shit! I should have thought of that! There must be more than one way out of backstage. And just as I was about to stand from our hiding spot, the door opened again.

I could smell no blood. Vampires cannot scent one another. It is the very absence of aroma that exposes us to each other. This guy had no scent!

"He's evil."

Purity had no chance to say more before he took off in a wide arc past us and down 6th Street.

"Hold on!" I grabbed her and introduced her to the floating technique.

This was a relatively new undead we were following. One of Jack's boy toys. Or Claude's, I just realized. Even he would be able to create an apprentice. This one had speed, but no knowledge of his powers. Not too smart yet, but still deadly. Very like Claude.

We bounded just far enough behind and over him to keep him from scenting Purity. Not that he would have paid too much attention to her blood unless he was desperate or had already fed.

The hunting vampire can only stay strong with the blood of the same sex. Baum and White had described them as *hemo*sexuals. It was as much the hormones in the blood as the blood itself that mattered. Only a strong, virile young man could keep a male vampire young, virile and strong. Just as the females of our kind needed human women.

Baum and White had told me the story of a young, noble Englishman, Edward Graymore, who was transformed by Phillipe at Charnac. It turned out that young Graymore was not homosexual, a situation Phillipe had overlooked, blinded by Edward 's extreme beauty. I had seen the reproduction of Phillipe's sculpture of him. He looked like a young Clint Eastwood. Clean, beautiful features forever frozen in time before they could grow haggard or craggy, tired or old.

Phillipe fascinated him, but not his overtures. Still, the vampire maker never dawdled over his feast and Graymore, a houseguest, was starting to exasperate him. Phillipe went into the guest chambers and overpowered him in his bed. He simultaneously fed upon and raped the young lord repeatedly, mortifying him unto his death. His final retribution for being spurned was to transform the youth. A bit of nastiness Jack must have learned from him. In his rebirth as vampyr, Phillipe told Graymore how he would need to secure the life's blood he would always require. Only through seducing other men—as young and strong and handsome as he had been in life—would he be able to heighten their normal hormonal secretions and, in drinking the enriched blood, remain eternally perfect.

Edward Graymore, lord and vampire, nobly refused. He went for his first few nights at the chateau not feeding. A dangerous thing. When he could stand the craving no longer, he was sent out. He had no trouble finding a homosexual young male and went with him back to his lodgings. The sight of the well-built naked man did nothing for the nude apprentice vampire. But the scent of a hungering vampire is like an enhanced pheromone. The magnified sexual aroma had the requisite effect on the human. But Graymore was appalled by the man's erection. Disgusted by his

ministrations. The kisses and the hugs, the tickling and the tongu-
ing. The grappling and groping.

Graymore broke the young man's neck, then tore at his throat
and drank. Naked, he reclined atop the naked man and experienced the ecstasy of the vampire. And when he pulled away and
acknowledged where he was and with whom, he also noticed his
own sturdy tumescence. And vomited blood.

He barely made it back to Chateau Charnac. He had not retained
enough of the human's blood. Still, in his weakness and disgust, he
cursed Phillipe, his maker. With each epithet, each malediction,
Phillipe became more enraged. Young Edward cursed his savior
even as he begged for salvation.

Phillipe brought him down to the worn stone staircase to the
Roman baths, carrying him like the sickly newborn he was. He
stepped into the hot water with his charge. Once submerged, he
undressed them both, tearing away their clothes. Graymore could
not fight.

The young lord was still erect from his earlier encounter and
Phillipe greedily took advantage of it. He knew it was a further torment. The undead can find no release from their tumescence but in
the sleep that mocks death. The torture was deliberate.

Why don't you kill me? These were the last words of Edward,
Lord Graymore as told to me by Baum and White.

Gladly, was the response he received.

Phillipe did the unthinkable. He was the only hunter vampire in
their history to commit such an act. He sunk his experienced fangs
into the neck of young Edward. And drained him of vampiric
blood.

Taboo. Forbidden, unthinkable. No undead had ever fed upon
another. Not even a master vampire like Phillipe.

And doing so drove Phillipe mad.

Purity was still caught up in my narrative when she looked
down to the street below her.

"There!"

I dropped to the sidewalk on Joe W. Brown Drive. There, between the Hilton, the Country Club, and the Convention Center,
our vampire had found his victim.

In his assault of the young man, this new vampire rid himself of
his black leather duster and the hat that hid his face from us. A little half-naked redhead! This was not the big blond from the performance. Here was yet another vampire.

I concealed Purity in an architectural recess of the building where we alit. Twenty yards, perhaps, from this nosferatu and his victim. I flew off and dropped to his side.

"I would stop doing that if I were you."

Corny? Probably. But I had used worse lines on perps when I was at the Tenth. Good cop, bad cop, painfully humorless cop.

"Get back!" he insisted, his speech distorted by the emergent fangs and glotted blood.

A feeding vampire makes an ugly expression. I probably did too, but I fed alone. Yet despite that, this was one cute-looking undead. I wish I had seen him alive.

I took his right wrist in my left hand and peeled him off his prey. He was cute no more. He dropped the guy and threw himself at me.

Was he still smelling the vic? Or did he not see me for what I was? Either way, he could not tell he was outmatched. He threw his head back to reveal his fangs, so I threw open my jaws to show mine. Size matters, especially in this. And I won the tale of the tape. Like any other vampire, I could make my fangs appear at will; I never needed to do it in public before. As I had grown in strength, they had grown in size. Quite impressive, even to the rare discerning eye.

But this little redhead with the killer bod was none too smart. He attacked me. I was bigger, stronger, faster, and better trained. It took me little time to subdue him. But even in my steely bear hug, he continued to fight me. He thrashed his head back and forth whipping it into my cheeks from side to side. He kicked at my kneecaps and scratched my forearms.

"This would be a good time to help," I called out into the dismal emptiness of this space. I had already started to notice that no part of Vegas was empty for very long. Hookers and vagrants, misguided tourists and drug dealers haunted these streets more constantly, more extensively, and more densely than in my hometown. The Strip might be the beaten track for the common tourists and the regular players, but there was no off place away from it. Constant traffic, vehicular and ambulatory, was as part of this town as poker chips, Elvis impersonators and quickie weddings.

"Precisely my plan."

I knew we would not be alone for long. I was just surprised by the interloper's speed and silence.

Apollo did not bother to sneak up behind me, so sure he was of his superiority.

"Good evening, Michael." A step.

"I am surprised to see you looking so well." Another.

"I am more surprised to see you at all." And closer still.

And time and I stood immobile.

He still looked enough like Jack to me, this "Apollo," to satisfy my discomfort. Bigger, yes, and more flagrantly muscular, but the same beautiful fiend nonetheless.

His hair framed his face and neck and reached for his shoulders. The streetlight made it gleam like a golden halo. Lucifer. The shining one.

His cowboy boots clicked intentionally, concrete against leather. Tony Lama's. His black, glove leather jacket purred against white cashmere turtleneck and crisp blue jeans. These were good clothes, but not overly expensive. More like mine.

Wait! Exactly like mine! Exactly the point!

Jack had seen me in the theater and duplicated my wardrobe. I was whelmed, but not overly. I shifted my gaze to Purity and saw what he had planned for her to see. She could not tell us apart. He played the "twin card," and successfully. Damn!

"Purity!" And I knew at the moment I called her name that it was a fatal mistake.

Jack turned to exactly where I had called. She was not hidden well enough from a vampire's sight.

"Servez-moi, mes enfants," he called to the shadows, to the deep recesses denied light. *"Servez-moi et l'obéissez."*

Small dust devils rose from the shade of the buildings, from the dim alcoves, from the darkness, from the gloom. Trash and refuse merged in the umbra. All manner of detritus rose from unconscious abandonment to reach through the penumbra for the light.

Better than my feeble attempts, nearer to Noel's grand accomplishments, Jack had formed a horde of golem. From the ashes, from the dust. Mindless they were and bent on destruction; they drifted with casual sentience to Purity. With the lazy intelligence of low-level gangland assassins, they moved on Purity with sluggish intent.

They formed into creatures at least ten feet tall, yet they were as incorporeal as whirlwinds. They had objective, but only the suggestion of form. Grayish tornadoes with glints of perception that lit them from the interior.

I attempted to move toward them, to intercept them before they reached Purity, but Jack prevented me. The last thing I saw of Purity was the curtain of fear that lifted off of her face. She had an idea, a good one. She was not afraid. Then I heard the first crack. Jack had grabbed me and broken my right wrist. I released the red-head.

Purity called to a protective spirit.

"Hear me, O Tharsis. Look favorably upon your supplicant and grant my prayer."

Purity was calling to one of the elemental angels. The Archangel Tharsis who ruled the waters.

From out of nowhere, an unseen cloud burst and deluged this small strip of Las Vegas with rain. Purity had surmised correctly. Jack's creatures were born of earth, wind and fire. Only water could contain them.

The angered Jack broke my hip.

"Shoot!"

It was less than a second.

Less than a second for me to look from Jack to Purity and to Jack again. Less than a second for her to react to my voice instead of my image and adjust her cuff out of the way of her concealed weapon.

It took less than a second for Jack to again play upon me, for Purity to shoot. For the dart—rosewood tipped with pure silver—to fly from her wrist and into the chest of the apprentice vampire. Less than a second.

And in that piece of time, that tiny piece of time, all the players committed to the scene.

Our human victim—for whatever his occupation in this rough neighborhood on this cruel night, he was still an innocent—shuddered and rattled into a personal association with the afterlife. We had lost him.

The fledgling vampire. He was neither fast enough nor alert enough to withdraw his master from the path of Purity's deadly dart. Instead, he threw himself in the way. The inch-long, solid silver tip embedded itself between his clavicle and his nipple. Four inches of shaft showed. More than three inside of him. Purity had missed his heart, but found his core.

His fangs pulsed in a palpable reflection of his agony. The argent sickness had already claimed him. The twinkle left his glittering green cat's eyes. His pupils dulled from hypnotic black diamonds to a cruder, colder gray. No longer enticing succubus, he no longer controlled invading stimulus. The dart's tip had surely poisoned him as its wooden shaft had rendered him unable to fight off the onslaught.

As I released my grip on him, Jack increased the pressure on me. We all watched him fall to the ground, Purity, Jack and I. Each sensing his pain.

The moon was full. And in its fullness, filled him. Lunacy made apparent, made flesh.

"Cody," Jack whispered. And we knew his name.

He screamed at the sound of it, at the aural assault, and we knew his pain.

His eyes grew wide and wider still, as if he were not merely looking at the lunar plane, but absorbing it. His jaws widened, displaying his sharp and deadly fangs. Pointed, now pointless, incisors nevermore to inflict themselves on an unsuspecting donor. Never again to pave the path to immortality.

And as I watched him in my pity, Jack squeezed my frame, shattering each breakable bone—humerus, rib and vertebra.

Purity moved quickly and tossed a small glass vial. It shattered near us. The smell—rose attar and garlic juice—rose like a cloud from the street. Not just the scent. The odor, invisible, took actual form. It loomed over us both. The form developed physique. Through Purity's magick, it had become a life form. And, as one in essence repugnant to us both, it had become a threat.

Purity had created a magick that protected her as it threatened Jack. Cream and red in color, it already had the look of battle-scarred flesh. Jack would never deliberately pass through it. Nor would I.

The Red Witch spoke through her creation, "Release him!"

Jack knew this human woman had outmaneuvered him. She had created a magical shield, one he could not penetrate. She had effectively neutralized his progeny. The golems were again garbage. The fledgling was already lost in a hallucinogenic web of extreme synesthesia. The former weatherman had yielded all control.

He tossed me, through the creature, sixty feet or so to Purity's feet. I landed, crumpled, collapsed. He scooped up the vampire called Cody like a child.

"We will meet again, Michael. And the witch as well. Run if you will, I will follow and find you. You have taken what was mine!"

And just like that, they were gone.

I looked up at Purity who was standing stock-still.

"You did good," I told her.

And she doubled over away from me and retched.

"Purity? I need you to buck up now. Get ahold of yourself. We have to go and I need you to help me get away."

She straightened and reached out for me.

"Careful," I told her. "I have a lot of broken bones and I need to heal correctly."

"What should I do?"

"First, stand aside."

I turned my attention to her disgorge and commanded it to burn. I looked at her puzzled eyes.

"When the police get here, I don't want them to lab test your last meal. The DNA will prove that you were here."

"That's a long shot."

"Not long enough."

"But we have to . . ."

"Purity," I started, knowing what she was going to say. "We can't stay and wait for them. This guy's been murdered. They'll hold us for questioning. I can't stay out that long!"

"But we have a responsibility!"

"Yes, we do! But not to these cops. Do you really want to point the finger at Apollo and Loki and get God-knows-how-many more people killed? We can't involve anyone else in our fight, Purity."

I saw submission in the subtle slump of her shoulders. She hated it, but she would go along for the greater good. We heard the sirens. Someone had called 911 and we were about to have company.

"O'Donald, what should I do?"

"Grab me under my arms and around my chest. Levitate and I'll do the rest."

Purity learned the floating technique fairly easily. I had not thought it was something mortals could learn, but Purity was not your everyday human. She improved on the bounding technique and the long-and-low technique by effectively marrying them. And in doing so, achieved what even Phillipe had not.

Purity St. Martin could fly.

chapter

13

If the magical charm and corporate precision of Disneyland were married to the surreal debauchery of Bourbon Street at Mardi Gras and then shoved inside a small-town America neighborhood's Fourth of July block party, the result might compare with the Fremont Street Experience in downtown Las Vegas.

A ninety-foot high electronic canopy made of more than two million lights roofed Fremont Street for four city blocks. Coupled with a half-million watt sound system, it was the largest light-and-sound show in the world. This open-air pedestrian mall provided nonstop entertainment every night from revue-quality singers and dancers to plumed and sequined showgirls to country-and-western hoedowns. But, The Experience wasn't the only show in Vegas to start daily at dusk.

They marched in from Main Street. Black leather boots marked their progress in steady percussion. Apollo and Loki had dressed identically, a grisly, glorious Gemini. Their black leather dusters surged around them like rising storms. The voluminous coats and skintight black leather trousers framed their naked torsos. The softness of the glove leather emphasized their hard, muscular physiques, while the dark color accentuated pale skin. Even on this jam-packed pedestrian promenade, the duo commanded space. Under a panoply of light, they shone.

It was not simply a walk; Apollo and Loki were a parade. They sauntered to the supplied music—the Supremes, Smokey Robinson and Aretha Franklin—as if it were chosen just for them. They strutted with the tribute to Elvis and other Vegas legends. They swayed to country music and classical music and rock. They imitated the jugglers and mimes, kidded with the clowns and stilt-walkers. They drew a crowd into procession from Main Street to Las Vegas

Boulevard, as was their intent. Not just consciously for who they were, but instinctively because of what they were.

Past the hotels and casinos, the retail shops and souvenir stands. Past the stages and kiosks and carts. Apollo and Loki led and the people followed—tourists and locals, performers and spectators. The black leather dusters billowed, wafting their scent as a lure to men and women alike.

Then, at the intersection of Las Vegas Boulevard, they turned back to face the crowd. And simply disappeared.

Some thought that the lights from the Space Frame strobed for a moment, giving the magicians a planned moment to escape. Others imagined that they got into an awaiting vehicle. One way or another, the mysterious magicians were on everyone's tongue again. And again in plain sight, hid the truth.

A moment later, the pair walked into Sulfur Sally's, a saloon about two blocks away near Carson and 6th. Sally was behind the small bar as always. Telling her story, as always, to a bar crowd more fixture than customer.

Sally had come to Vegas in the Swinging Sixties to audition as a showgirl; she had bleached her hair platinum blonde for the occasion. She wore the requisite bathing suit, also new, under her light coat. She wore her highest heels.

"Take a number and stand over there, Blondie." The line had become classic.

Sally had arrived for her scheduled audition to find dozens of other hopefuls lined up around the outdoor pool, each waiting in the searing sun for her chance to be inspected by Anthony "Loverboy" Lavellia.

But Sally hadn't forfeited everything in Norman, Oklahoma, just to become a number. She paraded over to the pool, kicked off her shoes, dropped her coat and dove in.

"Gedda hellatta dawarder!" She loved doing her impression of Loverboy, even after all these years. At first, in thanksgiving, then as parody, and finally, kaddish.

"Make me!" she still said with the same coquettish eyes and pout.

"Ya can't sign no contract soakin' wet, Blondie!"

Sally swam over to the ladder and slowly came out of the pool. She flicked her hair in smug rejoinder to the gaping stares of the other applicants. She refused the towel one of them offered her and put her hands on her hips saying, "What are you staring at?"

Loverboy came over with a towel and held it up to her.

"Ya coitins don't match ya carpet, dollface."

Sally laughed so hard she couldn't finish her story; she almost had to put down her drink. No matter, everyone in the club had heard it before. None of them was young anymore. It wasn't so much the story, but the telling of it that was funny anyway.

Sally had made her white bathing suit herself, but hadn't remembered to line it. Once it got wet, it became transparent. And once you could see through it, you could tell she wasn't a natural blonde. Collars and cuffs.

But if that was a surprise, her hair was a shock. As it dried, it turned a greenish blonde. The effect chlorine had on peroxide. Not a soul would come near her. Only Loverboy.

He came up to her with a contract for the show. He asked her name. Like a schoolgirl, she gave her last name first. Suffern, Sally.

"Sulfur Sally?" And the chlorine chorine was born.

She stayed with Loverboy's show until her lack of talent for singing and dancing became overly apparent. She stayed with Loverboy until it was also apparent she move on. He set her up in her own little club where her burgeoning abilities as a raconteur thrived. Sally continued to temper her peroxide job with a little chlorine rinse, keeping her hair the same shade of "sulfur" blonde. But these days she also had to dye her other lucky charm. Just so her carpet never matched her curtains!

"Hiya, boys," she said to Apollo and Loki as they made their way through the barroom, past the old regulars. She had no idea who they were. She never knew any of the young men who made their way through her sad and unintentionally retro club and descended her secret back stairs to the private club below.

Brimstone.

Members only. And to become a member, you had to be invited by the owner or another member. You had to be handsome. You had to be gay. And you had to like sex—lots of it and all kinds.

Apollo and Loki pressed the discreet little buzzer at the bottom of the stairs. The large tufted red leather door opened. They joined the doorman in his small, blazingly bright antechamber. As big as they both were, he was larger still. They could hear music muted by another tufted door.

"Keys?"

The magicians produced two gold-colored plastic keys, each bearing a magnetic strip like a credit card.

"Sponsor?"

"Derringer," they both answered at once.

The big bruiser confirmed the authenticity of the cards and reached for the doorknob of the inner door.

"Derringer is inside, gentlemen. Enjoy yourselves."

He opened the door and the music instantly became ten times louder. They stepped inside and the door was sealed behind them.

Brimstone was designed to test newcomers. The hallway was bordered with one-way mirrors, so that the members could preview arrivals. The lighting was intentionally too dim to proceed without assistance. Apollo and Loki played along.

"This way, gentlemen," a second voice requested.

Both Apollo and Loki saw him perfectly in the apparent darkness. He was not as big as the first man, but much more handsome. He was naked to display the obvious reason for his employment as aperitif. Apollo and Loki looked at each other and smirked, their cat's eyes glittering in the dark.

"What was that?"

"What?" Loki asked.

"I thought I saw something flicker. It's gone now."

Even with narrowed eyes they could see their guide's puzzlement. Without his speaking, knew of his intent to check the lights for loose connections.

"Brimstone is a private club for professional men. If you are accepted after this initial meeting, your dues will be paid immediately and only once yearly. There are no clothes allowed inside the club proper," he instructed. "By coming with me to the changing room, you agree to our terms."

"Proceed."

The guide opened the door to a well-appointed changing room. The red lights were a higher wattage, but just barely. The walls, like the doors, were of tufted red leather. The furnishings were dark mahogany. He walked over to one wall and explained, "These are individual lockers. Each member gets a numbered key and a code name for protection. No member can wear any clothing past this point. No member may refuse the advances of another member. No sex act is forbidden."

He turned, as he always did at this point, to see what effect his instruction had on the new guests. They were completely naked.

It is disconcerting for one who has worked his entire adult life towards physical perfection to encounter another who is utterly perfect. Overwhelming to encounter two at once. Hunter Daniels stopped still. He couldn't move, couldn't breathe. The room was getting warmer, growing dimmer, closing in. The magicians—he recognized them—came closer.

He couldn't tell which was the more beautiful, more perfect. The big blond was stunning, like a classical statue come to life. His muscles, his skin, his hair, his face, his voice—all beautiful. He absolutely was the Sun God. He moved as beauty does in a dream.

The dark one touched his face and Hunter turned in slowest motion. Sexual tropism. His experience had corkscrewed from buoyant frisson to carnal quagmire. Time had become a palpable force; desire, a physical hunger. If the blond was pure grace, this one was sin in waiting. His green eyes had a gravitational pull. His deep, full lips parted in unspoken promise. He shook his head and Hunter could smell a scent released from his hair. It called to him. Peaches and olives.

Hunter came closer to Loki, drawn by the scent, the warmth, the beauty. He bent down to nuzzle the dark one's hair on head and cheek and chest. The hairs were like sentient cilia; they seemed to reach for him, cleave to him. Loki raised his arm and rubbed his armpit on Hunter's face.

"That's enough, gentlemen."

Apollo and Loki turned to see the intruder. Their movement had the quality of fantasy, each effort caught at its most perfect moment. The deliberate action captivated the new arrival. And he was drawn to the room's enhanced scent. He drew back to dispel the illusion.

"Please come inside. Welcome to Brimstone." The words fell in hollow echo as if he could not himself believe them.

Loki responded first.

"I'm not finished in here yet." He indicated the attendant who was kneeling before Loki, his face buried in the young god's pubic hair.

"Hunter, get up!"

The attendant fell backwards as if out of a dream. The dressing room cooled, brightened.

"I'm sorry! I don't know what happened."

"Take a break. Tell Isaac to take over for you. You gentlemen come with me please."

As he led them out of the changing room, the very handsome man with the coppery bronze skin said, "I am called Apache. All members choose an alias when they enter."

"I assume 'Hunter' is taken?"

Apache stiffened. He was not accustomed to being challenged. Certainly not in his own club. But these two famous beauties would add stature to Brimstone, so he let it ride.

"The employees use their own names for legal reasons. It is cause for expulsion to touch an employee. They are here to work. Accepted?"

Loki grabbed the handsome Native American in a very intimate way. He massaged Apache's cleft with that state of physical excitement both vampires had achieved by feeding before arriving. His attentions were not unwelcome. Lust and loathing on the same coin.

Apache arched his back to press it against Loki's chest and belly, a stimulus response. He clenched the dark one between his largest muscles. He reached back with both hands to cup Loki's buttocks. It was like intimacy with a fevered stone. Never again would Apache think of hot and hard in the same terms.

Apollo moved around before Apache. Together the magicians bent him to receive them both. And at their command, the lights flared bright.

All around the large and well-appointed basement room, naked men stared at the trio. This broke tradition. Apache, as the club's owner, had never before engaged a new member, much less two, before introducing the others. Whatever their occupation prior, dozens of naked beauties stopped and watched in admiration and jealousy. The music overwhelmed them all. Cool jazz on hot flesh. Soft blues and red leather.

Apollo turned to the nearest nonparticipant and said, "Come."

A simple word, a siren's song.

And Keith Hawthorn, the big, boyish, ob/gyn who went under the nickname "Captain America," joined him. Dr. Keith's all-American good looks were in direct contrast to the exotic group he joined. At six-two, Captain America had light brown hair cut conservatively short and baby blue eyes magnified by gold-rimmed glasses. He worked out as much as his busy schedule would allow, exaggerating his muscles to make up for his other, more personal smallness. He had the look of a shy choirboy and his look was deceiving. As any member present could attest.

Keith came up behind Loki and inserted himself without prelude.

Adding another tonal layer to the living sculpture, the café-au-lait, professional center fielder, Andre Douglass, slid on his back under his favorite partner, Apache. The other members called him "Genius" for his inventiveness. And he displayed it well. Chisom—a famous Hollywood actor who could ride as well as he was ridden, Columbus—always first in discovery, and man-about-town Derringer joined in. Solos joined into pairs, pairs merged into groups, and the groups married the main. All linked as one in response to Apollo's call. In no time, they had become one complex chain of debauchers stretching out and folding back upon itself. A grunting, groaning, undulating, muscular body of desire and need, assault and receipt.

Apollo looked to Loki and nodded. It was time. Together they chanted, low and slowly:

"Lo, Barbatas, I set loose my shaft, my shaft finds his target and makes the Moon to rise;

"See, Nuberus, I fire my arrow, my arrow's tip buries itself and makes the Sun to shine;

"Behold, Gusoyen, I propel my lance, my lance finds its opening and makes the Stars to glow;

"Attest, Spirits! Not Moon nor Sun nor Stars shoot as I shoot, shine as I shine, command as I command!

"I pierce the flesh of men! I pierce their hearts! I pierce their minds!

"Their souls are mine, by the power of my rod!"

And with their final word, all present were bound in mutual climax. Each thrashed in concert with all others. Every individual moment of ecstasy was felt by all. Their communal cry was a primitive "so be it," an agreement envoiced from their basest part. They were bound to Apollo and Loki and to each other as well.

After a moment, they slowly began to move. And with regret and with reticence, disentangled themselves from one another. They rose from their prone positions, still clutching and cuddling, and looked upon their gods in languorous afterglow. Some whimpered still or sighed. Some clutched furtively, fruitlessly, for the passion to continue.

"Have I made you jubilant?"

"Yes, Apollo." He had passed the need for introduction.

"Will you continue with us?"

"Yes, Loki." He had joined Apollo's ranks.

"Will you remain with us always, remain like this always?"

"We will."

"Then follow."

Apollo and Loki moved towards the dressing room. And without question the others joined them. Wordlessly in afterglow, each unlocked his closet and dressed. Foregoing the showers, all carried the tang of recent sex.

They emerged at the top of the stairs in Armani and Varvatos, in Brooks Brothers and Prada, in Gucci, Zegna, Klein and Lauren. And each expensive outfit, every costly fabric reeked like the fitted sheets of a by-the-hour motel. Sulfur Sally's aging clientele had never seen "the boys" looking so disheveled, so crude. The men tramped through the dingy barroom and onto 6th Street. They left behind Jaguar and BMW, ignored Hummer and Cadillac, disregarded Lincoln and Lexus, and walked south

The Vegas breeze, pre-sirocco, lashed their naked faces; faces buffed free of age-reversing lotion, moisturizer, face protector and pore cleanser by each other's flesh. They were oblivious to their wind-mussed hair—ungelled, unmoussed, unsprayed—as they marched behind their twin gods. They paraded down to Charleston and over to Paradise. Down Paradise and past Sahara, past Twain, past Flamingo, this was already the longest walk any of them had taken in Las Vegas. They not only ignored the first scuffs on Magli shoes and Fennix's, Mauri and Banfi, and D & G, they disregarded the pinch and crush of footwear not intended as hiking shoes. Blistering and then bleeding, they continued unswayed.

Parallel to the University of Nevada, they walked to the side of a non-descript building, opened the steel outer door and entered the Stoker. Force had joined ambition.

Bob Taylor, ever aware of his environment, was first to notice the invasion. He had been spared the physical assault of the mated gods in exchange for a psychic slavery. Opposites may attract, but only like recognizes like. And Maverick saw slaves.

He changed "Suck the Mainstream" by Bleakclown, without segue, to alert the attending clans of the arrival of their deities. The blistering music just halted, for a second only, but long enough. Then he slowly pulled into the flitting and fey opening of the overture to Felix Mendelssohn's "A Midsummer Night's Dream."

Each attending Goth sidled back to his parent clan like spiders retreating from daylight. The Clan Dracul stepped back to the bar.

moon. Shortly, none of us could die. It was not safe to go with John to Vows and Secrets, but at least it would not be fatal.

I led John out to the helipad and to the edge of the skyscraper. I had little time to teach him the floating maneuver; we could not be late for this performance. I held him across the chest with one arm and held his spine close to my sternum and belly. He remembered the position and responded. But not only did I no longer desire his backside, I could not get aroused by a dead man. John had lost his ability to produce hormones and without them could not attract me with a human scent.

"By the way, John, how are your teeth?"

He flashed his pure white, burgeoning canines at me.

"Perfect," he grinned in an all too boyish way. "I've never had a cavity in my life!"

And so, no fillings either. That is too bad, John.

"Fly with me, John!"

And we were over the rooftop and sailing through the velvet night.

I did not make this flight smooth; I did not want John to develop a liking for it. Still, I could tell that he was beginning to acquire some of the synesthesia and that the sensation of floating was being reinterpreted in his mind.

"Stay with me, John."

"I am with you, Mike."

"I need you to pay attention to *me*, now." I forcibly turned his head to make him fix upon my eyes. I had the greater strength, the greater control and the greater knowledge. I insisted to his mind. Me. Give your attention to me.

We touched ground on the side street opposite the stage entrance to Vows and Secrets. John began to recognize his surroundings.

"This is Park Paseo. That's the stage door over there."

"Can you get us in there, John?"

"Of course."

As I began to drift across the street, I noticed the clumsiness in John's step. He was not floating. This did not bode well.

"Are you all right, John?"

"Yeah, fine. Just a bit nauseous, I guess. Maybe I'm hungry."

I hope not.

Try as he might, John could not get the door open and I did not wish to attract attention by ripping it off its hinges or breaking it down.

"The performance must have started already. They don't like anyone coming backstage during the show."

"Is there another way in?"

John looked at me as if I needed to have simple things explained.

"The front door?"

They had planned this well. I would have to come in the way they wanted me to. No surprises. Well, I would have to make do.

We walked around the corner as I whispered my command to any mortals in the lobby. Sleep. And walked up the broad and shallow steps to the grand and oversize gilt doors. Something was different. This was not how they looked the last time I was here.

The bright gold had contrasted strongly with the deep, rich black when first I came to Vows and Secrets. Now there was a shabbiness to the beautiful ebony, a grayish patina. And the gold had cheapened to a dingy, brassy gilt. This theater was aging. Dying.

We stepped inside the nearly deserted lobby of the theater. And what was true outside was echoed within. The hint of bat's wings over the bars was suggestion no longer. These creatures loomed now with obvious intent. This was still a house of magic, but it had definitely become black magick.

The gleam had diminished from the bar tops, a griminess had shadowed the exquisite carpeting. Fleur-de-lis had hardened into sharpened spear. Even the air seemed clogged with dust and tasted of ash. This was a crypt.

We gingerly overstepped the bodies of the unconscious staff; their impeccable uniforms decayed into cheap costume. Their beauty faded as well. I heard the music emanating from inside the theater. I had heard it before. Baum and White had educated me well.

Love is like a rebellious bird.

It was a message meant for me, I knew. And knowing that, understood that they knew I was here. It was Bizet's "Carmen." The "Habanera." And I knew the next verse was just as prophetic.

The bird you thought to catch unawares, beat its wing and flew away.

But who? Was Jack meant to be the bird? Purity?

I tried the lobby door to the theater and found it locked. No surprise. We hurried up the grand staircase to the balcony and found the door open. I ordered the exterior lights out and we slipped into the theater.

All slept as the magick played out on stage. Yes, there were humans here; I could smell them. But, this theater was not solely populated with the living. There were other things about.

I looked over the railing and down at the stage. Once again, Jack's theatrics surprised, a bait and switch. What I expected to see was a scene from medieval Spain. Ghosts of Don Quixote and El Cid. But instead I found a very common and contemporary gay leather bar. Muted red and amber lights toned down by deep blue and steel-gelled supplements.

The stage was a cruel confection of leather, wood and chain. The bar "employees" and bar "patrons" alike showed no true emotion, no sense of worth. Of being. They moved listlessly in their mutual seductions, personal revelations. There was a sense of sexuality upon the stage, but not one that compelled. Not one that attracted.

There was a sense of danger in these leather-clad men. A violence seething below the stagnant surface. If sex were to be had, it would be cruel and sadistic. Joy was not an option.

They moved in intricate patterns. A true pavane, but lacking majesty in its lack of restraint. The strong mauled at the lesser. They carved a new scene by degradation and mockery, through pain and fear. An aggressor tore the clothing from a submissive and rammed him hard into the bar surface. Another at the prop pool table. Another over a stool. And another and another. The perfect symmetry and classic steps were replaced by more individualized and brutalized forms of flamenco and fandango, by bolero and tango.

Over the sweet sadness of the Spanish guitar solo, the stage of Vows and Secrets was torn apart and rebuilt by the naked dominators through cruel sex acts that mistook reconstruction for recreation. The contrived wooden walls transformed into the stone walls of a ruined castle. Its long bar, a pathway inside. The pool table became a sacrificial altar. And as the rapists finished their aggressions, Apollo and Loki made their joint appearance.

They, too, were dressed in leather, but with each step they took towards center stage, Loki's leather morphed into mail and armor. Apollo's into velvet and fur. And as they got closer, the chorus redressed. In their own armor now, the leather quite changed.

Trees, gnarled and saddened, grew from crevices and cracks in the far mountain backdrop. Moldy pennants and faded standards blew where pornographic posters once hung. The wooden floor changed to step-worn stone.

"I hope you enjoyed our little set change," Apollo traded for a rousing cheer. "We have a new magic for you. One I like to call 'Alchemy.' And for the first time on this stage, I will require another assistant."

This was it. This is what he lured me for. I turned to grab John and head for a safer space, but behind me was all emptiness. John was gone.

"You," he pointed. "Will you come and aid me in a simple magic?"

But he was not pointing up. I looked down to where his out-stretched hand indicated. Over the ledge and into the center of the audience.

There was Purity.

She rose solemnly, looking neither right nor left, down or over, to make her way across the row of patrons and down the aisle to the stage.

She was dressed in one of her lounging-around robes. A fairly simple affair, floor length with long sleeves and a v-neck that did not plunge very far. It was a dark raspberry color and made of crushed velvet. Her hair hung simply. She reached the stage and he guided her up the steps.

I had only just then realized that I stood silently watching, making no attempt to interfere.

"This will never do for this scene," Apollo told Purity, much for the sake of his crowing audience. There was no living man or woman moving in this congregation; they sat shock-still. He had indeed created a small army of vampires. They sat in groups of two and four. How many? Two dozen? Three?

"I will require a costume a little more pretty, a little more regal for this piece."

He waved a hand at Purity and she was transformed. Her hair shone like newly wrought copper as it plaited itself amongst gems and pearls. Her dress softened in color and texture and shrunk to fit tightly to her form.

Apollo threw his hand back and caught Loki, the dark knight. The heavy leather of his jupon and leggings and the carbon black metal of his cuirass and brassard, greave and tasset, thickened and grew. They took on a slick and leathery, deep green sheen. At hands and feet, his gauntlets and sabatons lengthened as well as they altered into razor-sharp talons. His helmet grew scaly too, the visor separating into two orbs of fire.

Loki's gorget and helmet grew longer into an alligator-like snout, bright white inside with massive yellowed fangs. And from behind his lengthening brassard, two leathery wings grew. A dragon, formerly Loki, filled the rear of the stage. The very menace that destroyed the castle and, I was certain, threatened to destroy Purity as well.

That was when I heard the clear, sad music.

Pavane for a Dead Princess.

This was not magick; I knew what this was. Murder.

I jumped down off the balcony and landed on the main floor. I raced past the grabbing hands of the not long undead to the stage. Purity was heading, unconsciously, to the altar. This could not continue. The closer I got, the closer she got to her doom. The demon dragon sat at rest, but only so long as the newly reformed sorcerer, Apollo, allowed.

"Stop!"

My shout reverberated the theater, flashing the lights. They all knew I was here now and they all knew why. And I damn well did not care. This was between Jack and me.

I jumped upon the stage and headed for Purity at its center, not realizing that I was the final piece to this puzzle. Here we had the evil magician, the demonic familiar, the bewitched princess. And then, before I realized, I saw.

First, my feet adhered to the stage. My perp shoes hardening into a bright metal. It grew up, overwhelming the legs of my jeans, making it nearly impossible for me to move forward. Up the material of my jeans' thighs, hips and waist. It devoured the trunk of my jacket. Hardened down my arms. I was encased in thick, inflexible, solid metal.

It was not until the metal overtook the collar of my jacket and started forming a captive helmet, that I knew what it was. Saw Jack's ploy.

Silver.

He had magically constructed a trap of silver! He did not realize.

I saw the smirk pull at the Merlin-like face he had created for himself. His eyes had positively ignited from the adulation of his fans. Both of us—Purity and I—caught at last, trapped by the superior power of Apollo.

In a flash, I threw my bare hands up to my throat and tore at the heavy metal armor. I rent the breast of the cuirass and threw chunks of the silver at both the dragon and the wizard. As I did, I turned my face to the audience and demanded of those standing, the undead, "Burn."

It all happened at once.

Although in this crowd, that did not much matter. We all saw each instance of time as a frozen moment. A snapshot instead of a film. Each grimace, every shriek, all movements strung together like a string of translucent pearls on the eternal necklace of time.

Initially, the apprentices just glared, doubting the strength of my abilities and daring my aggression within sight of their master. Their glare was replaced by confused wonder as inaugural, small bursts of flame emitted from wrist and shoulder, from foot and face. The tiny flashes reflected in their unbelieving eyes as they struggled to swat each other out. In horrified realization, they pulled apart from their confederates to save themselves from burning in communion. But the command was too complete for any one of them to save himself or harm another. The flame too hot, the conflagration too brief in its intensity. They went up like a magician's flash paper, their newfound abilities alone recording the destruction in an altered, elongated sense of time. The tyros fled the theater seeking relief from my magic, abandoning their gods.

In my peripheral vision, I could also see the simultaneous events onstage. With the novices gone, I turned my full attention to the weapons I had launched. Even as a mortal can freeze a selected moment in time, encapsulate it and confine it, the undead could all the more. I could see as nearly simultaneous the tearing of my armor, hurling its pieces and the other, accompanying horror.

Each silver slab sliced through the air as a blue-white whir that sang of destruction. The rightward chunk should have hit Jack first, but the dragon that was Claude slithered in closer. He sensed my attack even as I mounted it. He snapped back his spine in serpentine undulation even as he threw his ferocious jaws open and forward. The wedge of silver struck as he struck. And it tore into the leathery flesh of his left wing as he snapped his huge jaws over the recumbent body of the unconscious Purity.

Jack's Apollo-as-sorcerer took the smaller shim of silver directly into his gut. But even as he did, he stomped the stage floor with his magus's staff. The wooden stage rippled below us, erupting at my feet. It grew up from the floor and vined around my feet, my calves, my thighs, my hips. It thorned as it vined, vined as it grew. It caged me completely, a rose brier.

What feared silver could not do to me, a simple rosebush could. I was trapped as I could be in no other way. The armor protected me from immediate danger, but for how long?

At that moment, Jack returned to his original form, in the simple leather outfit he had first worn on stage. He commanded the mortal audience to rise, leave and notice nothing. In the same instant that Jack returned, Claude was himself again as well, and Loki no more.

I was also dressed as I was when I left the penthouse, but for the pieces I had torn from my jacket. I was in trouble now. If I moved, if I breathed deeply, the thorns would pierce. That would be sure death, if excruciatingly slow until the cycle returned the full moon.

But worse yet, Purity was nowhere to be seen. The dragon had swallowed her and the dragon was no more. Purity was simply, inexplicably, gone. I had failed to save another innocent life.

And worse had come to worst. The soft wrenching of inevitable life touched my ears. This magick had taken new form. From each nodule of the bush's canes, a shoot emerged. It budded and grew. With painful slowness, the petals opened and released their scent. It was more than heady; it was overpowering. It caught at my senses and bewildered them. I was blinded and deafened and left insensate. I was enshrouded in a soft pink coma. But, I no longer cared. I had lost Purity. I had lost. Completely.

chapter

17

He watched the captive open his eyes.

"Now, where were we?" It came as a disembodied, almost feline, utterance from the dark depths of their new location. Lazy, but with a calculated design. He knew movement would be Mike's reflexive reaction and he was not disappointed.

"Careful, Michael. You do not want to scratch yourself."

Jack watched from the darkness as Mike scanned his prison; neither moved. Mike was confined to a modified cage; the inch thick bars and crossbars looked to be set at parallels of four inches.

"Those rods are rosewood, Michael. They are the canes of the bush that trapped you."

This was no longer some wild plant, but a jail with design.

It encapsulated him in a perfect oval. Not a full sphere, it was elongated and fit him exactly. Close as a coffin. A deadly lozenge overgrown with thorns. Thorns that faced inward only.

"Burn," Jack purred to insure that Mike could see the fullness of his failure. Small stout beeswax candles vented his intent. Soft light bathed hard features. Mike could see just cage and captive, although he sensed a greater audience.

"The thorny capsule you are in is fit into an even stouter rosewood ring more than six feet in diameter. You can be turned in a complete circle. Then that ring, as you can see, fits into another, just larger, so that you could be spun horizontally as well as vertically. And finally, that one into two more in opposing obliques. My personal version of an armillary sphere."

Jack rose from the neighboring darkness and moved close into the glow that played upon the crafty cage alone. He saw the realization in Mike's eyes. And in that realization, the fury. Mike had finally seen the cage as no mere restraint, but as a play toy for a confirmed sadist. The confirmation lived in the cold gray eyes that absorbed, rather than reflected, the warm candlelight.

"You were protected from the thorns while you slept, Michael. But now that you are awake, you will have to protect yourself."

With a quick and smart jarring, the oval began to turn.

"Witness my subjects, Michael. Those you harmed with your gifts."

And with that decree, hundreds of candles sacrificed themselves to a common end.

The cage moved slowly, allowing Mike to view the apprentice vampires. Here was Jack's legion. Dozens of them looking like perfect ghouls. The flames he had visited upon them had destroyed much flesh. Oozing flesh and blistering boils suppurated with a glistening discharge. Human blood stained, dark red, arms and bellies, faces and thighs in an attempt to regenerate the dead army.

Eyes hung loose in fleshless sockets, teeth showed from cheekless jaws. Bone and muscle were revealed through patches of missing tissue.

Mike laughed.

"The bloodbath, I see, came *after* the inferno."

The cage swirled faster for his impertinence. Mike was compelled to grip with hands and feet, fingers and toes and push against the rose stalks in order to avoid the sleek, sharp thorns.

"Do not think to anger them further, Michael. They control your cage," Jack informed him.

"What do you want from me, Jack?"

"Want?" Jack softly padded through the shallow sea of his acolytes. He drew Mike's attention to the spots where his feet alit. And he gloried in Mike's repulsion.

The bruised baby vampires entertained themselves in various ways even as they witnessed the main event. They were coupled and grouped in the manner of an encounter at Brimstone and many of them were those same participants. Their blood-infused nakedness excited them, while the sight and condition of the captive, coupled with the perversity of their own nature, pushed them even further into cruel grottoes of sadism and masochism. They had become an undead allegory of a principle they could no longer recall.

And as they writhed and undulated, they unconsciously created an irregular walkway for their lord and master.

"I want what Noel would have wanted from your friend, Laura

Wilcox. What Phillipe would have wanted from your own lover, Teddy . . ."

Jack could see in Mike's eyes that he was beginning to understand the sequence.

"I want you to fulfill the promise of the grimoire, Michael, as only you can."

Jack watched as Mike's pupils locked. The subdermal deciphering of an age-old puzzle.

"Teddy wasn't necessary, was he, Jack? He was just there. Not someone in particular, just available."

"He was a diner meal and no more, Michael," Jack sneered as he turned his naked back to him. He knew Mike had seen his perfection. What Mike had done to him on the pier was of no consequence. Jack had found a way of regrowing his precious organ and he knew it tormented Mike. As much as the new, searing scar on his belly tormented him. Mike had given him another argent infection.

"But Laura! Certainly Noel saw her opportunity in Laura."

"She certainly would have, if she had read the grimoire while Laura was alive. To mock me, my mother destroyed her true chance at immortality."

"Then why kill her?" Mike shouted. The quivering sea of voluptuaries echoed the sound waves as physical writhings of their own. And in response, ordered the "rose maiden" to spin aggressively.

Jack's soft laughter betrayed no residual human joy. It bit like steel wool, scratched like Fiberglas, burnt like iodine. It tormented with a promise of a deeper laugh.

"I killed her because she would have killed me! I killed her because she had been hunting me for decades. I killed her because eventually she would have solved the puzzle! I killed her for the exact opposite reason to why I am going to kill you."

The silence in the room began as the small eerie reverberating echo of an Alpine pass. But, with time it grew, as all silences do. It developed into a gummy fog. Cloying in its false sense of security, clawing in its threat of eternal separation.

Again it grew with promises kept.

The sad silence of twenty minutes past the hour became a malicious mist, a fatal fog. A desperately primitive attempt to rejoin the clan. The lonely reassurance that you are foregone.

Michael O'Donald could not utter a word. There were none to

be said. Jack knew that Mike had come to the realization that he had lost everyone and everything that was important to him. That he was to be sacrificed for the purpose of finally destroying the world.

"You have one consolation, Michael. At least there would be no one left to remember you badly as the final betrayer of the human race."

He knew that Mike wanted to plead one last entreaty. Mike licked his lips and opened his mouth and . . . shouted "Ohhh . . . noooo!"

Jack had finished his procession and sunk into a divan pillowed with his devotees. Up from their midst they lifted the weak and pliable body of John Cabot Cox.

"Oh, yes, of course, you know each other, Michael."

Mike O'Donald shook his head slightly in the confines of his cage.

"Would you like him, Michael?"

Mike looked up with a hope that asked if Jack was brokering some sort of deal. But what sort? What did he have left to bargain with?

"Mister Cox is the same as when you last saw him. Drained of human blood, infected with vampire blood, but not yet of the undead."

He has not yet taken human blood!

"He has not yet taken human blood, Michael. But each day he grows weaker. There will come the day when what is left of him will not be worth saving."

"Again, what do you want from me, Jack?"

"I want to know what you did with your witch. Where did you place Purity St. Martin after Claude's dragon swallowed her?"

Mike stood immobile.

"She was completely under my control. There is a possibility, but the least likely, that she slipped away when the silver struck me. I just cannot make myself believe it. So, what I do believe is that either *you* removed her or someone else did. Either way, I want to know where she is."

He watched Mike's eyes. He watched Mike's skin. He watched for an indication, any indication—a twitch, a flinch, a pulse—of his knowledge of Purity's whereabouts. The witch was his enemy and needed to be subdued. But Mike was giving up no hint. Either he did not know or would not say.

Jack decided to force the issue.

"Hunter."

He watched Mike quake at the term. And was pleased. He knew without knowing that Purity referred to Mike that way. He enjoyed, even more so, Mike's reaction to the hulk who answered the call.

Hunter Daniels stood tall from the supine orgy. Six feet even and two hundred and five pounds of gym-blasted and sun-kissed beauty. The tiny patch of white skin rising from his scrotum up over his hips revealed his true colors. And inside the imprint of the smallest swim trunks flourished an even smaller patch of golden brown hair. The same bright brown of his neat sideburns, trimmed to the exact end of his earlobes, and hinted at in his pert moustache, his lashes, brows and in the sun-dappled streaks of his thick mane. Except for a faint, fair brush at each armpit, the rest of Hunter's body was strikingly hairless.

"Come."

Hunter went immediately to his lord and master. He nuzzled his huge form onto the couch made of Jack and John both.

"Attend!"

And he did.

Hunter paid his first attentions to the dissipating, but still attractive, form of John Cabot Cox. Just as he was instructed. And John reacted in a still-human way.

Jack watched his minions as they inadvertently tormented Mike with their mutual interest. And he watched Mike in his involuntarily suffering.

But the anguish had just begun.

Jack leaned over Hunter's thighs, much in the same way that Hunter's face was caught between John's. He hovered over Hunter's femoral muscle and struck. And in striking, drew first blood.

The scent drove the multitude wild. Virgin blood. Unmarked by any other vampire. Jack looked up and dangled before Mike his little toy. A small, sharp, stainless steel penknife stained with Hunter's blood. Just enough.

Jack watched Mike as Mike watched John. The scent and the hunger, both watchers knew, were driving the tyro mad. Soon, he would defy even his own master to take first blood.

"How do *you* feed, Michael? I do not sense in you a desire to take human blood. Still, you must feed somehow. Tell me!"

Mike shook his head almost imperceptibly and Jack could not

tell whether he was unable or unwilling to share his secret. Jack flashed his knife and struck again.

"Your precious John will suffer for your silence, Michael. Tell me or lose him."

Mike O'Donald sunk in his cage, the tips of the thorns pushed against his skin, nearly pricking.

His body language told everything. He had lost. He had not saved Purity. Could his honesty yet save John? He had no choice. He had to make a decision.

He began to whisper.

"I feed, Jack, as you cannot. You created the monster I am. The beast you are not. But it was a mistake, an accident born of arrogance. You did not recreate as you were created. You, because of your curse, must feed off of the blood of the living. I, because of mine, am *still* living. I never quite completely died. I am not like you."

Mike raised his voice just slightly. He had to have known that Jack could hear him. He was announcing now.

"Phillipe insured that he had drained you of your blood as he, in turn, had been drained of his. He was assured that you were dead before he supplied you his form of salvation. And you, in turn, became nosferatu exactly as he did."

He again raised his voice.

"But not me, Jack. I never went through that process. Not in that same way. It was your 'curse' on me. Remember? To leave me as an infected mortal. To leave me with the knowledge that my death would never release me. To leave me with the decision of when to die and the consequence."

Now he yelled. And the timbre of his voice made all things animate and inanimate shiver and quake.

"But you could not foresee what would happen later, could you, Jack? You never foresaw the addition of Noel's blood."

Jack's eyes flared. He had been lied to. And perfectly. But before he could demonstrate his anger, Mike continued in a loud voice.

"Nor could you anticipate Claude's deliberate disobedience. How could your ego ever envision a sycophant's betrayal? And of all the methods of rebellious destruction, how could you have known that Claude would choose the worst one and *suffocate* me?"

Jack's aftershock of anger was revealed to all the room. Club Stoker flared into vivid brightness, forcing Claude to cower in the draped shadows of the High King's throne.

That could wait.

But Jack wanted retribution and Jack needed release. He took his small blade of surgical sharpness and incised small pricks into Hunter's calves and thighs, punctured his buttocks and abdomen. Into Hunter's chest, he jabbed. And to his shoulders and biceps, pierced and punctured. He created a blood frenzy by his actions and prevented it by his will.

"You do understand the implication, Jack. Suffocation cannot kill a vampire. Claude did not know that, because Noel never really taught him. But, then again, Claude did not know what you had done to me on the pier. You never confided in him. He could not have known that I already had vampiric blood running through my veins. First, you deceived him and then, I deceived you. And finally, Claude double-crossed us both.

"And because of all the deception and double-cross, the arrogance and accidents, I did not turn into a simple 'hunter' vampire, one who must replenish his blood supply from the living. No, Jack, I do not need to feed as you do. I do not need to hunt at all. I am my own prize, my own salvation.

"You were right, that night of our first meeting on the pier, when you called me 'The New Orion.' Although, what I became was not what you had in mind. I am a different type. And it is all your own fault!"

"Scatter!"

Jack's seething command emptied the dance floor of the club. His acolytes fled his wrath, skittering backward across the floor as if in a movie played in a reversed and irregular speed. Some disappeared into the disk jockey's booth, a few hid behind the bar, others withdrew into the folds of the velvets and laces of the Brahmin's quarter. The rest melted into the shadow of the staircase.

Jack alone remained near the center of the floor, lounging on the pillowed divan. Alone with his toys, Hunter Daniels and John Cabot Cox.

He rose from them by no apparent physical means. And as he rose the candles brightened. And he never took his eyes from the eyes of Michael O'Donald.

"Feast!" he hissed, nearly spat, between his angry canines.

And with that word, he set John free and enslaved him just the same. It was not a feast; it was a fray.

John's fangs had been growing, uneducated, to a point past painful. And in their stinging numbness, he had no command. He went for Hunter's open wounds, his open mouth centered on the cuts. But his unwieldy, untrained incisors blocked him from satisfaction and tore ribbons of flesh from the formerly perfect form.

Each frustrated attempt brought Mike more misery and Hunter less hope. Jack finally got what he wanted. He saw how terrible it was for Mike to witness the slow and sustained murder of an innocent man, to watch another partake in the horrific method of sustenance that he had barely avoided, and to withstand the sight of a former lover descending to the final stage in an inescapable spiral to hell.

John Cabot Cox looked only into his master's eyes. But all saw.

A mortal's eyes might be called "sapphire blue," but the term was inexact in the human specification. In the undead, it was quite accurate.

John's eyes glittered like the gems they were named for. Their charm had crystallized. And as they hardened, his knowledge grew. John Cabot Cox knew what he had become. What he had lost and where he was going. And none of that knowledge pleased him.

"Michael!"

He flew as he shouted, having no control of either. He threw himself. He knew nothing of the purpose of rosewood. Nothing of what it could do to him or to its captive. He was upon the cage in a moment. The force of his disturbance pushed deadly thorns into the flesh of the one he loved. And in gripping the bars, he pierced his own skin with fatal barbs as well.

The scratch turned to itch; the itch, a burn. The burning grew into consummation. Nothing existed for John Cabot Cox but the sensation; the abstraction became reality. The tickling became prickling. Each prick, a new and different sensation. Burning became craving. Then thirst and hunger. A crawling, wriggling lust. A supplicated yearning. And as it itched, the inability to scratch became paramount.

He could not, would not, pry himself from the barbs. All John could do was stare into the eyes of Mike O'Donald, forever beseeching in mute interrogation, "Why?"

Mike's eyes began to fill with blood-tinted tears. Tears for those whom he had lost, tears for those he could not save. And through his tears, he looked into John's eyes as he slowly pried loose his fingers from the deadly thorns. He saw nothing of his remembered John Cabot Cox in those eyes. Nothing human, not even nosferatu. John had gone. He was lost in a world where Mike would soon follow. A world more taxing than that of the argent sickness. An inner world of tormented sensations where nothing existed but pain.

And as he levered his former lover from the apparatus that would eventually kill them both, he sensed a silent, horrid change in the cellar. John's own weight finally freed him from the grip of the remaining thorns and his ultimate disassociation caused him to fall to the ground below Mike's cage.

Jack stood alone in witness to the destruction of his kingdom. All of his followers had fled from him in fear. His own consort hid in distrust of his mercy.

And his doppelganger, his twin and key to immortality, slumped in the bottom of his cage, lethally wounded.

Slowly, he walked to the base of the cage and lifted the stout leather gloves from its base. He put them on and rotated the rings himself, lowering the center sphere to the ground. He opened the door and lifted Mike's body from his jail.

We must be quite the eerie image, he thought. *I, flushed from my recent feed and he, ashen from the rose poisoning. Identical in every way, but for our apparent health.*

"Still, Michael," Jack said aloud. "All will progress as planned. You cannot die until the next full moon. And I had planned on killing you then at any rate.

"Bring the tub," he shouted to his underlings. And the men of Brimstone, along with the vampretenders of Club Stoker, emerged from their concealment. Those behind the bar lifted the long aluminum tub as the others hurried to assist. None wanted to be left out, to appear to be unwilling, unhelpful.

Even Claude hurried from his self-imposed separation in a desperate show of faithfulness and support. He made great show of directing the placement of the tub, of his return to the position of co-command. As if nothing had ever changed.

Jack smiled at him. And again Claude was taken in by that smile. The sweet curve of lips that implied "you are loved, you are safe."

"Thank you, my dear, devoted Claude. Am I to take it that you will be first to aid me?"

Claude could not but answer, "All I am is yours." He had, again, been outmaneuvered.

Jack arranged Mike in the tub so that only his head was out of it. He positioned his damaged arms and pierced legs so that they sat as low as possible. He turned to Claude and took his hands in his own. In an unsubstantial part of a second, he swooped low and pierced with his distended fangs the medial vein of Claude's forearm. He darted with preternatural speed to the right arm and did the same.

Jack just watched as Claude stood in a stunned, silent amazement at the sight of his blood spurting into Mike's tub. Claude finally saw what ultimate betrayal looked like. And it was the stealing of one person's lifeblood to another's nefarious ends. And Jack knew that Claude could not see the irony in the theft.

Claude hated Jack for being a vampire. So be it.

Jack repeated the attack upon each of his subjects—mortal and vampire.

Soon the level of the dark liquid began to rise and cover the ashen form of Michael O'Donald. He remained unconscious in his poisoned fever, alternately shivering and sweating. Always emitting little groans. Calls to spirits he had lost, to Laura and to Teddy; calls to spirits he could not save, Purity and John.

"I will bathe him every day in our blood. It is vital that he be kept this way until I perform the necessary ritual. The one he and I were born to fulfill. Phillipe, the maker of vampires, searched in vain for his mortal twin over centuries and continents. Noel, my mother, the supreme witch, wasted all of her energy and time, when the very things she sought were always before her. They failed, but I shall not fail! On the warm, clear evening of the coming full moon, I will achieve what they both sought. I shall become one with the immortals and I shall rule the earth. You must all join me in this last rite. The ultimate ritual that will free me of human concerns. All of my people, those absent as well as you present, will assemble with me on the top of Sunrise Mountain. There, you will join me in the ultimate celebration of the Black Mass. Bind yourselves to me and I promise an everlasting reward."

Bathed in the glittering sensation of the communal affirmation and adulation, Jack failed to notice one who did not applaud. The single one who heard "I," when he was listening for "we."

chapter

18

Blackness surrounded me. Was it newly past dusk or was I still in that same, long darkness? I tried to clear my head, hoped for light, wished I could recall. Where was I? What was I doing here? And just where was here? I felt as if I should be doing something, accomplishing something. If I only knew what that was.

Had I been unconscious long? I ached. A thousand small throbbings delineated my frame. I thought I could remember lying very still, engulfed somehow in . . . something. There had been people around me and then . . . nothing. Damnit, no recollection, nothing at all.

Yet, even in this absolute, dank blackness, I could see. Well, not exactly see. Still, it was vision of sorts. Like a bat's radar sense, its . . . echolocation. Strange word for me to remember. It had to have meaning for me. Because I was not actually seeing with my eyes at all, but with my whole being. It was as if the synesthesia had mutated into a new and different sense. *Synesthesia?* There's another odd word. But this one I knew well. I'll take "vocabulary" for a thou. Hell, I'll make it a true daily double. I possessed this synesthesia. I could exchange and appreciate a single stimulus with all my other senses. And now, it was as if they were all collaborating to fill in for my inability to see in this enveloping darkness. My hearing and sense of touch worked together to create a sense of space. This was a large area, almost the size of a house. Taste and smell convinced me that I was underground. Was I in a basement? No. Although I could feel the dampness, I could also sense the soil, smell the blood. But didn't every vampire smell blood?

Vampire. Yes, damn me, that I remembered. And I rolled my tongue around my stunted fangs just to assure myself.

But, no, this scent was not blood! A very similar aroma, but inorganic. What smells like that? What is not blood, but still tastes like blood and is found in heavy, damp air and musty, dank soil?

Copper! Blood tastes like copper. That's it! Dark and dank and damp. Earthy and coppery both. Complete darkness with a heavy stagnation to the damp air. This was a copper mine.

But how did I get into a copper mine? And what else had I forgotten? I was developing a sickening fear that what I couldn't recall was exactly what I desperately needed to.

Wait! I remembered—was it recently?—seeing bright lights against an ink-black sky. Marvelous jewel-toned lights that glittered and twinkled. And sharp, shocking neon in awesome arcs and delicate arabesques. And as they glowed, they sang to me. And in their song they tasted of rare and wondrous fruits. Fuck! I was being distracted by the synesthesia!

I pulled myself back and remembered images. Shapes strange and familiar. Pyramids and gondolas, lions and pirate ships. And striking names. Names I knew—on huge signs. Place names! New York and Paris, Mandalay and Caesar's Palace.

Las Vegas!

And with that thought, in that instant, it all came back. Like a silent movie version of an acid trip, my life flickered and raced through my mind. Like a hallucination married to a nightmare, my memory retraced all of the horrors of the past months. First, in New York, then France. Back to New York and then, here, in Vegas. I remembered it all.

And then, Purity was kidnapped from the penthouse. And John Cabot Cox showed up as a vampire fledgling. Vows and Secrets. And then John disappeared. A magic act before a sleeping audience. Apprentice vampires applauding, admiring. And then burning. The dragon that was Claude. Purity, a sleepwalking princess. Jack as Merlin. Me in knight's armor. The magickal rosebush. And then, John again.

It was like a spinning wheel or a whirlwind. One of those crazy tilt-a-whirl rides—light and dark, up and down. Only occasionally would an image stand out and have meaning between the blasts of color and the gray vacuum. Purity: I lost her. To the snapping dragon. John Cabot Cox. I lost him, too. To the dragon? Yes. And yet, no. At least, not in the theater. Underground somewhere.

But not here. In that basement.

Somehow, Jack and Claude had moved me from that secret

basement, away from the spherical cage and the tub of blood. That blood! Mixed bloods of humans and vampires. I absorbed them into my wounds. What did that mean now? Now that I had absorbed blood. How had it changed me? Who was I now?

And then they hid me here. But where was here? A copper mine, obviously, but there were many of them in Clark County, close to the Las Vegas city limits. But knowing that did not really help. It was not so much the *where* that was important, but the *why*.

It had all come back. Losing Purity to Claude's dragon in Vows and Secrets. Getting trapped in Jack's magical rosebush. Losing John to its thorns in that basement. I was now truly and utterly alone here. But, damn it, I would not sit alone in the dark!

"Arise," I called in my lowest audible voice. I had not just remembered who I was, but what I was capable of doing.

From a radius of about twenty-five feet, with me as the epicenter, they began as vague wishes. Dim and dark honey-color, they grew as they rose until they were about the size of softballs. I saw them in front of me and arcing, equidistant, to either side. I was not ready to turn my head just yet. I did not think it wise to move until I knew it was safe. But since I could see seven of my plasmic, phosphorus creations, I judged there to be another five behind me I could not yet see. A dozen seemed right.

"Come," I whispered. A sound born of uncertainty. I was not sure I was alone in this cave. I was not sure of my ability to control these entities. Unsure of everything. Yet, they responded.

They had life. Perhaps, if I allowed it, personality. But I would not allow it. I was not about to play God. Not today anyway. Still, I did feel the responsibility of a creator as I watched them near. And enlarge as they neared. Slowly and steadily, they brightened as well. Paler now, a softer, brighter, yellowed honey, they also honored me with some warmth, although I was not aware I had wished for it. They might not have individual persona, but they had more graciousness than many I had known who did possess personality.

They ceased their advance at about six feet away and brightened to reveal why. I was in another rose cage; this one was a hemisphere like the domes designed by Buckminster Fuller. There was probably just enough room to stand. Maybe not.

"Come," I commanded them. And they approached my thorny prison. But as soon as their plasma touched the woody stalks, my jail reacted and grew inward, their lethal thorns reaching towards me. My living lanterns trembled with fear for me. Kind and caring? Well, I could solve this without upsetting them.

"Burn!"

I was fairly certain I saw my fellows recoil. Apparently, they were also more intelligent than I. My attempt to destroy my prison was greeted with angry rebuke by the cage itself. Not only did it not burn, but also decidedly disliked my intention.

It grew at a dazzling speed. Out of anger, I was sure. The individual bars that were touched by my creations curved inward towards me, their thorns growing longer and sharper as they did. This plant was retaliating! Reaching for me! I rolled backward in an attempt to evade them. I remembered too well their sting.

I scampered and got to my knees. I tucked in to make myself a smaller target, watching it as I did. I made a small sigil in the air. It shifted in avoidance as easily as a fencing master. Jack had apparently imbued it magically with some ability to protect itself.

"*Étonnant, n'est pas?*" Jack had arrived, silent as the grave. And the jail halted in recognition of his mastery. "Maybe not really as astonishing as all that, Michael. Did you know that rosebuds naturally recoil from a gardener who was about to clip it for a bouquet?"

I could do nothing but stare at him. He had, apparently, foregone his "Apollo" guise permanently and again looked just like me. He was dressed in a kind of monk's robe, like the one I had seen him wear at Charnac. Long sleeves that completely covered his hands, a hooded cowl that would have totally obliterated his head and face if he'd had it up, and a hemline that brushed against the dirt floor. But instead of completing it with a dye and fabric appropriate to a dour cleric, Jack's robe was of gold lame. You might take the vampire out of Vegas . . .

"Not that the human eye could discern the rosebud's movement," Jack continued. "But they have done elaborate, scientific tests to verify the fact. I would imagine that disproves the expression 'dumb as a plant,' doesn't it?"

"So, Jack, are you saying it acted like this of its own volition?"

"Well, maybe not entirely, Michael. There is only so much it could do on its own. I gave it a boost. It was to attack the practitioner, if magick was used against it. Self-defense, really."

"Yes, but yours or its?"

We studied each other for a quick moment. Neither of us all that pleased to be in the company of the other.

"So, what happens next, Jack?"

"Come, Michael," he said in a softer tone. "You know how this goes."

Jack moved closer to my prison. He was so sure he had the upper hand. He grew chatty and relaxed and spoke to me as if we were colleagues or old friends. He stopped before actually touching the rose cage.

"As we speak, the June moon is climbing in the night sky. Just before it reaches its apex, we will go out to greet the disciples and begin the ritual . . ."

"The ritual?"

"Don't play the fool, Michael. It's unbecoming to you. You achieved much in your fight against me. More than any other could have done. Content yourself that you saved your witch friend and go peacefully to the altar."

The altar . . . and the full moon. They mean something to me. Something I have read or seen. They are major pieces to the puzzle. But what? And what piece am I? And what did he mean about Purity being saved? We both watched Claude's dragon swoop down and swallow her whole. Purity was certainly gone. Why was he playing with me?

Just then, Claude neared the outer edge of the light. I could not tell if he had been listening to us or not; he wore his same vacant look of inexpressive beauty. It was a fearsome look, beauty undeserved. I had always unconsciously preferred the presence of a small flaw to point up natural beauty. Something that said: I have seen it; I have been there. Something like a crooked smile, crinkle-edged eyes, a cowlick.

Damn! I was describing Teddy. And all of a sudden, I felt weary and sad. I could not recall the last time I thought of him. My life mate, my soul mate. A perfect innocent. From back when I had a life, had a soul. I will never see him again. Still, I had made him a promise. But how, Teddy? How do I destroy these two? If only I . . .

Get him ready, Claude.

You'll have to remove the rosewood first, Jack.

What is this? I heard what they were thinking. How could I hear what Jack and Claude were thinking, if it was impossible for a vampire to read another vampire's mind? Baum and White said so. Right? Something really strange was happening here.

Look at him, Jack. He's really scared. He looks like he's trying to figure out what's going to happen to him.

He does look alarmed, Claude. Make sure he remains when I remove the cage.

"So, how you doin', Mikey?" Claude fully entered the light. Still an utter show-off. Claude had intentionally left his robe open and, of course, he was utterly naked beneath it, except for an odd, soft, leather belt at his waist.

"Just do what you came here to do, Claude. Kill me and get it over with. Just try not to fuck it up like last time!"

I saw the quick scowl that let me know I got to him. Even his erection seemed to bob a moment. Self-doubt. Good, I could work with that.

Cocksucker!

Enough, Claude! He is trying to rile you. Can you not see that? Get on with it!

"Okay!"

Claude said it aloud, but was it meant for Jack or for me? Maybe if I could keep him off balance, it would give me enough time to figure this out.

Claude stepped closer and as his robe swayed, I saw the reason for Claude's seemingly useless belt. It held a sheath. There was a fairly large knife in it. Stainless steel, by the look of the guard and the pommel, with a hilt of bone. An athame. Okay, I knew how this was going to play out. I had to go along until my moment. I had ridden in this rodeo before.

"Thanks to you, Claude, I have no one left and nothing to live for. You won. I have no fight left in me. Do what you want."

Even as I said it, I saw them enter. A dozen men, all beauties, in matching black monk's robes, entered this chamber of the cave with short, lit torches. Apparently, they had their instructions, for they went right to work.

Half of them handed their torches to the six others. They came up to the cage and began to unlatch particular panels. I could see then that it was a doorway of sorts. And, apparently, they were the ones who had sealed it, for they knew just how to open it. It seemed that the cage had been instructed to defend itself only from my magic.

They disassembled just enough of it to allow me to stand up and out of it. Free, I took a long look at Jack.

"Do not think on it, Michael. You have living loved ones. You wish them to remain that way, *n'est pas*?"

I knew what he meant and I could not risk my mother or sisters.

Killing them would be the kindest thing Jack would do. It would please them much more to steal their souls. I closed my eyes briefly, shook my head and smiled.

"Then, let us get this over with, Jack," I said.

"Here, Michael, this is for you."

Jack handed me a soft robe. It was exactly like theirs, but for the fabric and the color. White wool. A lamb for the slaughter? Jack should have known I was no lamb. A lion for the slaughter? Where had I seen that image before?

I dismissed the thought and put on the robe. I was grateful for some covering in this cool dampness.

The twelve black-robed men began the procession out of the cave and we followed, Jack ahead and Claude behind me.

It felt strange to be walking again. I was unsure of the terrain, of the direction. But for now, I was walking. Walking uphill and out of here. But, unfortunately, not alone.

I heard the sounds of other disciples in the darkness before me. They walked silently, but made inadvertent, natural noises. The whoosh of fabric. An orchestra of cloth. The shuffle, scratch of sandals. Leather percussion.

"I know something you don't know," Claude whispered to me. "And it will really ruin your day."

I turned my head to whisper back, "Is it that Jack left the rosewood cage intact? Do you think he left that for me?"

Claude shut up instantly. But I could still read his thoughts and they satisfied me.

The incline had grown steeper. And all was silent, dead silent. Then a new sound began and I sensed a much greater group of people and feared a singular intent. With a soft shift of my head, I slipped the hood back from my eyes. I feared making too obvious a gesture. I felt a breeze against my face. Warm and dry, but fresh, air. We had exited the cave.

In my distraction, I looked up into the inky, indigo sky. What lights!

The black celestial bowl was pricked and punctuated by bright, blue-white stars. God's fingerprint, Purity called it. They were dazzling and overpowering, out here, away from the city's fripperies. And they told a story, one important to me right here, right now. The same story the ancients had seen in them. In clusters and constellations, they related that story still. There, straight above, were Perseus, Andromeda, and Pegasus. Gemini was in the eastern sky and Capricorn was to the west. Draco was in the northern sky and Phoenix to the south. I knew this! This understanding was a gift from Charnac. This was Midsummer Night. The sabbat of Litha had begun. That accounted for the altar and the robes. They had come for the solstice.

But the single brightest light, blue-white, dominated the sky. The Mead Moon. The Honey Moon. If I remembered Baum and White's teachings, different cultures had different names for this very special full moon. The Rose Moon, the Strawberry Moon, the Rotten and the Windy Moon. It was even called the Dyad Moon for its associating two individuals as a pair. I was beginning to remember everything the lovers ever taught me. And Purity's contribution as well. And with the memory came understanding. And with understanding came strength. I knew what was to be done.

I looked down. We had exited onto a hillside. I could just make out other hills in the distance. I could see many dozens of like-hooded and robed members moving uphill in front of me. From the sound they were making, a kind of wordless chant, I could sense a great many more whom I could not see. There could easily be a few hundred in this strange group, about one tenth of whom carried oil lamps. But since the hillside was only brightened in those small patches of lamplight, I could not tell exactly how many had come.

Our march gradually slowed. The leaders of the procession, the black robes, had apparently arrived at their designated place. The leaders, as I had begun to call those men in black, made a circle at the summit. The large, handsome men dropped back their black hoods. They were big and strong. They worked at assembling a large, flat table from slabs of granite that had been left, hidden by brambles, in a heap at the apex of the mount. They positioned two long, rectangular slabs and two short, square ones to form a sort of box or frame. The very weight of the stones held them upright. I had seen something like this before. The twelve black-robed men hoisted the final long slab and placed it atop the frame, making a large stone table.

An altar! I had seen this before. This exact image.

Those below, those in red and gray and brown, increased their chanting. It was something I vaguely recognized. Like Gregorian chant, but not. This chant did not simultaneously elevate and relax one as the other did. This intonation seemed to have the opposite effect. It was constrained and yet agitated. Not contemplative, but vacuous. Void of emotion, yet full of intent.

And just then, the chanting increased. The black-robed leaders lit larger torches—eight feet tall—with their shorter ones. They positioned the torches as a long aisle, a pathway, and stood and waited.

But I moved.

The chanting grew as the torches flared. The torches flared as the moon ascended. And as the moon ascended to its apex, we approached the altar.

Jack, in glistening gold, and Claude, in a muted silver-gray, walked as if in a regal procession, bestowing glances and small smiles on their subjects. But they were not kings; they were jailers, for they held me between them.

Then, the chanting began in earnest. I could feel the tempo in the very beat of my pulse. This congregation was not calling to mere kings; they were beseeching demigods. Jack and Claude moved forward, alone, to accept the accolades.

A half-dozen of the black-robed supplicants went to the blond with the golden robe and another six to the dark-haired one in silver. They opened their masters's robes and exposed them to the congregation. They were perfect men. Their faces and bodies had attained a state of flawless beauty. They were more than mere men, more than flawless sculptures. They were godlike.

They acknowledged the chanted adulation of the crowd. They bowed, but in complete and obvious self-satisfaction. They knew who they were and what they wanted.

And now, so did I.

Twelve black-robed servants took me and led me to the altar. With six on one side and six on the other, they lifted me above the slab for all to see. The congregation cheered the sacrifice. For sacrifice was what I was. They all knew it. They all knew me.

O'Donald!

And I knew one of them!

Purity? Is that you? Are you all right?

O'Donald, have you traded yourself to Jack Courbet and Claude Halloran? Traded yourself for me?

Don't worry about that right now, Purity. Are you all right? How did you get here?

I'm fine, but I don't know how I got here. The last thing I remember is when Jack and Claude entered the penthouse with one other vampire.

You don't remember Vows and Secrets? You don't remember the magic show?

No, O'Donald. None of that.

You don't remember the dragon?

My God! I do! I do remember dreaming of a dragon attacking me.

That was no dream, Purity. It was Claude, magickally trans-formed. But, where did you go? Where have you been?

O'Donald, I have no idea how I got to this place dressed as I am. I have no idea where I've been, but I do know I'm going to save you. Or my name is not Purity St. Martin and I am not the Red Witch!

The men in the black robes stripped me of mine and revealed my ashen body with a multitude of small, still bleeding, punctures on my frame. They stood me, naked, upon the altar top. For all to see.

Oh, my God, O'Donald! What have they done to you? I've failed you.

Not now, Purity! I need you to do something for me now.

The congregants had grown louder and wilder in their revelry. They were singing aloud and twirling about, singly, in couples and in groups. Good! No one would even notice what would happen now.

You have a plan, O'Donald?

Yes, Purity, but I need your help. You must stay right where you are. Can you set up a protective shield between the altar up here and the congregation on the hillside?

I think so.

Don't think, Purity! Do it!

But what about you? You won't be inside the protection.

I know what I'm doing. Trust me!

I picked out Purity on the hillside. In a field of neutral tones, she was the only one in a wine-colored robe.

Still the "Red Witch," huh? Had to wear a red robe.

Honestly, O'Donald, I don't know how I got to be dressed like this. I don't know how I got here. One moment, Jack and Claude came into the penthouse, the next, I was walking up this mountainside. Now, be quiet. I have to work.

She threw her hood back from her head and her red hair glinted in the moonlight.

Careful, Purity, they might recognize you.

I have to reveal myself to the goddess, who is the Moon. She is Arianrhod, O'Donald, who rules over the space between life and death, who rules over reincarnation. She rules over this sacred night as well. Her dominion is over sovereignty and fertility and cosmic time. It was she who created the cosmic tapestry and wove lives into the weft and weave of the cosmos. Only she can return a soul for another life or send it on to another existence altogether. She is fate and she is fury. She is the goddess of a thousand names. And great is her strength that she could show her full face at the moment of the summer solstice. And now I must call to her, O'Donald.

Unheard by the noisy congregation, Purity beseeched her goddess aloud.

"Sacred Mother, called Selene, called Artemis, hear my prayer! As all sovereignty is yours to bestow or revoke, all life is yours to protect or expose. Grant me your strength! Give me favor that I may act as your instrument and retrieve what was stolen from you. Lay claim to the lives that are, by right, yours. And punish those who would usurp the privilege that is yours alone. So mote it be!"

Purity, quiet! Don't let them find you.

I feel the goddess, as I have never felt her before, O'Donald. My skin horripilates as each cilia, every pore, reaches out for her. I can feel my hair go static in reaction to her blessing.

She can well afford to reveal herself; you cannot.

Understood.

Quietly, Purity begged her, "Blessed Mother, she who gives me strength and purpose, shield me from thine enemies, that I may perform your works in shadow and in silence. I am but your supplicant and your instrument and seek no greater renown."

Still standing upon the altar, I prayed along with Purity and, for my reward, I felt Selene's silver smile upon my face. Then I felt another presence as well.

Purity? What's happening?

Do you feel it too, O'Donald?

What's going on?

For some reason, my feet feel as much a part of the ground as my head does of the skies.

Torn between them?

No, not torn, but shared, a conduit between equal forces. Arianrhod has called her sister to assist her.

What sister? Who? Purity, what's going on?

She is Gaia. She is Prthivi. She is called Geb and Coatlicue, Hou Ji, and Pachamama. She is called Bacabs and Papa and Midgard and Enlil.

And that was what I felt too. The Mother. Earth.

I felt her swell up from the ground, through the stone, and into my feet. Up and into the whole of me. She rose through me, filling me with her solid strength and surety. Her command and her patience. I looked at Purity and knew she was undergoing the same experience. The goddesses were truly at work, and we were merely their tools.

I watched as Purity lightly stomped her right foot and slowly lifted her hands from her side. And as she did, a mist rose from the ground itself. Quite faint, at first, then slightly denser. It grew, as translucent tendrils, up the legs of the communicants and covered like a dim, gossamer shield. And all throughout this mystical fog, tiny specks glittered. Like the faint motes that dance in sunbeams, these particles were the mingling of moonbeam and dust. The goddesses spoke together and made magick. I cannot believe that the vampires surrounding me could not recognize the enchantment, but they showed no notice. The magick was complete.

Jack took to one side of the altar and motioned Claude to the opposite. One naked vampire each on either side of me, they laid me down and stretched me full out. No one but I, it seemed, noticed the pale, glimmering cloud that encompassed the onlookers. No one else seemed to perceive the vague gray-black shadows that rose beside the altar and its celebrants. Jack nodded to Claude and he began.

"*Gratias Deo.*"

Then back and forth they traded rejoinders. And while they prayed, the fog grew thicker and the shadows grew bolder. Unnoticed.

"*Est Missa Ite.*"

"*Tuo Spiritu cum et.*"

"*Vobiscum Dominus.*"

I lay prone upon the stone tablet, my arms and legs extended over the edges. I made no sound or movement, but I was bathed in the blue-white light of the goddess as she grew into the full majesty of her peak.

"*Saeculorum saecula in regnas et vivis qui. Sacramenta refecerunt sancta et pura quem.*"

"*. . . Macula scelerum remaneat non me in ut et praesta . . .*"

"*Meis visceribus adhaereat povati quem. Sanguis et sumpsi quod Domine tuum Corpus.*"

Loudly and assuredly, they continued the Black Mass. This time they thought it would not be disturbed. They worked backwards from the Benediction; they would finish at the Introit. They spoke each word in reverse order, somberly and distinctly. Goaded by dark specters, invisible to all save me. I had to know.

Purity?

I'm here O'Donald. Can you still see me?

No, except for the immediate area, all has dimmed from sight.

Will they notice the magick?

I think not. These demons are quite busy.

But she was not aware that I spoke of other demons. The goddesses were sparing her for my sake. And the vampire lords continued with a violent cruelty that found reflection in the clash of the preternatural and the primordial.

Everywhere, small forks of lightning cracked into the foothills. Large groans of thunder filled the surrounding valleys. The scene was awesome, electrifying. Again, the Immortals fought the Ancients on a playing space that was life itself.

Jack beseeched his gods, just as Noel had. Currying favor, promising tithe, with fawning flattery and noblesse oblige.

Sharp winds cut and burned. Shadows wailed in the sad joy of imminent release. Bullets of hail pitched and plummeted, tumbled and teemed. And still the aegis of the sister gods held the innocent safe. And all trembled unaware in the presence of the unseen Dark Ones. The demons threw down their fury in full force. For their pact required sacrifice. The ground began to quake.

Jack had prepared for this as his mother had. He called to Claude, "Give me the athame!"

Claude withdrew the solid steel ceremonial knife with a bone hilt from within the folds of his robe. He proffered it above his head. Jack took hold and when he tried to wrench it away, Claude would not relinquish his grasp.

"Give it to me, Claude!"

"Hold onto it, Claude," I goaded him. "This is as much your sacrifice as his!"

Claude glared at me; his eyes glowed. But I could see that the idea had taken root.

"Yes. If we are to truly be partners, Jack, we must do this together," Claude said.

"You must give me the knife. It may not work if two hold the athame," Jack answered.

"Nonsense," I threw in just to roil the waters.

Now it was Jack's turn to glare. He knew that if this sacrifice was to be made, now was the only time. They would have to make it together. He had been outmaneuvered in underestimating Claude. He had been arrogant in his negligence to sedate me into silence. He was being forced to comply.

"What is it, Jack? Unable to share regency?" He didn't like my taunt. But, oddly, neither did Claude.

"I can handle this without you, Mikey! I don't need your help!" Claude screamed.

O'Donald, can you hear me? Can you help me? I am here for you, but I am at a loss. I am prevented from coming to you without assistance.

Stay where you are, Purity. Don't attempt to come closer. This is going exactly as planned.

What plan? I don't understand.

The celebrants were isolated from the congregation by a pale and vaguely pink fog that ringed the entire mountaintop. It was like a swirling storm, a vortex with the altar as its eye and pith. But instead of being tossed like detritus in a tempest, all were cleft to their place. I, only I, could clearly see the entire conflict that soon would become a battle royal.

All humanity was at stake. Jack and Claude could not be allowed their success. How did they dare agree to yield a race that was no longer theirs? How could they risk the forfeiture of our advances to a new Dark Age? The blackest of all darkness. I would stop them. And thanks to their stupidity, I finally knew how.

Naked, they grappled with each other over my naked body. Jack's fist closed over Claude's, which held tight to the athame. With their free hands, each tried to pry the other off of the prize.

"Release, Claude! You will be my consort. What more do you want?"

"I will be coregent, Jack. Coregent or nothing!"

Their naked bodies were slipping as they fought over me for the sacrificial knife. I could not interfere. I had to have them this way for my plan to work.

O'Donald!

I could not answer Purity. This was my game now. Mine alone.

I cannot move forward to advance up the hill. I'm trapped in the shield I assisted in creating. I am not simply protecting the bystanders; I have prohibited myself from further engagement. Help me, O'Donald. I must come to you.

I refused to answer. I hoped Purity would think that because of the shield, I could not. I hated to do this to her. Abandon her. But it was for her own good. For everyone's. Then I heard her. Not in my head, but aloud.

"Goddess sisters! Free me from your care! Allow me to be your sword against the Dark Ones. Pray, permit me to contend against the weapons of evil."

And I watched to see what magick she was up to now. But the goddesses did not let go. She was held inside the cloud just like all the others. I saw her proud shoulders slump. Heard her sadness.

I have not been found worthy of the task. I have failed you, O'Donald.

The swirling fog grew faster and denser. The flashes of light inside grew brighter, larger and more frequent. Jack and Claude, naked over their naked victim, each held me down with one hand and shared control of the knife with the other. The pebbles and hailstones that swirled close around us could not penetrate the divine fog. Purity was safe. Lightning clashed only inside the storm's eye, barely avoiding we three. This war had chosen its battleground and all nonparticipants were being kept at bay.

With one mind, one voice, Jack and Claude screamed their final invocation over the fray. With their conjoined hands, they raised the athame high above them, hilt to the sky.

I seized my moment. I threw up my arms and grabbed the wrists of both Jack and Claude at once. All they could see was the sly smirk that took hold of my face. The smirk that revealed intent and defied contradiction.

With all their strength, Jack and Claude together could not oppose me. They could not overpower me nor could they free themselves.

"Come to me now, Selene," I called.

A single, sleek bolt reached from the deepest heavens for the exposed metal at the heel of the hilt. The mountaintop flared alight.

"Transmute!" I cried as it touched. And the goddess gave me her gift, blessed my strange alchemy and turned the steel into her own prized metal.

Silver.

Jack and Claude both felt the argent sting at the same moment. I could see the shock and surprise on their faces. But, Jack was not about to give in.

He shouted over the storm, "You thought that would stop me,

Michael? The argent sickness? In another moment, that will be a thing of the past. I will be well beyond that!"

"We!" Claude insisted. He was forever through with being ignored.

"I have done everything for you, Jack! I have lied. I have cheated. I have stolen and murdered. There is not a sin left that I have not committed to gain you! And still, it is not enough! All you have ever thought about was you!"

"Claude, you can have whatever you want. But the time is now! Let us make an end of it!"

I couldn't have agreed more.

Collapsing back upon the altar stone, I held onto their wrists and dragged them down with my weight. I pulled the silver athame close and plunged it into my heart.

"Free!"

That single shout echoed throughout all space.

The moment was crowned in confusion. Too much had happened at once for full appreciation. It seemed as if the heavens opened and rained a blue-white fire upon the altar. As if the full moon itself burst forth and drew that single spot up to it. A column of electrified cloud stretched from the earth to the heavens. And through it all, I saw but one thing; the constellations as they danced in the void to tell their story.

I looked down to watch the horrified faces of my tormentors, my creators. They were fiends, indeed, but cowards just the same. They struggled to free themselves from my death grip. To let go of the athame, let go of one another. But free themselves, they could not. For the fire that surrounded us, bound us.

Or, to be more correct, the scorching fire did not surround, but emanated from within my heart. The goddesses helped me to fulfill my destiny. To recreate the July shield in Phillipe's chapel. I was the lion to be sacrificed by the two naked men. But more to Phillipe's prophetic point, I was the doorway.

I watched the sacred flame leap from my chest to consume them. First, their fingers as they gripped the athame they so desperately tried to release. Fingertips blackened and fingernails curled. The flesh and meat of each digit charred and broiled. And as much as it must have hurt, it stunk. Up, knuckle-by-knuckle, it consumed each finger to the palm of each hand. Jack's skeletal hands and wrists and forearms pulled at the offending silver blade as they pushed against the even more offensive me. Claude, ever ineffectual, simply shook his head back and forth in an attempt to avoid witnessing this final treachery.

Still, the screams were worse than the smell.

It was then that I silently thanked the goddesses for preventing those below—mostly Purity—from having to fully witness this destruction by virtue of their magic screen. And for blunting my hearing from Purity's cries. I did not think I could bear her feeling of betrayal. I turned for a moment to look down towards Purity. I gave her my last smile.

The now-scarlet flame—stunning in its personification—seemed to pick and choose what it would take next. Would it be flawless hair and flawless skin? No. I watched as their perfect flesh burned from their perfect biceps, perfect triceps from perfect bones. As the fine cinders swirled away. Cinder that had been beautiful blond and black hairs. The fire persisted, layer by layer. First, skin; then, flesh; then, bone. It even evaporated the blood borrowed from innocent victims as it incinerated the very black blood that was the vampires' birthright.

And even as it claimed them, they fought on.

The fire crawled past shoulders, up neck and onto chin. It melted the perfect, creamy flesh of flawless faces. Faces that intrigued and attracted men and women both. Faces that had once drawn victims close, now offered nothing but repulsion as they burnt and blackened and blew away, leaving exposed jaw and tooth and fang. Their once perfect teeth chattered, in unison, in jaws that could no longer bring darkness and death. Tongues that seduced through speech and suckle, now lolled—bright red—in blackened caverns. The screaming was over.

The flames ascended. The higher they edged up nose and cheek, the less the vampires looked undead. Twin flames darted into matching nostrils.

Jack suddenly looked very surprised. His stunning gray eyes, the very core of his seductive form, sat in a bloody red bed. His lashes evaporated and his lids melted away, revealing overextended orbs barely held in place by charred and cracking bones. Suddenly, they exploded outward into a gelatinous scud. They met with fragments of Claude's shattered emeralds just above my chin. No longer would they enchant, enamor, deceive. Unworried brows began to furrow, as forehead, and then scalp, sizzled, snapped and split. Their craniums buckled and broke, having no charges to protect.

They were dissolving above me. Even as I evaporated below. Maybe it was a last gift from the goddess, that I should be able to see the final destruction of those two who had destroyed so many. The victim had become the victor.

Jack and Claude collapsed upon me. I relinquished their wrists and thrust my hands inside their rib cages, grasping their hearts.

And I knew no more.

epilogue

Michael O'Donald had found his solution. Without me. Not to just the one problem that drew him to Las Vegas, but to his own concerns for life everlasting. O'Donald fused all he'd ever learned—from Baum and White, from Phillipe's books, and from my own pale teachings—to present the ultimate resolution.

Michael Flannery O'Donald had self-immolated.

The brilliant scarlet and gold flames brought to mind the classic symbol of sacrificial fire, the phoenix, whose constellation glittered above. How like that bird he was. A paragon, a symbol of excellence.

O'Donald's flame burned true—bright and hot. It illuminated him at first, casting a glow upon his handsome, smiling face. I did not feel the wind or the hail, protected as I was, but I did feel O'Donald's heat. And felt his joy. He didn't simply wish to foil the vampires who had tormented him; he demanded release. And so, he destroyed himself, kamikaze-style. Jack Courbet and Claude Halloran were also consumed in the mystical flame. And, blown away by that divine wind.

And when the supernatural fire abated, all it left behind was a bleached mound of large stones and a scant cloud of swirling ash moving up and away from the summit of Sunrise Mountain. No Jack. No Claude.

And no Michael O'Donald.

O'Donald had offered himself as the ultimate sacrifice. A thing I was either unwilling or unable to do. The goddesses recognized their champion and it was not I.

I stood, stock-still, unable to move in my utter sadness. I had lost in winning. I heard a vague shuffling and muttering around and behind me in the near-twilight. It would be dawn soon. I had truly lost him.

The apprentice vampires scurried away to seek shelter before the sun did to them what the moon had done to their masters. Good. I had no desire to look upon more demons.

The humans were leaving, too. And now I finally recognized them. The Goth role-players of Club Stoker and the gay business-men of Brimstone. Chorus girls from huge resorts and the drag queens from seedy dives. Bartenders and accountants and wait-resses and teachers. All of the would-bes and wannabes recruited into Jack and Claude's dark army. Those with no self-esteem, now with no fulfillment. Their gods were gone and forgotten. They all retreated from a failed attempt to become something other than their self-perception. But, would they start anew or just begin again where they had left off? I just didn't care. I simply wanted them away from here. This sacred site. The burial place of their savior, whether they knew it or not.

They dispersed as they wandered downhill. None seemed to re-member why they had gathered here, but neither did they wish to recall. No recognition, no conversation. They hurried away.

But I could do no more than stand and stare at the pile of rocks that moments ago held ashes. Disseminating ashes that were all that remained of a great evil and an even greater good.

"I'll miss you, Mike," I whispered to the dusty whirlwind as it moved out of sight towards the retreating night. I simply could not call him O'Donald any longer. Not when there was no longer any-one to hear the playful teasing. And the chaste flirting.

"And he will miss you, Miss St. Martin. *Sans doubt.*"

I froze at the expression. I felt the presence the moment I heard the words spoken and it frightened me that I had not sensed my company arriving.

I could not turn, could not move. How was I supposed to deal with this?

"Have no fear, Miss St. Martin. I wish you no harm."

Mike was right. It was very disconcerting to hear two mature men refer to themselves as a single being. Two distinct baritones blended so perfectly as to sound as one.

Baum and White moved around to face me. They were every-thing Mike said they were. And so much more. I had the distinct impression that I knew them already.

"Aspros and Dentro, I presume?" Reflexively, I made a small protective sigil behind my back.

They smiled at me. And the smile told the tale. They had not been called by these names in quite a very long time. And they missed it.

"We shall get along quite well, you and I," they told me.

"Forgive me for saying so, gentlemen, but you are vampires. And, even if you do not murder to stay alive and you subsist in a manner like Michael O'Donald did, I still cannot bring myself to trust you."

They ignored my bluntness to say what was important to their minds instead.

"Purity, dawn nears. I must pass over New York on my way home to Charnac. You may travel with me, if you wish, but I must shield myself now. I do not hunt, it is true, but I am not immune to the sun's rays. Please, come into the conveyance with me. I must go inside, into the shade."

I'd been so wrapped up in what was happening that I hadn't noticed their "ride." Neither helicopter nor jet, I was certain this vehicle wasn't for sale anywhere.

"No, it's an experimental prototype."

They'd read my mind. Even after I'd made the protection. They're very strong. And that was not something I was altogether comfortable with.

"Where did you get it?" The question, I knew, was awkward past schoolgirlish. They didn't trade glances. I was beginning to understand that they needn't. Theirs was no affectation. They were truly one in all ways.

"Please, enter."

They stood outside the door, waiting gallantly for me to enter first. Even though the sky brightened and day was imminent.

I entered the helicopter. I didn't know what else to call it. Neither a Harrier nor a CRW, it was like a flying yacht. A billionaire's plaything, an alien craft. Even the exterior color was indescribable. Somewhere between silver and black, like a gleaming pewter with a vague iridescence.

"What is this thing?"

"I call it the Hummingbird. It is virtually soundless. And the unique materials and structure make it almost indiscernible while aloft."

"Why would you need a thing like this?"

"Surely you understand my need for discretion. It is important that I come and go without attracting attention. And Nellis Air Force Base is all too close. Please. Let us leave now; it grows light."

I noticed the same pilots behind the controls in this abbreviated cockpit as were in the Charnac jet. I could not remember their names.

"You remember the pilot, M. Grandet, and his co-pilot, Goriot?"

They were mindreading again. But this time they helped me to save face. How could I get annoyed?

"Of course. Good to see you again."

We turned from the small, ergonomic cockpit to look at the ship's interior.

The craft itself was stunning. Not as opulent as the Dassault Falcon, it was trimmer and more modern. But it had been expertly outfitted. It wanted for nothing. Nor did I.

The windows were small ovals, eighteen inches wide and a foot tall. The moment the door was shut and the motor started, they sealed completely. The thick Plexiglas was covered with a blackout shield, a liquid crystal display screen. Each could project the image directly outside the window or one from any of hundreds of satellite links. Rather than the rich gray, brass and cherry wood of the diplomatic jet, this craft's interior was a soft fleshy-beige. A womb. No harsh angles or hard surfaces, everything was amorphous. Feminine?

Baum and White explained the workings of the airship to me in exacting detail. They showed me each button and demonstrated its purpose. Showed me each hidden door, hidden compartment, hidden reason. They took their time and made sure I understood each and every thing. Overly polite.

They showed me modern conveniences unavailable in current markets. They cooked for me in an oven that combined light wave and magnetic wave technology with something they called bio-technology.

"Are you saying it's alive?"

"Not simply living, but cognizant."

I stood staring in bland refusal to comprehend.

"I do not prepare your meal, Purity. The oven does."

"Of course, the oven cooks it; that's what ovens do. There's nothing special about that."

"There is about this oven. It knows, for instance, exactly what is inside of it. In this instance, breast of turkey, a vegetarian quiche and an angel food cake. It knows not only what is inside, but how each needs to be cooked and when each should be ready."

"It's . . ."

"Impossible? Not for Charnac. And, there is so much more."

They began to explain the workings of Charnac. They described their history and their function. And what life was like on the vast estate.

They told me of the extraordinary collections, the extent of both the art collection and the library.

They sat on either side of me and each took a hand.

"You will come back to Charnac with me, Purity," they stated.

I was a little amused by their extreme courtesy and dogmatic confidence. Even without vampiric powers, I was sure these two pale giants could squash me like a bug, if they chose. And still . . .

"No, gentlemen, I will *not*! I am returning to New York. My home."

"Charnac could be your home. It is outstanding!"

They proceeded to outline business holdings and real estate. If anyone were ever able to outwit them and connect the dots, they would find the Marquis de Charnac to be the wealthiest man in the world.

The lovers described for me the ruses perpetrated throughout the history of Charnac. Imaginary births and deaths. Invented marriages. False documents littering a counterfeit paper trail.

"Gentlemen! This is all fascinating. I would love to see it. One day. But not now. Now, I'm going home!"

"But you *promised* to return with me."

"I? Promised you? And just when, may I ask, was that?"

I could not quite get over their impudent behavior. This was beginning to irritate me.

"When I conjured you from the jaws of the dragon . . ."

Oh, shit!

". . . And removed you, with my magick, to Chateau Charnac, where you have been for a full cycle of the moon."

Shit, no!

"You promised that if I brought you here, for this, you would return with me."

Please don't let this be true!

"Gentlemen, whatever has or has not happened before, I cannot think of one good reason why I should return to Charnac with you."

They did not even need to look at one another before answering, "For Phillipe's grimoire?"

Phillipe, they explained, had the only transcript in the world of the actual Black Mass. The library also owned the only true "Necronomicon." They had been the engineers of the rumors about it. They themselves had written the fake. They had carefully orchestrated all that had been believed about black magic for centuries.

"Would you like to see the truth of the matter? See what Phillipe had spent many centuries collecting?"

"Why don't you leave it with me and I'll study it in New York? I promise I'll return it when I'm done."

They took my refusal in stride. They were not about to give up easily.

"For this, then."

They showed me a complex, legal-looking document. But since it was written in French, I didn't care to spend my time trying to translate it.

"What is this?"

"It is the document that proclaims you as the Marquise de Charnac."

I looked where they directed. I could decipher what it said. I was the legal wife of the Marquis of Charnac.

"It's a forgery!"

"Of course. As I said, I have been creating documents such as this for centuries! But it is signed and sealed. It is all quite binding in the French courts. You are Charnac!"

"I am Charnac?"

Then silence.

I said it. Shit! They tricked me. Shit! I'd used the phrase that Phillipe used, that Jack used and Michael had used to proclaim their power. No matter my tone, I'd said it. And that's all that was important. Shit, shit, shit, shit, shit!

"Charnac welcomes you." The rejoinder. "I am yours to command."

"That's not what I meant! You know I didn't mean to say that!"

They just smiled, like two people who knew they'd won a bet.

"You might wish to say *'merde'* when you are at Charnac."

"What's so goddamn important about my returning with you to Charnac that you'd trick me into it?" I was yelling at them.

"It is safest."

"Look! The bad guys are dead. It's over!"

"No, I am sorry, but it is far from over. All of the "bad guys," as you say, are not dead. Still, it is not for you to deal with them."

"I agree. They are not my problem anymore. And I don't believe that I'm theirs. So, I don't need the safety of Charnac. And I don't need your protection!"

"Possibly not. You are, as I have observed, a very strong witch. And the vampires at large are but apprentices without mentor . . ."

I was tiring of this verbal scrimmage. I should never have come this far with them. There is nothing I have to fear from the novices. I don't require any more help.

"However, Madame la Marquise, the child you are carrying does."

Everything I thought I knew left my mind like a television being turned off. All I saw were scratchy, fluttering little lights being sucked inward to a tiny, white dot. I wanted to debate them, but I had lost my footing.

"You look confused, Madame la Marquise."

"Don't call me that again! You know it's not true!" I paused to formulate a further argument. "And I am not pregnant!"

"You are. You know you are."

"My husband never gave me a baby."

"But he did."

"It's not possible."

"It was your own magic, mistress. Surely you remember that."

The universe stopped and I had become its epicenter. It was like whatever the opposite of tunnel vision was. It was opposed to all I wanted.

"Is it truly, mistress?"

I stopped for a moment to mentally gasp. And then to catch my breath. And try to understand.

"I am not offended. Your intentions are good. Still, I must insist that I am not pregnant. I cannot be carrying Patrick's child."

"Well, as *you* state it, mistress, you are not."

"Good. Then we are agreed. I do *not* carry Patrick's child."

"Of course not. Patrick Xenopoulos died before he could father a child. But, Michael O'Donald, the Marquis de Charnac, as you certainly read on this paper, is your legal husband. It is his child you carry."

Mike. His child.

"It just can't be! Mike was a vampire; he could not be a father; he was the undead!"

"Mistress, surely he explained to you that he never *actually* died as others do. Never came back as other vampires had. As Phillipe and Noel had. As Jean-Luc and Claude had. Not even in the way that Aspros and Dentro had. The Black Gift did not *rescue* him from death as it had for all of the other vampires. He possessed that gift *before* he died. Michael O'Donald still carried many of his human traits and abilities into his singular state of nosferatu. He could cry, for example. He could leave a fingerprint. And, *he could* father a child."

It was true. I had to admit it. What I believed had gone "wrong" at the rite of Tantric magick was this. It was the entire reason why I couldn't control my powers. I had unconsciously used them—used Mike—to get what I never got from Patrick. A baby.

"Not just a baby, a son."

I looked directly into their eyes. Twenty-four carat brown gold. Beautiful.

"It's a boy?"

"So I believe. Your son will have the entire world at his feet! There is nothing he can want, nothing he could want to do, that is out of his reach. Think on it!"

I pressed my burning brow on the cool window panel. As the screen related, the bright lights of Manhattan were extinguished during the day. I barely noticed, flying overhead. Flying past. I was on my way to a new home. A new life.

What would I be going home to in New York? Wasn't this the better plan? Privacy and untold riches in which to raise my son. What new mother wouldn't want this?

I smiled at my caretakers. I was going with them.

Home.

We had traveled from the near-dawn of Las Vegas to France's Cognac region. The stunning airship had landed right on the rear patio. Baum and White had ushered me inside.

There had been so much that occupied me during the flight. I finally thought to ask about Mike.

"Mike told me that he could hear Jack's and Claude's thoughts on the mountain. I didn't think vampires could read each other's minds."

"We can still transfer our thoughts to communicate without speaking," they answered.

"No. Mike heard them speak to one another. Not to him."

"It could have been caused by the influx of all that blood. Michael never needed another's blood. And to have so much—human and vampiric—who knows what that did to him? Think about it, Purity. We cannot transmute metals either. As unique as Michael had been, he possessed even more abilities this day."

And I did think about it. I thought about that and more. Thoughts of Patrick, who had unknowingly involved me in this affair. Thoughts of Jack and Claude. I should have spent more time at our first meeting at the theater. Seen them for what they truly were. Done something about it. And my thoughts of Michael O'Donald. All that he was to me without knowing. All he would be for my future. Our future. Our son.

There had been much to occupy me during these past seven months at Chateau Charnac. I had improved my fluency in French. I had my formal portrait painted. I had greeted my tenantry in the sunlight, a thing no other Charnac had ever done.

Michel de Charnac's death had not been announced for the first few months of my residency. By then, my people had already accepted me and grieved for my loss. And our affection for one another grew as my belly did.

I had taken to calling my chamberlains, the chief officers of Charnac International, Aspros and Dentro, when we were alone, and M. Baum and M. White, when we were not. They had assisted me in everything. They had become my best friends. What remained of my friendships from New York—mostly Patrick's old friends anyway—grew distant. How could I marry again so soon after his death? And lose a second husband while pregnant with his child? There was no doubt about it. The Red Witch was a jinx. God bless the child!

Only a few of my fellow practitioners felt there was more to the story. I had to make excuses to keep them from Charnac. The moment they saw me or set foot in the chateau, they would know the truth, a truth I could not afford to have revealed. Not now, not ever.

Wasn't it all too strange? A copycat of "The Horror of West Street" murdered Patrick. I married the original killer's younger brother. He died mysteriously and I inherited the title and the estate. Those witches would have instinctively understood the surroundings. They would immediately have understood the nature of Baum and White. No. They could not ever come.

So, I had spent these past seven months in virtual isolation. I saw only the workers who had come to the chateau or the townspeople, when I had thought I should be seen in public. I had gone to a few nearby chateaux to meet my august neighbors. After all, I would be looking to make a good marriage in twenty years or so. Ah, the silliness of it!

Aspros and Dentro were to be my midwives. What they knew of medical science far outweighed the local physicians and hospitals. One of the guest suites had been renovated into a combination clinic and maternity ward. They had to get used to my human needs in preparation for the future needs of my son. My son.

He, the yet unnamed, would be a modern-day French nobleman. A consort of royalty. The lovers and I had spent many days outlining his education. We would educate him at home until he was old enough to keep the secrets of Charnac to himself. Aspros and Dentro had created a book of Mike's genealogy. Mostly for me, I suppose. It would be quite some time before my son would be able to juggle the multiple truths.

The three of us, together, would teach him everything. The origins, however bleak, of the House of Charnac. All of it. But for him to learn it all, so must I.

"Do you know how Phillipe became a vampire?" I asked one night at dinner.

"Do you mean how he was changed and by whom?"

"You know quite well what I mean." I wasn't up to their wordplay.

"Phillipe left other books, mistress. He did not only compile his books of magick; he also wrote his history."

Why did this astonish me? Except for the two of them and Mike, all the vampires I'd heard of or met were extremely self-involved. It was the core of their nature.

"Phillipe has an autobiography? I want to see it!"

"Not simply an autobiography, mistress. Phillipe was not that simple a being. Phillipe chronicled, not only his long life, but the very origins of the vampire!"

This cannot be! Surely, it was more than I ever expected.

"My God! Are you telling me that here, in this house, there is a book about how vampirism began?"

They had kept this a secret from me. They choose now to reveal it. Why? Will I ever truly understand these two? Oh, the things I'll have to teach my son before my eventual death.

"Then, right now, I wish to . . ."

The sensation was overwhelming. Unlike anything I'd heard said. It was as if the whole core of my being was separating from me. I'd been pregnant for so long, it seemed my natural state. Not this!

"Mistress! We must get you to the clinic!"

They lifted me gently from my lounge. They were not embarrassed, as I was, about the wetness. They flew me upstairs.

It was as if I was watching a movie of the events, not as if I was living them. I felt a newer, more immediate heaviness in my belly. And the heaviness wanted out! This child was going to be born no matter how ill prepared I was. And, I'd just discovered just how ill that preparation was!

I'd admired the chateau's ceiling before. It's beauty. But, I'd never flown prone under it, watching it speed dizzily over my head. I tried to shut my eyes, but it made the nausea grow, the pain quicker. Is that what they meant by quickening? I laughed, even though I didn't feel like laughing. The ache in my hips was outstanding. Only to be measured against the pain in my lower back and my legs. My neck and headache. I couldn't feel my fingers or toes.

Thirsty. I did feel thirsty. I didn't know why.

I had taken to wearing a type of hostess pajama set in the last few weeks. The waistband was greatly expandable and the overgown was long-sleeved and calf-length.

They laid me gently upon the examining table and removed my soiled clothing.

It was an ordeal; don't let anyone say different. I could live fully each of its excruciating seconds, each interminable minute. The hours, the countless hours.

I could relate the feel of the spasms, the painful throes that should be spelled "throws." The flashes of hot and cold. Forgetting how to breathe! The desire to vomit. I felt a tension in my muscles that I wasn't sure was of my doing. An implacable external stiffness and interior thrashing. And all through, the pain of a new creature demanding release. A new son or daughter.

Please be a daughter! I have a name for you! Grace, I thought, or Hope. A name like mine. How, I wonder, do you say those in French? I can't think anymore.

I couldn't believe I was trying to think of this now. That I'd not made the slightest attempt to determine this before. What if it truly *was* a boy?

Crowning was not anything I could have been told. It was meant only to be experienced. There were no proper words. And yet, in its way, it was only the beginning.

"The head is out now," they said as if they were helping in some way.

Should I call it after Mike, if it's a boy?

"I have the shoulders!"

I chuckled to myself. None of us had been through anything like this before. We had no idea what we were doing.

I guess I should call him Patrick. It's only fair. No, Charity! I shall call her Charity.

"Almost done! Keep pushing!"

As if I needed to be told! Men! Honestly!

"Here you go. Here you go; this is it!"

I felt, for a moment, like a deflated balloon. As if I'd achieved my purpose. I was exhausted and exhilarated, happy and depressed. And, caught up in the moment, I almost forgot to . . .

"ω θεοί!" Aspros had shouted in Greek.

"What is it?"

"Oh, my god!" Dentro added, unconsciously explaining.

"Please! Is it a boy?"

They looked at me, the swaddled newborn in their shared grasp. I wanted to take the baby, but I was too tired to reach out my arms.

"He is a hemming."

And all I remembered as I fell unconscious was that one word. Hemming.

Hemming. What a beautiful name! I shall call him Hemming.